CUP

OF

LOVE

ALSO BY FRANKLIN WHITE

Fed Up with the Fanny

CUP

 OF

LOVE

franklin white

POCKET BOOKS
New York   London   Toronto   Sydney   Singapore

This book is a work of fiction. Names, characters, places and incidents are products of the author's imagination or are used fictitiously. Any resemblance to actual events or locales or persons, living or dead, is entirely coincidental.

 POCKET BOOKS, a division of Simon & Schuster, Inc.
1230 Avenue of the Americas, New York, NY 10020

Copyright © 1999 by Franklin White

Originally published in hardcover in 1999 by Simon & Schuster, Inc.

ISBN: 0-7434-8241-7

First Pocket Books printing June 2003

10 9 8 7 6 5 4 3 2 1

POCKET and colophon are registered trademarks of Simon & Schuster, Inc.

For information regarding special discounts for bulk purchases, please contact Simon & Schuster Special Sales at 1-800-456-6798 or business@simonandschuster.com

Cover design by David J. High and Ralph C. Del Pozzo, High Design, NYC
Cover photographs © Tony Stone Images

Printed in the U.S.A.

A c k n o w l e d g m e n t s

As always I give thanks to the Father, Son, and Holy Spirit.

Thanks go out to: Miea, for keeping me together when everything seems unbearable; William Clark, for being on an entirely immeasurable level from anything I've known in the past; you're astronomical! Many writers search their entire careers for what I have attained: editor Laurie Chittenden, who has once again motivated me to put it on the page and visualized my idea before one word was ever written. Thanks for being God's vessel for allowing me to break into this business, and good luck in your new endeavors! Thanks to Zoe Wolff for stepping in like a true professional.

Of course thanks goes out to Mom and Dad, for covering me with your love *all the time—no matter what—*and cultivating a mind-set to do great things, as you both have done. Much love to my entire family and to my friends.

✦ ✦ ✦

Okay . . . I wasn't going to do this. But so so so so so so many people have been in my corner that I just had to give you all shout-outs. Plus, I might need a dollar one day! First, thanks go out to the family! Sandy, Baby Brea, Karla, Cleo, Dennee, Brandon, Ericka, Chaka, Chandler, and Julie, Clarrettae, Sue, Richard, Emma, Reva, Uncle Warner Parsons, Carmen, Danny, Tyke, Sandra, Phil, Jeff, Stephanie, Jerry, Uncle Amos, Emma Moore, Reva Walker, and everybody else

Acknowledgments

. . . anybody I missed? PROBABLY SO . . . but the love goes out, so keep praying for me.

The fish-frying, turkey-smoking, football-watching Dirty Bird fans on the hill. Billy and Sonia Greer, Chris and Diane Patterson, John and Yvete McKenzie, Brian and Linda Banks—Linda good lookin' out with those typing skills—I'll be back! Hey, when is the next fish fry? Somebody let a brutha know! Can't forget Roy Johnson—making those millions! James Param. Thanks to Anne Killcrease for reading. Darryle Melson. To all the peeps from back home living close by— Richale Watkins, Lisa Starks, Eric Kirkland, Bidea, and those Perfect Thugs— Keith, Ed, and Tee—young brothers keep working at it and get those grades! Mark and Latina Anthony, SFC Boxton, Terry Poindexter and clan, Kaloa Hearne, James and Carol Brown and family, Lisa Durroh and family, Pastor Todd and Mrs. Todd, Rosita Page, Frank Tatum, Sandy Jackson, Lee Craft, Lamonte Waugh, Randy Clarkson, Alvin Dent, Ronald Steward, Mark Stinson, Garland Williams, David Dungy, Rick Carter, Michael Washington—look for me in L.A.! To those of you I missed on the first one—Eric Shephard, Jay Brown, Eric Crump, Bill Harrington—these bruthas used to sit around and listen to me tell stories! And call me crazy at the same time! Michelle Blake, Linda Sawyer—Pops told me what ya said! Kim Lee, and that bass-playin' Foley—waiting on that album, brutha! Troy Jones, Nate Beach, Joy Eubanks, Karen Wilson, Teresa House, Maricruz E. Andeme. Big ups to the New York Connection—Reggie English, Bill Bolden, Sheryl Jones, Ernestine Callender, Tonya Anderson, Wilton Cedeno, Vaughn Graham, Pam Mason, Joann Christian. All those writers who I've met on this journey: Keep up the pace and keep getting betta and betta. You are all making a brutha proud! Eric Jerome Dickey—waitin' on my tickets to the premiere! (2) ya heard! Lolita Files—I know you're going to be there—so make sure I get mine . . . watch my back! Walter Mosley, Victoria Christopher Murry, Sheneska Jackson, Yolanda Joe, Tim McCann, Omar Tyree, Thomas Green, Patricia Haley-Brown, Camika Spencer, Sharon Mitchell, Colin Channer, Sister Souljah. And all those booksellers who always sell those books! Keep up the good work! Oh, yeah, almost forgot—there's only one thing right about the comparison—I am male. Everything else is propaganda, baby! And the name is Franklin White, please . . . please . . . stop dat mess, as Stubbs would say! How many remember the eighties? Do me a favor: Please register to vote—then vote!—and that's for real. Check out the Web site: FranklinWhite.com.

Peace and Courage to all!

*To every ounce of blood
that has paved the way*

Just looking at it doesn't absolutely tell you what it is. If touched from the top and the contour followed, it becomes a circle no matter what direction you travel. But when you make up your mind to taste the ingredients of understanding, loyalty, communication with a splash of passion, then you know it must be a Cup of Love.

— FRANKLIN WHITE

What Ya Goin' to Do?

Vance Butler stood frozen still. The reflection of his light-skinned face against the dark-tinted windows inside the airport showed signs of worry and deep trouble. Drama and conflict had once again moved into his life like a slithering snake and he was the only one to blame. He was seriously guilt trippin'. Vance was almost certain someone had stood on the tip-top of one of the few skyscrapers in Columbus, Ohio, and zoomed down on him with the most powerful lens ever made. His every move through the night had been brought to light, unmasking the dirt he'd done to his beloved Artise. When the evidence was laid in front of him and blow-by-blow accounts of his stealth unveiled, Vance had no defense from the excess drooling, stunned-eyed, wobbly-standing, eight-count posture he'd immediately fallen into. Round one: room verification. Round two: time of day. Round three: name of lady friend. Round four: confirmation that a well-hyped fabricated mandatory business meeting didn't take place. These were the counterpunches Artise had thrown in his face that broke Vance down into submission. Her flurry had instantly made her live-in lover concede and acknowledge wrongdoing. So quickly in fact, that Vance's mind hadn't had a chance to register to lie if he had chosen to.

"Who in the hell could have saw me?" Vance continuously pounded while his eyes were glued to the airport runway. He was so deep into his thought, the sounds of the roaring engines of the airplanes barely registered. "Damn—the topic of scandal again." He sighed, checking his watch then doing a double take at his timepiece when he realized he had been standing in the same spot for three hours. Vance had been daydreaming and tormenting himself at the same time. The continual flash of Artise's wounded face playing over and over again in his mind made Vance feel like he wanted to go out onto the runway and sprawl out underneath the landing gear of a 747.

Vance was sick about letting his guard down and letting the traits and mannerisms of a nasty, ill-fated, hapless dog with razor-sharp teeth take over his mind and control him like it was able to do. He wondered how ferocious he must have looked to Artise, his love of ten years, when she found out that once again he couldn't handle lurking lust. Vance and all of his five-foot-ten, hazel-eyed, wavy-haired, thin-bearded, light-skinned self was unable to do what he promised to himself and to Artise after his last bout with the devil . . . *not fool around.*

"Can a brutha get a 'hello, how was your flight' or something?" Ethan Davis said as he stood eye to eye with his best friend, smiling with his arms extended. Ethan was dressed in a black, half-length leather jacket, blue jeans, and a pair of Lugz loafers. His sparkling teeth stood out against his dark skin, and his brown bedroom eyes narrowed nicely when he smiled. His arching eyebrows were dark, close to wavy. Ethan looked like he had maybe gotten a haircut before he boarded the plane. His hair was cut coarse and close and his goatee was lined perfectly, touching his thin mustache at the exact same spot on each side. He still appeared like he could be a better-than-average sprinter, his body was lean and looked as though he worked out from time to time. Vance was so into his thoughts that he hadn't even realized the flight he was waiting on had finally landed.

"What's up . . . you all right?" Vance said, reaching out to Ethan and greeting him with a halfhearted hug.

Ethan stepped back from the careless embrace and tapped Vance on the arm. "Yeah, I'm all right. . . . The question is, are you all right?"

Vance looked around; he was still feeling irritated, like the zoom lens was still on his ass. "Come on, let's get your bags and get the hell out of here, Ethan," Vance suggested.

The wait for the luggage seemed longer to Vance than the entire time he had spent at the airport. He remained in his zone. His eyes were glued to the conveyor belt, waiting for it to spit out the bags. Ethan looked at the conveyor belt, then at Vance. Then at the conveyor belt and back at Vance again.

"Fascinated with that, huh?" Vance didn't respond. "Vance? . . . Vance?" Ethan called out. Vance took his hand and ran it down his beard, then placed his hands in his pants pockets as he huffed, trying to release his tightening love tensions.

"Yeah . . . you say something?" Vance asked.

"Yes . . . I did," Ethan announced.

"What? . . . What is it?"

"Man, what the hell is goin' on with you?"

Vance just shook his head.

"You know what? You're acting the same way you were when I left. . . ."

Vance looked at Ethan and Ethan read his eyes.

"Awwww, man . . . don't tell me . . . do not tell me," Ethan stiffly pronounced.

"I won't then." Just then the bags began to emerge from the conveyor belt and Vance kept his eyes on the bags as Ethan moved a couple of steps away from him. He looked back at Vance, wondering how he could have let this happen again. Ethan had a hell of a memory, and it was like déjà vu; but the last time this had happened he was moving to Atlanta. Now here he was back in Columbus, Ohio, and nothing had changed. Ethan just shook his head as his mind took him back to July, in 1996.

Ethan had decided that he'd had enough of Columbus, at least that's what he'd led Vance to believe and his excuse had gone over unexpectedly well. Without warning he was moving to Atlanta to get away from it all and journey to the black mecca of the United States. Ethan's vision of Vance's stained eyes and nervous motions was unforgettable.

Vance had been the most sorrowful, dejected, heartbroken brother that Ethan had ever seen. And the most important element of it all was that Vance didn't contemplate or investigate why Ethan was leaving town. He'd been way too involved with the drama he had caused Artise. So when Ethan had asked Vance to take him to the airport, that was exactly what he did. Vance's look now was identical to the moment when Ethan had stepped on the plane—all depressed and blue. At one point Ethan had thought he was going to cry. It had been the first time Vance had fooled around on Artise. They had been together for seven years. Ethan had been behind the scenes of the matter and easily could've been called one of the denominators for Vance's problem. Ethan had run into an old friend who was with her girlfriend while he and Vance were enjoying a Clippers game down at the stadium. Vance hadn't given Terry a second thought when they sat down and began chatting while the minor league team of the Yankees pounded away at Cleveland's minor league squad. But when he received a call from Terry at his place of employment and then told Ethan about it, things had quickly changed.

"Yo . . . guess who called me?"

"Who?" Ethan remembered asking.

"Terry."

"Terry? . . . Terry who?"

"You know who I'm talkin' about, Ethan."

"Oh . . . that Terry. I wonder how she got your number?"

"Don't front, Ethan. Why did you give her my number?"

"I don't know. . . . I just thought you might want to talk to her."

"Talk to her about what? I don't have anything to talk to her about."

"That's what I told her." Ethan recalled his deviousness and smiled.

"You told her that?"

"Yep. I told her you were married."

"Married?"

"Yep."

"When did you attend my wedding, Negro?"

"Look, I just told her you were deeply involved. Maybe she took it as that, I don't really recall."

"Is that all you recall?"

"And that you weren't interested in sleeping with another woman."

"You don't know what's on my mind."

"Man, I was just trying to help you out because she said you looked like a good fuck."

"She said that?"

"Yep. But I told her she was probably wrong."

Vance had laughed. "You told her what!"

"I just told her that you've been with Artise so long, you probably don't even know how to romance another woman."

"You must be out of your mind!"

"So I'm right, then?"

"No, you're wrong."

"Yeah, right."

That's how things had started between the two, Ethan remembered. And a couple of months later Vance took the plunge and brought Terry to the hotel and knocked boots with her. Terry didn't have an inkling of the personality, charm, or grace that had always blown Vance's mind about Artise. But she did have a way with words. Terry was blunt, to the point, plain old exact. She was an expert with flirtatious expressions, movements, and suggestions. She always smiled and was carefree, not afraid to tell how good her sex was. Vance's zest for Terry had been strictly of the sexual nature. Her lanky legs and "so good" strut had been too appealing for Vance to let pass by. When she had said to him while they stood in front of the hotel door, "Don't take one step in there . . . if you're not going to give it to me right," it was the last straw and he opened the door, and for five nonstop hours, that's what Vance did. Seven years of commitment and truth had gone down the drain for three hundred minutes of nonstop sex.

Terry had a loud mouth, though, to go along with her personality. Something Vance would have found out if he hadn't jumped in the bed with her so soon. Terry noticed Vance and Artise out dancing and didn't know the bartender was Artise's first cousin as she sat and watched the two having a good time. She'd opened up to the bartender while she sat downing Absolut citron vodka and before Vance and Artise laid their heads on their pillows that same night, Artise had known the who, what, when, where, and why of Terry and Vance and how they got their groove on.

"Are your bags going to jump off this thing and walk over to you or what?" Vance hollered over to Ethan.

"Man, grab the bags and let's go," Ethan mouthed over to Vance.

"So what happened?" Ethan asked as soon as Vance slammed his car door shut.

"Nothin' . . . nothin' but Artise finding out about me and Sheryl, then the two of them having a three-hour conversation over the phone about everything Sheryl and I did last week. Besides that, nothin' . . . nothin's wrong. I just love my boring-ass life in this ugly-ass city. I don't even know why you came back. Just look at this place, Ethan, the sun hasn't shined in almost a week."

Ethan didn't want to hear any bad comments about Columbus. It was bad enough he wasn't just visiting. He took a long extended breath, trying to get over his reality. At the same time it was hard not to compare Columbus to Atlanta. The lifeless and dull atmosphere in Columbus hadn't changed a bit. It was just like he remembered and exactly like what he and all of his friends complained about on a continuous basis years ago. First of all Columbus was gloomy as hell and everybody loved to walk around with the same damn attitude of, "Ohhh . . . I'm just trying . . . to make it" or "I'm still living." The city always seemed dim and depressing and really didn't deserve the label of the "capital city" of Ohio. Nothing vital or grand ever happened there, except for an occasional KKK rally that didn't benefit anyone. It reminded Ethan of a high-class railroad town filled with people who were happy just being okay and whose spirit had the power to easily rub off on anyone who laid their hat in the city overnight. Not to mention the nightlife. Columbus was nothing like other major cities where a variety of nightspots could be found. The nightlife consisted of a few broken-down establishments in buildings that should have been condemned and made into parking lots. The only club even worth mentioning was Whispers, which served dinner and drinks at a nice price. There had never been any genuine camaraderie between the black citizens and anyone who was born and raised in Columbus and had achieved national popularity or celebrity did it someplace else because Columbus lacked the means for anybody to do anything. Only the Ohio State University football and basketball programs kept the outside world from forgetting all together that the city was on the map. There was only one black radio station on the FM frequency. And if you traveled too far away from its reach, *five miles or so,* you would be tapping your fingers on your steering wheel wondering what the hell happened to what you were listening to—and singing your own damn song. At the same time, the black leadership was so out of touch with the issues and circumstances happening in the city that no one even cared if they spoke up about the injustices or not because their word didn't mean a damn thing. The only politician who had ever made any headway was David Norman and he was president of City Council and running for mayor. Over the last twenty years the inner city had decayed without the so-called leadership of the city saying a word, and no one had ever stood up to find out why. Meanwhile, the suburbs and outskirts of the city were continually becoming upgraded to a point where the disparity of black and white in the city was clear as day.

"How did she find out?" Ethan sighed, thinking about what he'd come back to.

"Ethan, I don't know."

Ethan could hear Vance's disgust with himself. "What do you mean . . . you don't know?" Ethan looked at Vance as though he was one of the dumbest cats in the city.

"She didn't say how she found out—and it doesn't matter anyway . . . she knows."

Ethan chuckled; he already knew the answer to the question he was about to ask. "Refresh my memory. . . . How many times have you cheated on Artise?"

Vance looked over at Ethan. "Three times. Sheryl makes the third time. . . . Why? You already know that."

"And how many times have you been caught?"

"Three times."

"Unbelievable, man."

"What?" Vance asked.

"I just don't understand how you could get caught every time you decide to fool around. I know some guys who've messed around—cheated, made booty calls, or whatever you want to call it—then washed their hands and been done with it . . . but *nooooo*, not you! You are just unbelievable. . . . You always get caught."

"This city is just too small. You can't go anywhere without seeing someone that you have met at one time or another . . . which brings me back to my question I asked you last night over the phone, Ethan. Why the hell you come back here?"

"We're not talking about me, Vance. We're talking about you. See, you cannot play Casanova in this town—especially if you have a lady that people have seen you all over the city with. That's rule number one!"

"You're right . . . you're right," Vance said dejectedly.

"See, this is not Atlanta. In Atlanta you can live in Buckhead and when you want to get your sneak on you can go to the Cascades or Stone Mountain and nobody would ever find out. I don't know how many times I have to tell you, Vance. If you're goin' to be a player, you got to think like one." Ethan noticed cassettes on the dashboard and picked them up.

"I'm not a player, Ethan." Vance tried his best to sound like he meant what he said.

"Oh, you ain't got to convince me! Believe that, okay?" Ethan said in a lower tone while checking out the tapes. "Cheat three times—get caught three times. You sure the hell ain't," Ethan mumbled. "What? You listening to church music now? What do we have here . . . Donnie McClurkin, Fred Hammond, Trin-i-tee, Marvin Sapp, Brother Ross & Positive Direction."

Vance looked over at the tapes and grabbed them from Ethan. "Give me those," he insisted. "It's not church music. It's inspirational."

Ethan huffed sarcastically. "So what did Artise say about all this?"

"That she was tired of it," Vance said.

"So she broke it off?"

"No . . . but she ain't having it anymore. Damn, I hate this! Do you know how long it takes to win a woman's trust back?" Then Vance realized it was Ethan he was talking to. A man who knew less about commitment than Vance did.

Vance's recollection of the reason Ethan left was uncertain. The two had never sat down after all these years to talk about it, because over the phone or Internet Ethan was so good at changing conversations and shifting discussions at any given moment. So Vance let it slide; he knew one day they would be face to face again. When Ethan left Columbus three years ago, Vance realized that Ethan ran away from a commitment to his then better half, Tassha. It was a surprise indeed when, as Vance sat in his kitchen days after taking Ethan to the airport, he was confronted by Artise's good friend Tassha.

"Vance?" Tassha said, storming into the kitchen.

"Yeah . . . hey, Tassha," Vance said to her; he was still hurting from his unkindness to Artise.

"Why would you do such a thing?" Tassha wanted to know.

"Look, Tassha, I don't know what Artise told you. But I really think that's between the two of us," Vance made clear.

"I'm not talking about that. Even though you have broken her heart."

"Then what are you talking about?"

"Don't act like that with me!" Tassha raised her voice.

"Wait a minute now, Tassha. You don't know me like that."

"Why did you help Ethan leave? You knew we were going to get married."

"Get what?"

"How could you let him just get up and leave two days after asking me to marry him! Ohhh, both of you are just pitiful excuses for men. That's all, pitiful!" Then Tassha turned around and walked away. Vance then understood the real reason for Ethan's instant departure.

"Never mind, scratch that," Vance said to Ethan after reviewing the facts. "Act like you didn't even hear my question."

"Whatever, but I'm sorry, Vance, I don't think Artise believes in you anymore. Especially after this episode. Three times you cheat . . . and get caught? A sista ain't forgiving like that. I don't care what you say."

"You think so?" Vance asked.

"I know so . . . and my question to you is—How can you think any different?"

"Well, Ethan . . . I'm hoping . . . okay? I just want her to give me one more chance so I can make it up to her, make her proud of me. I've been thinking. I want to marry Artise, make her my wife."

Ethan didn't give what Vance said a second thought. His eyes became fixed through the windshield at a very symmetrical lady walking across the street holding the hand of a little girl. She had on a very tight pair of jeans and a denim jacket.

"Yeah, I hear you, Vance," Ethan muttered. "But I'm telling you . . . don't even try proposing now. She will definitely turn you down," Ethan said, enjoying what his eyes were watching.

"My mind is telling me it's the right thing to do, though."

"Man, if I was Artise and you asked me to marry you . . . I would leave your ass at the altar."

"Yeah, I bet you can tell me some things about that," Vance fired. Ethan gave Vance a look that only true friends can give—then he pointed toward the lady who now had stepped onto the sidewalk and begun to strut down Broad Street. Ethan nodded his head toward her.

"See . . . now that's what you should be focusing your attention on. WWKs!"

"Nope . . . that's okay," Vance insisted sharply.

"Look . . . you are not going to change, Vance, so why put yourself through the trouble of trying to settle down now? 'Women with kids' are better anyway. You act like what I have realized about them is so out of touch or something. But let me tell you I really do hate to see women all alone trying their best to take care of kids without a man being there. I have a soft spot for that shit. Plus to simplify matters, when I approach them I'm up-front about my intentions and surprising as it may seem, they not only understand but they want exactly the same thing as I do. They want me for the moment, then they get along with their nonstop lives and I pretty much do the same. It's understood by both parties, that's what it is."

"Forget that, Ethan. Artise is right."

"Right about what?"

"She's right about us and our lives. Just look at us, man. We're in our thirties and still running around here like we don't have a care in the world. It's really getting old."

"It's funny to me how people get in trouble, then all of a sudden miraculously begin to want to do the right thing after being caught," Ethan said.

"There's nothing wrong with that, Ethan. At least I've realized I need to make a change." Vance ran his hand down his beard.

"The only thing you've realized, Vance, is the fact you don't know how to go out and get laid on the down low without getting caught." Ethan scoffed.

"I'm serious, Ethan. Look at us man . . . walking around beginning to look like our fathers and their fathers and not even trying to make a legacy for others to follow. We're about to become just another unknown fixture of this city, and I always told myself I wouldn't settle for that. Look at me—working for a dairy manufacturer, booking orders for stores all across the state and still living in a one-bathroom, cramped-ass four-room house that doesn't have air-conditioning. That ain't no kind of legacy, and I definitely didn't finish college with that in mind. Hell, I don't even have a kid to leave a legacy to!"

Ethan scratched the top of his head.

"On top of that, Ethan, do you know how long I've been with Artise?"

"I have an idea."

"Almost ten years and I don't have nothin' to show for it except some stupid-ass arguments and failed goals. And the funny thing about it is, we ain't getting no younger, so it's not going to get any easier."

"Just like I said. Every time a brutha gets caught up in a scandal, they want to perpetrate and do the marriage thang."

"Nope, don't even try it, Ethan. You know for the longest I've been talking about doing this."

"Yeah . . . I'll give you that you have. But you haven't, and you still doing what we all do. First it was your songwriting, and what has happened with that? Nothing. All I ever see is notes scattered all over your car with words on them." Ethan held a piece of paper up. "Vance, the words are not supposed to be on paper . . . they are supposed to be on someone's record. Then it was your little business ventures that never have materialized. Man, please . . . I stopped listening to you years ago . . . so I know Artise has."

"Well that's too bad. Because this time, I'm serious."

"Serious about what, Vance? If you were going to change, you would have done so long ago."

"Ethan, things take time," Vance declared. "But I'm going to show you and Artise I can change."

"What ya goin' to do, Vance. What ya goin' to do?"

A Little Lunch

The echoes of Artise's shoes as she walked through the halls of City Hall were quick and uneasy. They possessed a clamorous tone which caused her to pause. The sound was so loud she felt like she was violating the great minds that were inside the confinements of the stunning white rock structure. So she waited for a second where she stood. Her eyes focused on the pictures of the great men and women that decorated the walls of the city's Hall of Fame. A few of the black-and-white photos were icons from her era. A two-time Heisman-trophy winner, the first man to walk on the moon, the heavyweight champion of the world, an Olympic-gold boxer, and mayors who had led the city. Artise didn't get much of a charge from the photos' existence and could not figure out why. Maybe it was the lighting, the order, the presentation. Artise wondered if the pictures would give more of a charge if they were placed on a higher level so that those who were from the same existence could be proud. *Oh well,* she thought. Artise looked around and decided her reverberations bouncing off the walls were not as much of a nuisance as she believed them to be. So she continued on her journey through the corridors, wondering why the most important building in the city always seemed to be so dull and diminished. Of course it was the middle of the day. Lunchtime to be exact. But the ambience within City Hall at that particular moment was identical to every time she stepped foot through the heavy doors of city government. *What a bummer,* Artise thought. The immediate atmosphere was doing nothing to lift her spirits. She was still upset about finding out about Vance and his infidelity. When she saw his face that morning she fought like hell with herself to not bring up the subject of his affair. And Vance fought even harder to stay the hell out of her way. When she went into the kitchen to get a cup of juice, he hid his face behind the newspaper. When she walked into their cramped bathroom to splash on her favorite perfume while he was shaving, Vance put his face under the running water and pretended to wash his face. Vance knew Artise was tired of crying, tired of trying, and downright worn out from the pain he'd caused. Artise had invested pure quality time into their relationship and they both knew this time, this mistake, this dis, was going to have to be dealt with—no matter what.

Artise and Vance had first met on a hot steamy night at the Ohio State Fair. It was so hot in the grandstand that eyes in the upper portion of the outdoor venue could see the humidity hovering over the concert-goers' heads below them. Patti Labelle was in concert and began to sing "If Only You Knew." Her stunning voice put the whole grandstand in a daze. Vance was standing two rows in back of Artise, and as their arms were flowing from side to side under the direction of Patti, Vance turned his head left and Artise turned hers right. And their eyes met. Then they smiled. Vance dropped his arms and walked over to Artise. Her soft eyes, luscious full lips, and bronze skin blew Vance away.

"Hello . . . my name is Vance." He extended his hand.

"Hi . . . I'm Artise." And she placed her hand into his and they stayed that way until the end of the song and then some.

Artise and Vance spent a helluva night together talking, laughing, and riding every single contraption the fair had to offer. Artise knew this was the man for her right away because up to that point she had only been on the merry-go-round and that was when she was ten years old. Vance was the man she had been looking for. One that would entice her to take chances—one who could convince her to put her feet in the deepest waters. Man enough to scream just as loud as she did when they were at the highest point of a roller coaster. A man that would take the straight drops and highs and lows with her while never letting go of her hand. And in the beginning that was what Vance was. A man.

Vance was Artise's first. He was the first man that she'd ever thought about every hour of the day. The first man she ever introduced to her mother. The first man to make her feel like she was the most special person a man could ever imagine being with. The first man she felt comfortable around. The first man she ever thought about having children with. The first and only man she ever had sex with. Artise had wondered if all the "firsts" were the reasons Vance was tearing up their relationship. She questioned, if she were a wild, overbearing, big-hoop-earring-wearing hoochie who called him on his every move, would he treat her the same way? Artise had thought about changing her style many times—each and every time Vance had strayed. But that was not Artise. Artise was a gentle, reserved, caring soul who wanted to be in love. She wanted to grow with her man and build a solid foundation. In the beginning Vance was full of ambition and enterprise, and they moved in with each other a year and a half after meeting. First there was the insurance claims business that he thought would be a huge success. He planned to run it right out of the house. Vance convinced Artise to attend a six-month insurance claims course with him while they both had full-time jobs. After three months, Artise expelled any doubts that she might have had and was sure that it could be done. But all of a sudden, and for no apparent reason, Vance did not feel like it was for him any longer, and at the beginning of the sixth month he dropped out and began to look into other ventures. Then there was the space for the downtown hair salon that Vance just knew would bring in money by the truckloads. But after going through all the paperwork to lease the space, Vance changed his mind again and left everything at the wayside.

"Nothin' but talk!" Artise said to herself. Artise pulled on the heavy brass door leading into one of the offices in City Hall. Instantly her eyes focused on who she'd come to see. "Now don't you look like every bit of N'Bushe Wright!" Artise said, looking her girlfriend up and down.

Tassha's looks were definitely paying the bills. Her tall, caramel, skinny self, which was already past the point of being labeled "skinny fat," was standing with a stack of papers in her arms and her eyes open wide. When she smiled, her entire face lit up the room. Tassha loved to dress in provocative clothing and hid the flaws of her thin lips and small nose well with makeup. She sometimes wished she was as short as Artise though. They joked all the time about what they would do if Tassha could switch her five-nine frame with Artise's five-three short-haircut-wearing self. Tassha was an outgoing sista. She could have easily been in a public relations position or something. When she spoke, her mannerisms and disposition brought her listeners close to her, and when she knew her counterpart was listening she would turn on her charm. Tassha knew she had the total package as she stood in the office of Councilman Norman in her opal pleated skirt and white silk blouse. She smiled at the sight of Artise, which instantly made Artise feel better.

"Hey . . . now!" Tassha cried out. "Did you take an extra hour of comp time for lunch today? It's just way too nice out for us to have to scarf our lunches down then go back to work. Uh-uh . . . not today," Tassha said, placing mail in the out box on her desk. Artise shook her head. She had been working for the state going on nine years and comp time was something she had plenty of.

"It's not like *you* have to really watch the clock anyway, Tassha," Artise teased as they held back their laughter when they noticed the huge wooden office door of City Councilman Norman opening up. Councilman Norman was fifty-nine years old, with light brown skin and a head full of salt-and-pepper hair. His three-button suit sat precisely on his wide shoulders and his shoes were spit-shined to perfection. Norman waited until the door was fully open and as he walked in, his distinguished presence took over the entire room. Looking up from the paperwork he held in his left hand he began to move his coffee cup up to his lips . . . then paused.

"Oh. . . . Hello, Artise," he said as he looked over the top of the reading glasses that were sitting on the tip of his nose.

Artise smiled. "Hello, Councilman Norman, or would Mr. Mayor be too premature?"

He smiled. "Hmmm . . . I do like the sound of that, but call me

David. Any friend of Tassha's is a friend of mine." He looked at his paperwork for a second. "Baby girl . . . um . . . um." David quickly cleared his throat and corrected himself. "Tassha? Have you seen the reports from the treasurer's office as of yet?"

"Yes, they're right on your desk next to the morning paper, David. Ann had them here right on time."

"Oh . . . okay . . . great. Please be sure to thank Ann for me. I know she must have had her people working on this all week long. She's wonderful." David turned and began to go back into his office. "Nice seeing you again, Artise." David turned back. "Can I count on your vote?"

"I'll be the first one in line, David," Artise said, referring to the upcoming election in which David was running for mayor of Columbus.

"Great! . . . Bye." The door shut behind him.

"Baby girrrl? . . . Did he say baby girl?" Artise whispered.

"Be quiet." Tassha giggled. "It slipped."

The ladies made it to the statehouse lawn exactly at the peak of lunchtime. The sky was completely blue and the breeze was noticeably refreshing and calm. It seemed like everyone who worked downtown was on the lawn with their lunch. Tassha and Artise were overjoyed they found a spot on their favorite area of the lawn.

"Okay, girl . . . let's do this at the same time so these nasty men don't get a chance to look up under our dresses," Tassha said, almost laughing. Artise nudged her head in the direction of some looky-Lous.

"Yeah . . . I know. The group over there already are watching us. Just so damn trifling. They have clubs for that," Artise said, giving the group of men the evil eye as the two sat down.

"Now . . . that wasn't too bad," Tassha said.

"Uh-uh . . . not at all," Artise confirmed. They began to unfold their napkins.

"So . . . how you doin' . . . you feeling any better?"

"Yep. I told you I'm okay. At this point I could care less."

"Are you sure?" Tassha pried.

"I'm sure, Tassha. It's like it doesn't even matter anymore. Vance could come home tonight and tell me he was packing up all of his things and I wouldn't try to stop him one bit. It seems like he is turning into every other brother you meet on the street. No drive or ambition, just livin' day to day collecting his weekly checks. I ain't got time for that anymore."

"I hear you, girl. What do you think has gotten into Vance? There was never a time when you weren't tellin' me something he was trying to do. But the last couple of years—I don't know. That's the second chick that he's been with from his office. I bet every babe in that building probably knows his business by now. You know how gossip gets around—and then gets all twisted after a while. If I were a man, I couldn't walk around in a building where all the women in the company knew who I had slept with. Let me tell you . . . there's a brother in the purchasing department on the third floor in City Hall, and every time I turn around his name is connected to another woman. And I am tellin' you, I've heard everything from he's the best lover in the world to his name should be Captain Quick Draw. Don't get me wrong, 'cause I date someone I work with, but we're monogamous."

Artise looked at Tassha with wide eyes.

"We better be . . . you hear me?" Tassha said.

"Yeah, what you and David have is nice. I mean, you two are seeing each other right now. But me and Vance are too, and he's going out doing this crap with others. How does that make me look? My picture is the one on display all over his desk, no one else's. I've tried to understand him. I know he's not messing with these ladies because he's not getting it at home. I know that for a fact. You know I talked to this Sheryl babe."

"You did?"

"Yep, and she said Vance never once said anything negative about me. Nothing."

"At least he's not trashing your name. I wonder what's gotten into him, Artise?"

"I don't know. Sometimes I think he's embarrassed that he hasn't stood by any of the things that he's promised. I mean, sometimes he comes home and finds me working on our business venture, and it just drives him crazy. Like I'm moving on without him or something."

"Why?"

"Girl, you know Vance. He had planned for us to be so well off, with children running all over the place by now. I guess when he walks through that door and sees me covered in paperwork instead of with a smile on my face doing something with our kids like we had always planned . . . I think it's a big letdown for him."

"Well, why has he stopped trying to do something, then? That's what I want to know. I've always envisioned Vance being much stronger than that."

"I don't know; I guess he's just like everyone else in this city who finds a job that pays relatively well. You know what I mean?"

"I feel you," Tassha agreed.

"You know how the saying goes around here, 'If you get to wear a suit and make thirty thousand dollars a year—you have accomplished something,' " Artise explained.

"I know. It's a trip how thirty thousand dollars seems to be what everybody in this city has to have in order to feel like somebody." Tassha giggled. "Including us."

"Yep, we ain't too much different. That's for sure. And if you really want to get technical about it, it's only fifteen we're making, because the government gets damn near half," Artise said, looking at her watch.

"Well, to be truthful, I'm tired of it. We should be doing much better than we are, Artise. I think it's time we go ahead and unveil our project," Tassha said.

"You think so?"

"I do. Look, we have been at this for a year and a half now. We have more than enough material to do our seminars and have practiced hours and hours on our presentations."

"I have to agree with you on that. I was looking at how many presentations I've already come up with and it blew my mind. Don't you know I have thirty presentations finished!" Artise boasted.

"Shoot, I have about that many myself. Artise, it's time. I'm at a point now if we don't do something soon . . . I think I'm going to go crazy. All the bad stuff happening in this city . . . these people need to hear positive messages. David was telling me that just the other night."

"You're right. It's not like we have to quit our jobs right away. We can set up some engagements on the weekends and see how things work out." Artise turned to Tassha. "Are you sure we're ready?"

"With all my heart, Artise. I know we can do this." Tassha and Artise both smiled; Artise grabbed Tassha's hand and said a quick prayer over their decision.

"Whew! I feel much better now! I know where my life is headed," Artise said as she took a sip of her drink. "Oh yeah . . . by the way. Ethan's back."

Tassha took her mouth off of her sandwich. "Are you serious? Why? For what?" Tassha said forcefully.

"Girl, I don't even know. Vance mentioned to me that he was going to pick him up and that's all I heard. I don't know if he's visiting or what."

"Probably running away from something like he always does," Tassha barked.

"Yeah. Now that man . . . has issues," Artise said.

"Well, anyway . . . I don't care. Haven't seen him in three years and don't want to see him now."

"I hear you."

"I'm happy with what I'm doing now. Just think if that fool would have stayed here and we would've gotten married, Artise? When he left I was sooo . . . damn brokenhearted. But since, I've realized it was a blessing in disguise that we didn't actually get married."

"Yeah, that would have been a mess," Artise agreed.

"I'm not even goin' to waste my breath talking about that fool. So . . . do you think you might want to go out with one of David's friends now?"

"No . . . no thank you," Artise said, shaking her head. "I don't think so."

"Why not?"

"Because I told you already. It would be too much like goin' out with my father."

"Is that what you think?" Tassha teased. "Please. . . . Yes, it's a little different at first, but you get used to it. Older men try harder at being romantic, Artise."

"I wonder why?"

"Experience, girlfriend. . . . Experience. Look at David. He's fine . . . to be nearing his sixties. He's slim, in shape, dresses nice, and he's very wise. I don't have any complaints. He looks better than most of the younger men running around here. I'm telling you . . . he has a lot of good-looking friends who are looking."

"Hmmm . . . let me think about it," Artise said.

"Will you?"

"Yeah . . . I'll think about it. . . . Now let's eat a little lunch."

Can I Get You Something?

"Here you are, son," Mrs. Gloria Stubblefield said to Vance as he reached out for the crystal glass full of water. "Stubby hasn't said a peep all day; if he doesn't wake up good and strong by tomorrow morning, I'm calling the doctor."

"That's a good idea. I'll just go in and check on him for a while," Vance said back to her, almost whispering under the jazz which was playing in the living room on the well-kept, outdated, four-foot-long, three-foot-high oak record player. Vance smiled. The unique look of the record player, combined with the yellow circular plastic attachment to keep the old record spinning, seemed to give the music more distinct sound and feeling.

It was without question that when Vance found out Stubby wasn't feeling well he'd drop everything. Murry Stubblefield was his mentor, counselor, and teacher and he had to find out how he was doing.

"Can I get you something to eat?" Mrs. Stubblefield asked. She was five foot two, dark as Mississippi molasses, with a very slender build. She wore a fashionable short-cut wig that was so firmly in place Vance often did double takes to see if it was her real hair or not. She had on tan pants and a white short-sleeve shirt showing her slender arms, each of which had one thick vein running down it.

"No, no thank you," Vance answered, relieved that he could resist her awesome cooking this time around.

Mrs. Stubblefield removed her finger from her lips. She always put her index finger over her lips while thinking before she spoke. "Are you sure?"

"Yes . . . I'm sure. I'm trying to watch my weight," Vance responded.

"Okay, suit yourself," she said as she turned away. Vance began to walk up the steps toward Stubby's bedroom but stopped as he heard Gloria creating a poem to the jazz that amplified the downstairs. Her voice was strong and her words passionate. They blended well over the tapping snare and blaring trumpet.

> *"I've seen a lot of things in my dayyy*
> *Just so many things I could say*
> *Ain't no need worrying 'bout the past*
> *The life I've lived wasn't first class*
>
> *"So many things had to work out*
> *Never been afraid to gut it out*
> *Strength and power is how I got through*
> *Strength and power—ha-lay-lu."*

Vance smiled and continued on up. He had heard many poems throughout the years, and normally when she recited poetry it meant there was something laying heavily on her mind. Mrs. Stubblefield definitely knew how to create poetry. Back in the day when Langston Hughes would come to town, he would always call her up and let her open for him before a reading. Langston loved to hear the young Gloria stand up and rock the crowd with her poems, and though Gloria enjoyed every minute of it, she never wanted to venture off from home to pursue her craft. She was happy standing in front of Langston or any other author who visited Columbus—while at the same time helping her husband to become successful. Bottom line, Gloria Stubblefield loved her some Murry and would do anything for him. Even years before she and Murry went down to the justice of the peace to make their union official Gloria had been a visionary soul. She had seen the greatness of her man and loved him without attempting to make him. She never had thoughts of a molding process and jumped into the clay of love—blind but willing, full of love. Her outlook on life stayed positive every day of their lives together—she was definitely a woman in love.

Vance watched Stubby sleep but could not tell if this was going to be one of those nights where that's all he would do. There had been times when Stubby was in pain when Vance would come over to visit and he would never wake up. Vance would just sit beside his bed and doze off himself, watch him sleep, or wait for him to wake up. The last time Stubby took ill Vance thought he was going to check out and give up living. For days he didn't move, speak, or show any signs of breaking out of his illness. Vance looked at Stubby the way a motion picture camera pans its subject. He could see that Stubby was in great pain. He even grimaced himself as he wondered what it would feel like to be in his same situation. But Vance broke out of his deep thought. He didn't want to seem worried, especially if Stubby suddenly opened his eyes, but it really bothered Vance to see Stubby this way. Stubby always tried the best he could to conceal from his loved ones the excruciating aches his body was experiencing from his arthritis. But this time . . . this moment . . . the grimace on his face and the way Stubby clenched his jaws together every ten to fifteen seconds showed he wasn't doing very well at all. Without opening his eyes, Stubby reached for his leg and tried to move it but couldn't. Vance did it for him and then began to massage both of his legs.

"Thank you," Stubby said softly. Vance smiled at him.

"No problem," Vance said just as softly, then continued to rub his legs, applying a little more pressure each time. Vance tried to imagine what it would be like to be eighty-five years old as he massaged Stubby's long-tired legs. *What was his driving force?* Vance wondered. Stubbs had already outlived all of his brothers, sisters, and one and only son. Murry Stubblefield had indeed come a long way from Winston-Salem, North Carolina. He was the youngest of sixteen brothers and sisters, and had been the mastermind of numerous business deals that netted him two hundred acres of land located all over the city. He never boasted or flaunted his wealth though. Sure his neighbors knew he owned property in the neighborhood, but they knew nothing of his fortune. Stubbs was a very inspirational man, a true motivator with wisdom beyond wisdom, and he loved to share all that he knew with anyone who would listen. For years Stubby had reached out to the children in the neighborhood. He'd fallen head over heels with Vance because he always had dreams, unlike other kids who would shake their heads unknowingly or spout off about the usual basketball, football, or movie-star dreams that filled their heads when Stubby asked them what they wanted to do with their lives. But not Vance. When Stubby would ask him what he wanted to do with his life as he waited for his rent money from Vance's parents, Vance would give him a different answer each time; but all of Vance's answers to Stubby's questions were clear and to the point. Stubbs took notice when it seemed that Vance actually sat down from time to time and thought about his future. Stubby easily placed Vance on the top of his favorite list of kids in the neighborhood. He made it a point to make sure Vance kept out of trouble, and made sure he had dreams and ideas pumping in his head every time he saw him. Vance explained to Artise that the main reason he didn't miss his parents when they moved to Oakland after he graduated from high school was because he had the Stubblefields.

Vance watched Stubby closely, but still didn't say a word. It looked like Stubby wanted to say something to Vance; his eyes were wide open and his thin lips about to move. But suddenly he closed his eyes and dozed back off to sleep again. Vance arose from his chair, opened the blinds slightly, looked out the back window and began to think about Artise. He couldn't shake the image of Artise and her wounded heart. He took a deep breath and looked back at Stubby, then noticed how good the deep redwood floors in the bedroom looked. They were aged and worn but displayed a glowing shine. Vance decided that this was the best place for him at the moment . . . someplace nice and quiet where he could think about what he had done to Artise. His mind began to wander again. He looked at Stubby's half-tilled garden in the backyard. It was four feet wide and twenty feet long. *More than likely Artise has had all that she is going to take from me, and quite frankly . . . I'm getting tired of me too,* Vance told himself as he heard Stubby move around in the bed. He walked over to see if he was all right. Vance looked down and observed what he wanted to become: committed, responsible, and strong to the bone, able to withstand the advances and temptations of the world. Days before Vance had slept with Sheryl he thought about Artise and the love he had for her. He tussled with the decision that he and Sheryl had made, but still he didn't have enough discipline to resist the temptation. After his second affair Vance had sworn to himself that he would not hurt Artise again, because deep down inside he really wanted his relationship with her to work. Vance tried with all of his heart to stay true but he didn't know how to get past the boredom that was setting into the relationship. He wasn't tired of being with Artise, but he missed the excitement that they once shared, and at the same time he saw himself getting older. Vance remembered when they would go out and dance the night away like no other couple in the joint, sliding around the dance floor as though they were on skates. It didn't matter what song was playing—from Janet Jackson's "Funny How Time Flies" to Alexander O'Neal's "If You Were Here Tonight," he and Artise intertwined with one another, cheek to cheek, enjoying the stares of those who wanted what they had and seemed to cherish so much True Love. Artise and Vance were lost without one another. They never let anyone come in between their tightly tangled web of love and together challenged anyone who would try. They were determined to stay together and become examples of what a relationship was and is supposed to be. But now Vance felt that because he did those things with her for so long he was somehow liable for her happiness forever. Deep in his heart Vance wanted to bring the excitement back. He wanted to find a way to break out of the everyday rut that he and Artise had fallen into over the years. He wanted to miss her when he was away from her again and to share a passionate kiss with her, just because.

"What's wrong . . . you in trouble again?" Stubby whispered slowly like one of the Last Dons. Vance bent down and placed a pillow behind his back.

"No . . . no, I just came by to see how you were doing. The missus called me and said that your bones were tightening up on you again."

Stubby tried to reach for the glass of water sitting on the nightstand, but was unable to put his hands around the glass.

"Give me a hand, will you. Dis won't last . . . too long I can tell . . . it's just a mild flare up. I shouldn't have spent so much time out in da garden. Have you taken a look at it yet? Thisyearmypeppersgoingtobethetalkofthetown," Stubby finished with a burst of energy. His garden was his life. Vance shook his head and chuckled.

"Okay . . . okay, slow down. Stubbs, why do you insist on working so hard in the garden?"

Stubby swallowed a sip of water. "Ya know how I am. I love to work with my hands and da Bible says that a man who doesn't work should not eat." Stubby smiled. "You know how I like to eat. You sound like Gloria. She wants me to sit in da house all day and watch TV. Dat Jerry Springer and all dat. I can't do dat, those shows will kill me. I need to keep movin', something to do. Black folk ain't never got nothin' by sittin' down all day long listening to other people's problems. You understand?" Stubbs struggled to say.

"Uh-hmmm, I understand," Vance said, as he put the glass back down and smiled, feeling Stubby would soon be back to normal, walking around in his blue jean farmer's suit and Nike high-top sneakers, and going from property to property on the block that he owned, making sure things were clean and in an orderly fashion and collecting his rent.

"Did you get somethin' to eat?" Stubby wanted to know.

"No . . . sure didn't," Vance answered.

"Boy, you know Gloria's feelings get hurt when you come over and don't eat anything?"

"I know . . . I know. But she piles it up so high on the plate. So I figure if I don't get anything at all, it would be better than leaving most of the food untouched, 'cause her cooking is too good. It puts weight on a brother."

"Trust me. She won't mind. Gloria loves to cook."

"Okay, I'll get a bite a little later," Vance reassured him.

"How's Artise?" Stubbs looked at Vance with his eyebrows arched, making the question that much more powerful. Vance walked over to the console television and turned on the set.

"Is this the channel you want to watch?"

Stubby nodded his head yes, and didn't pressure Vance about Artise. Wisdom told him that since Vance didn't answer, there was trouble in paradise again.

"Ethan's back," Vance blurted out. Stubbs began to laugh then cough. Vance walked over to the bed and gave him more water. "Did I say something funny?"

"Yeah . . . you sure did. I told you that Negro was not going to last in that city, didn't I? I bet you he came back here because he thinks he can slide by doing whatever he can without any kind of agenda. So what's his sorry self going to do now?"

"I don't know. Work—maybe get a job someplace. He said something about a grocery store or something."

"I tried to tell him years ago, that he had to stop joking around, but he never was one to listen."

Vance didn't want Stubbs to get worked up over Ethan. Ethan had stuck into Stubbs like a thorn ever since he was in junior high. "Don't you ever watch any other station?" Vance asked.

"No. CNN is my favorite. I like to see what's going on in the world. I don't need to see what has happened in this city because the same thing happens all the time."

"Yeah, I know. It's so predictable here. You ever think about leaving this place when you were younger?" Vance sat back down beside the bed.

"Younger? Boy, what you talking 'bout? I thought about leaving this daggone place yesterday." Stubby grabbed the cover and put it over his legs. "Look at it. July and we gettin' frost at night. How my garden goin' to take that?"

Vance smiled. "You ain't goin' nowhere, Stubby—you know you love it here."

"It's okay only if you have something to keep you busy all the time. If I didn't have all this property I would have been gone long long time ago to Florida. One day I might surprise you though and just take off."

"I hear you," Vance said.

"Are you thinking about leaving again, Vance?" Stubby asked.

"I don't know. . . . I just feel like my life is standing still. Not movin', just doing the same thing every day."

"I can tell you this: no matta' where you live, if you are not doing anything worth while you goin' to keep feelin' dat way. There are just too many young people feelin' like you, son, who don't understand dat."

"I just don't know what I want to do. I surely don't like my job enough to be there until I retire."

"Vance I am surprised at you. Why did you go get that college education for? And let's not talk about Ethan quitting college during his senior year."

"What? I went to school so I can get a job." Stubby took his eyes off Vance and looked at the ceiling. Vance noticed his expression.

"What?"

"The education you received was not given to you so you could get out and just get a job. It should be used to make a difference. You are beyond just workin' for somebody. You should want to make a mark with your life. To me that's what an education should be used for."

"But I got bills to pay. I have things that I haven't even accomplished myself—let alone go out and try to change the world."

"I don't think you are listenin'. You have the smarts to go out dere and do some powerful things that this place needs around here."

Vance smiled. "Thanks."

"You just need a break or two, that's all, just a chance."

In no time at all Stubbs was asleep again. Vance waited around for a while and decided that Stubbs was out for the night. So he went down into the kitchen to get a little something to eat.

The Talk

"Hey," she said softly, almost singing to Vance. Artise was quiet and solemn, still hurting. It was already hours past the time she usually came home from work, and Vance dared not ask her where she had been. Her specialized way of getting back at him was so powerful that if Dr. Laura knew about the situation she would likely suggest Artise's tactics to her callers on a daily basis. She was cold as ice toward Vance—very unlike her usual bright-eyed, smiling self. It was quiet in the house, and Artise could see Vance out of the corner of her eye as she put down her keys and browsed through the mail. He was at the counter in the kitchen drinking a glass of water.

"Hi, Teese." Vance could barely get the two words out of his mouth. He was feeling every bit of her pain. He didn't want to trip the wires and ignite the bomb that he knew must really be laying heavily on Artise's mind. *Maybe this is better,* he thought. *I can handle this. I have to.* "You want something to drink?" Vance offered.

Artise looked up and shook her head no. It wasn't because he was hungry that Vance opened the bag of chips sitting next to him, took a chip out, placed it in his mouth, and began to chew. The crunching broke the ice between them.

"I thought you were going over to the Stubblefields' today," Artise said.

"Umm-hmmm, I did, baby . . ." Vance paused. His words were out of habit, and he and Artise locked eyes for the first time. Vance thought maybe she would blow, but Artise didn't seem to mind. "I had a small bite to eat. I told Mrs. Stubblefield she just can't keep tryin' to feed me like she does."

"How was the old man doing?" Artise asked, not taking her eyes off Vance.

"He's doing fine. Just a flare-up, that's all." Vance took another chip out of the bag. "How was your day?" Artise hadn't called him as usual just to say hi.

"It was okay," Artise said, her voice cracking from emotion. She wanted to just break down and cry. She had yet to really explode from the devastation of her surprise. She hadn't talked to Vance about the situation yet and didn't know if she could. Artise didn't realize the reason she was so hush-hush about the situation was because she didn't want to accept the fact that Vance had betrayed her again in the same way he had promised not to in the past. It was almost like an old vinyl Michael Henderson record that had a scratch on it—the same words repeating over and over again. Even though the words that Vance skipped had sounded so sweet to her in the past, she knew it was time to take the stylus off of the record. Artise became agitated and just shook her head at Vance as her eyes filled.

"Vance, I can't believe you," Artise said with a grimace and grin and snicker rolled into one. "I honestly thought you were not going to put me through this again. What makes you think I can just sit back and let you continue to do this to me?"

Vance was still.

"All of the years I've put into this to make things work, and when I finally think I'm over the last thing you've done to me, you hit me with something else."

Vance looked at Artise with a blank face. He was tense and didn't know how to explain his actions to Artise as she stood there waiting for his answer, looking deep into his eyes, trying to figure out just what the hell was going on inside his head. "I know you're tired of this, Artise, and I'm willing to do whatever you choose. It's your call."

Artise nodded her head in agreement. "Yes . . . yes, it is my call, Vance, and I have already thought about it."

Vance tried to read her mind. She began to cry. Vance got off his stool and moved toward her.

Artise stepped away from him. "I can't take this anymore, but at the same time I don't want to lose you, because I've made you a part of my life that I've never imagined being away from. Look how long we've been together, and we have planned and planned, and it's getting to the point where we decided that we were going to get married and have children." Artise paused. "Are you doing this to me so we don't have to go on with our plan? Are you using me, Vance?"

"No, baby, that's not it at all," Vance assured her.

Artise broke down in exhaustion in Vance's arms. Vance's conscience began to lash at him. *Look what I've done not once, not twice, but for the third time. Damn I hate this. I hate to make her hurt like this. No more, damn it. No more!* Vance thought to himself. His words seemed to beat him and sting throughout his body. He dared not say anything. His words meant no more to Artise. The time had come for him to do as he said. Artise looked up at Vance as he tried to find the words to console her. She waited, but the reassurance never came, never materialized. Vance was too ashamed, and Artise took his silence to mean "Yes, affirmative, you're so right." Artise removed herself from his arms and walked away. Vance wanted to call Artise back to him, but didn't know what to say. He'd had his chance, but as he heard Artise shut the bedroom door, he realized once again he'd blown it.

Hard Workin'

After Artise finished crying her eyes out, she called Tassha and told her that she would be over in the morning. Tassha hung up the phone and rolled over, thinking Artise would show up around eleven, even after twelve. So when Artise knocked on her door at exactly seven in the morning Tassha thought she was dreaming. She couldn't even remember the last time she'd been up at seven on a Saturday. It had always been her sacred time—stretch time. Artise could tell Tassha was sleepy when she opened the door—but after telling her about her conversation with Vance, Tassha had understood why she had wanted to get out of the house. So they quickly made some coffee and went right to work on their business venture. The two sat around all day finalizing their business plan. So they were sitting at the kitchen table, Artise with her knees bent in the chair, concentrating like an elementary school child coloring for the first time. Though Tassha was too tall to get into the same position, she sat in the chair upright, poised in deep concentration with her head tilted in her hand. Artise looked up at Tassha.

"This really feels good."

"Doesn't it!" Tassha said, smiling from ear to ear. "I think this is going to work out, girlfriend."

"You mean you know this is going to work out. We're motivational souls now. We send everything into the atmosphere and claim it. Positive thinking all the time, sista!" Artise said.

"That's right . . . that's right. . . . We're going to set this place on fire!" Tassha declared.

Tassha and Artise were quite a team with just the right pizzazz, charm, and experience to make their dream come true. Their business plan consisted of using their God-given talents and becoming motivational speakers to corporations, high schools, colleges, and private industries. They had split up their workload months ago in the areas where they felt each was the strongest. Artise was working more on the spiritual side of getting souls and minds focused on God while Tassha concentrated on the motivational get-up-and-go aspect of achieving goals. Christian academies played a large role in Artise's life. She had attended private schools until she went to college, where she met Vance. Her mother had wanted her to attend Notre Dame, but Artise wanted to try something completely different so she chose to stay home and go to Ohio State University. At OSU she no longer had to attend mandatory church services, but she went anyway because of her love and faith in God. Now Artise wanted to provide a forum to teach others what she had learned about the Creator and how He could work in daily lives. Artise was interested in educating folks about spirituality on the job, in families, and in achieving goals. She knew firsthand how her spirituality had gotten her through college and helped in dealing with the dreary everyday predictability of her job. Not to mention helping with Vance and her on-again off-again relationship with her mother, which always devastated her more than anything because she was an only child.

Tassha on the other hand was a daughter of a schoolteacher and a civil rights activist. Her father worked in the housing industry, fighting mortgage and loan discrimination cases. His huge success set the good-ol'-boy network in Columbus on fire, and he soon found himself and his organization being monitored by the FBI. The experience Tassha went through worrying about the safety of her father after he was shot at numerous times only elevated her ability to articulate about troublesome situations. Tassha took most of her father's characteristics. She wasn't afraid to speak up herself when she saw injustice or someone not being treated right, a trait that David loved about her. Tassha's latest feat was when she overheard a store clerk at a department store call three young black males "restless natives" as they walked through the store on their way out to the mall. The store clerk was talking to the store manager, and as they both laughed at her comments, Tassha let them know that she didn't appreciate being in the store and having to listen to such ignorance and bigotry. She called the store's headquarters right from the store office and in a matter of minutes received an apology and an assurance the manager and clerk would be disciplined and sent to diversity training. That was just the type of person Tassha was—a strong-willed, talkative, outgoing woman able to get her point across and make others follow her. Her belief in her abilities was confirmed by working with David. He and Tassha were at odds on the issue of persuading the state to turn over regulatory control of welfare to the city so that they could more closely monitor single mothers and how the money they received was used. Tassha persuaded David not to vote for the measure, because the city council was going to put the extra responsibility on the city treasury office, which was already understaffed. David's vote was the deciding one and wasn't an easy decision for him to make, but he listened to Tassha's well-thought-out conclusions and decided she was right.

Artise put down her pen and turned to Tassha. "How long have we known each other?"

" 'Bout six years, almost seven. Why?"

" 'Cause it just seems so much longer," Artise said.

"Oh thanks, I think," Tassha said, laughing and looking at Artise in a strange kind of way.

"No, don't take it like that. I'm just saying, it's really nice to have someone in your corner who shares your dreams. You know?"

"I feel ya, girl. It's funny how two people who aren't even related can become so close," Tassha said; then she noticed Artise daydreaming, her hazel eyes fixed on the ceiling. "What's on your mind?"

"Me and my mother got into it again after I called you last night. I called her to talk about Vance and she started off with all this I-told-you-so nonsense that I was not going to hear. All I did was call her to talk, you know? And then we got into an argument."

"You and Cathy?"

"Sure did and it shouldn't even be like that. I should be able to talk to her without us getting into an argument about my life. That's why I was sitting here thinking about how me and you come from the same womb."

"What do you mean?"

"I mean the womb of sistahood. We've had some of the same trials and tribulations and can relate to each other just like—if not better than—mothers and daughters or even sisters who've come out of the same maternal womb. A lot of born sisters don't speak, are jealous of each other, and fight constantly, and we do none of that. In all the years I've known you, if we had something we didn't agree on we've never fought about it. You have your opinions and I have mine and we have unconsciously agreed to disagree without all the drama. I think most people are afraid to do that, which is why they have so many problems."

"You know, that's pretty good, Artise. I never looked at it that way. You should save that thought and write a presentation on it, 'cause some of these sistas need to know that we're all in the same game. I realized a long time ago it ain't going to get me anywhere if I sleep with a married man or dislike a sista who has gotten her life together and is doing well. When we do that to each other it makes us look so bad and only keeps the person who is jealous in a rut."

Artise jotted down a reminder to put Tassha's thoughts down on paper.

"Well, next week we should hear something from Nationwide and the Women's Rotary Club," said Tassha. "I called them both last week, and they seem to like our presentation ideas. David was even nice enough to recommend us, and I think they're going to come up with the money we asked for."

"That is going to feel sooooo nice. Getting paid for what we like to do, instead of what we have to do," Artise confirmed.

"Yeah and just think, after they hear us and word gets around, we're going to have all the engagements we can handle. 'Cause lawd knows we have something to give!" Tassha screamed and Artise laughed along. Artise looked at the clock on the wall.

"It's eleven o'clock already?"

"Time has flown by!" Tassha said.

"Yeah, but when you're sitting behind that desk nine to five, it takes forever."

"I know that's right."

"So you want something to eat?" Tassha asked.

"No, not me, I'm fasting today." Artise looked down at her work again, and Tassha's face went blank for a couple of seconds.

"How long have you been fasting?" Tassha asked.

"I started back in college when I would see a lot of sisters begin to gain weight. But as I started to read more about it in the Bible it's become so spiritual for me. It makes me stronger."

"I just don't understand how fasting can make you stronger. I've heard about it, but to me if you don't eat you get weak. Not that I eat a lot," Tassha said as she looked down at her body and noticed the rising poof around her midsection. "Well, not that much."

Artise smiled. "But it does make you stronger. It's like denying yourself something that you really enjoy, for the Creator. I fast for Him and it's so good for my body. You can fast just about anything, though."

Tassha dropped her pen on the table. "Interesting."

"Yeah—if watching television is one of your favorite things to do, don't watch it and spend that time praying and getting in touch with your spirituality."

"Some people do that?" Tassha wanted to know.

"Yep. My friend in college did," Artise said.

"Hmmm."

"But I personally fast meals because of how it cleans the body and how strong it makes the mind. See, if your body says it wants something and your mind tells your body it doesn't, your mind has control over your body. Like these men. If they let their mind control what's in their pants instead of vice versa I would probably be with my man right now."

"And maybe I would've still been with one or two myself," Tassha suggested.

"Why don't you try it with me?"

"You mean not eat?"

"Yes."

"Are you serious? I've never fasted before, and I've been craving some hot wings all day!"

"Well, don't eat the wings. If you really need something to eat, eat something else—a salad or soup."

"Girrrl, ain't no salad or soup up in here. I haven't been to the grocery store in weeks!"

"What have you been eating all week?"

"Monday I had a sandwich from the deli for lunch and didn't eat it all, so I ate that for dinner. On Tuesday David took me out to the Palace. Wednesday I ate those leftovers that I brought home with me from Tuesday, and Thursday I had Chinese, and last night a couple of slices of pizza." Tassha laughed and began holding her stomach.

"Well, try this. Since you want your wings so bad, don't eat them, and it will help you to understand fasting a little better. It's just taking something away that we really want, for God. You can eat a salad instead."

"I don't know, Artise."

"Trust me—you'll understand what I'm talking about."

"But I want some sloppy, zesty, greasy wiiiiings!" Tassha cried.

"Come on, Tassha, this is one of the things I'm going to talk about in all of my presentations, and I can use you as an example."

"Well, let's start tomorrow. I have no problem being your example, but right now I want some tasty hot wings with sour cream on the side and some fries. You can't tell me it doesn't sound good?"

"Come on, Tassha, pleeease. We can't talk right and walk left. We have to live what we speak," Artise begged. Tassha stomped her foot on the floor and smiled.

"Okay, I'll do this, but I'm going over to the grocery store and get myself the ingredients to make me the biggest salad you've ever seen." Tassha grabbed her purse and quickly headed for the door.

"Don't you want me to go with you?" Artise asked.

"No, that's all right, the store is right next door. You keep working. I'll be right back."

"All right, now, don't come back here with no hot wing sauce all around your mouth," Artise teased. Tassha opened the door and gave her comment some thought as she could almost taste the spicy sauce she had been craving.

"I won't. . . . I promise I won't."

Tassha actually enjoyed the three-minute walk it took her to get to the grocery store. She had always loved convenience. She'd spent all of her summers as a teenager in Manhattan with family, where it never took her more than a couple of minutes to get to any place she wanted to go. If she wanted pizza it was three blocks down. Movies were two blocks east. A turkey sandwich was across the street. Ice cream right next door. She had grown to love it, so when David offered to rent his condo to her, she didn't hesitate one second, because of all the conveniences it was surrounded by.

It would have had to happen like this, Tassha thought as soon as she walked into the store. The deli was the first department she came to after pulling out a basket. And the very first thing Tassha saw waving to her through the glass behind the counter was a freshly cooked batch of hot chicken wings that were still steaming. Tassha's first impulse was to go straight to the counter and order a dozen or two. But she stopped herself, and just for the sake of trying something new, she looked but didn't order any and felt good about it. She licked her lips and took a big whiff of the aroma, almost tasting the glistening sauce. Tassha fought off her desire and turned away, heading straight for the fruit and vegetable section. Tassha huffed and puffed, not because she was out of shape but because all the goodies in the store were getting to her. She wanted to hurry up and get the hell out of there before she grabbed a big box of Famous Amos peanut butter cookies or a double bag of barbecue chips and opened them up on the spot. It seemed like eternity, but she finally reached the vegetable section and looked at all the different types of lettuce that she could choose from. There were heads of lettuce, bags of wilted lettuce, and bags of lettuce mixed with nuts and carrots. Tassha put the wilted lettuce in her basket then turned around to see what else she could add to her salad. Onion, cucumber, tomato, and carrots all found their place in the basket, and Tassha decided that she was going to add a little cheese. On her way to the dairy department it was like she had been dragged back to her childhood when her mother wanted to go on a diet and would insist that Tassha join her. She had hated it. It seemed as though her mother went on a different diet every other month for weeks at a time and it drove her crazy. Tassha grabbed the cheese and stood in line behind a lady who had a full basket. Not the ordinary "It's eleven o'clock at night Blue Bell ice cream and cookies." She had the "Saturday afternoon ain't nuffin' left in the fridge I have five kids and school starts Monday" shopping cart that runneth over. And the bad thing about it, it was the only line open. Tassha knew it was going to be a while so she grabbed a *Sister 2 Sister* magazine off the rack and started to leaf through the pages. Then she heard a commotion.

"Oh no she didn't. Oh no she isn't," Kyle said to the slim grocery bagger standing behind him. Kyle was the store clerk. He stood around five foot eleven, very slim, with dark skin, a bald head, and an immaculate complexion. He began to suck his teeth each time he ran an item through the scanner while looking at the lady in bewilderment. Tassha could sense he definitely had an attitude and didn't want to do his job, so she stood by and watched his shenanigans.

"Child, what would make you want to come to the grocery store this late at night and do all this shoppin'?" Kyle asked.

"Excuse me?" the lady said back to him, shocked. Kyle stopped scanning the groceries and put his hand on his hip.

"Oh, you didn't hear me? Well let me ask you again, 'cause I don't have a problem with saying it again. I said, Why . . . did . . . you . . . wait . . . so . . . late . . . to come . . . up in here . . . and buy . . . all of this shit? Did you understand that?" Kyle rolled his eyes, then grabbed a box of detergent and ran it over the scanner. The petite sister's face became flushed and annoyed. She looked like she was getting ready to tell Kyle where he could go but got sidetracked as she tried for the second time to run her bank card through the debit machine. She tried for a third and then fourth time, then showed her frustration with the machine by taking a deep, agitated breath. She read the instructions again, swiped her card again, and stood there waiting for it to prompt her.

Kyle glared at the lady devilishly and slowly looked back at the bagger and smiled.

"It doesn't work," Kyle finally told her, and the bagger let out a muffled laugh. Kyle looked as if he had accomplished something.

"So what am I supposed to do?" the lady asked, surveying all of her groceries.

"Well, if you want my opinion," Kyle barked, "you shouldn't have come out this late buying all this shit. Maybe you'll have to put it all back up." Tassha put her *Sister 2 Sister* in her basket and made eye contact with the woman in front of her. They were both stunned.

"Look, is there another machine around so I can pay for all of this?"

Kyle didn't answer, and the bagger acted as though he hadn't heard what she'd asked.

"Sista, there's one right in front of the store," Tassha said, pointing to where the machine was. The lady picked up her purse from the basket.

"Thank you. I'll be right back." She briskly walked out, and Kyle followed her with his eyes.

"You would think with all these damn groceries she's buying she would be able to at least come out of the house lookin' better than that," Kyle said to Tassha, getting another snicker from his coworker.

"Excuse me?" Tassha said, not believing what was transpiring right in front of her eyes.

"I'm just saying, girlfriend, her outfit is outdated like a mutha!"

"First of all, I'm not your girlfriend. I'm a customer in this store and so is she, and I would appreciate you showing me and that sista some respect."

Kyle gave Tassha a glaring look.

"You have a serious problem," Tassha said.

"Yes, I have a problem," Kyle said.

Tassha confirmed it. "You sure do."

"And what do you mean 'I'm not your girlfriend?' I am what I am, so don't tell me any different," Kyle said.

"Look, I don't know what your problem is, but my eyes are looking at a man, *brutha,* and I have twenty-twenty vision."

"Oh no, she didn't say that, Kyle," the bagger said, agitating the situation, then looking out to the swinging doors as the lady came back from the debit machine. Kyle was getting ready to say something back to Tassha, but as soon as he opened his mouth the lady caught his attention.

"So how much is it?"

"One hundred and thirty-five dollars and thirty-two cents."

"Okay, thanks," she said, and she began to count out her money onto the counter. "Twenty, forty, sixty, eighty . . ."

"Damn, could you hurry up? I get off at six in the morning," Kyle said. Tassha held herself back, but the lady in line had had enough.

"Look, sweetie," she said. Kyle gave a "see there" look to Tassha, letting her know that he was recognized as feminine. Tassha shook her head in disgust with his attitude. "I don't know what your problem is, but that is the last time you are going to talk to me that way. I didn't come in here for that, so you better just take this money and shut the hell up!"

Kyle snatched the money and the bagger began to laugh as the lady stood there with her hand out waiting for her change. Kyle took the change from the drawer, ripped the receipt off of the register, and laid her change down on the counter.

"Who's next?" Kyle said, looking at Tassha. Tassha opened her purse to get her money. Kyle noticed the store doors open and for a brief second he looked a young lady up and down. She had on a tight pair of blue jeans, a red half-shirt, and her nipples were fighting their way for attention. Kyle shook his head when she noticed his stare. Then he looked back at Tassha. "Is this all you're eating, girlfriend?"

Tassha didn't answer.

"I know you're not on a diet. If you ask me, you need to put a few pounds on dat ass."

Tassha squinted at him and tried not to blow up. She exhaled.

"That will be eight dollars and ten cents."

Tassha started to hand him the money then stopped. "Can I see the manager please?"

The bagger looked at Kyle and put his hand over his mouth.

"Eight dollars and ten cents please," Kyle demanded.

"Look, I'm not giving you a damn thing until I see the manager."

Kyle sighed and snatched up the telephone then punched the intercom.

"Manager to register five. Manager to register five."

"What? You don't have enough money or something?"

"Don't you worry about it!" Tassha shouted.

"Oh, I'm worried . . . because if you don't, I'm the one who's going to have to put all this shit back."

"Kyle, what's the problem?"

Tassha turned around, and as soon as she saw the manager she put her money back into her purse and began to walk out.

"No wonder this place is such a mess!" Tassha shouted at the top of her lungs as she went through the swinging doors.

"Tassha . . . wait a minute!" Ethan hollered out to her.

"You know her?" Kyle asked.

When Tassha got back to the apartment she was out of breath and didn't have one single bag under her arm.

"What, you changed your mind?" Artise asked.

"Yeah, I think I'll fast after all," Tassha said.

Not In Here

 Ethan stood looking at Kyle.

"What? Why are you looking at me?"

"Kyle, what just happened in here?" Kyle huffed then shifted most of his weight to his right leg.

"Beats the hell out of me, Ethan. If you ask me, that heifer that just left here needs to check herself, because I don't have to put up with this." Kyle turned to the bagger. "Wasn't she trippin', Horace?"

Horace smiled and then tried to act like he was busy stacking bags under the counter. "I'm not in it," Horace said.

"Well fuck you, then. . . ." Kyle whined.

"It seems to me that you've been into a lot of altercations tonight. What's the problem?" Ethan asked as he walked over to Kyle's empty lane.

"Oh, so you think I was in the wrong?"

"I didn't say that."

"You don't have to say it, Ethan," Kyle snapped back. "You know what, Ethan, I don't know what kind of strings you pulled to come up in here and just take over as manager, but you're going to have to realize these customers are nasty."

"Strings . . . I didn't have to pull any strings. You ever heard of credentials . . . experience . . . work-related skills?"

"Yes I have, college boy," Kyle snapped.

Ethan and Kyle's relationship hadn't changed since they graduated from East High in 1982. The looks and snarls they gave each other were evidence that their longtime feud had not been put to rest after all these years. If Ethan didn't have to pay rent for his new apartment, he probably wouldn't have taken the job at Snyders Market once he found out that Kyle was on the payroll. Ethan simply didn't like Kyle Bennet.

"Listen, Kyle. I have a pretty good idea what happened out here tonight. And I'm going to tell you right now. You better shape up, because I won't have a problem with getting you out of here."

"Getting me out of here? Please. . . . See, I can tell you're raw, because it's not that easy. Maybe the union rep can break it down for you. I can call the office and have him down tomorrow."

"Your union rep doesn't have to break anything down, because I'm not like the coward who just left this job. I'll fire your ass first, Kyle, then your rep can talk to me all he wants to try to get your job back and believe me, it won't be easy. Now, is that raw enough for you?"

"Ethan, don't try to come out here and act like you have a problem with me and the way I do my job. Let's be real about this. You don't like me because I'm gay. You have never liked me."

"For the record, Kyle, I'm out here because of your job performance. For the first three days I've been on this job, your cash register has come up short each time, you've been late all three times, and the phone constantly rings for you like you were at home or something. But if you want to get personal—no, I don't agree with your lifestyle."

"What the hell you talking about—you don't like my lifestyle?"

"You heard me." Ethan looked at Horace. "Horace, did you hear me?"

"Yeah—I heard you," Horace said, walking away. Horace was on the chubby side, dark skinned and of average height, and wore a medium-length Afro.

"Good, because I don't like yours either," Ethan said. Horace was gay too. "But you do your work around here, so we don't have a problem. I have a problem with Kyle because he's trying to push his sexuality on every person that comes through those doors, and I ain't having it. People don't care about you like that, Kyle. You need to get it through your head."

"Look, you don't know me like that, Ethan."

"Come on, Kyle. I know you better than you would like. I know you enough to know that you need this job so you can take care of the child you and Stacey had right before we graduated from high school. What's that make your daughter now, seventeen, eighteen years old?"

"You have a daughter?" Horace blurted out.

"Yeah, I have a daughter, so what?" Kyle said, looking at Horace then back at Ethan.

"That's why I ain't buying this gay thing you're trying to push over on me, Kyle. You're just confused, man, get through it."

Kyle looked at his watch and then began to take off his apron. "Look, I'm on break. All I can say about this is you trippin', Ethan, you trippin'." Kyle began to walk out the front doors of the store and he paused for a second and looked at Ethan. "You would think you could accept gay men by now after living in Atlanta all those years. Shit, Atlanta ain't nothin' but the East Coast San Francisco," Kyle said, continuing out into the front of the store. Then he stopped again and turned back. "And, if you haven't heard, we have a national gay month now. So I suggest you get over it—cause we're here to stay. Just check your calendar."

Ethan began to walk through the store checking on the workers who were responsible for stocking the shelves. Ethan wasn't exactly happy to be working in the same damn store he had bagged groceries in as a teenager, but he needed the money. The owner gave him a very nice salary, and Ethan could work with it—for now. After he finished checking on the nighttime crew, he walked back to his office to begin on the receipts for the day.

"Ethan . . . Ethan, is that you?" a sweet, sexy voice rang out. Ethan turned around and showed his wide smile, then focused his eyes on the shapely figure that stood in the middle of aisle eleven in her blue jeans and tight-fitting red shirt.

"Monica. . . . Oh my goodness. Come here and give me a hug!" Ethan demanded.

"When did you get back home?" Monica asked.

"Couple of days ago. I'm back for good; this is where I work."

"For real?"

"That's right."

"Where were you again?" Monica said, holding on tight to Ethan's hand.

"In Atlanta. . . . Lived there for over three years."

"Ohhh, I hear it is sooo nice there."

"It has its moments. So how's your son?"

Monica paused for a moment, like she wanted to tell Ethan something. "Oh, he's fine. . . . He just turned four, but he's going on twenty-three."

"Is that right?"

"Umm-hmmm," Monica said, flirting with Ethan.

"I know somebody has snatched you up, as good as you're looking," Ethan said, catching on to Monica's hand caresses and playful come-on.

"Nope," she said with lightning speed.

Ethan smiled. "Well, looks like we're going to have to start off where we left off."

"If I remember, you promised to take me out."

Ethan chuckled. "You remember that?"

"Yes, I do. I also remember you telling me that I was too young for you—when you left."

"I said that?" Ethan said, looking Monica up and down and having a very hard time keeping his eyes away from her exposed midsection.

"You sure did."

"Well, how old are you now?" Ethan joked.

"I'm twenty-three."

"Old enough for me!"

"Are you sure?"

"Yes. . . . Why don't you call me here a little later. We'll hook something up, okay?"

"Okay . . . I will. Talk to you later," Monica relayed back to Ethan, then she let go of his hand.

Oh yeah . . . talk to you later, Ethan thought as he watched Monica in her tight jeans shift from side to side until she was out of view.

Giving Guidance

It couldn't have been a more beautiful day. Sun shining at its fullest, air fresh and crisp. Vance stepped out of his car and looked at Stubby, who was standing in the middle of his garden. The seventy-eight-degree day had Vance envisioning a nap once his eyes focused on Stubby's hammock, which was free and clear of a body.

"You might as well take dem eyes off my hammock! I might be old. But I ain't blind. . . . Remove dem eyeballs, partner!" Stubbs giggled at his own joke. "I haven't been able to lift my legs high enough to get in it for the last five weeks and I just lowered it a bit. When Gloria brings me my cool tea, I ain't going to be no good to nobody!" Stubbs began to laugh again—almost uncontrollably.

"Don't nobody want to lay in your hammock. Keep working!" Vance joked as he moved in closer to the garden. "What's happening, old man?"

"Just lookin' over da garden dat's all. You know I must have did a damn good job puttin' in dat fertilizer, 'cause my collards look like I might have to give some of these away dis year," Stubby boasted.

"Well, you know you don't have to worry about that—the way your wife cooks. She'll be able to put them bad boys in a pot. Shoot, the way you worked in that garden and the pain you went through . . . you deserve a nice garden."

"Dat's righ', boy. You reap what you sow. I'ma say it again. You reap what ya sow. And just look, my harvest is plentiful." Stubbs grinned. "Looks like Gloria goin' to be a while wit' dat iced tea. But I'm goin' to lay on back anyway . . . don't want to waste this beautiful day." Stubbs looked up into the heavens; there wasn't a cloud to be seen.

Vance grinned at Stubbs. He always did when Stubbs wore his farmer's suit. Stubbs still had a lively glow about him. His golden brown face with the two small moles under his wide eyes and his completely bald, clean-shaven head made you keep your eye on him at all times. Vance's eyes traveled down to his shoes. "Stubbs, you went and got you a new pair of sneakers, didn't you! Every time I turn around you got a new pair. You as bad as these young boys running around here."

Stubbs looked down at his shoes. "Oh yeah—had to git me a pair of dem Jordans. You know he got his own line of clothes now. Got me a warm-up suit too. Probably wear dat next week when I do a little barbecuing for the block party. You welcome to join us."

"Thanks, you know I'll stop by."

Stubbs maneuvered himself into a comfortable position in his hammock and looked down at his shoes again. "Um-um-ummm if dey only made dese when I was comin' up. I would've been in da Hall a Fame, boy."

Vance smiled.

"So what you doing? Coming over to check on the old man or what?"

"Yeah—had to see how you were coming along. But I see you're all right."

Stubbs's eyes lit up—he was grateful. "So where is dat Artise, huh? You know I like to see her hangin' all on your arm, don't ya?"

Vance moved his eyes off Stubbs then to the ground. His foot kicked at the grass. "Yeah, I know. . . . But we ain't doing too good right now."

"What did you do?" Stubbs asked. Vance looked up at Stubbs.

"What did I do?"

"Yep. . . . What did ya do? Don't no lady stop hangin' around ya if ya didn't do nuffin'."

"How do you know so much?" Vance teased.

"What did that rapper—wit' those slick jitterbug dancers dat we used to watch over and over again—say? Used to remind me of my swinging days."

"Who are you talking about?" Vance chuckled.

"You know, dat music movie I taped. I still got it—in my room. It didn't last but 'bout four or five minutes."

"Music movie? Ohhhh. Dr. Dre, in his music video," Vance remembered.

"Yeah, yeah . . . dat's him. . . . I know so much because I'm like him. I been dere and done dat." Stubbs chuckled.

"You crazy!" Vance suggested.

"Well I have, Vance, and I been studying yo' face the last couple of weeks. Somethin' is troublin' you. And I got a good idea what it is."

"Is that right?"

"Yup, and I ain't goin' to judge you either."

Vance took a deep breath. His relationship with Artise was sinking fast. It had been weeks since they'd held a decent conversation. Vance was in the process of putting more pressure on himself for his mistake than she was.

"Well, Stubbs, tell me. How do you do it? How do you stay away from being tempted?"

A chuckle came out of Stubbs's mouth.

"See, dat's your first mistake. You have an illusion dat you won't ever be tempted." Stubbs lifted his head up and made sure Gloria wasn't on her way over. "Take my word—you're *always* going to be tempted, but it's what you do with the temptation that counts. You can believe it or not—but I get tempted. Not as much as you get tempted . . . but ol' man Stubbs gets tempted, boy!" Stubbs looked around again then laid his head back down. Vance snickered.

"You? What's that all about?"

"It's about being human . . . not a man . . . but human. I bet you my wife get tempted too. But you got to work through it, Vance. . . . It's a constant battle." Vance ran his hand over his beard then put his hand on his chin and listened intently; this was exactly what he needed. "Dat's why I tell you . . . you need to find you a real good pastor who talks about dese things. It's a fight wit' dat devil. The devil knows where people are weak. And dat's in da flesh—it's something else."

"That's for sure," Vance said.

"Take Mr. Clinton for example. I know we done heard a lot about him lately, much more than some can stomach. But dat man—well, I say human to get my point across—is the highest-ranking official in da free world. Now some of my ol' buddies around town feel like he deserved what he got from dat girl. The economy doin' fine . . . everybody workin'—them people I talk to say he deserved that girl getting down on her knees for him. But dey thinking like humans. The devil done went into dat man's life and set him up and had dis whole country in a uproar. Dat's how da devil work, Vance. He will find your weak points and keep workin' dem until you tame them or until Jesus get tired of you being used. Then the wages of sin . . . is death. You understand?"

"Yeah . . . I understand, but I try, Stubbs. I tried my heart out."

"Boy, you ain't got to confess to me." Then a light went off in Stubbs's head. "What you mean, 'tried'?" Vance gave Stubbs an embarrassed fake-ass smile. "Awww, Vance. Dang on it!"

"I know . . . I know. How do you think I feel?" Vance pleaded.

"I hope really really bad. And I mean dat, son. I thought you loved Artise?"

"I do!" Vance answered back quickly.

"Well dat ain't no way to show her, boy." Vance nodded his head. "You got to let her know she's all you're living for—ya know what I mean?"

"Yeah . . . I know," Vance answered. "And I'm trying, that's all I can say. I'm tryin' and I'm going to do better."

"At least you recognized it, son. Some people never do dat. All you got to do is just work on becoming strong—mentally and spiritually. And I tell ya, it ain't no easy thing to do, especially da way dese young womans be dressin' up nowadays . . . I'm tellin' ya, Vance, it ain't easy." Vance began soaking up Stubbs's words of wisdom, and Gloria, dressed in an all-white dress, came out to the hammock and handed Stubby a glass of iced tea.

"Hi there, Vance," she said. "You want a glass of tea and a chicken sandwich?"

Stubby looked at Vance before he took a sip of his drink. Vance saw the look. "Sure! Thank you very much."

Gloria started to make her way back into the house and Stubbs hollered out.

"Gloria . . . do me a fava' when ya come back out. Git dat envelope on my nightstand wit' Vance's name on it."

Gloria threw her right arm in the air, acknowledging Stubby as she carefully tried her best to walk back up the three steps that were in between her and the door. Vance put his hands in his pocket and looked down at Stubby, who was into his tea.

"What envelope?" It seemed like Stubby phased Vance out for a minute, because his eyes gazed up to the clear sky.

"Ya know . . . life ain't the same as it used to be, Vance. I've been living a very, very long time, and I've seen so many things in this world change. Mainly people." Stubbs looked at Vance, wiped the sweat from his face with his handkerchief, and snickered. "Includin' you."

"Me?" Vance pointed to himself.

"Yup, you. It use to be a time—and not too many people still round that could back me up on dis—but it use to be a time when things mattered, people mattered and cared about what was happening in their lives. Not a lot of folk can say dis." Vance noticed the neighborhood seemed to become strangely quiet. "But I have seen it all. The Great Depression. Understood and agreed with the Kerner Report. Seen great men murdered because of hatred and how the press holds as much blame for the destruction of our community as the government itself. I've even known black men who couldn't even get a shot at the big leagues and was betta' than Jackie Robinson or Roy Campanella. And now, thirty, forty years lata' they talkin' 'bout the Negro leagues like it was one of America's most treasured pastimes. It's just convenient for them to do that now because those pictures and history are moneymakers." Stubbs shook his head. "Just been one hell of a life and sometime I don't know how I endured it all. When things take a turn and look like dey goin' to get betta' . . . something else comes along and sets everyone back ten years. When dey lay me to rest, one thing they goin' to know 'bout me, I lived my life to the fullest and I made good of a whole lot of bad that's been done to me and my people."

Vance didn't know where Stubby was going with this. Sometimes Stubbs would rattle on about things on his mind—have another quick thought and be off and talking about something else—but not this time; he stayed the course and it kept Vance's attention.

"I can't recall if I ever told you this story before, but I was told it over and over by my father."

"I'm listening," Vance assured Stubby.

"Well, two months before I was born in Mississippi in 1914 there was a lynching dat was as bad as dey came back in dem days. I can remember being told about it at the age of five and from then over and over again until it was a fixture in my brain like da alphabet. There was a black man named Samuel Petty who lived in Leland, Mississippi, and he got into a scrap wit' one of dem white-boy deputy sheriffs, and they accused him of killing dat deputy. I don't know if he did or he didn't, but when word spread of da fight and killin', a big mob just came to his home and pulled Petty by a rope to the center of the city." Stubbs began using his right hand to help him get his point across while he held the glass of tea in his left hand. "Even in my old age, son, I can still imagine how he musta felt knowing dat he was going to be tied up by a rope and killed. All da white people of the town had a meeting and decided what to do wit' him. It musta been at least four hundred people in the city, and da men and boys all had guns and rifles and helped to fill a box up wit' straw drenched in oil. Dat boy Petty pleaded for his life, and as he screamed and begged they turned him upside down so dat his head was inside the box, den set him afire. Dat boy Petty was strong, though; he was determined not to be burned by dem flames, and somehow, dat man got himself free of da box and back on his feet, but his body was ablaze. Still tied to the rope Petty tried to run and da fools dat tied him up was still holdin' the rope and let him run until the slack ran out of dat rope. They just stood there pointing deir guns and pistols at him." Stubbs's old hand began to tremble. He was shaken and didn't even notice his worn hand was showing how much he was being touched inside his old soul. "Den . . . a voice rang out from dat crowd. Shoot him! Shoot him! someone hollered. And don't you know dem fools shot him until dey didn't have any mo' bullets. He was on da ground and his body still ablaze and dem white boys walked up to him and shot him some mo' and he was already dead. Imagine dat." Stubby grabbed the side of the hammock and just looked up into the sky. Vance looked at Stubby, took a deep breath, and rubbed the back of his own neck. It was hard to swallow. Most of the time when Stubby told stories they all were connected to an incident that happened in the news or in the community. But this time Stubby was way out there, and Vance couldn't comprehend why he'd brought up the subject of the lynching. Gloria came out and brought them out of their silence. She handed Stubby an envelope and placed a pitcher of tea and Vance's sandwich on a nearby table. Vance looked at Stubbs.

"You okay?"

"Yeah . . . yeah, I'll be fine. Dat story always tears me up inside," Stubby confessed. "And to think we still got people in this very neighborhood doing worse things den dat to their own brothers and sisters." Stubbs just shook his head and looked like he was going back into his thoughts, but the envelope blew to the ground and caught his attention. Vance bent down and picked it up and attempted to give it to Stubbs. Stubby looked at Vance. "No, no, you go ahead and keep dat." Vance looked at the manila envelope.

"What is it?"

"Don't worry about it right now. You'll find out after I finish tellin' you my story." This time Vance took a seat next to Stubby on the grass. "So during da lynching dere was a man who saw the entire episode. He was a black man. He hid so dem white boys didn't see him, and he witnessed da whole thang. He was so disturbed how dem people just took it upon themselves and judged dat man and decided what should happen to him in a matta' of minutes 'cause he was black. After he witnessed what happen' to Petty he knew in his heart dat he had to tell someone just what happened so dat the other blacks in town would know and many others around the nation would too. So what dat man did was wrote down word for word what he saw and sent letters out all across the country. Dat man risked his life and told everyone what happened, and it even made some of da black folk up North angry and dey wanted to go in dat city and burn it down. They decided against it though . . . but his letter brought about a new mindset in a whole lot of black folks, and dey started to fight back after dat. . . . They didn't want to take it anymore." Stubbs slurped some of his tea.

"Hmm . . . it must have been a real hard living back then with all them fools lynching blacks."

Stubby nodded his head yes. "Yep . . . it was. Dat's why I want to do what I need to do and see the difference I make. See, the man didn't have to go out on no limb and tell people what was goin' on down South. He didn't have to take da risk of getting him and his family killed. But he did it. 'Cause he knew it was da right thing to do. He spread the word. And that's what I want you to do at some point in your life," Stubby said, looking at Vance and pointing toward the envelope.

"What are you talking about?" Vance wanted to know.

"Go ahead and open her up." Stubbs pointed at the envelope.

Vance looked at the envelope before opening it, then at Stubby again.

"Just something I wrote," Stubbs joked—he had never learned to write. Gloria had written all his correspondence. Vance looked at the contents.

"Whose handwriting is this? I know it isn't yours. I've seen your handwriting."

"Okay, you got me. . . . It's Gloria's that's a writer's pen. You know I can't scribble like dat." Vance looked over and noticed Gloria appear through the screen door, looking at him. He began to read.

Vance,

Me and Gloria can't explain how much you have meant to us all these years. After we lost our son, it seemed like you just stepped right in and knew that we needed someone in our lives. We have cherished every day that you have come over to see us just to say hello. We thank you so very much for doing things around the house when Stubby has been laid up in that bed when his bones stiffen up on him. We always say to each other how thankful to God we are to have you and look upon you just like a son. You treat us better than most sons do their own parents. You always come over on the holidays when most people don't care, you never forget our birthdays even when we do. You truly give us a reason to live because you are nothing like the many other people in the world that have forgotten about the older generation. You always ask our opinion on issues and want to know what we have done in our past in the same situations that you encounter yourself in these last days. We just want to say thank you so very much and to tell you that we love you so very much.

Love always—Murry and Gloria Stubblefield

Vance turned to Stubby. He could see there were tears forming in his eyes. Stubby was thinking of his one and only son who'd died in a car crash. Stubby missed him dearly and had never had a chance to share something like this with him. Now, through Vance, he was able to experience this father-son moment. It was pure happiness and joy. The expression on Stubbs's face told Vance that this moment was very precious to him, and he wanted to enjoy every second of the moment. Vance reached down and took Stubbs's brown trembling hand—a hand once filled with the physical power to protect him and his family. Vance could still feel the strong, dignified spirit that remained in his soul. Stubby shook his head, and Vance could see from Stubby's expression that this was a moment he would take to his grave. A tear fell from Vance's eyes onto the letter right before he bent down and gave Stubbs a hug. Vance cleared his throat.

"Thank you. . . . That was very nice," he said, turning his head to wipe the tears from his face. Gloria was now by his side; standing firm and strong like this was the moment she'd always dreamed of having with her own son. Vance bowed gracefully to her, then took her hand and pulled her into him as Stubbs pulled out his handkerchief and wiped his eyes. "Thank you . . . thank you very much," Vance said again. Making someone feel good cleared his mind from the trouble that he had caused Artise.

"You're welcome, and every last word is the truth. You just don't have people in your life as good as you, boy. A very rare commodity indeed." Gloria continued to pat Vance on his back as they embraced. "Now look at the next page," she said. Vance looked into her teary eyes, then began to read. Gloria and Stubbs looked at each other, full of pride, and Gloria reached for her husband's hand while they waited.

"You must be kiddin' me! Stubby? . . . Miz Gloria?" They had smiles on their faces. "I can't take this. . . . Uh-uh . . . ain't no way."

Gloria became stern and impassioned. "Now, Vance, this is what we wanted to do. We talked about it and prayed over it for a while now. The Bible says we're to leave an inheritance and see it work while we are still living. We want to show you how to work this gift if you don't know how." Then she smiled. "Plus, boy, you deserve it."

Vance smiled.

"Take her words, boy, like dey was comin' out of my mouth," Stubby said. "What you have there is a deed to some very important land—precious land right here in this city, most of it located downtown. Not many people around here even knew we owned it. We bought some of that land from a white gentleman who right before he passed away felt bad about all the bad things he had done to black folk. Gloria worked for him and his wife, and you know I was dibblin' and dabblin' in real estate, and when dat ol' boy asked me if I wanted to buy it then asked me to name the price . . ." Stubby began to laugh. "I just couldn't turn it down. So I reached in my left-hand pocket and pulled out a dollar and he took it—no questions asked." Gloria walked over and patted Stubby on his chest. "Vance, you have just become a very rich man. A very rich man," Stubby assured him.

Big Willy

The dark hollow surroundings of the parking garage had always made David leery when he walked out to his car after work. The underground parking, which was available for City Hall top brass and their guests, was dark on the brightest of days and the aura of under-the-table business dealings filled the air. It was close to seven-thirty in the evening and David was on his way to meet with his campaign manager to discuss financial matters for his campaign before a late dinner with Tassha.

"How are you, Councilman?" a firm cocky voice rang out from the direction of David's car. David stopped and tried to focus on the silhouette standing beside his car. "Very difficult to see down here, isn't it?" Then there was a chuckle. David still didn't recognize the voice or the shadowed face, so he stood still, hoping it wasn't some reporter from the *Dispatch*. "Councilman, please, I would like to have a couple minutes of your time," the man said, then he began to approach David. With each step he took an echo followed him. Intuition told David to look behind himself. When he did he noticed a dark sedan rolling very slowly toward him with its parking lights on—then it stopped.

"Doesn't look like I have a choice, does it?" David said as his eyes focused on the features walking through the murkiness. Out from the gloom came a man slightly shorter than David, well-dressed in a dark pinstripe suit. He had brownish red hair and eyebrows that were even lighter, a pointed nose, a crooked smile, and a deceitful standing disposition. David pushed his head forward to confirm his notion. "Tenner?" David said.

"Well now . . . you finally recognized me," Tenner said, raising his hands shoulder high. "This lighting is really bad on the eyes of men our age, David. I hope you get that fixed when you become mayor. Hey . . . that would be a helluva campaign slogan for you." Tenner laughed. "I can see it now. 'Hey, Mr. Mayor, get us out of the dark!' Imagine that on an all-black TV screen, David. I bet a message like that would put your counterpart on point!" Tenner laughed again and saw that David wasn't amused. "Well think about it." Tenner took a deep breath and put his hands in his pockets, and David looked around to see if anyone else was in the garage with them. "David, relax. I just finished meeting with the mayor—everyone knows that I'm down here. No need to worry at all." Tenner didn't calm David's nerves.

"What do you want, Tenner?" David looked around again. "One picture of us together down here alone and any chance I have for being mayor is washed away."

Tenner became sarcastic. "Is my reputation that bad, David?" Tenner tilted his head to the side and rocked his head back and forth. "I'm going to see what I can do to improve my image. I'm starting to hear that too much."

David was becoming edgy. Ronald Tenner was the richest man in the city of Columbus. And he was not only powerful in the city but he had ruthless connections worldwide. He was the chairman-CEO of the largest real estate firm ever established in the state of Ohio and had a hand in every business and political endeavor in the past twenty years. And he was proud to be known as a die-hard ladies' man. Over the years his public persona had declined. The residents of the state—particularly those in the city of Columbus—were tired of his cutthroat business tactics, which were leaving them footing the bill on proposed malls, airport renovations, and the promise of bringing the city a professional sports team. The money he flaunted was very old money. The Tenner empire had been passed down generation to generation from his father's Irish heritage. Tenner had grown up watching his father and grandfather handle their empire and didn't have a hard time continuing their business dealings.

"So how's the campaign coming along?" Tenner asked. David nodded his head.

"It's coming. What can I say?"

"Outstanding, David. I'm really glad to hear that. You know it's no big secret I was here today to talk to Mayor Causwell. You know—just to feel him out. I'm trying to decide if I want to support him again or not. But something about him . . . I don't know, but a little voice in me is telling me not to work with that scum again and to choose another contender. Do you believe in little voices, David?" David didn't respond, but he took a step toward Tenner. Tenner placed his hand on his cheek and looked up at David. "You know, this voice is telling me to back someone else in the election, and the way I see it, there's only two legitimate parties running for the seat—and one of the parties is standing before me. Now, David . . . we have locked horns many times in the past, but I really think we could come together on a couple of issues, and if so, I can get you the money you need to finance your campaign. I know you could use the money, David."

"How do you know that?" David asked.

"Everyone can use money, David. . . . Everyone."

"I'm listening."

"Well, David, it goes without saying that I have great sway in this city, and all over the state for that matter."

"More than a few argue that point, Tenner."

"Come on, David. You know it's true. Regardless of what anyone says. Now hear me out. My endorsement would not only put my thousands of faithful citizens in your corner, but the city police, fire department, and Jaycees are all ready to support you on my command."

"Tenner, I already have their support, along with the entire black community and a good portion of the white Democrats. I think that alone will get me in the seat."

Tenner shook his head slowly and chuckled. "Look, David. We're both businessmen. Don't for one second think the black community in this city and the small amount of white Democrats who will vote for you will be enough to win this election."

David knew Tenner had a legitimate argument. It happened to be David's biggest concern when he had decided to run for office. He decided to hear Tenner out.

"So what do you want? How can I help you, Tenner?"

Tenner smiled. "Well, David . . . I want to support a candidate that has my same feeling and vision concerning crime and the penal system. This city just hasn't been the same since they tore down the state penitentiary. This entire country is being bombarded by crime and roguish criminals every day, and our city's crime rate isn't what you want to call appealing. What I want to do is back a candidate who steps up to bat for mandatory minimum sentencing, abolishing parole for minor crimes, and who will fight for a new private prison that will house men and women right here in our great city. If I could find me a candidate with those intentions, I would back him with all I have to get him elected."

David began to laugh. "You must think I'm just a dumb fuck, huh, Tenner?"

"Now, David, why would you say that?"

"What will you get out of this private prison?"

Tenner smirked. "I get to own it."

"I thought so."

"So you're aware of the profits in private prisons, huh, David?"

"It's my job to be aware."

"Good—so I won't have to tell you about all of the wonderful moneymaking opportunities there are through contracting the facility out."

"Not to mention the expenditures that come along with the deal. Especially if you're the one supplying the prison with its necessities," David said.

"Well, David . . . you sound like you've done your homework. My privately owned T.E.N. Group will own and run the facility. With the new mandatory sentencing and the abolishment of parole my friends in the statehouse are preparing to pass in the next few months, overcrowding in jails will develop and they will have to come to my prison—of course, for a fee," Tenner said confidently.

"That's so gracious of you, Tenner," David said. "How am I going to explain building a new privately owned prison in the city?"

"Now, David, come on. You're one of the biggest salesmen this city has to offer. I still remember when you peddled vacuum cleaners back in the good old days. Just use your charm," Tenner sang. "Use your charisma!" Tenner snapped his fingers together. "Just do what you do best. You know, a Stop the Violence and Crime campaign. You're perfect for it."

"And where do you propose on building this prison?" David asked.

"Downtown. Where else? It's already abandoned and we already have the new sheriff's facility there, the juvenile center, the new city jail—hell, a high-tech prison is all we need."

"There's no room for that," David argued.

"There will be," Tenner said.

"What are you talking about?" David could only imagine what Tenner was up to.

The lights on Tenner's car flashed and broke the two out of their dealings. "Well . . . duty calls. Just think about what I said, David. . . . Full financing for your campaign. You can't fuckin' beat it. You just can't." Tenner walked past David. David stood still until Tenner's car was out of sight.

More Meat

 "Thanks for the interview, Mr. Davis."

"Please call me Ethan—my father is Mr. Davis," Ethan insisted.

"Okay, no problem," said the dark-haired white girl. She was wearing beige Dockers, low-heeled brown shoes, and a brown button-down shirt. She had strong cheekbone structure and her full lips allowed her to get away without plastering makeup all over her face.

"So, Casey, you're interested in working here at Snyders?" Ethan said, shuffling through her application papers.

"Very much so. In fact, the assistant manager position will help me out with my thesis paper for the graduate work I'm doing."

Ethan looked down at Casey's credentials. Then he was interrupted by the intercom system. "Yes, Tina, what is it?"

"Sorry to bother you, Ethan, but your favorite employee is at it again. He's on his break in the deli."

"Okay, I'll be there as soon as I can," Ethan told the front-end clerk. He turned back to Casey. "Sorry about that. . . . Sooo, you graduated in ninety-two and you were born in sixty-seven?"

"Umm-hmm, yes."

Ethan had a look of bewilderment on his face. Then he took a quick glance at Casey again.

"Is there a problem?" Casey wanted to know.

"You just don't look a day over twenty-five. Not that it's a bad thing, but when I first took a look at you, I thought you were younger. That's all."

"I'm a vegetarian and love to work out."

"That will do it. Well, would you look here . . ." Ethan said, looking at her résumé. "I went to OSU myself."

"You did?"

"Sure did—and dropped out the last quarter of my senior year."

"I've thought about it myself plenty of times. Actually I received a scholarship for vocal music. But I took a long look at the chances of ever making it in that business and I had a change of heart," Casey said.

Ethan smiled. "So tell me, who do you sound like? My girl Celine or Shania Twain?"

"Neither," Casey answered bluntly. "Put it like this: If I had to compare, which I really hate to do, I would say Mary J. mixed in with some Tina Marie with a splash of Minnie Riperton."

"Oh . . . it's like that!" Ethan responded.

"Like I said. If I had to compare," Casey giggled.

"Well, your résumé looks fabulous. I'm really trying to change the attitude around this place. This market could really double its take on a weekly basis if the workers would put out a little more. But most of them have been here for a while, and the union they belong to has the upper hand, and they try to get away with murder."

"Union? Oh my," Casey blurted out.

"Does that scare you?"

"No, but I've heard so many things about unions."

"Believe me, they all are true," Ethan joked. "You just have to go by the letter in the store policies; it eliminates problems with the workers. If you have a problem—lateness, nonproductivity, whatever—it's right here in this blue book that corporate and the union came up with." Ethan held up the small pocket-size book and showed it briefly to Casey.

"Well, I would really like to work here, Ethan."

Ethan looked at Casey. "I don't see anything here that gives me any indication that you can't." He put down her résumé. "So when can you start?"

"As soon as possible wouldn't be soon enough."

"You'll be working directly under me, and I'll be happy to answer any questions that you have. First we have to get you drug tested. When we get back the results we can work on your schedule. Here's the address to the drug-testing location. Give me a call in two days; I should have the results. Any questions?"

"No, I think that will do it," Casey said, getting up from her chair. Then they were interrupted.

"Ethan, I think you need to come into the deli," Tina said over the intercom. Ethan looked down at the intercom and pushed the button.

"Okay, Tina . . . I'll be right there." Ethan stood up from his chair.

"Thanks a lot, Ethan, I'll see you later," Casey said as they walked out of the door together.

"You heard me. . . . Give me some meat, nigga!"

"Kyle, you better get out of here with that," Horace instructed.

"Horace, I can't eat no sandwich wit'out no meat. You know I like meat. And hurry up. I waited twenty minutes for you to make this one and I only got twenty minutes left on my break. I can't understand it. . . . You get moved from placing groceries in a bag to putting meat on a piece of bread and you think your whole damn life has changed."

"Look at all of these customers, Kyle," Horace whined.

"I see them," Kyle whined back. "And they see me. . . . They can wait. You fixed this sandwich and I don't like how it's made, so you goin' to do it right. I'm a customer too, damn it."

"Kyle, why don't you come behind the counter and put whatever you like on it. You're not going to get me caught up in your games, because I'm not baggin' no more groceries."

"Look . . . you're the one making sandwiches, nigga . . . so, here, finish making this one." Kyle slid the sandwich closer to Horace. The customers waiting in line were beginning to get upset. "So what you goin' to do?" Kyle asked Horace.

"What does it look like I'm doing? I'm going to finish making this man's sandwich, and when I'm done I'm goin' to start on the next one," Horace answered.

"Oh no you're not!"

"You just watch me."

"What's the problem?" Ethan said as he made his way up to the counter.

"Nothing, why?" Kyle snapped back. Horace pointed at Kyle then continued working.

"I'm just waiting here for him to redo my sandwich so I can go on my break."

"Look at all of these people in line, Ethan. Kyle is tripping. If he wants more meat, he can come behind the counter and get it," Horace said. Kyle took a deep breath then rested his head in his hand on the counter and started to tap his foot.

"Kyle, you need to go on break because it's too busy out here for this nonsense," Ethan said. "Plus you're making a scene."

"A scene . . . You haven't seen a scene. I'm on my break. Therefore I'm a customer, therefore I want my sandwich made right, damn it!" Kyle said righteously.

"Man, would you hurry up!" said a young male who was standing in line with his friends. Ethan sighed. Kyle turned and looked at the heckler.

"Man. . . . Man? Now somebody done told him wrong." Kyle pointed to the young brother as he and his friends began to laugh.

"Kyle, I want to see you in my office right now," Ethan said. Kyle gave Horace a dirty look then turned it on everyone in line.

"I'll be back," he whispered, then pointed to his sandwich. "Punk, put some meat on it."

Ethan was already sitting down when Kyle entered his office. Kyle made himself comfortable and waited for Ethan to say something. Ethan opened his cabinet drawer and pulled out a piece of paper. "What the hell is wrong with you?" Ethan asked.

"I don't know what you mean."

"Oh . . . you don't?"

"No . . . I don't."

"I think you do," Ethan said as he began filling out the paperwork.

"I just told you . . . I don't." Then there was a pause. "What's that? Another write-up?" Kyle asked.

"I don't know what you mean," Ethan said, angered that he had to take the time to fill out an employee discipline form. Ethan pushed the form aside then angrily folded his hands together. "Kyle, look . . . you're going to have to stop walking around this store like you own the place."

"I do that?"

"That's right. And you know you do it."

"No, you're mistaken. You might perceive that I do that. . . . But I don't."

"Well, Kyle, here's the deal. This is your second time in my office since I've been working here, and like I told you the first time, you need to control your outbursts, because like it or not customers come first. From here on out there isn't going to be any excuse for you to continue to disrespect this store and my customers."

"So what you sayin', Ethan?"

"I'm saying I want you to stop with the bullshit. That's what I'm saying. You're here to do your job."

"See now, Ethan, you need to stop thinking you have a damn doctorate in store management or something. I've already heard about you on the block. You're still up to your same old games, then you're coming in here like you are completely the shit. You need to stop it. 'Cause you're not fooling me."

"I'm not trying to fool you. This is my job and I'm going to do it. Put yourself in my shoes. Do that for a second and tell me, what would you do with you?"

"They don't pay me to do your job. So this is an interview, huh? Because if it is, I need to get a shop steward," Kyle said, crossing his legs. The intercom interrupted Kyle's answer.

"Ethan, Vance is here to see you. Should I send him back?" Tina asked.

"Yeah . . . okay . . . send him on back," Ethan requested.

"So, can I go?" Kyle said.

"Go ahead . . . man. Go on," Ethan said as Kyle raised slowly from his chair and started to walk out. He looked back with piercing eyes at Ethan. "What? Did I say something wrong?" Ethan wanted to know. Kyle rolled his eyes and sucked his teeth. The sound irritated Ethan. Kyle jerked open the door then stopped like he had forgotten something, and pointed toward the chair.

"Oh yeah—who was that short, dark-haired white girl in here earlier?" Kyle asked with lightning speed.

"None of your business," Ethan told him.

"Forget you, then. . . . And I'm still on my lunch break," Kyle said as he strutted out the door.

Ethan hadn't seen Vance smile so big since he'd come back to Columbus. Vance shut the door and looked around the small cluttered office.

"Why so happy? Finally get laid without getting caught?" Ethan wanted to know.

"Don't start, Ethan," Vance said.

"Artise forgive you or something?"

"Nope . . . not yet. She's still pissed."

"Well why the hell are you smiling from ear to ear?"

Vance plopped down into the chair across from Ethan's desk. "Whewwwww!" Vance blurted out; burdens within were finally being raised from his being.

"You did get laid, didn't you?" Ethan asked again.

"No, man. I just can't believe what happened to me today. It's like a dream. I went to see Stubby today, right . . . and, man . . . he and Gloria—God bless their souls—did me right!"

"Did you right?"

"Sure did. . . . I went over there earlier this afternoon to see how he was making out, and we were sitting down talking . . . about this and that and the next thing, you know. Stubby hands me an envelope with the deeds to some of the land he owns and four hundred thousand dollars to go along with it!"

Ethan's eyes popped wide open. "Get out of here, Vance!"

"Man, I'm serious! The Stubblefields gave me three million dollars' worth of land and four hundred thousand dollars cash. It's unbelievable!"

"Vance, I knew Stubbs owned property, but I always thought that old man was talking out the side of his neck. And how the hell does his land add up to that much?"

"Of course, it wasn't worth that much when he got it back in the day, man . . . but real estate goes up, and that's what it's worth now. Ethan, my brother . . . My brother, I have finally gotten the break I was looking for!"

"You are one lucky mutha—"

Vance interrupted. "No, blessed. Stubbs said that this was a blessing, and you know what? I believe him. There's no way this type of thing happens to just anyone."

"Awwww, man, your rent just went way—way up!" Ethan assured.

"What?"

"Your rent, brother. These honeys are not even going to know what to say to you."

"Ethan, you must be out of your mind. I'm going to propose to my girl, and I'm going to give her everything that she's ever wanted. Show a sista how much I love her."

"Have you told Artise yet?"

"Nope, I'm going to wait until the right moment. It has to be right, you know?"

"Vance, you don't want to propose right now. I'm telling you. The ladies are going to be all over you like you won't even believe."

"That's why I'm going to marry the lady I love so I don't even have to be worried about all that. When I told you I was going to change, Ethan, that's what I meant."

"I don't understand it . . . I really don't. A brother gets a chance to be the biggest player that this city has ever seen and you want to rush off and get married."

"Man, Stubby ain't give me this to be no damn player! He gave it to me because he believes that I can make good with it, and that's what I'm going to do!" Vance certified.

"Well, what I don't understand is, why would they give all that to you?"

"I told you, man . . . just a blessing. They told me they're just so happy they've lived as long as they have, and they want to see a blessing work. That's it, man. Stubbs said that he didn't know how much time he had left to live and he wants to see his legacy before he's called home."

"Are you sure that your name is the only one on them deeds, man?" Ethan questioned.

"Who else's name would be on them?" Vance asked.

"Mine . . . who do you think?"

"Yeah, right . . ." Vance shrugged it off. "Not a chance."

Heartache

Every time the doorbell rang Artise looked up with anxious eyes, expecting to see her mother walk through the door and join the family dinner. Not since childhood could Artise remember the entire family gathered to break bread together for no other reason than to enjoy each other's company. The last time everyone gathered it was for the funeral of a distant cousin who had died of cancer. But then Sharon, the youngest of Artise's aunts on her mother's side, finally rented the movie *Soul Food* and she decided that their family needed to have a family meal together every two weeks. Artise was so enthused about the plan that she volunteered to make her favorite potato salad and broccoli with cheese. This was a first for Artise. She was never around her family members without Vance, and she knew they were going to ask her where her beau was. Artise had another dilemma. She and her mother had exchanged heated words after her mother found out that once again Vance had not been faithful.

"So what was his excuse this time?" Artise's mother had wanted to know as they talked over the phone.

"Mama—I don't know. He doesn't even know. All I know is I'm trying to get my life together and I can no longer live like this."

"Well, Artise, all I can say is—"

"No, Mama—I don't want to hear that," Artise interrupted.

"Artise, you need to hear it. I told you Vance was not good for you a long time ago. I tried to tell you he was doing nothing but steering you in the wrong direction, but you just don't want to listen."

"Mama, this is my life."

"I know it is. But I'm tired of him making you go through this. Vance is nothing but a bum and I wish you would recognize it." Artise couldn't take the pressure.

"Mama, you don't know!" Artise screamed into the phone, then she slammed down the phone in her mother's ear.

"Thadious, are you ready to bless the food?" Sharon screamed over to her husband, who was sitting on the couch, tickling his nephew and making him sound like a soprano in a concert hall.

"Sho' you righ'," Thadious amplified back to his wife. "All right now, everyone, let's gather around the table and join hands." The entire family gathered around the table in no time at all. The appetizers had been devoured an hour ago, and they'd done nothing but make everyone more hungry than they already were. "Okay . . . everyone ready?" Everyone nodded. "Let us bow our heads and give thanks. Heavenly Father, thank you for this precious moment we . . ." Thadious stopped and everyone lifted up their head as the door opened.

"Hi, Aunt Cathy!" one of the children screamed out. Cathy wore a wine-colored dress with a matching scarf. Her hair was pulled back, exposing her tightly sculptured brown cheekbones. Her brown eyes were lined perfectly and there was a thin layer of gloss on her lips. She was a portrait of an aged Artise.

"Come on over here and get in this prayer, girrrl!" Thadious said. Artise smiled and looked at her mother, wondering if the others saw the incredible likeness between them.

"Hi, Mama!" Artise said. Cathy looked at Artise and took off her scarf without saying a word, then joined the family circle far from where Artise was standing. Artise was shocked by her mother's silence. She unintentionally squeezed Sharon's hand so tightly it made Sharon take notice. Thadious finished the prayer.

"Amen!" the entire family said in unison. Sharon looked over to Artise.

"You okay?"

"Yes, I'm fine. Just fine." Artise stood in her spot as the family grabbed their plates and began to eat. "But I'm going to ask her why she couldn't speak to me."

"No . . . not now, Artise," Sharon pleaded softly, so the others wouldn't hear. "I've never seen your mother do something like that before, and to not speak to you in front of the whole family is telling me she's pretty upset about something. I don't want our family dinner ruined. Just give it a chance."

Artise gave her mother another glance. "You're right. I don't want to start a scene. After all, Sharon, you worked so hard to get all of us together. Yeah . . . let's have something to eat."

If a stranger had been at the dinner party and didn't know that Catherine was Artise's mother they would've thought the two didn't know one another. Cathy made it a point to stay away from Artise and avoided even looking her way. For a brief moment Artise and her mother were alone in the kitchen together. Artise was pouring a glass of water and she turned around to see her mother come into the kitchen. But when Cathy saw her daughter she quickly turned around to leave.

"Mom . . . wait a minute. Where you goin'?"

Cathy took a deep breath as though Artise was inconveniencing her, but for the first time all night she looked Artise in the eyes.

"Mom, what is the problem? Why are you not speaking to me?"

"Artise, when you hung up the phone on me I thought you just didn't want to talk," Cathy snapped.

"Mom, you always hang up on me and I've never once walked into a room and not acknowledged your being. Why did you do that in front of the whole family?"

"Because I'm tired of you calling me, talking about Vance, then when I tell you what I think, you get upset. That's why I didn't speak to you."

"Oh that's the reason, huh? You're still always trying to run my life."

"I'm not trying to run your life. I'm trying to help you out. That's all—help."

"Well you don't have to worry about me and Vance anymore, because I'm making a change in my life. But it's not because you want me to do it. I just think it's best."

"Are you leaving him?" Cathy wanted to know.

"No. But I'm moving on with my life. That's all I'm saying. It's just time for me to look after me."

Cathy eased a little. "What are you talking about, Artise?"

"I'm going to concentrate on doing something with my life instead of waiting on Vance, that's all. I think it's time I really do."

"Well, I'm happy for you, Artise—but like I've always said, 'Once a cheat, always a cheat.' Now give me a hug."

Here It Is

Vance was gleaming equal to a schoolboy on Christmas Day. He could see his new residence atop the hill. It was a bright white vision of a luxurious castle above a forest of enormous oak trees and green vegetation. It was identical to the home he'd promised to Artise over and over again they would one day share together. Vance had been to the house many times in the last month; nevertheless, his gaze remained on his new domain as though it were the first time he had ever laid eyes on it. He was pleased, gratified—plain old tickled to death with the sight progressing toward his eyes. Vance was so astonished by his home, he wasn't paying any attention to the wisdom Stubby was trying to place into Ethan's head.

"I'ma tell you how it is, boy, and I don't know why you don't want to listen. I'ma show dis boy righ' here how to spen' dat money he was given. Den make mo' over and over again before I die," Stubby testified from the back seat of the car as he looked at the house himself.

"Well, I still say he needs to go buy a new car," Ethan declared, looking back at Stubbs.

"A ca'. A ca'? What's wrong wit' da one we in? Wha's wrong wit' what we ridin' in now? See, dat's what's wrong. You git some money and da first thing everybody want to go git is a new ca'. A Lexus, or one of dem BMWs. Ethan, I know you smarter dan dat, boy. He should just git dis house then put all his money up and watch it work. Vance, do you got a car payment on dis?" Vance was putting the car in park and soaking in the grand view of his estate, still not paying attention to the conversation.

"See, me myself . . . I coulda moved out here in da fifties and sixties . . . but what was I goin' to do out here all by myself? I wanted to be close to all my peoples, dat's why I didn't move. Don't you boys know? Dis part of da city used to be all white? My, my, my . . . how times have changed," Stubbs reminisced.

"I still think he should get rid of this damn Taurus. This car is over ten years old. The paint is chippin', the seats are worn out," Ethan reiterated, trying to get his point across.

"Dat's all right, Vance. Drive it until it falls out on ya, den you will need a new ca'," Stubby repeated before realizing his words were not being heard.

"Here we are!" Vance finally said. "Welcome to my new home."

"So it's all yours now, huh? You done signed all da paperwork and everything?" Stubbs asked. Ethan was already halfway out of the car.

"Yep . . . everything is set. All I have to do is propose to Artise and we're moving in here and goin' to start planning our wedding."

"Dat's good, Vance. I'm glad dat you ain't sitting back and contemplating yo' future wit' dat young lady, because I'm telling you, money will get you in trouble if you don't have a steady love in your life." Stubby planted his feet on the ground then began to get out of the car.

"Well, if it was me, I think I would be a bachelor for a year or two or three. No reason to rush it, now," Ethan expressed.

Vance ran his hand down his thin beard. "Nawww . . . I don't think so, Ethan. I'm ready, man, it's time for us."

"My feelings exactly," Stubbs agreed. "Me and my Gloria been together for many many years and I've never wished I stayed single one mo' day than I did."

"That's how I want to be," Vance confirmed as they all stood looking at the house from a distance. "I can see me and my lady and all our kids living the rest of our lives here. Running all through that yard . . . chasing my sons around the house with our dogs following close behind, while Artise looks at us through the window."

"Well I can see myself tonight, as a matter of fact. Going out with a fine young brown-skin lady who I hadn't seen for years and is cuckoo for Ethan."

Vance turned to Ethan. "Who you going out with tonight?"

"Just another one of my WWKs who I promised a little something to tonight."

"You are wild! Just out of control!" Vance said.

"Li'l bit too wild, you ask me," Stubbs said. Ethan looked over at him.

"Stubbs, why after all these years . . . you still don't like me?" Ethan joked, but deep down inside was serious.

"I never said I ain't like ya, Ethan. I just don't like what ya do," Stubbs said tight-lipped without blinking an eye. "You always playin' some type of game every since you been a little boy. You got to change sometime, son."

Ethan pointed to Vance. "I ain't no different than Vance."

"What?" Vance blurted out.

"Oh yes, you are. Now see, Vance is a go-getta' and he cares about people. That thing you do wit' yo' ladies who got kids is just sorry . . . sorry, I'm tellin' you."

"Look, we're all men here. We're standing out in the suburbs where can't anybody hear us, and I want to know why what I do is so wrong? I don't want to bring you into this, Vance, but . . . how can I be any different from what he has done in the past? Somebody talk to me?" Ethan demanded.

"Come on you two. Let's go in the house," Vance said.

"Wait a minute, son . . . now, we both been in dere enough times. Why you bring us out here anyway?" Stubby joked. "Let me answer his question."

"Yeah, I want to hear this," Ethan protested. Stubby didn't hesitate.

"Well, Ethan, I think you different from Vance 'cause what he went through wit' his mate is just bad judgment and lust. He don't never go out and intentionally do his Artise no harm. He just can't keep zipped up."

"Okay . . . what about me, then?" Ethan questioned. He put his hands in his pocket and began twisting his midsection, waiting on the answer.

"Well, you . . . you go out dere and hunt. You hunt on the most prized women who should be the most respected in our community. Then when you get them you just move on about yo' sorry little bidness, and dese women have kids who need more than that, Ethan."

"You got it all wrong, Stubby—this is a new day. These ladies want me to do what I do. Plus let their daddies take care of them. I'm not their father."

"Why you go there, Ethan?" Vance mumbled. Stubby began to stoop down to take a seat in the grass; Vance gave him a hand. Then Stubby motioned for Vance and Ethan to have a seat. Their heads were all forward, on the house.

"I know that ain't what you think, Ethan. Dem ladies wit' dem childrens don't think like dat. And don't ya know if dey had the kids' daddy to take care of dem they wouldn't be wit' you. Now I know you crazy. Don't you think for one minute dese ladies are carryin' on wit' you because of yo' lovin' or dat dey need lovin'."

"Everybody need lovin', now," Ethan confessed.

"Not dat kind of lovin', boy. You can't tell me dat dese women ain't somewhere someplace in deir mind thinking—hoping, even prayin'— you just might stick around to help with their childrens and help dem make somethin' out dey life like couples supposed to do."

"Nope, this time you got it all wrong, Stubbs. Women nowadays just want the physical taken care of. What they need me for if they already have children? Why would they want me around when they're doing the job of mother and father? It's just more complicated in the nineties than it was when you were in love," Ethan explained.

"Young buck. Let me tell you something. First of all—dat's an illiterate excuse. Using time to verify da reason for yo' season. But more importantly than dat, I'm still in love. Now what dat tell ya? Ain't no difference in the game of love. Love is love no matta' how ya look at it. Been here for the longest. Goin' to be here longer than you and I know. Not even dat cloning thing everybody up in arms about goin' to be able to take love away from a human being. It's what make us human, Ethan. But dat dere thing you doing wit' all dese lady friends of yours goin' to get you in trouble 'cause it ain't right."

"Okay, you say it ain't right. If it ain't right, what am I supposed to do?"

"I don't tell no man what he should do. Dat ain't right. I just recommend and tell you what I know from my experience. But if I was you, put it like dat . . . I would find me a nice young lady and quit all dis nonsense and carrying on dat you do."

"Well, I ain't ready to be tied down right now," Ethan said.

"Nobody suggesting that you tie down right away. But find someone that you could love. Someone that you could live your life with and try your best to work things out with dem and get to know who you spending time with."

"It sounds good, Stubby. But . . . hell, I ain't ready for all that yet."

Stubby looked at Vance, who was still gazing toward his new home. "Well, what ya ready for? Boy, you in your thirties and I'm telling you through my experience. You don't want to live dis life as a man without love. A real man searches for love, wants a family, and craves to provide."

"I just want to keep my freedom—do whatever I want to do. When I want to do it and with whoever I want to do it with. That's what I want to do. And that's what I'm going to do," Ethan snapped.

"Vance, listen to his words—told ya he's suspect for what ya got in mind," Stubby said.

"What's that, Stubby?" Vance was clearly distracted.

"Yeah, what are you talking about?" Ethan asked.

"Vance, have you been paying any attention to us at all?" Stubby hounded him.

"No . . . not really."

"Stubbs said I wouldn't be good for what you had in mind."

"I said 'suspect' . . ." Stubbs clarified.

"Ready for what?" Ethan was getting curious.

"Ethan, I brought your name up when we were discussing something I want to do for Mrs. Stubblefield," Vance answered.

"What is it?" Ethan pursued.

"Something special dat will make my Gloria so happy. . . . Something she has always talked 'bout doin', but she's always been by my side helping me out with what I want to do so she never got a chance to get things rollin' herself."

Ethan still didn't have a clue and gestured with his hands toward Vance.

"I'm going to open up a museum that will house books from every black author that we've had in America—along with a coffee shop—in the very spot where Mrs. Stubbs would recite poetry when opening up for Langston Hughes, Chester Himes, and all the other great writers who made their way through the city back in the day."

"Yep, da ol' *Chapter* was the name of it," Stubbs blurted out. "I got some photos of it back at the house."

"Chapter?" Ethan looked confused.

"Yes sir, dat use to be da place where all of our writers would come and read some of deir works. It used to be the talk of da town!"

"And that's important to Mrs. Stubblefield?"

"Yep, sure is. It's the place where she worked before she started cleaning houses and helped me git on my feet. It's where she just watched her career as a poet dwindle right before her eyes because she did more workin' at dem tables than perfectin' her craft. She did have her moments there, though. Especially when she opened up all dem times for Langston. I almost thought dat ol' boy was sweet on my ol' Gloria, but me and him had a sit-down. Man to man."

"You and Langston Hughes had a sit-down?" Ethan asked, in disbelief.

"Oh yeah . . . wit'out a doubt. We used to do dat back in our day. Sit down and talk it out. See what was on another man's mind before deciding if he had to be dealt with. And back den, see, my size at six feet three was big, and just about any man I told to meet me in da back of da club, he came to see what I wanted. But anyway . . . he told me dem eyes he was givin' my Gloria wasn't nothin' but eyes of harmony, eyes of love for what dey did for people back in dem days. He just enjoyed her poetry so much, and I loved it too . . . so I understood why he wouldn't take his eyes off her when she read. . . . And, ohhh, dat Mr. Himes . . . ol' Chester Himes used to come down from Cleveland and tell stories like you couldn't believe—have the whole place beggin' for mo'! Gloria always talked about getting that place started again. So I bought da land where it once stood many many years ago, and that's just one of the things we have not done dat we said we was goin' to do."

"And I've decided I want to take the building sitting on the land that Stubbs leased out and make a cultural dynasty out of it. Just picture it, Ethan. A twenty-five-story building with all the books that black authors have ever written."

"From Hughes, Booker T. Washington, W.E.B. DuBois, Zora Neale Hurston, James Baldwin, Gwendolyn Brooks, and anybody else dat came before them or after dem," Stubbs interrupted with passion. Vance smiled at the old man's passion.

"We want to have a centralized place where people can come and see the works. Not a library, but a place where you can read all the great works among others—to get that vibe back, that passion for the written word in our lives. And to make it that much more special, I'm going to add on a stage so that Artise and Tassha can give their motivation seminars and where groups can perform plays."

"Now that ain't a bad idea," Ethan conceded. "But what has it got to do with me?"

"I told Stubbs that I was thinking about making you head of personnel at the High Hopes Center."

Ethan's eyes lit up. Vance and Stubbs both looked back at him and nodded yes, confirming the idea.

"You was thinking of me like that, partner?" Ethan asked Vance.

"Yep, sure was. But I can't have you in there trying to hit on every woman you see walking in the door with a kid. I need you to uphold the standard that we're going to set, because the place has to be immaculate day in and day out. Physically and spiritually."

"Dat's righ'. People can sense when things ain't right in a place as soon as dey walk in da door," Stubbs said.

"Well, I am getting tired of this damn grocery store already. This daggone union stuff is beginning to get on my damn nerves."

"Now, Ethan, you can't just say you want to do it just to get away from what you're doin' now. This center is goin' to be da only one like it in the world. Right here in Columbus, and it has to be ran right. Vance is going to be able to get some of that federal money to keep it going, plus pay good money to the employees who goin' to be working dere. He needs your head to be right," Stubbs explained.

"You know I'm a completely different person at work," Ethan said.

"Yeah, but when you act different ways in different places den, boy, dat's when you have problems. We need you acting the same way . . . all the time. And leave dem dang-on ladies wit' dese kids alone."

Vance looked at Ethan expectantly.

"I don't know. I don't know if I can do that," Ethan confessed. They all became quiet and looked up at the estate.

"So, Vance . . . you figure out what kind of fertilizer you goin' to use on dat grass yet?" Stubby wanted to know.

The Simple

Ethan sat across from Monica and was all smiles. She looked awesome, drinkable, just so inviting. Vance's suggestion that he do a "new thing" and dismiss his play with WWKs, was not something he was going to contemplate at the moment, even though he'd given it some deliberation while he showered and rubbed Polo Sport all over his body before his date.

"So here we are!" Monica said, showing her brown dimples to Ethan.

"Yeah, we finally have a chance to sit down and talk," Ethan replied. "Wow."

"What?"

"You look good, Monica," he admitted to her. Monica had on an all-black dress with spaghetti straps, very low cut in the front and showing the top portions of her breasts, which were like magnets to Ethan's eyes. Her hair was pulled back and her dark lip gloss brought out her bright, wide, magnificent eyes.

"Thank you, Ethan. You look nice, too, in your black three-button suit and wing tips. You always could dress." Ethan coyly adjusted his black tie. Then Monica giggled. "You just sittin' up in here, looking like a Mafia gangster."

"You think it's too much?"

"Nooo, matter of fact I like it."

"Thanks."

"You sure can get a sista all hot and bothered." Monica narrowed her wide eyes.

Ethan licked his lips and placed his hand on his chest. "I do that?"

"You know you do. Especially over the phone."

"I do that to you?"

"Yes, all the time."

"I don't mean to," Ethan said flirtatiously.

"Yes you do. . . . I know you do," Monica insisted.

"Well if I do, I apologize."

"Ummm-hmmm, sure you do." Suddenly Monica was reminded of something. "Oh yeah, I'm sorry about last night over the phone. My son kept touching my leg—talking about 'you dead . . . You dead.' "

"What?"

Ethan didn't have a clue and just shook his head back and forth.

"He kept touching my leg and saying it over and over again," Monica explained.

"So what did you say to him?"

"I told him that I was very much alive and made him stop playing that stupid game."

Ethan gave an amused shrug. "I don't know where they get their imaginations from," he said.

"Probably from television. But that's the reason I was occupied."

"It's all right. You're mine right now."

"That's right, I am." Monica felt a burst of energy. "So how do you like being back here?" she asked.

"It's okay. I thought I was going to come back here and be bored out of my damn mind. But so far it hasn't been too bad."

"Just wait a couple of months—I bet you pack up and go back to Atlanta. Why did you leave anyway?"

"You know, my partner asks me that all the time. I don't know. I got down there and it was cool at first, but those people are so much into cliques. I mean everything is where do you work . . . who do you know . . . even what church do you go to."

"You didn't like that, huh?"

"Nope. I found myself spending all my damn time wondering what clique I should try and get attached to. Don't get me wrong. Atlanta has it going on. It's just not for me."

"Well I'm glad to see you back. Before you left we were seeing each other all the time downtown."

"Every day almost," Ethan said.

"And when you told me you were leaving I was like, 'Damn, why now?' My baby was almost a year old, and it took all I had not to go out with you. But I had to concentrate on my baby boy."

Ethan grinned. "I know I must have asked you to go out with me at least three times every time I saw you."

"Yeah, you were all over me," Monica joked. "But I'm glad you were."

"So where's the baby tonight?" Ethan wanted to know. Monica paused for a brief moment.

"You mean my big man. . . . You should see him. He's over at a girl-friend's tonight."

"Oh, okay. . . . So do you like being a mother?"

"Ethan, I'm telling you it's definitely a challenge, you know? Every day it's something different, but I'm managing all right."

Her answer made Ethan think. He didn't like the opinion Stubbs had of him and wanted to find out from someone who had already been told the rules. "Can I ask you a question?"

"Sure," Monica said.

"Do you think I'm scandalous?"

"Scandalous. What do you mean?"

"You know I've exclusively been going out only with ladies that have kids . . . right?" Monica nodded her head yes. "I want to know how you feel about it. Do you think I'm trying to take advantage of you and your son?"

Monica squinted. "Nooooo . . . Ethan, why would you think that?"

"I've been told what I do is wrong, and I want to get your opinion, that's all."

"Okay, answer this question for me?" Monica requested.

"Okay . . . I'll try."

"Why do you only date women with kids?"

Ethan thought for a minute. Then took a deep breath. "Do you think they'll ever bring us our drinks? This is supposed to be one of the best restaurants in the city." Ethan motioned for a waitress. "Ahh . . . here she comes." Ethan had ordered cognac and Monica had ordered Long Island Tea. While they waited for their drinks, Ethan wondered about her question.

"Are you going to tell me?" Monica asked, getting the conversation back on track.

"You want the truth, huh?"

"Of course."

"Okay. It's kinda hard to explain, and on the other hand it's very simple."

"So what version are you going to give me?"

"The simple one, tonight," Ethan said.

"All eyes are on you." Monica winked at him as their drinks arrived. Ethan raised his glass.

"Here's to the simple."

"We're cuttin' through the entire chase up in here," Monica pronounced as she and Ethan touched glasses. Then Ethan looked at Monica more intensely. Monica enjoyed his look.

"Respectfully, Monica, the simple of it is, I prefer women with kids because I enjoy spending time with them. I truly feel they deserve to get away from it all from time to time. There hasn't been a woman I've dated who hasn't told me how nice it is, getting away for a few hours."

"Amen to that."

"See what I mean? Plus it's more of an understanding. Most of the women are having baby-daddy drama or are afraid to have their children around other men. But they all still need to get out and . . ." Ethan chuckled. "Get their maintenance on."

"Hey . . ." Monica sang. "So your choice has nothing to do with wanting to stay single or avoiding a relationship, huh?"

"That's what people seem to think. But hey—I've been in relationships before. I can love," Ethan submitted.

"Do you ever think you'll love again?" Monica put her hand over her mouth. "Listen to me sounding like a damn sick love song." Their laughter made the conversation easier.

"Hey, anything is possible," Ethan said. Monica lifted up her glass and smiled. It was all she needed to hear.

The Deal

David was seething. He abruptly jammed his car into park at the top of a steep hill, turned it off, and grabbed his keys damn near in one motion. He was on his way into the Chinese restaurant to see Tenner. The restaurant was the kind of place where all the big ballers in the city went, and David knew he'd find Tenner among them. Earlier in the day David had put two and two together and realized that Mr. Tenner had put the squeeze on his most reliable campaign financiers. One minute David was on the phone with the police union trying to make sense of their change of heart and decision not to back him. Then his strongest supporters, the Ministers Union, who had been very vocal in support of his campaign, called and notified David they had decided to renege on their support as well. There was only one man in the city of Columbus who could get the men in blue to change their decision, and convince the men of the cloth as well.

The restaurant door was opened for David as he approached, and after taking a couple of steps inside he stopped and glanced through the dimly lit eatery. "Mr. Tenner has been awaiting you," the hostess said, directing David to the stairs that led to the upper half of the restaurant. David looked up the stairs with apprehension before he began his journey; he knew if he was seen by a reporter or anyone of influence in the community he was finished before the election. But without his supporters there wasn't going to be any race, and he would lose without a doubt. David glanced around again then made the journey up the stairs. A large robust man greeted him with a welcoming snarl as he reached the top step. He spotted Tenner on the other side of the room. He was talking to someone, but David could only see the back of her head.

"Casey, I really think you're wasting your time," Tenner said.

"Ronald, it's too late, I already took the job. Listen, I can't put what I do for you on my résumé. Do I look completely ignorant to you or something? I want a career; that's why I went to college in the first place. What I've been doing for you couldn't in a million years give me credit for on-the-job training."

"I'm not going to tell you what—"

"Thank you," Casey interrupted with attitude.

"Not this time I won't," Tenner clarified. "But you still owe me and I want you to understand. When I tell you I need you, that's exactly what I mean. Do you understand, Casey?"

"Not really."

"No?" Tenner asked.

"No . . . I want to know when my so-called debt is going to be paid in full."

"I didn't mean to . . ." Tenner motioned with his hand to silence Casey, then lit a cigarette.

"When I say it is. And how many times must I ask you not to start rambling deranged concerning the matter? It's over and done with now; when our business is finished you'll know. Now give me a minute, I have other business," Tenner barked. Casey gazed at Tenner with hateful eyes then walked away. Tenner took a sip of his wine then stood up, motioning David over to the table. David checked out the guard. Within seconds, he was standing in front of Tenner.

"Nice suit. Glad to see you could make it," Tenner said.

"Didn't feel like I had too much choice in the situation, Tenner. Let's get down to business; I don't have a lot of time."

"Excellent, David . . . excellent. I'm very happy to hear that you've finally come around."

"Listen, Tenner, I'm not here for any bullshit. I know what you did. And you are forcing my hand here."

Tenner smirked then took a sip of his wine and picked up his cigarette. "You know what I did? Is there any evidence for whatever you're talking about, David?"

"No—as usual, Ronald, you covered your tracks."

"Whew . . ." Smoke came out of Tenner's mouth as he exhaled. "I thought I was slipping. So I take it you're here about my proposal?"

"You mean your strong-arm tactics," David said.

"Look, David. I want what I want. Getting that prison means everything to me. It's definitely a moneymaker, and I'm determined to get it done. Besides, don't you know my people are already working on the plans, David?" Tenner finished off his wine. David noticed Tenner's bodyguard motion to Casey, who was sitting at a nearby table. Suddenly she walked over to the table and picked up the bottle of wine. She poured Tenner another glass, and Tenner's eyes ran up and down her body. Casey grabbed David's untouched glass and turned it right side up then tipped the bottle.

"No . . . no thank you," David insisted as he placed his hand over his glass.

"Are you sure?" Tenner asked. David nodded yes.

"Thank you." Casey placed the bottle on the table firmly, making sure it would be heard. Tenner chuckled and watched her walk away again.

"Your daughter?" David asked.

"Why? . . . Does she remind you of yours? Tassha's her name, right?" Tenner lit up another cigarette. "See—that's why I like you, David. You have lots of nerve, and that's the making of a great mayor. So you've realized what I can do for you and you're here to take my offer, huh?"

"No. I'm here because you have leaned on all of my campaign contributors and I don't have any money for my fuckin' campaign."

Tenner took his cigarette from his mouth and blew a smoke ring directly over David's head. "Like I said, David, you've realized what I can do for you. Here's the deal. Time is wasting and I have some very important people waiting on me to secure the building for my prison so we can get things under way. My people downtown tell me the deed has changed hands from old man Stubblefield to some loser. It looks like I'm going to have to strong-arm this kid."

"Why don't you buy the property like you do everything else?"

"Don't have the time. I told you, I want what I want. Plus I've already tried," Tenner answered.

"Sounds just like you," David charged. Tenner took another drag off his cigarette and blew another smoke ring. "So what are you going to do to get the property?"

"I have a couple of options for dealing with this new guy. But you need not worry yourself about that. I just need to know if you're going to make this prison a part of your campaign. And, can get the city behind it?"

David put his hands over his face and rubbed his eyes. "Tenner, this city doesn't need a prison."

Tenner picked up his briefcase, laid it on the table, plopped it open, and took out an envelope and then placed it on the table. "But you need a campaign financier." David, knowing what it was, looked at the package; then their eyes locked. "Here's some start-up money for the campaign. Three hundred thousand—all cash, completely untraceable. There's enough here to get things rolling for your campaign, and there will be more to come when I see you've announced your agenda for my prison through the media to the people of the city. If things get sticky you might even get to do it at the site." David seemed skeptical. "Don't worry about it—you're a very savvy man, David, and when the opportunity arises I know you'll take the bull by the horns." The envelope hadn't been touched yet, but David's eyes had looked down at it more than once. Tenner slid the envelope even closer to David's hands. "Mr. Mayor, please . . . take it?" David looked at Tenner with a clear understanding that this would be the beginning of a never-ending relationship. His hand began to move toward the envelope. Thoughts of the biggest campaign ever launched in the city began to ease any guilt David felt about his first under-the-table dealing. David's hand stopped just short of the money.

"I'm going to need a complete report on this prison."

"Done," Tenner said. David looked at the money and nodded toward the cash.

"Does it come with a list of names for my records?"

Tenner smiled. "David—I'm not a bad man." He chuckled. "All of the financiers that you were working with assured me they'll assume responsibility for all campaign contributions for the record. I'm just paying the bills. Everyone's on board."

"I'm going to need a report of everyone involved with accountability sent to my campaign manager by the end of the week. Do you understand, Tenner?" Tenner's beady eyes followed as David again moved his hand toward the money. He placed his hand on top of David's when David touched the envelope.

"I understand. But you need to understand as well. Once you pick it up, it's yours, and that means we have a deal. I want to hear something about my prison the next time you're in the media, David. Deal?"

"Deal."

Happy Hour

Tassha was excited. She squirmed comfortably into her seat, put her napkin on her lap, then finally began to relax, holding onto her delightful expression. It was finally a girls' night out. Artise was not so fast. She looked around to survey the territory before she took her seat. She felt unsteady since it had been several years since she'd been out as a single woman.

"So here we are!" Tassha announced.

"Yup . . . here we are," Artise verified. "Tassha, I have to tell you. I'm not feeling this at all."

"What's wrong?"

"The only reason I agreed to come out here tonight was because I wanted the word to get back to Vance. That's all. It's been a month, and it's like our situation is not bothering him one bit," Artise complained while she looked around.

"Well, I'm sure it will. You know how it is around here, word travels fast," Tassha suggested as she looked around the diner. "You want to meet some of David's friends? There're a lot of them here tonight. I can introduce you now or we can wait until David gets here."

"That's okay," Artise said quickly.

"I don't see how you're doing it, myself, Artise."

"What?"

"Still living in the house with Vance without talking to him."

Artise tried to smile. "I thought it would be worse. But after he found out that I was serious about us doing our own thing, I think I got my point across. I'm just pissed because he's taking it so well. It's like he's hiding something from me. Probably someone; I guess he never planned on marrying me all along."

"Why do you say that?"

" 'Cause he's never there anymore. I hear him coming in the house around eleven-thirty at night, and when I'm in the bed I can feel him peek into the room and make sure that I'm okay. But he just goes and lays down on the couch. He must be having a good time with his lady friends or something. I thought not having me whenever he wanted was going to be the icing on the cake—a way to make him really feel what he's been missing. But shoot . . . Vance hasn't missed a beat. He's doing his thing."

"Well, you need to do yours." Tassha motioned across the room. "See the brother standing over there at the bar?" Artise forced herself to look. "That's Charlie Reeves." Reeves caught Artise's and Tassha's eyes then tipped his glass toward them.

"Ahh, see now, Tassha, now he knows we're over here talking about him," Artise whined.

"That's all right. He likes that. I can invite him over if you like."

"No—that's okay. I can't."

"You're going to have to start sometime, Artise. You said it yourself that you have to start doing your own thing. Don't let Vance's silence play mind games with you. Are you sure he's having a good time?"

"Oh, I'm sure. Matter of fact, I know he is. I called him at work today and they told me he wasn't in."

"Wasn't in?"

"Yup."

"That's strange."

"Isn't it. But I know one thing. If he doesn't have his half of that mortgage, we're going to go at it."

"I bet you Ethan has gotten into his head since he's been back. And for Vance's sake, I hope not."

Artise kind of giggled. "It cracks me up to think you two were going to be married, Tassha."

"Yeah, me too. Ethan would have drove me crazy with the games he plays."

"You think?"

"Girl, yes! Now that brutha would've had me admitted. But David has been putting on the pressure lately himself."

"How so?" Artise questioned.

"He's been all over me about being with him on a more permanent basis."

"He wants to get married?"

"He didn't actually say that. But he's been talking about kids. And he knows that I ain't the one to be having no children without being married. The whole idea does sound inviting; but see, Artise, this is where his age is coming in to play with our relationship. He's getting older, and I don't know if it's right to bring a child into this world under those circumstances. I've tried to discuss it with David, but his mindset is that he's not old. And when you look at his demeanor I have to agree with him on that. He says that he's in his seasoned sixties, and he would make the best father in the world. David is wonderful, but I cannot just jump at the idea without thinking it all the way through— kids need to be able to enjoy their father too."

"See, that's how I feel about dating an older guy period, Tassha. Psychologically I don't know how I would be able to handle it." Artise paused a moment. "At least you're happy."

"Thanks, girl. You're going to be happy again too. It's just going to take you a little time. You've been with Vance for too long to just say okay it's finished overnight. Ending a relationship like that needs healing time. I went through the same thing with Ethan. It took me forever to figure out why he did me the way he did. But I never truly understood the reason why, because I didn't talk to him about it. I thought going after him was a waste of my time. So I was left out in the cold. I made myself handle it, though, by becoming stronger and stronger every day. And I think this place right here would be a great start for you." Tassha began to scan the room again, then followed Artise's eyes when she noticed her looking too. "See anyone interesting?" Tassha encouraged.

"No . . . not really."

Tassha smiled. "That's Ray Perkins. Talking about prestige? He's the president of the National Bank and sits on so many boards in the city that you can't even keep track of them all. He's sixty-four and one of David's golfing partners. Matter of fact, we know his daughters. Michelle and Trai Perkins."

Artise shook her head. "That's all right, Tassha. I am not trying to meet that man. Not when I used to talk about men with his daughters at the hair salon."

"Now that would be kind of odd . . . wouldn't it?" Tassha asked.

"I would say so." Artise laughed it off.

"Okay . . . so what about meeting a younger guy. I know of some prospects."

"No, that's okay . . . I can't right now," Artise said.

"Why do you keep saying that, Artise? You can do anything you want," Tassha insisted.

"I don't think so, Tassha."

"Why not?"

Artise took a deep breath. "Because I just found out that I'm pregnant, that's why."

Tassha's mouth dropped open.

"Yep . . . pregnant, Tassha."

Tassha was stunned. "You're pregnant, Artise?" Artise took a sip of water and nodded yes. A million thoughts ran through Tassha's mind.

"I know. That's how I was when I found out, Tassha," Artise said solemnly.

"You're going to have the baby, right?" Tassha whispered.

"Without a doubt. I'll just have to do this all alone. It's funny how your whole life can change in a matter of weeks, isn't it?"

"Mine just changed in a matter of seconds," Tassha joked. "Well, I'm happy for you, girlfriend. This is wonderful news!"

"Thank you." Artise blushed. "I'm still in a state of shock," she confessed.

"Well, with Vance still living in the house—he's sure to find out sooner or later. When are you going to tell him?"

"I don't know. I just might wait until he can see it with his own eyes."

"Are you serious?"

"Yep, that's how he did me. Kept me in the dark about things. I feel like doing the same thing to him. Then when he finds out he'll know exactly what it feels like to be blindsided."

"I know you're hurt, Artise . . . but this is so important."

"I hear you, Tassha. But why should I always take the high ground when it's time to do something right? For once I would like to get back at him."

"That makes sense, but that's not even your nature, Artise. You care how people feel. You don't like to hurt people."

"So you think I should tell him instead of letting him find out on his own?"

Tassha nodded her head yes. "No matter how messed up Vance has been acting."

Artise thought about her answer. "Okay . . . I will. . . . Just not right away. I'm not in the mood to discuss anything with him right now."

"Well, if it's anything that I've seen turn many a man around and make them do right, one of them is children . . . and that's a fact," Tassha confessed.

"Yeah . . . but some get even worse. They begin to think that you have to depend on them for every little thing, then they go and get more scandalous than they were before. And I don't want that to happen."

"Come on, Artise. Be optimistic and full of hope. You need every bit of that right now."

Artise thought about Tassha's kind words. "I guess we're going to have to put things on hold with our business venture, huh?" Artise said.

"Now that's entirely up to you, sista. If you say we can go along with it, then we will. We can still line things up and get things in order, so when we say together it's time to take this plunge, we'll take it together. I know you have a million things to think about now, and starting a new job shouldn't be one of them. Not right now. . . . You need every little benefit and penny you can get, because things can get pretty expensive."

"Thanks, Tassha."

"Believe me, it's no problem at all. I need to do some soul-searching anyway. I know David is going to ask me again about our situation, and I have a feeling he's getting tired of me brushing him off."

"Well, do me a favor and keep this a secret? You're the only person that knows. I haven't even told my mother yet."

"Artise, she's going to be so happy!"

"I hope so." Artise blushed.

"Awww, she will. Her first grandbaby!" Tassha gushed.

"Umm-hmmm, her very first one." Artise and Tassha turned their heads as they heard the men sitting around the bar start to applaud when David walked in.

"Hello, Mayor!" a friend of David's shouted.

"Well there's your man," Artise announced. Tassha smiled and caught David's eye.

2-2-7-2 Straight Box

"Wait a minute . . . just wait a minute," Kyle screamed as the customers in line were becoming ever more impatient with his lack of skills working the lotto machine. Kyle had complained to Ethan about Horace's move to the deli and asked for the same treatment—another position to break the monotony of ringing up the groceries on the register. Kyle solicited for days, and Ethan had grown so tired of hearing his nagging and complaining that he decided to give Kyle what he asked for; in his own words, "The plush cozy job of entering numbers on the lotto machine." Kyle thought he was in heaven until the lotto reached $35 million.

"Now let's do this, please. I have to get back to work," a customer emphasized to Kyle as he handed him his lotto card. Kyle snatched the card and put it in the machine, but the card came back out without printing the tickets.

"Now what the hell is wrong with this machine?" Kyle wondered aloud while he looked over the machine for problems. He finished his inspection then looked at the customer's card, and with his hand on his hip looked directly at the customer. "What the hell is wrong with you? You're supposed to fill out the entire damn card . . . six numbers, fool, not five! Take this card and get at the end of the line." Kyle gave the card back, but his customer stood still and began to complete his ticket.

At that same time a small, middle-aged man who was next in line stepped up and handed Kyle his card.

"Sorry, but these are not the numbers I had on my card," he said. Kyle squinted his eyes.

"What are you talking about?" The gentleman showed Kyle his tickets. "If these are not the numbers that you gave me, then where did I get them?" Kyle asked.

"I don't know where you got them. But not one of those numbers on these printed tickets match the numbers I gave you."

Kyle huffed and tried to compose himself. "So what do you want me to do?"

"I want the numbers I gave you to be printed on my tickets."

"Do you have the numbers?"

"No," the man said. "You kept my card for some reason."

"You sure are blaming me for a lot of shit—you know that?" Kyle shot as he scanned the numbers.

"Well, if the numbers I gave you were on my ticket I wouldn't be here complaining at all, would I? Now I'm going to have to sit down and fill out another card because you don't know what you're doing." The man began to fill out his card right on the counter.

"Excuse me, but you're going to have to do that in the designated spots we have available to mark the cards. Then when you're done you need to get back in line—all the way in the back." Kyle pointed. "Then come see me." At that same point the other gentleman before him finished filling out his card and handed it to Kyle.

"Okay, here you are," he said.

"I thought I told you to get at the end of the line; we already completed our transaction, and if you want to go at it again you're going to have to get at the end of the line. I don't think I can make myself any clearer." The gentleman began to sneer and looked at the other customer who was standing at the counter.

"Do you believe this guy?"

"He's a class act, isn't he?" the other one said, then looked down at one of his tickets again. "Look here? I told him to give me two-two-seven-two straight box and he gave me two-two-two-seven straight three times, no box whatsoever. Never in my life have I seen someone profess to work the lotto machine who doesn't know a damn thing about it!"

"You two couldn't be talking about me?" Kyle interjected.

"Oh yes . . . yes sir . . . we are." They laughed.

"Sir?" Kyle was getting really pissed off.

"And that term is being used very loosely at the moment," one of the men indicated.

"You don't know me!" Kyle shouted.

"I wish that was true. Now what you going to do about our tickets so we can get out of here," one of the gentlemen said, becoming angry.

"I'm going to take the next person in line and watch both of your asses get in the back of the line. . . . See ya!" Kyle said.

"I'm not going anywhere—you're going to fix these damn mistakes. I've already waited in line forty-five minutes waiting for you to learn how to use the damn machine and I am not waiting any longer."

"That's right. . . . I've been here too long myself," the other man cried. Kyle looked at both of them.

"Well I'll tell you what. I'm not doing shit until both of you move out the way and get at the end of the line." Kyle picked up his closed sign and put it on the counter and sat down.

"You better get your ass up!" someone yelled from the back of the line. Kyle turned in another direction. His back was now facing the customers.

"Now he's done gone crazy!" someone else shouted after him.

"You know?" Casey asked Ethan as they went through the files in his office.

"What's that?"

"This business is not as boring as some might think. All this paperwork for verifying freshness dates is enough to keep you busy all day."

"It usually does. But I tell you, it's better to keep ahead of it than to let it get behind. Because if you let some bad meat get out of here, that's a federal offense. People's lives are at stake."

"Well, thanks for showing me the ropes," Casey said.

"No problem. You need to know."

"You know we've been working together for a couple of weeks now, and you've been quiet lately. Not your ordinary get-out-and-go self. What's on your mind?"

"Just have some things to consider. . . . A business opportunity," Ethan said.

"That's great. Anything promising?"

"Well, it sounds good, but I'm going to be expected to take my personal life to a higher level. That's why I'm having second thoughts."

"The employer said that to you? How can they say that?"

"No, my best friend said it. It's his business."

"Oh, now that's understandable. Friends and business can be tricky. They know you inside out."

"Who you telling? Not just anybody could tell me that I have to change in order to work with them."

"That's why they're called friends."

"Ya think?" Ethan said.

"I sure do," Casey confirmed.

"Well, I might as well tell you now."

"What?"

"I'm real close to taking it," Ethan said bluntly.

"That's wonderful."

"Yeah, it's a real good opportunity." Ethan sounded a little hesitant.

"Well I say go for it," Casey enthused.

"I'm really considering it. But you know if I take it, that's going to leave you here to take my position. I haven't talked to the owner yet and don't know what his plans will be. But I think you're a fast learner and I can put in a good word for you—if I decide to leave."

"You would do that?" Casey asked, flattered.

"Yeah, why not?"

"Thanks Ethan, that would be great."

"No problem." Ethan closed the file cabinet. Then the intercom rang.

"Can you get that?" Ethan asked.

"Sure. . . . Yes? This is Casey."

"Ahhhh . . . Casey, this is Kyle. I need to talk to Ethan." Casey looked over to Ethan.

"What is it, Kyle?" Ethan asked, sensing trouble.

"You need to get out here and control these customers, because I'm not punching in one more number until these fools learn to respect me," Kyle sniveled. Ethan and Casey shook their heads.

"Listen, Kyle, I'm not in the mood for this. You asked me to give you another job and I did. So do it."

"Like I said, Ethan, I am not doing anything until you come out here and control these fools."

"Okay, I'll be out there in a minute."

"Well, I'm waiting, and so are the customers," Kyle said. Ethan sighed as he turned away from the intercom.

"I do not feel like dealing with him tonight. I'm to a point with him where I might lose it."

"I can handle it—if you want me to?"

Ethan looked at Casey. "I wouldn't do that to you. I went to school with him, and he doesn't care about anything or anybody."

"Well, let's see—we can chalk this up as on-the-job training."

Ethan thought about it for a second. "Okay . . . if you want to. But I'm telling you, sometimes he can get really nasty."

"I think I can handle him."

"Think so?"

"Sure."

"Okay, but I'll go along and eavesdrop a little," Ethan said.

Kyle hadn't moved one inch. His legs were crossed and he was glaring at the displeased customers who were angrily waiting for him to reopen the line. Ethan stood back out of sight as Casey approached Kyle behind the counter.

"Kyle, what's going on?" Casey asked calmly, looking at the displeased customers. Kyle looked up at her, remaining seated.

"Am I mistaken or did I ask for Ethan?"

"Ethan's tied up right now. Why is your line closed?" Casey asked. Then the customers became riled.

"Because he doesn't know what the hell he's doing!" someone shouted.

"See, that's what I'm talking about, Casey. They're not respecting me."

"Kyle, I don't know what's going on here, but you're going to have to open the line back up and continue working, okay?"

Kyle stood up like a fire had been ignited. "Hell no . . . it's not okay. These broke-ass people need to take their asses home and save their money anyway!" he shouted out.

"Kyle, I'm going to ask you again to forget about it and get back to work," Casey demanded.

"Listen, little white girl. I ain't doin' a damn thing!"

Ethan couldn't take any more and moved behind the counter.

"Oh, now here you are. What are you—her knight in shining armor? Go ahead, Ethan, and tell me you don't like my attitude like you always do. Go ahead."

"Look, Kyle, I don't like your behavior, okay. You're either going to open back up or be suspended. And I mean it."

"You goin' to suspend me?"

"That's right. I don't have time for you and the customers are waiting. So what are you going to do?"

Kyle got up from his chair, rolled his eyes, and walked away. People in the line began to clap. Ethan looked at Casey and shook his head, then took the closed sign down.

"Who's next?" Ethan asked.

"I am," the gentleman in line said. "First of all, let me have two-two-seven-two straight box." And Ethan rolled up his sleeves and went to work.

Settin' Up

Vance was a nervous wreck. The time of truth had arrived and stared him in the face. He was beyond the hyperventilating stage—the promise he was ready to make to his beloved had him in an excited trance. In the past when he'd thought about proposing, he never imagined it would have him in such an uproar. Back when he'd mentioned it to Ethan, his proposal to Artise was going to be short and sweet, not too extravagant. But with his newfound wealth, it was only appropriate that he splurge—make it the most important start to their beginning. He had three larger-than-life carats ready to slide on her finger when he knelt on one knee. Vance stood tense in the bare living room of his new home with two pillows and a blanket trying to decide where to place them for the most romantic effect.

"Right there!" Ethan's voice was amplified by the hollowness in the house.

"What?" An echo followed Vance's response.

"Right there, man. Drop those pillows right there—spread out the blanket then line this whole room with the candles and the roses. Now that's romance," Ethan said.

"Right here?" Vance rubbed his clean-shaven face. He couldn't wait to splash more after-shave on it to stop its stinging. . . . "Are you sure, Ethan?" Vance asked.

"That's the spot," Ethan assured him.

"Okay . . . right here. Damn right. This is romance at its finest—and it's my idea, so don't even think about trying to claim this one, play-boy," Vance joked. Vance arranged his props on the floor and stepped back to survey the scene he'd created.

"You know I wouldn't do that. I'm just trying to help a brother out." Ethan sat against the wall in the far corner of the room. "So Artise hasn't got a clue?"

"Nope," Vance replied confidently. "Nada."

"Vance, I don't know how the hell you've kept all of this from her. I know if it was me, the cat would have been out the bag a long time ago."

"Well . . . me and Artise have been going through some rough times so that made it a little easier."

"She hasn't forgave you yet?"

"I haven't even asked her. Last thing she told me was 'I'm going to start doing my thing and you can do whatever.' I've been trying to stay away from her because I've damn near spoiled the surprise and told her everything. But after tonight she's going to realize that she's the only one for me." Vance paused for a second, shifting the pillows slightly.

"At least you know she's not in it for the money. I couldn't imagine you married to another woman anyway because you two sure have been through some rough times."

"Yeah, she was with me when I didn't have a dime in my pocket."

"You don't have to question her love and that's for sho'," Ethan confided.

"So you think I'm making the right choice?"

"Yeah, man—I mean if you want to get married. You have to marry Artise—no doubt about it."

"And that's exactly what I'm going to do." Vance stepped back and looked at his setup one more time. "So what was the deal with you at work when I called?"

"Man . . . I had to suspend Kyle at work. He really pissed a brutha off today. That attitude just got him in trouble. I would have suspended him a long time ago but those damn union rules are a trip. One frequency . . . two frequencies, warning, and then suspension. You don't know how that affects the workplace."

"I could imagine."

"Let me ask you something."

"Go 'head."

"You remember Kyle, don't you?"

"Yeah, I remember him. Didn't know too much about him. But yeah."

"So what you think about him?"

"I couldn't even form an opinion. Why?"

"You know he's gay, right?"

"That's what they've always said about him. But I remember he had a kid or two."

"Yeah, he did. Then afterwards—he just flipped the script."

"Hey, it happens."

"Well I have a serious problem with him."

" 'Cause he's gay?"

"Naww, man. 'Cause he's always trying to push his lifestyle off on everyone and makes it such a big deal. I could care less about what he's doing, as long as it don't interfere with what I do."

"You tell him?"

"All the time. But he starts off with all this homophobic nonsense and rambles on and on about me being homophobic—like he's rehearsed it over and over again. You wouldn't believe some of the things he does at the store, man. Just outrageous."

"Maybe something else is on his mind. You never know."

"Maybe?" Ethan quickly dismissed

"I'll tell you one thing, there aren't going to be any unions working up in my place of business, and you can write the employee handbook yourself."

"You know what I thought about the other day?"

"What's that?"

"I remembered that Jesse stands on that corner in front of your building selling his peanuts." Ethan put his hands up over his mouth to imitate Jesse's high-pitched voice. "Hey! How ya' doin'? I ain't seen you since high school! I got fresh-roasted peanuts, best made anywhere in da city!"

"You sound just like him!" Vance laughed.

"Man, every day he says the same old thing to everybody! What are you going to do with my man?"

"I'm going to leave him right there. I might even get him a nice stand out there. It will bring flava' to the place. That vibe I'm looking for. If he wants, I'll even move him into the coffee shop."

"He's about, what? . . . Seventy-two?" Ethan asked.

"Probably. But tell the truth: when he says, 'Hey, I haven't seen you since high school,' doesn't it make you look at him?"

"It does. . . . I can't lie about that." Ethan paused, growing more serious. "I just don't know for sure about taking the job yet, Vance, but I can tell you this. It's definitely been on my mind."

"Well, you're going to have to make up your mind, Ethan. 'Cause I am going to need you to help with this thing from ground zero. And you know the money we agreed upon is right there."

"I hear you. But, Vance, I got to be straight. I took offense to that crap Stubby was running down at me last time we were out here. Man, ain't nobody going to tell me how to live my life."

Vance chuckled. "Ethan, you ain't never once listened to him. I don't see why you don't try to understand what he's saying to you."

" 'Cause it's my life and I do what I want to do. You know how I am. When I'm at work, I work. And when I play . . . I play!" Vance shook his head knowingly, feeling Ethan's vibe.

"So, my brutha, who you playin' with tonight?"

Ethan smiled then looked at his watch.

"Awww, man . . . Monica again."

"Another WWK?"

"Act like ya know, Vance," Ethan said back.

"How many does she have?"

"Just one. And she is on the move, Vance. Work during the day, school on the weekends, has her own place."

"She's in the game like you. Does she know how you do things?"

"You know I'm up-front with my females. When you're up-front with them, they're up-front with you."

"So what are you two going to do tonight?"

"Get a room," Ethan said without hesitation.

"Just like that?" Vance asked.

"Just like you and Sheryl did," Ethan teased. "But I ain't going to be hiding and ducking."

"Forget you, man," Vance said while he checked out his setup from every angle in the room.

"I'm just saying . . . she has the sitter all set and she told me she was ready tonight. So it's on, you know what I mean?"

Ethan followed Vance's movement with his eyes. Vance had moved to the front door and had both his hands shaped into L's like a movie director to see how Artise would take in the picture he'd painted for her. "Yeah, I know. . . . I know what you mean. 'Cause it's going to be on here too!" Vance shouted and his voice echoed through the entire house.

The Night—the North Side

Artise didn't have a clue where Vance was driving to. Vance had called and asked her out to dinner minutes after she returned from happy hour with Tassha. *Why not?*, Artise thought. The happy hour scene did nothing for her, and strangely, she felt bad for going. She hated the looks and stares she received from the men and swore that no matter what type of situation she found herself in down the road, happy hour and after-hours joints were not going to be a part of her life. The first thought that came to Artise's mind after Vance asked her to dinner was flat-out no. But she thought for a second and decided to see where Vance's head was at. Her objective was to see if Vance was enjoying this lull in their relationship. She decided that if he was passionate and sincere about making changes in his life, and honestly sorry for what he had done, she would tell him about the baby. If not, she would wait until another day. Artise sat in the passenger's seat and looked out both windows. There wasn't a single restaurant on this side of town that they had ever been to. *Who has the money to eat out here?* Artise thought, looking curiously at Vance out of the corner of her eye. They were in a part of the city where those with big money laid their hats at night. Artise tried to think of how many times she had been on this side of town. Twice, she remembered. Once when she had a volleyball game in high school, and the second time to visit a boutique where there was not one dress she could afford. Vance seemed like he knew where he was going, so Artise played the stillness-and-serenity game right along with him: But when he turned off onto a dark wooded road, she decided to find out what was going on.

"Vance?"

"Um-hmmm?"

"Where are you taking me?"

"To get a bite to eat."

"Way out here?"

"Yeah . . . I think you'll enjoy this place."

"Well, how did you hear about it?" Artise asked skeptically.

"Oh . . . Ethan stumbled onto it and told me all about it." Vance could see the lights magnifying the house as they approached. "See, here it is through the wood line." Vance pointed in the direction of the house, which was still about a half mile away.

"Oh, okay, now I see it. This looks expensive, Vance."

"Don't worry about it. I've been saving a couple of dollars just to bring you out here." Vance smiled as they stopped far enough from the house so that the entire estate could be seen in all of its splendor and majesty.

"Wow! You mean to tell me someone turned this place into a restaurant?" Artise wanted to know.

"Ummm-hmmm."

"I bet you it's gorgeous inside."

"It is," Vance blurted out. Artise turned sharply toward him. "Ethan told me it was," he clarified.

Vance began to maneuver the car over to the side of the driveway into the grass, and Artise became a little worried when she heard the rocks under the car ravel.

"You sure this is okay?"

"If someone tells us to move, I will. But I think we'll be okay," Vance said as he stopped the car and turned off the ignition. "Now this is better." He tried to get as comfortable as he could behind the steering wheel of his Taurus, taking his notebook of lyrics and placing them in the back seat. Artise had her eyes fixed on the house.

Vance was lost for words. In no time at all he got caught up in the scenery right along with Artise, and it became more and more difficult for him to keep his composure. He knew what was going on—Artise didn't. He looked at all the windows in the house and wondered who had come up with the idea to accent the windowpanes with crystalline lights. He thought it was a very nice touch; it helped in setting the romantic mood he was trying to capture. He glanced over at Artise. She had an expression of awe painted over her face. *Good,* Vance thought; it was exactly how he wanted Artise to feel. He wanted the house and ambience to break the silence between them. The silence of love is what he was trying to unravel. Tonight's sky reminded him of all the nights he and Artise had taken long soul-searching walks discussing their future under the stars. Vance took a deep breath and struggled to contain his romantic impulses. He considered it best to let Artise start things off. He wanted to know what was on her mind.

Artise began to relax. It was good that she did. She decided to take Tassha's advice and tell Vance about the pregnancy as soon as possible. This wasn't exactly the way she wanted to tell him though. She never dreamed that she would have to tell him while sitting in the front seat of his ten-year-old Taurus. They had both dreamed the pregnancy would be announced in a house similar to the one before her eyes. Their plan was to be married first and have at least seven months of car, house, and utility bills paid so Artise could take off from work and enjoy and nurture the newborn correctly. But things hadn't worked out that way. They were living in an old house on the east side that was beginning to need repairs, and they were in a relationship that needed mending as well.

Vance couldn't take it anymore. "Looks nice doesn't it?" he called out to Artise.

She paused a beat, returning from her thoughts. "Sure does. Could you imagine living in a place like that?"

"Now that would be something . . . huh?" Vance said, continuing the game.

"It sure would be," Artise fantasized before her voice went an octave lower. She knew there wasn't a chance. "You know . . . we always dreamed of living together in a house like that one, Vance." Artise pointed, then her hand went back down into her lap like it was exhausted. She'd sounded happy when she spoke of their past—and at the same time, weary with disappointment that things had not turned out as they'd hoped.

"Yeah . . . I know, Teese," Vance said, though with less fatigue. "Who would have imagined that it would've been this difficult for us to get on track." Artise looked over at Vance and he continued. "And I can say it's been all my fault—and that's for sure. Sometimes your dreams outweigh what you can accomplish, I guess."

"Do you really believe that, Vance?" Artise fixed her eyes on him, waiting for his answer. When her body turned the car seat squeaked.

"Well I mean in a certain time period, yes. You can't always accomplish what you set out to do," Vance explained.

"It could be that people quit trying to reach their goals and they use that as an excuse."

"I feel where you're coming from, Artise, and I can honestly say that I take all the responsibility of us being here in this old Taurus . . . instead of living in a house like that," Vance confessed.

"You're willing to take that responsibility?" Artise asked.

"Yes . . . I am."

"Well, Vance, there's a whole lot more that I want you to take responsibility for."

"Oh, what's that?"

"We're having a child together—and I pray that you take all the responsibility in the world for our baby." Vance sat up from his position, accidentally honking the horn.

"Artise . . . you're pregnant? Baby, when did this happen? When did you find out?"

"A couple of days ago," she said. Vance reached over and hugged her. Artise's eyes just looked at the ceiling of the old car while her lips crumpled.

"You know . . . Stubbs always told me things would work out for the better between us," Vance said proudly. Artise didn't understand him and pulled away from him.

"Vance, I know you're happy about this. But we aren't ready for a child. I mean, this is not how we planned it at all."

"Yes it is, Artise. We couldn't have planned it any better!" Vance reached into his pockets. He was rushing now, his mind and his pulse racing two hundred miles per hour. He had brought Artise out to surprise her, and what he got in return was the most precious surprise he could ever have asked for.

"What are you talking about, Vance?"

"I'm talking about this." Vance pulled a key from his pocket and handed it to Artise.

"What's this for?"

"Look up there, Artise." Vance nodded toward the house. "This is the key to the front door." Artise looked at Vance and her breathing became heavier.

"What?"

Vance's smile was as wide as Artise had ever seen it in her life.

"Yes, this land we're sitting on—ours. That house—ours. All ours, baby!" Vance was delighted.

"Vance, how . . . what are you talking about!" Artise tried to stop her hand from hitting him on the arm.

"Baby, I'll explain it to you later." Vance got out of the car and ran to open the door for Artise. "Come on—let's go inside."

"Vance, this is crazy!" Artise protested.

"Baby, you're right, it is crazy, but right now . . . let's go look at our new house!" Vance grabbed her hand and pulled her out of the car and Artise began to laugh in disbelief. He put his arm around her and they stood looking at the house, both of them anxious and enthusiastic and reflective about what could be. Artise looked at Vance, making sure she had his eyes.

"Vance, are you for real?"

"As real as real can be."

She smiled. "Are you serious?"

"Absolutely . . . positively." Then he kissed Artise on the cheek.

"You shaved!" Artise said, kissing him back.

"It's a brand-new me, baby. Shall we?"

Artise nodded. "Ummmm-hmmmm, we should." Then they began walking toward the house, and their steps turned into a trot, which turned into a full-blown sprint all the way down the driveway to the front door.

South Side—My . . . My . . . My

Monica was sure that Ethan knew the time had come. She'd made it unmistakably clear she had one thing on her mind for the night. Making love. She had explained over the phone to Ethan that it was time for maintenance—the legendary supreme oil change, complete with filter and pressure check. Their last meeting put her over the top and was the deciding factor. Ethan's answers to her questions concerning commitment and children were open-ended enough to give her a glimmer of hope, an inkling of a chance that she could make this man like what he would be given. Like it so much, in fact, he would smile and say, "That's okay, I want to be with you anyway," after she broke the news about the twin boys she'd had while he was away. It was the first time Monica hadn't acknowledged the twins' existence to a man who showed some type of interest in her. In the past her truthfulness had backfired. The minute she would say "I have three boys," the men would put on their coats and run to find their hats. So just this once—for all of their sakes—she hadn't told.

"Okay, Brent . . . I want you to take good care of your brothers, okay?" Monica said, looking down at her four-year-old son who was soon to be five. Monica grabbed all three of her sons in front of her and put her arms around their waists as though they were having a family conference. "I know Mommy told you that I wouldn't leave you guys by yourself anymore . . . but Mommy doesn't have anyone to baby-sit and I know how much you have heard Mommy talk about Ethan. He's really special to me, and after tonight he's going to realize that. And soon he'll be here for all of us. So you guys bear with me, okay? You did a wonderful job the last time, and Mommy just asks you to stay here and be good just one more time." Monica looked at all three of her sons. They all had blank expressions on their faces. Then the eldest spoke.

"Mommy, I want to take a bath and play with my toys. I don't want to watch them again."

"Brent, you're going to have to wait until Mommy comes back, okay? What I need you to do is to stay in the back room with your brothers and make sure they behave. That's what big brothers do, didn't I explain that to you?" Brent sighed and nodded his head yes. "Now are all of you clear—everyone is okay with this, right?" Monica asked. The twins were now on the floor playing with blocks and Brent just blinked his eyes. "Brent . . . you understand, don't you?" He blinked again, and Monica grabbed him and gave him a big hug then began to tickle him until he smiled.

"That's my boy. I promise you. Tomorrow you can play in the tub with your toys all you want. Now Mommy has to get ready to leave, okay?" Brent grabbed Vernon and Keith by the hands and took them into the back room. Monica watched and smiled. "Do not let them out of your sight, Brent." *What am I going to do?* Monica said to herself silently. *I can't take them with me—hell, if I did, there would be no reason to leave in the first place.* Monica glanced toward the back. *This is the last time, anyway. There won't be a reason for me and Ethan to go to a hotel, because after I finish with him he'll be here all the time. I just have to show him—give him what he needs first.* The doorbell rang. Monica ran to the back room, kissed her boys good-bye, and opened the door. When Ethan saw her face he attempted to step in, but Monica put her hand into his chest and he stood still.

"Hey, baby, you ready?" she asked.

"Umm-hmm . . ." Ethan said with a strange look on his face.

"Me too! Brent's at the sitter's and I'm all yours!" Ethan's bizarre look quickly disappeared with Monica's openness combined with the hot red dress that sat perfectly on her body.

"All mine?" Ethan asked.

"That's right!" And they were on their way.

Monica was grooving to Michel'le's new CD as the lovers made their way to the hotel. She didn't want to give herself up and let Ethan find out that she was more interested in him than this one night might indicate. But she wanted to find out where Ethan's mind was.

"This sure is a nice CD!"

"Yeah . . . she's still *nicety!* Ethan joked. Monica looked at him.

"You remember that?" she asked.

"Yep . . . I sure do!"

Monica hummed along with the music. "So you think you'll ever settle down?"

"I don't know. Yeah . . . maybe. I thought we already discussed that?"

Monica soaked his answer in. *Not what I absolutely wanted to hear,* she thought. *But at least he's undecided and didn't say no.* "What about children? Do you have any or want any?" she asked Ethan.

"Uh-uh. No kids," Ethan said. "Maybe one day though . . . you never know. It might be fun to have a little me running around."

Hmmm, Monica thought. *I could have one more. Plus mine are young enough to get used to calling him daddy.*

The lust and electricity between Monica and Ethan was thick when they got situated in the room at the Doubletree Hotel. While in the elevator they were all over each other, and as soon as the door opened Monica went for Ethan's shirt and they began kissing.

"Hold on a second." Ethan pulled back. "I need to get some ice for the wine—it took me two hours at the store just to pick out the right bottle for us. I'll be right back."

Monica kissed him. "You promise?"

"Oh yeah . . . I promise." Ethan went out the door and Monica began to undress. Her eyes looked at the phone and she decided to call home.

"He-llo!" Brent said.

"Hi, baby! It's Mama," Monica said. "Is everything okay?"

"Yep," he reassured her.

"Where are your brothers?" she asked.

"Sleep."

Good, Monica thought. "Do me a favor and climb into the bed right next to them and go to bed. I'll be back home shortly, okay?"

"Okay, Mom," he said.

"See you later . . ." she said.

Ethan came back into the room with a bucket of ice and placed the bottle into it. Monica's lace panties and bra caught his attention.

"My . . . my . . . my," Ethan exalted.

"If you like what you see . . . you can have all you want."

"Well I do. And I will," Ethan lusted.

Back to the North Side

"So Stubby just came right out and did that for you, Vance?" Artise wanted to know. Vance had just finished telling her about the Stubblefields' goodness.

"Yes, baby . . . yes!" Vance exclaimed. A grin covered his face. He took his bank book out from under one of the pillows. He'd kind of known that he was going to have to prove himself. "Here, look. . . . What did I tell you?" Artise's eyes lit up. "We are set!"

"They must really love you, Vance," she said.

"I know. . . . When they explained everything to me, I didn't even believe I was rich until about two or three weeks later. I kept going to work and everything until Stubby called me one day and asked me what was I doing there."

"So you quit?"

"Uh-uh. Not yet. I'm out sick." Vance laughed. "But Monday I'm outta there!"

Artise smiled. "But you were able to keep it from me?"

"I know. And it was the hardest thing I ever had to do in my life."

"Why?"

"Because, Artise. I'm so used to having you around, that's why," Vance said. Artise checked out the house again.

"So you already bought this, huh?"

"Yep." Vance smiled, pleased with himself.

"And the check cleared?"

"Artise, will you stop!" he laughed.

"I'm just making sure. You know how things can get messed up sometimes," Artise joked.

"So do you like how I decorated?"

"Yes, it's nice. Was this your idea?"

Vance nodded. "Come on. Let's light the candles," he said.

"Okay, why not," Artise agreed.

Vance walked over to the first candle in its marble holder on the mantel. He picked up a box of matches, struck a match, and looked directly at Artise.

"Damn."

"What?"

"It's you. You look so nice."

Artise blushed. "Thank you," she said. She had on a little skirt and a white short-sleeved shirt.

"You know, I was beginning to think we would never get to this point in our lives, Artise. I was beginning to feel like a loser." Vance lit the candle, then they walked two steps to the next one. "All the things that I'd ever promised you seemed like they would never be obtainable, and baby, I couldn't handle it."

Artise smiled. "But look what you've done. You've made people feel good when you didn't even know what you were doing. And they're the ones who rewarded you," she said supportively. Vance lit another candle and the dim room became a little lighter.

"Why, thank you," he said.

"You're welcome."

Artise and Vance slowly walked around the entire living room lighting all the candles. The mood that Vance was searching for—hoping for—was among him and his love. It was soft . . . it was romantic . . . it was gentle, it was passion at its best. The two found their way into the middle of the room and sat on the pillows, amid the flickering candlelight.

"I could sit here all night," Artise said.

"I could too. You want to know why?" Vance asked.

"Yes, I do."

"Because I love you. And because you're the only person in the whole world who can make me feel like I do at this very moment."

"And how is that?"

"It's like when you have everything you need in your cup to make the perfect cup of tea. But I'll call it a cup of love."

"A cup of love?"

"Yes. You have all the ingredients I need in my cup to get me through all of my fears, misfortunes, and happiness. Your understanding, loyalty, and love is divine, Artise, and I wouldn't want anyone else to enjoy all this with. You know what I mean?"

"Yeah, I know what you mean," Artise said, blushing. "But I want to know, how do I taste?" she asked seductively.

"Hmmm. . . ." Vance leaned over and kissed Artise right on her lips. Then Vance eased off and smiled. "You taste so . . . so good."

"Ummm. That was nice," Artise purred.

"It really was," he said back. Then they just sat on their pillows, relishing the moment. Vance had an idea. "Do me a favor?" he asked.

"Yes," Artise said.

"Put your hand behind your pillow and grab whatever your hand touches."

"What?"

"Put your hand behind the pillow and bring out whatever is behind it."

Artise hesitated then did as Vance asked. She tried to get a feel for what it was by looking into Vance's eyes, but she didn't have a clue—and Vance didn't give her any.

"Go ahead, it's okay," Vance explained.

Artise moved her little body so she could reach behind the pillow. Her tiny hands fought their way through the pillows and finally touched something. She brought her hand forward to reveal a package.

"Okay, now open it," Vance suggested.

"Open it?"

"Yes . . . open it."

Artise took another look at Vance and tried to read his mind. He smiled. She took a deep breath and began to open the package. Vance's heart began to pump. Artise took the ribbon off the box and the paper landed on the floor. "Now stop," he ordered.

"Stop?"

"Yes. . . . Artise, before you open that all the way, I want you to know that I love you with all my heart."

Artise was glowing. "Thank you, Vance. . . . That's so sweet of you."

Vance felt tears forming in his eyes. The moment was turning out to be better than he had ever dreamed. "Okay, open it," Vance said.

"Are you sure?"

"Yes."

Artise opened the box and it was as if the entire room had gotten a shade lighter from the diamonds that were set in the ring that Artise now held.

"Ohhhhh!" Artise began to tremble, and Vance put his hand over her face to silence her.

"Teese, I've been waiting for so long to do this for you and here is my chance." Vance cleared his tight throat. "Baby girl?"

"Umm-hmm," Artise whimpered.

"Will you marry me?" Artise's eyes filled with tears immediately, and Vance saw the first tear fall from her eye. He took his hand and wiped it away as Artise looked at the ring again. "Will you marry me, sweetheart?" Vance asked again. Artise took the ring out of the box and stared. She was beginning to cry uncontrollably. Vance moved as close as he could to her and placed his forehead upon hers. They were one. Artise looked at him, still tearful. She exhaled, then placed the ring back in the box—Vance's heart stopped beating.

"No, Vance. I just can't do it," Artise said. "Do you mind taking me home now?"

In His Arms

Five hours and four sessions of lovemaking is what Ethan and Monica accomplished in their get-together. Ethan's hunch that Monica was special in bed was right. Even though she was seven years younger, her confidence was as strong as he had ever run across—she walked the talk. Ethan was exhausted, but happy. His content grin lasted all the way until they got back to Monica's house and it was time to call it a night.

"Well, here we are," Ethan said, putting his car in park. "I have to say—this night is going to go down in history."

"So I get a page in your little black book?" Monica joked.

"No way. You've made a brother want to start his own personal diary about a sister!"

"You would do that for me?" Monica felt good that she was not just one of his girls. She leaned over and began to kiss Ethan, and it lasted awhile. Then Ethan backed away.

"Ummm . . . sweetheart."

"What's wrong?"

"Do you mind if I go inside? I have to use the restroom something awful," Ethan struggled to say.

"Right now?"

"Of course, and very quickly." Ethan tried to keep the situation funny.

"Let me make sure the bathroom is at least presentable. You know how we girls are sometimes when we get in a rush."

"Please hurry, okay, Monica." Ethan tiptoed up to the front door with her as she toyed with him.

"Wait here, okay?" Monica said.

"I'm not going anywhere . . . except around to the side of this house if you don't hurry up . . . trust that," Ethan said.

Monica went ahead inside to check on her boys. She wanted to make sure they were asleep and wouldn't come running out from the back as soon as they heard her voice. Monica walked back to their room and opened their door. She thought maybe they were under the covers, because the air did have a bit of a chill, but when she pulled the covers back, they weren't there. She smiled *That's right; they're in my bed waiting on me,* she thought. But when she reached her room they weren't there. Worried, she began to call out.

"Brent! Brent! Where are you, sweetheart?"

Ethan became concerned when he heard Monica calling out. He walked in the house and saw her come into the living room. "Monica . . . what's the problem?" Monica didn't answer. She was beginning to panic.

"Brent!" Monica called out. "Vernon? Keith?"

"Monica, what is going on?" Monica began running through the house. She finally walked down the hallway to the only room she hadn't checked—the bathroom. Ethan followed closely behind her. They both stopped when they saw water flowing out from underneath the bathroom door.

Monica investigated the water as she continued walking toward the bathroom. Ethan still was without a clue and had a puzzled look on his face. A steady flow of water could be heard running in the tub.

"Oh . . . oh no!" Monica yelled frantically. "Oh . . . no . . . not my babies!"

"Babies?" Ethan mumbled.

"I said wait until tomorrow—I said not until tomorrow!" Monica screamed. "Please God, no!" Monica pleaded as she made her last step to the bathroom door. She looked back at Ethan, then opened the door.

"Nooooo! Nooooo!" Monica sang in pain. "Nooooo!" Ethan moved in front of her and saw three small boys submerged in the water. Vernon and Keith were sitting on each side of Brent, completely stiff and blue. Ethan gasped when he saw Brent holding his brothers in his arms. He too was stiff. Then a bubble relinquished from Brent's mouth. It was his last breath.

"Oh my God!" Ethan shouted and he reached into the water and pulled the little ones out with one swoop. "Call nine-one-one, Monica! . . . Call nine-one-one," he screamed as he began trying to bring them back to life. But Monica didn't move. Instead she began to cry uncontrollably. She knew all through her being her boys were already in His arms, then silently Monica began to explain to the spirit as it clutched onto her sons as she only wished she could.

> *Oh my child*
> *My child*
> *Knowing I've done wrong*
> *My child*
> *My child*
> *He's taken you home*
>
> *Oh my child*
> *My child*
> *To a place*
> *We all long to see*
> *My child*
> *My child*
> *Never dreamed my babies*
> *Would see it before me*
>
> *Oh my child*
> *My child*
> *It's all my fault*

My child
My child
never asked to be here
Now washed away like a pillar of salt

Oh my child
My child
Tears of pain
Are all I have left
My child
My child
To show you I care
As you lay to rest

Oh my child
My child
Please understand
I really do care
My child
My child
and tell Jesus
I didn't mean this to happen
soon as you get there

Oh my child . . . my child

Talk to Me

Artise hadn't changed a bit since she was a little girl. When things were troubling her mind she would always go to Mama, and that's exactly what she did when she woke up the next morning sluggish and dazed from all the events that had happened to her the night before. She headed right for her security blanket, her shield away from the world—a place where she could clear her mind. Her favorite spot in the world—her old bedroom at her mama's house. Artise hadn't bothered to call, so when she saw her mother's eyes peek through the shades when she knocked at the door, it reminded her of what she had been trying to convince her mother of doing. Cathy opened the door and Artise made her move inside.

"Artise . . . don't you know you scared the living daylights out of me, girl. What are you doing here this time of morning?" Cathy said, catching her breath.

"Mama, when are you goin' to get a dog?"

"A dog?"

"Yes, a dog, Mama. I thought we already discussed it?" Artise shut the door behind her.

"We discussed it? Well, are *we* going to clean up after it?"

"No, we're not. But at least you won't be scared out of your mind everytime someone knocks at the door."

"I'm not scared."

"Mama . . . yes you are, and I hate it that you live here all alone."

"Well, forget about a dog . . . and get me a man!" Cathy chuckled.

"Mama, you're terrible."

"Well, there's nothing to worry about. Did you lock the door back?"

"Yes, Mama," Artise said.

"So you still haven't answered my question."

"What question?" Artise asked.

"What are you doing here? What's wrong? And I hope you're not here to lay on your bed, because I'm making a new dress back there," Cathy said bluntly as the two walked into the kitchen where Cathy was fixing herself breakfast. Artise smiled.

"Dang, you already have breakfast done and everything."

"Yep . . . it doesn't take long. Now, quit holding the conversation up. What brings you over here so early this morning?"

"Well, I'm pregnant," Artise said swiftly. "Vance asked me to marry him, I told him no, and the Stubblefields gave him over three million dollars in real estate and cash. And if I was betting this morning, I would say he's sitting in his brand-new house where I left him."

Cathy dropped the spoon she was stirring her coffee with. "Wait a minute . . . wait a minute. Run that by me again?"

"I said I'm pregnant and—"

Cathy interrupted. "Stop right there. Artise, you're going to have a baby?"

"Yes, Mama, that's what usually comes out after nine months, unless there has been some major changes in the human biological system that I don't know of." Artise smiled and her mother reached out to hug her.

"Ohhh . . . my baby . . . is having a baby!" Cathy boasted. "When did you find out? Is everything okay?"

"Yes, Mama . . . everything is fine. I just found out a couple of days ago. I have another appointment next month," Artise said.

"You know, I had a dream about fish the other night."

"Oh, Mama, please! What does dreaming about fish mean?" Artise giggled.

"Your grandmother told me when you dream about fish someone

close to you is pregnant. And I dreamed about fish and you're pregnant—so she must have been right!"

"Well, I'm glad I went to the doctor first to verify it before I told you," Artise said.

"Well, I could have saved you some money," Cathy said, putting her hand on Artise's stomach. "You're going to be such a pretty mother, Artise."

"Thank you, Mama."

"Now what else were you saying?"

"Well, last night Vance asked me to marry him and he told me the Stubblefields gave him a bunch of money—the inheritance that they were going to give to their real son but he passed away."

"Let me get this right—he asked to marry you and you said no? And he finally has some money, plus you're pregnant?"

"That's right, Mama. I said no. . . . I almost said yes. But I started to think about something he said last night, and it made me realize that I wasn't ready."

"Well, what did he say?"

"He said that I was his every ingredient in his cup of love."

"Cup of love? That's kind of romantic . . . even for Vance, if you ask me." Artise shot her mother a reprimanding look.

"Mama . . . you know Vance is romantic. If nothing else he's romantic."

"If you say so."

"But I just don't feel the same way. I thought about what he said, and it doesn't feel the same way for me. What about my cup? Why should I marry him when my cup is not filled to capacity. I don't trust Vance right now . . . as far as I can see him. And think about it . . . if I have this baby and he goes and cheats on me again, I'll be a divorced wife with a kid to take care of all on my lonesome. Plus all this money he has now. You know how tempting things will be."

"Mama ain't raise no fool, did she?" Cathy asked, smiling proudly.

"Uh-uh. Sure didn't," Artise insisted. "But get this, Mama. Vance went out and bought a house just like the one we've always talked about living in."

"You did have a fun night, didn't you."

"Mama, you should see this house. . . . It took everything I had not to say yes to Vance. But I'm glad that I didn't."

"Me too, baby! So, do you want to move back home with me?"

"Move back here?"

"Yes. You can move back in here with me and we'll take care of the baby together."

"Mama . . . uh-uh. I can't do that to you. Plus, I have a place to stay."

"But you're going to need some help, Artise. How are you going to work and take care of the baby too?"

"Well, maybe I'll bring the baby over in the morning or something . . . but I have time to decide."

"Artise, I think you should decide now, because you have never been pregnant before, and baby . . . you are about to go through some changes and you're going to need help."

"Well, let me try first, on my own, Mama."

"If that's what you want to do. But be careful of Vance. I can see him putting pressure on you to get married now. You have to be ready to get married, and if you're not ready to be married now, you're not going to be ready anytime before you have this baby."

Artise became quiet. She knew that her mother was never fond of Vance, so she just let her words pass. "So, Mama, what's for breakfast?" she asked, putting a halt to the conversation.

"You know how I like my breakfast, Artise. I made me some eggs, bacon, and oatmeal."

Artise smiled. "Mama, as long as I can remember, you have eaten oatmeal," she said playfully, turning on the small television that sat on the counter.

Suddenly they were both drawn to the television and the sadness in the newscaster's voice.

"Three small children, one age four and twins of eighteen months, were found late last night by their mother in a tub full of running water. Few details are known at this point, but the Channel Ten investigative team has learned that the children's mother was out on a date and left the four-year-old boy in charge of watching his little brothers. We do know the mother has been taken into custody. We expect more details at six and later tonight as this story unfolds."

"Would you look at that?" Cathy cried. "What has gotten into these ladies out here? In my day the children came first. Now we have women going out and leaving their babies at home alone. They should put that lady in jail for life."

"They sure should. What kind of woman would go out and leave her kids at home for a date? I wouldn't leave my kids at home for anybody."

"See, Artise, these women think men can do everything for them. This woman was thinking with her silk panties and forgot all about her kids. . . . I bet you that's what happened."

"There ain't no man that good . . . and that's for sure," Artise said as she got up and turned off the television. "I don't even want to see any more news. It's too depressing."

"Poor babies," Cathy said, pushing her coffee away. "Poor, poor babies."

Eight Weeks Later . . .

Time seemed to blow through the city of Columbus with rapid speed. Since Vance's failed proposal, he'd done nothing but grueling work to get the museum project started. In addition, he was filled with endless heartache and lost sleep from all the worrying he had done over Artise and his child. But Vance stayed the course. He didn't move out of the house he and Artise shared together. *I'm going to stay right here with her until she decides that she wants to be with me in our new home. I did not buy the house for me. I bought it for the both of us, and I want our family to be happy there and we will,* Vance told himself daily. He had a hard time going out to see their new domain after Artise had told him she didn't want to marry him, and forced himself to take the drive up to Upper Arlington every seven or eight days just to check things out. When he opened the doors of the house his mind filled with the joy the home could bring him and his family, but after looking around and soaking in all of the imagined special moments, Vance would become depressed and downhearted from his dream not being a reality.

At least he and Artise were speaking. Artise explained to Vance that her mother wanted her to move back in with her and that she was considering it—so Vance kept the pressure on by demonstrating how much he loved her. He was home and in the kitchen cooking Artise something nutritional when Artise returned from work every night. He placed love letters in her briefcase and sent roses to her office daily. He did everything he possibly could to help Artise get through her dizzy spells and morning sickness. He even called repairmen to fix the neglected problems that had plagued their house for years.

At first Artise had felt like she couldn't explain herself to Vance. His newfound money and opportunity made her distrustful—Vance was a new man. But she soon got over the tangible items and told Vance what was really on her mind. *I knew him when he was dead broke and didn't have anything at all. I'm going to speak my mind,* she told herself and she did. "You have not provided the ingredients that I need in the cup of love you talked about when you proposed to me," Artise told him.

Vance understood. He'd always known he would have to prove his love to Artise because of his rocky past. He knew he had to change and that it wouldn't happen overnight. He pressed on and worked hard, determined to fulfill his promise to Stubby. He would construct the most exquisite museum for literature the country had ever seen. He would make Gloria proud of her husband and of him.

The more Vance accomplished the more he wanted to finish his project. The situation with Artise had him picking up his lyrics notebook every night. His mind was on love—the words he wrote were about love. He had become obsessed with achieving his lifetime goal, to write a song of love. As he sat at the kitchen table at night after looking in on Artise, he realized that words needed to come from substance, things that mattered. His situation with Artise made him realize that all along he had spent years and years writing words about women who didn't have any meaning to him. But now his words flowed freely on his pad. He had experienced an awakening, his heart had bled, and he wanted back what he never fully realized he'd always had. Vance was in love. "Surprising" is the word Vance used to describe to Stubby how easily things seemed to be going. Shelves for the museum and featured artwork by Jacob Lawrence, Faith Ringold, Horace Pippin, and many others were being placed on every floor, and a PA system was being placed inside so jazz could be heard throughout the entire building.

Stubbs could see the pain and transition Vance was going through. "A brokenhearted soul is easy to pick out," he told Vance. They had been talking about the shocking death of Monica's sons and the grief and heartache it was causing Ethan. "You two need to focus on the important things, get settled, become men." Vance knew Stubby was right.

Guiding Vance in the right direction concerning his money and everyday life was now Stubby's main goal. He not only wanted to show Vance how to work his newfound fortune, but he wanted to make sure Vance's life was based on a more spiritual level. The majority of the spiritual tapes he had given Vance over the years had gone barely listened to at all. Stubby told Vance it was time for him to have a sit-down, one-on-one, with the Creator. "Let God know what's on your mind, son. Ask him for his help in really committing to Artise," Stubby encouraged. "No more fooling around . . . no more lying. You got to be there for Artise like a husband should." Stubby prophesied that if Vance did these things, Artise would soon be back in his arms.

Vance believed in Stubby and his wisdom so much that he finally decided to take his advice. Vance wanted his Teese back. He began a new life in spirituality even though, as he explained to Stubby, he was at odds with the church as a foundation. Mostly because of the matters that were playing out in the news about the Baptist convention and all the fraud that had taken place. "My mother took me to a Baptist church growing up, Stubbs, and if corruption is going on there, it must be going on everywhere. I just don't know if I would be comfortable in the church right now."

But Stubby explained, "Vance, the church is there to give us direction, and until you become comfortable with the church's direction, you can serve the Lord on a personal level and you'll still be blessed. Don't let the devil take the one you love and your child away from you because of the problems the church is having. You must endure, son."

Vance began to open his Bible every morning instead of just looking at it. In the past he had been scared of the words it contained; but instantly Vance began to feel the change in his attitude and turned to reading the Bible along with daily meditation. Vance knew he was a long, long way from being perfect and realized he wasn't going to become perfect just because he was leading a new life. "Just remember,

Vance, the more you get into the spiritual side of yourself, the more the devil tries you. You have to continue to pray and stay strong 'cause, son, the devil is a liar," Stubby told him.

Artise noticed the subtle change in Vance and that was the main reason she stayed at home and didn't rush off to move in with her mother. She was impressed, intrigued, amazed, and happy to see what Vance was attempting to do. Artise wasn't spying, but she began to notice Vance take time with his Bible, and sometimes she would hear inspirational music in the morning before he left for the day instead of the early morning R&B stations he usually listened to. So she didn't have a problem when Vance told her the Stubblefields were planning a Sunday dinner and asked if she would like to come. Artise thought it would be nice to get out of the house and taste some of Mrs. Stubblefield's cooking—after all, she was with child, and the cravings were beginning to kick in.

Eight weeks after seeing Monica's children lying in the tub, submerged in water, definitely was not enough time for Ethan to clear his head and get over the traumatic scene he had witnessed. Ethan was strong enough not to go into a deep depression, but he was upset that Monica had lied to him about having only one child, and for deciding to go out with him and leaving her children alone to fend for themselves. Ethan felt sick inside that her children lost their lives, but he was not going to let his conscience make him believe blood was on his hands as well. It was a fight he swore he'd battle to his death. There were many times the recounting of the situation frequented his soul during his sleep, and Ethan would rise from his slumber, walk, shake, and denounce its presence. The situation convinced Ethan to visit Monica in jail, though. He wanted to hear the words come out of her mouth, to hear her say he was innocent. When he saw her, Monica looked worn and in a state of shock. She looked nothing like she had the incredible night they had spent together. She was completely shabby and deteriorated, and looked ten years older and fifteen pounds lighter. Her eyes were barely open, but you could see the redness around her eyeballs. Her lips, hands, and hair were extra dry from the coldness of her cell. Her body movements, as if locked in handcuffs and shackles, were weary and well spent.

"I am dead, Ethan," she said into the phone as she looked at Ethan through the Plexiglas.

"What?" Ethan said, squinting his eyes, trying to understand her words.

"Don't look at me like that," she instructed sharply. She had already been made hard. "I'm dead."

Ethan looked at the prison guard who was standing nearby. The guard turned away from him. Ethan removed the astonished look from his face and turned his head slightly to the side, almost looking at her from one eye.

"I finally understand what my oldest was trying to tell me, Ethan. I was dead all along. Dead," Monica said without blinking. "I was living inside of flesh and wanted a man more than God."

"Look, Monica. I don't know what you're talking about. I just came down here to see how you're doing," Ethan said.

"You! Did! Not!" Monica screamed. Then she smiled, but the force of her bellow made her cough. "You came down here for the same reasons I'm locked up!" she shouted. "I know you haven't been sleeping." Monica smiled again. "You've been up like me. You've been thinking like me. You've been wondering what my babies are telling God, haven't you?" Ethan swallowed. *How could she know?* Monica began to speak slower. "I know . . . because they have already spoken to me. Brent, Vernon, and Keith—all three of my babies, Ethan. They all spoke to me." Ethan thought about hanging up the phone and walking away. "Don't do it," Monica fired. "The word in here is that there will soon be a new prison built and we won't be able to have any visitors, so you better listen to what I have to say while you can. I know your fate, Ethan," she snickered.

Ethan raised his eyebrows, then looked to see if any other visitors noticed his trembling hands. "What are you talking about?"

"My boys told me—they've been told your fate."

Ethan became flustered. This was not what he came to hear. "So you blame me for this, Monica?" he asked.

"Or do you mean do they blame you for this," Monica corrected.

"I'm not taking the blame for anything. You understand that? I didn't know," Ethan testified.

"You're right. You didn't know—but, Ethan, did you really care? In all of our conversations, all the questions that I asked you, did you answer for you, or for me?"

Ethan started to speak. "I . . ."

"Hush," Monica said. "You answered for yourself, Ethan, to get me. And I fell for it and we both have to pay." Monica smiled again. "I will pay here." Her eyes penetrated Ethan's soul. He wanted to speak but he couldn't. He needed to know what her sons had told her about his fate. Still smiling, she said, "You will pay. You will." Ethan stood up from his chair.

"It was not my fault," he said, shaken. Then he put down the phone and began to walk away. Monica began screaming at the top of her voice.

"Did you think this was all about a good fuck, Ethan? Did you think I wanted to leave my children alone—just because of what we did? Did you ever stop to think that maybe somebody, someone wanted you to help? Damn it, Ethan! You're going to pay . . . trust me, motherfucker! You are going to pay!"

As fate would have it, Ethan found himself over at the Stubblefields', helping Vance touch up the white baseboards throughout the house. He had been much more quiet than usual, and Vance took it as him wanting to hurry and finish to do other things.

"You're sure working fast. What, you got a date?"

Ethan looked at Vance. "You trying to be funny or something?"

"Naww—I just know you. That's why I asked," Vance snapped back.

"Umph . . . everybody think they know me now."

Vance put down his paintbrush. "Negro, if anybody in this world knows you, I do. What the hell is on your mind?"

"Nothin'," Ethan snapped. "Let's just finish this."

Stubby must have heard the two, because he came inside like he couldn't hold his tongue any longer, and looked down at Ethan.

"You know, Ethan? When Vance told me that you were the man that went out with that young girl who left her childrens in the house by their lonesome, it didn't surprise me one bit." Ethan looked up from his baseboard and didn't say anything. He thought he had heard everything to this point. But he was truly surprised at Stubbs's frankness.

"See, what did I tell ya? And don't give me dat expression like Stubby is one of those peoples who likes to say I told you so . . . 'cause I ain't. Boy, I don't have too much air left in me, so what satisfaction would I git out of it anyway. I'm trying to save all da air I have to say something to peoples dat want to listen and care about life. You know it really makes me mad dat three childrens had to lose their life because their mama thought dat you—you, Ethan—was goin' to be part of their lives. I don't know how you goin' to live wit' yourself wit' dat on your conscience, son, I really don't." Stubby walked out of the room.

Ethan was speechless and felt like it was his daddy giving him a tongue-lashing. His mouth was wide open.

"Vance, did you bring me over for this or what?"

Vance wiped some paint off his forehead. "Nope . . . didn't have anything to do with it. Ethan, you know how that old man is. If he feels a certain way, he's going to tell you."

"You're right . . . you're right," Ethan said. "So how do you feel about it? You haven't said one thing to me about it since it happened."

Vance looked at Ethan. "Look, man—we all make mistakes. I know you told me that you didn't give her any reason to believe that you were going to be a part of her and her babies' life. But some people take what's not said in a positive way. You know what I mean?"

"Yeah, I know," Ethan said.

"You got caught up. That's all I'm saying." Vance paused. "But I do have a suggestion for you."

"What's that?"

"Stubbs loves you, man. No matter what you think. All he wants for everyone is the best. So when he asks you to attend his dinner that he's planning, do me a favor and tell him you'll come . . . okay?" Vance gave Ethan a serious look.

"Okay . . . yeah . . . I'll come."

"Good. And I'll talk to him about being easy on you, okay?"

"Yeah, do that, man. I would appreciate it," Ethan said. "So that job offer still available or what? I think I want to do this."

Vance smiled. "You sure?"

"Yeah—I need a change. All I have to do is finish training my assistant at the supermarket, and I'll be able to start full time."

"Good. . . . 'cause I thought I was going to have to look for someone else," Vance admitted.

"Naww . . . just take some people a little longer to make decisions, that's all."

"Cool," Vance said.

"Speaking of making decisions—what's up with you and Artise?"

Vance looked at Ethan, beaming with confidence. "God will make a way, brutha, he will make a way," he said, then continued to paint.

Good Food, Good Meat

When the Stubblefields announced they were having a dinner party, they meant exactly what they said. Mrs. Stubby was standing in the dining room, draped in a spicy black dress, with a delightful expression on her face. She loved gatherings and the fellowship that was attached when bringing people together. It reminded her of when families sat down as a lineage and enjoyed one another's company. She had spent long hours preparing all the food and the dining room table looked fabulous. Her best china had been removed from the cabinet, shined, and placed on the table for all her guests. There were ten plates sitting on the table and every last person who was invited had arrived. Vance, Ethan, Artise, and Tassha plus four of the Stubbys' closest friends.

"Thanks for coming with me, Tassha," Artise said apologetically when she noticed Tassha look at Ethan from the corner of her eye. "I didn't know Ethan was going to be here; if I did I would have warned you."

"That's all right. I've completely gotten over Ethan. I don't feel any pressure at all. I'm just here for you. How are you doing so far?" Tassha wanted to know.

"I'm fine. I had a little morning sickness today. It scared me, Tassha, 'cause I didn't put two and two together. But my mother happened to call when I was laying across the bed and told me what it was."

"So are you going to move back in with her?" Tassha asked.

"The last time we talked I told her I would. But I haven't told her when. You should see her, Tassha. She's so excited about the idea."

"How is Vance taking all of this?"

"He's doing okay—I've even seen some positive change."

"Oh really, now?"

"Umm-hmm. But it's still the most awkward situation. You know, Vance told me that he's not moving into the new house until I come with him?"

"That's a lot of pressure, Artise," Tassha sympathized.

"Yeah, I know. And he's serious about it too."

"He still hasn't said anything about you moving back in with your mother, then, huh?"

"Not since I first mentioned it to him. It was almost like he didn't hear me. When I told him, he had the strangest look on his face. Like he was trying to defeat something. Like he was in a battle."

"Hmm—I don't know what that's all about. But I've never seen him so excited and so broken at the same time," Tassha said.

"Yeah. Vance has always wanted children. And it's probably killing him inside knowing that our situation has not turned out the way he's always planned. But I've seen some change. I can tell that he's trying."

"How so?"

"He's just more focused on what he's doing. I think he's trying to show me how committed he can be."

"Well, friend to friend: Don't close all of your options. I'm not being selfish or anything . . . but all that Vance has gotten with this inheritance? I think you deserve it too. . . . You have been with him for years, Artise. So do me a favor and think about every decision you make, you hear me?"

Artise smiled. "I hear you. Thanks."

Vance and Ethan were on the other side of the room.

"Have you spoken to Tassha yet?" Vance asked.

"Nope . . . but I've seen her look this way a couple of times," Ethan uttered, wondering if she was still bitter about him leaving her at the altar or if she thought he was trash for going out with a woman who left her kids at home all by themselves.

"So you goin' to speak?" Vance wanted to know.

"Probably not. Unless she speaks to me or it's absolutely necessary."

"Man, that's not polite."

"I know . . . but what should I do? Walk over to her and say 'Hello. How have you been? You know, we haven't spoken since I asked you to marry me, and by the way, did you hear about the crazy-ass fool I took out on a date who left her kids in the house by themselves to drown to death?"

Vance looked at Ethan. "Yeah, you're right. You shouldn't say anything at all unless spoken to," Vance determined.

"Okay, everybody. Dinner is served!" Stubby shouted, gathering everyone's attention. Stubbs was looking good. He had on his black-and-white three-piece suit, with his timepiece dangling from the vest pocket, and spit-shined shoes. Stubby was busy greeting his guests. He blended in well with the atmosphere. The house, though old, had lots and lots of history. There were old pictures from the thirties and forties sitting on different tables in the house which were destined to be collector's items, especially the ones of the railroad workers covered in sweat as they labored. The hardwood floors were old and worn but had just the right finish and sparkled in their own way, along with the original heavy sliding doors with the gold-painted handles that led into the dining room.

"Ohhh . . . look at Stubby, y'all! You sure are sharp tonight!" Stubbs's dear friend Otis exclaimed.

"He sure is looking good!" Mrs. Stubblefield said and Stubbs's eyes lit up. "That man could always dress!" Stubbs made sure his tie was straight and sat down at the head of the table.

"Well, you know. I still know how to dress up a pair of britches . . . from time to time." He chuckled. "But you all look nice. Thanks for coming." Everyone smiled and thanked the Stubblefields for the invite. Everyone took their seats, and right away Vance felt awkward because he wasn't sitting next to Artise. But it wasn't so bad. They were sitting right across from one another. Vance right next to Ethan. Tassha right next to Artise in the middle of the table. "Does everyone know each other?" Stubby wanted to know. Everyone nodded yes.

"Good, because you should always know who you break bread wit'. Will everyone please bow deir heads so I can bless this wonderful food?" They did as asked. "Heavenly Father, thank you for this opportunity to sit in fellowship. We know dat nothing at all is promised to us. But we do know, Lord, dat your grace is always within our hearts. Amen." Everyone lifted their heads. "Now somebody pass me dem collards!" Stubby demanded.

"Here you go," Vance said as the guests began putting food on their plates.

Otis had worked as a barber for forty years and knew how to get a conversation going. "Well, Stubbs, looks like ol' boy Clinton has been cooked and basted."

Stubbs smirked as he placed the collards on his plate. "I knew it was going to come up, and, Otis, I have to say, I have never in my life seen people so dang-on happy to find out what dat man did with dat *woman.*" Stubby snickered. "Ms. Lewinsky."

"You would think people would be tired of it by now," Otis's wife Marilyn said.

"I know I am. That's all you hear about day in and day out. What he did, what she said," Mrs. Stubby said, and everyone agreed whole-heartedly.

"Well, you know. It's just the way of the world. In my view I think every president has done some bad things; but this case—this nonsense is getting out of hand. Who's got the collards?" Otis wanted to know. Artise looked at Tassha and smiled at the older guests. Vance had always told her about how they act and talk, but being up close and personal gave her another perspective.

"It's all a dang-on smoke screen. And I'm not telling you what I heard. I'm telling you what I know," Stubby said, making room for his sweet potatoes then reaching for the rolls. "Now listen to what I tell you— this is what I want you to know." Stubby pointed around the table with his fork. "There's a report dat should have been out months ago." Vance looked at the other guests. He knew Stubby was getting ready to tell everyone something that they probably hadn't even thought about.

"And this report is based on the Iran-Contra situation dat was going on back in the eighties. See, these Republicans are smart—dey have tried everything dey know how to keep dat report out of the hands of the American people . . . particularly us black folk—and I'm going to tell you why. Dat report has some stunning information in it about our government selling dat crack cocaine in the inner cities in order to fund the Contras in their conflict. Now dat congresswoman . . . dat brilliant black woman from California. Uh . . . uh . . ."

"Maxine Waters?" Tassha said.

"Yeah, yeah, dat's her," Stubby remembered. "She's right on the government's case about the situation because it affects her people in her districts. Now, we saw what happened with dat Rodney King incident. The town went up in flames. Just think what's going to happen when it gets out dat our own government infested our streets and communities with crack cocaine. It's going to be civil unrest. But look who was in control of the White House when all this happened. Mr. Bush and his friends. Now doesn't dat look like a good reason to use a smoke screen—and attack Clinton for his personal affairs so dat people won't be interested in what happened with Bush? And it's my understanding the report is being released right under our noses while we watch all this nonsense in the White House."

"You got a point there. . . ." Otis agreed.

"Yeah . . . I been around too long to not see da games dat go on. But I tell you this: Our people better wake up, 'cause there are a lot of things coming up that's going to affect this country."

"Like?" Otis asked.

"Now don't quote me on this, 'cause Stubby still has some research to do. But since I got everyone here, I will just throw it out dere so you all can do your own research and if you find something out, get back to me and we'll put two and two together. But I hear in the year 2007 dey got to give blacks the clearance to continue to vote in this country."

"Now that would be something, wouldn't it?" Mrs. Stubby said, shaking her head in disgust.

"Are you serious?" Vance asked. "They have to take a vote in order for us to be able to vote?"

Stubby nodded his head. "That's what I'm investigating now and trying to find out. It alarmed me so bad I just had to bring it up. You see, back in sixty-five—were any of you young souls born back then?" Ethan, Artise, Vance, and Tassha all nodded.

"I wasn't walking though," Vance joked.

"Well, you were probably too young to remember anyhow. But I hear the bill President Johnson signed in sixty-five expires in the year 2007. Dat's when Congress has to vote again. Dat's not a long time from now."

Ethan was surprised at the information. "You mean to tell me Congress has to vote to decide whether black people can still vote?" he said, very displeased.

"If all this is true, it will be right before another presidential campaign kicks off," Otis said as he put a piece of roast in his mouth.

"I didn't mean to scare anybody, but my point is this. If all of this is true or even if it ain't, one of our so-called black leaders needs to stand up and find out and let us know. Damn shame we still talking about this and it's almost the year 2000. If Congress has such an easy time doing whatever they want to the president, you know they can do whatever they want to people of color. So let's find out what's really going on," Stubbs pleaded. "And I got one more thing to say about this racial profiling thing that's going on all over the country."

"Oh . . . yeah . . . yeah." The entire table followed.

"It's happening on da roads, airports, everyplace. Police saying dey stopping folk 'cause dey look suspicious or dey fit some kind of profile. Shoot, if being black is the profile, I'm surprised that any of you ain't been stopped yet cause all of you sho'nuff black and fit that description."

"Especially you, Ethan," Vance let go. Ethan nudged Vance on the arm.

"Well dem policemans know what dey doing. Dey stopping folk just to stop dem, hoping to find something on a whim. But I tell you how we can put an end to dis business in a heartbeat."

"How?" Otis challenged.

"Shoot, all we got to do is everytime we see our people pulled over in the car or stopped at one of dese airports by da police, we should stop whatever we doin' just to let them know we have our eye on dem. While we standing there we do our own visual inspection. Get the name of the officer, the badge number even the vehicle number so da one being stopped don't even have to give the officer no funny looks or back talk, 'cause he know his brothers got his back." Stubbs looked at everyone sitting around the table. "I bet you with all our eyes watching dey would stop dat mess in no time at all."

"Now that's a good idea, Murry. I'm goin' to try that," Otis said.

The dinner went nonstop once everyone began to give their thoughts and opinions on the world of politics. But the coldness between Ethan and Tassha continued, as did the quietness and darting glances that Artise and Vance gave one another.

Tassha made it a point not to say a word to Ethan. Even when she wanted another helping of the potato salad that sat right next to his right hand. There was no way she was going to speak to the man she had planned to marry but had skipped town on her without any reason whatsoever. Tassha had wondered for years why Ethan did that to her. And as she sat across the table it seemed funny to her that he was right in front of her—within distance to throw her entire plate in his face and ask him any question she wanted. But she hadn't become bitter, just a hell of a lot stronger and wiser over the years, and she handled his presence. And the indifference and attitude that she displayed toward Ethan was just enough to get her through the night.

Ethan, on the other hand, was just happy that the long, drawn-out conversation didn't switch to local happenings. Ethan would probably have soiled his pants if the subject he was involved in had come up. So he sat quietly through most of dinner, trying his best not to draw any attention to himself.

Vance and Artise at least began to share pleasant smiles and obliging concerns with each other. Vance wanted to just get out of his chair, take Artise by the hand, and take her back into the kitchen and tell her how good she was looking to him. And Artise recognized the look in his eye, so she teased him in a way that only a petite brown sister can. She looked at him with her eyes, batted them once or twice, because she knew Vance loved the way she presented herself in front of others. If nothing else Artise wanted Vance to know she was at the top of her game regardless of their situation.

After dessert Stubby quickly changed the conversation to poetry and how much he missed the old days when poetry readings and get-togethers were the talk of the town. As he enjoyed a very short sip of wine, he tried over and over to get his wife to recite a couple of poems that she had done over the years. But Gloria refused him teasingly over and over again, until finally Otis and the others began to cheer her along as well.

"Now y'all know I'm serious about my poetry, now," Mrs. Stubby said.

"We know that, Gloria. I was there them nights Langston was in town. Now go ahead and do what you do for us." Otis laughed. Everyone else sat back, ready to enjoy her words.

"Wait a minute. . . . Wait a minute. How we goin' to set the mood wit'out some candles and darkness. You know it used to be full of candles and smoke back in them days. I can't take the smoke, but the candles I can handle," Stubbs said.

"I'll get them," Vance said. He knew exactly where they were, and as he set them up and began to light them, Artise watched him. It reminded her of the night he'd proposed to her. When the last candle was lit Mrs. Stubbs stood up from her seat and Vance inhaled sharply. He was dying. He wanted to go put his arm around Artise. But the fact that she had refused his proposal kept him away. So he sat still, trying, desperately trying, to deal with the romantic surroundings.

"Okay, I'll recite two poems. The first one is called 'Loving Love,'" Mrs. Stubbs said. She looked at her husband of many years. His gaze still made her blush, and everyone chuckled because they could see the love on both of their faces.

"Watch out, Stubby!" Otis said.

"Aren't they so romantic, Tassha?" Artise cooed.

"I was just about to ask you the same thing," Tassha said back. Mrs. Stubbs cleared her throat, then she found her groove by looking at all the lit candles in the silence.

> *"I love love, anytime, any day*
> *I love love, in the snow even in rain*
> *The love I've experienced*

I even love that too
Warm, caressing and blessed
All the way through

"Sometimes situations make you think
About love
Makes you dwell with
Emphasis—thoughts like
Are we really one?

"But when you truly love
There's no hesita-tion
A true love is known
Maybe not in the beginning
But definitely when it's all said
And done

"Absolutely, no doubt
Love is what I want
The feeling the passion
I can't live without."

Mrs. Stubbs looked at everyone as she reached for her glass of water. Halfway through her poem she'd gotten a rush. It took her back to her heyday, and she enjoyed the feeling. Something within told her that there would not be that many more opportunities to feel the rush she'd just enjoyed. So after her guests stopped applauding for her words she began to speak.

"I had no idea tonight was going to bring out my deep love for poetry as it has. And I want to do one more poem. It's one that I've never recited but has lived inside me since I married Murry. It's the most special poem I've ever written, because I wrote it when Stubby and I were first married. After we said our I-do's I went into a room and jotted it down. It means everything in the world to me . . . because I have never in my life read it to Stubby and I don't know if I'll ever get another chance to do it. So I hope you all bear with me. Just one more time."

After hearing Mrs. Stubbs's trembling voice, everyone sat in awe. Mrs. Stubbs's presence, tone, and diction were paramount to any; they were well rehearsed and refined to a point where they could not get any better.

"Okay . . . here we go. Are you all ready?" she asked.

"Go ahead and do your thang!" Otis cheered. Mrs. Stubbs held her head high, proud of the years which lined her face. Her eyes shifted onto her beloved husband and didn't move.

"This is called 'Our Love,' " Mrs. Stubby informed.

> *"I had to break away*
> *just to gather my thoughts*
> *it's been one hell of a day*
> *I committed to you*
> *in front of the cross*
>
> *"The hopes I have*
> *for us run through eternity*
> *like waves in an ocean*
> *moving with a steady breeze*
>
> *"Will it last?*
> *I hate to ask, but it laid*
> *heavily on my mind*
> *until you kissed me*
> *your sincerity answered*
> *my cry*
>
> *"I have vowed, pledged*
> *and assured you*
> *the incubus spirits*
> *that lurk will not approach*

"*Our bond which is tide like a knot*
without slack will never become lax
loose or limp

"*Those are the last words that you*
will ever hear me utter
concerning the contradictory
worries of love, you hear me, brother?

"*My love for you and I know it's*
    shared
is a stable, solid, condensed
reinforcing entity, which is sure
to take us there

"*To a point in our lives*
when we will be able to share
our success and wisdom
with all our babies and their
children's children if God
lets us . . . dear

"*I don't know, and no one can tell me He does*
see the future and what we will become
but as long as I put these words and keep them
close to my chest
God's goin' to take
Care of us, even after they lay us to rest."

"*God's goin' to take care of us*
even after they lay us to rest."

Something I Heard

Vance was pacing the kitchen floor. He was reminiscing about the sunny look Stubby had on his face as he sat in his chair keeping his eye on his dear wife while Vance helped Mrs. Stubbs clear off the dining room table. A delighted shock. A wonderful awe of appreciation. An ecstatic rapturous flow of love. Stubbs was flat-out moved by his beloved's poem. Her poem downright knocked him out for the count and made tears stream down his face. He hadn't known she had written the poem sixty-five years ago and was exalted that it meant even more sixty-five years later. Vance was astounded by what he'd felt while Mrs. Stubbs recited her words, with Artise so close to him but so far away from where he wanted her to be. When Vance noticed a tear fall from Stubby's eye in the middle of the poem, Vance understood that love could work. He realized that love was real, precious, and thoughtful, and he finally grasped what love was not. It was not how he had loved. Very far from what he had rendered to Artise. And at the end of the poem, Mrs. Stubbs had collapsed in her seat, full of joy from releasing words she had held for so long in her body. The sounds of her cry in the silent room full of electrified souls jolted Vance. For the first time he heard a voice within speak—he felt a spiritual awakening.

"*Vance, you have heard the words of true love. Words that were sent by me through my child. I have received your prayers, and it's time you ask your beloved again to join you in union. She is my child and loves you very much. You have been blessed and have received another chance."*

Vance blinked and the voice faded away. He realized that his prayers concerning his and Artise's future had been delivered.

"Hey, I didn't know you were still up," Artise said to Vance as she opened the refrigerator and took out a pitcher of water. Vance was startled. The squeakiness of the refrigerator door reminded Vance to hit it once or twice with WD-40.

"Yep, still up."

Artise poured her water, gave Vance a smile, and began to leave. "Uhh, can you give me a couple of minutes?" Vance wanted to know.

"Sure," Artise said.

Vance gathered his thoughts before he spoke. "Tonight was special, wasn't it?"

"Mrs. Stubbs sure knows how to move a soul," Artise agreed.

"That's what I wanted to talk to you about," Vance said. Artise waited for him to continue. "Well, tonight . . . really meant something to me. It really made me think, that's the first thing I wanted to say. And the second thing is, I wanted to discuss with you something that happened to me tonight."

Artise took a sip of her water. "Okay."

"Well, after the poem Mrs. Stubbs read to the old man, well . . . A voice spoke to me." Artise glanced up at Vance like she was in a meditative state of being. Her look forced him to stop.

"Vance, you too?" she asked.

"After the poem . . . a voice . . . a voice fell over me too! At first I thought it was just internal, me being so into what Gloria was saying, you know?" Artise took a deep breath. "What did the voice say, Vance?"

Vance smiled. "Artise, I'm sure it was God talking to me—giving me instruction on how to move on in my life. The voice told me to ask you a question, Artise." Artise's eyes began to water. "What's wrong?" Vance moved closer to her and took the glass of water out of her hand.

"Vance, the words I heard tonight told me to get ready for a question and said that when I hear it . . . it will be as genuine as the pure blue sky."

"So . . . ? So? You already know what I'm about to ask you, then?"

Artise smiled. "Y-y-yes," she stammered.

"This must be meant to be, baby! Because what I have to ask you is pure . . . and it's genuine as the bluest of all skies." Vance held on to Artise's hand and dropped to his knees right in the middle of the kitchen. Artise began to weep. "Artise . . . I want you to know that I've tried everything in my power to get myself on the right track. I've cleansed my life . . . and started off fresh . . . allowing and taking directions only from God." Vance kissed the womb that contained his baby then looked at Artise again as she put her arms around his neck. "Artise, would you marry me?" he asked, fighting back his emotions. "Artise, would you and my child marry me?"

"Yes, I'll marry you, Vance. Yes, we will marry you. Yes."

Another Meeting

David was livid—absolutely charged up that Tenner's assistant called his office in the middle of the day requesting his presence at a driving range thirty miles outside of the city. He had instructed Tenner never to call his office during business hours. It would have taken David forever to explain to Tassha why a man of Tenner's influence would be calling. This time David was lucky because Tassha had stepped out for a while. He had never once lied to Tassha. She knew nothing about the deal he and Tenner had arranged and David's plan was to keep it that way. David didn't know how he was going to explain to Tassha his support for the prison if he was ever forced to. David's whole political career had centered on change. It's what he told everyone in order to win the primary. The need to change the behavior and the old lock-'em-up-and-throw-away-the-key attitude of most politicians in the Midwest had been David's message. David thought if forced, he might explain to Tassha that dealing with Tenner was an old debt being paid back, and that once elected, he would never support the prison, simply politics, he would say. But Tassha knew better, and if she ever found out about the money he'd accepted, he'd have a major fight on his hands.

"Didn't you bring your clubs?" Tenner asked as David walked onto the platform overseeing the range. He extended his hand, but David walked right past him and reached for a nine iron.

"No, I'll just check the feel on one of these," David said, scanning the place to make sure there were no familiar faces around.

"Not a soul around, David. Relax and hit some balls. You know I wouldn't jeopardize what we have going." Tenner assumed his golf stance and addressed the ball, then swung. He hit the ball flush. He smiled then looked at David as he knocked a bucket of balls that were waiting for him into a tray. David was now facing him. "You know? I forgot you were a lefty!" Tenner said in the process of setting up for another shot.

"Yeah . . . have been all my life," David responded flatly. "So what's so important?" He set up to loft his ball.

"I just wanted to update you on how things are going with our plan for that property for the prison." Tenner took another swing. Flush again. Then David took his swing. His ball lofted perfectly out toward the one-hundred-yard stick.

"What do you mean 'our plan'?" David questioned, then moved another ball into position with his club. "My only deal with you was to set up a forum and alert the city of the need for a prison in exchange for the campaign dollars—which you originally stole from me in the first place." David swung again and Tenner watched his ball float beautifully into the air.

"Nice shot," Tenner said. "David, I'm surprised at you. Did you honestly think that's where our business dealings were going to cease?" Tenner sliced his next shot. "Damn it!" he wailed. "You know, I only do that when my blood pressure rises."

"Better go get that checked out," David said back to him.

"Well, I'll let you in on a little information, David." Tenner ran his hand through his full head of hair and put his body weight on his club. "I've sent some of my best agents in trying to get the owner to sell it to us."

"And?"

"And this guy isn't budging. As a matter of fact, he hasn't even returned any calls. If I know Stubblefield, and I do, he's probably trying to instill in this guy his 'a man is nothing in this country without land' philosophy."

"Sounds like you," David snapped. Tenner gave David a glaring look.

"Anyway, I hear he plans to open some type of fucking museum or something. Not many like them around."

"Doesn't sound like a bad idea to me. We need more tourists in this city anyway," David acknowledged. "Why don't you open a hotel? Damn same thing, don't you think?"

"Don't you know how many prisoners I can house in a twenty-five-floor skyscraper? You know, in seven-by-ten cells. It would be the best thing to ever hit this city. And get this, David."

"I'm listening."

"I'm going to put the exercise area on top of the building. Twenty-five stories above the ground. Now what fool would try to jump off of that. Talk about security!" Tenner boasted.

"Well, Tenner, to tell you the truth, without the building you can't have a prison. Now can you?" David reminded him.

"That's what I wanted to talk to you about."

"There's nothing to talk about," David said as he prepared to take another swing. Tenner moved David's ball right before he was about to swing and it got his attention.

"David, I don't think you understand. Money—lots and lots of money—is at stake here. Let me tell you a little story. The building that I want has special value to me. When my father was on his deathbed, with his mind failing, he let it go to the Stubblefields for so little I'm afraid to say, a whole lot less than it's worth. I was just getting into the family business dealings, so I wasn't aware. So technically it belongs to me. More than that, David, I do not squander money that is ready to be made when it only needs a facilitator to nourish it. In addition, it's the only building downtown that has enough space to do what I want to do. So I have to have it." David kept his eyes on Tenner. "David, if the prison populations weren't growing like they are and crime was down and if they were not such big ticket items, then of course"—Tenner smiled—"I would just let this idea blow past and enjoy the museum along with everyone else. But I can't, David. I just can't." Tenner set up to hit another ball. "Don't you know prisons have grossed over thirty billion dollars? I'm not a greedy man . . . I just want a piece of it. You'll benefit, of course, as well." Tenner was about to swing, but David stuck his club out and knocked his ball out of the way. Tenner looked up.

"So it's all about the money?" David asked.

"That's all, David. That's all I care about." Then Tenner reset his ball and took his swing.

Plain Ol' Rough

The one being banged, humiliated, and tormented was in a state of disbelief. It was much different from all the times before. Even the room was different—not the plush hotel with radiant, glistening furnishings. Instead they handled their business in an ugly, corroded, deteriorated room infested on the outside with drunks, thugs, and druggies. *What the hell is on his mind tonight?* Tenner's lover thought. Tenner was in a foul mood. He was unable to get David to call a spur-of-the-moment press conference to sell his prison to the city and he needed to release his frustrations to clear his mind. He was doing his thing—harsh and severe, coming ever closer to becoming brutal—while his bodyguards waited outside in a town car for him to finish his business.

"Is this what you want?" Tenner said, nearing exhaustion.

"Yes, Tee . . ." his lover answered.

"Is this how you like it!" Tenner shouted at the top of his voice.

"Yes!" his lover said hatefully. Tenner's movements became faster and harder before there was finally complete silence and idleness. Tenner caught his breath. His lover was afraid to move until the word was given to do so. Then there was a knock on the door. Tenner looked at his watch.

"Shit. . . . Ten minutes early." Tenner removed himself from the bed, and then noticed his lover's blouse lying on the floor. He threw it on the bed. "Go get dressed and fix yourself back up. I'll call for you when I'm ready." Tenner turned his back to retrieve his shirt, and before he could turn around his partner made out like a whirlwind into the bathroom.

Tenner walked over to the hotel room door and flung it open. "You're early. Don't you know being early can sometimes get you in trouble?" he asked.

"Whatever. What is your problem, dragging me out here?" Casey asked, looking around at the ugly room they were standing in. "You might have bodyguards to watch over you, but I don't, and I don't appreciate being called out here at night. Or any other time, for that matter."

Tenner shook his head and smirked at Casey's spunk. Over the past year she had really changed. She had gone from being a shy little college girl who obeyed his every command to a high-spirited lady who refused to be taken advantage of. "I had business to take care of with some of my agents and they prefer to do it on their own territory," Tenner said.

"What, your drug team?" Casey snapped back. She noticed Tenner's half-buttoned shirt and looked him directly in the eyes. "Nope. I'm sorry, not tonight and definitely not in here. I mean it, Ronald. . . ." Casey insisted, then her eyes focused through the dark room on a pair of red pumps on the floor next to his feet.

Tenner snickered. "You don't have to worry about me tonight. I've been taken care of."

Casey folded her arms and looked at him. "What's this all about?" she asked. Tenner looked at the bathroom door and Casey followed his eyes.

"It's about business, Casey. That's what it's all about—I'm a businessman."

"What type of business?"

"Serious business, Casey. This is business pertaining to my new prison."

"So what do you need me for?"

"I just wanted to alert you that you may be needed to do some undercover work for me soon. So keep your schedule clear."

"Undercover work?" Casey snapped. "I told you I have a job."

"And I told you, you still work for me, and when I tell you to do something I don't want to hear about anything else you think you might have to do. Don't forget, Casey, I'm the one who has kept you out of a long prison sentence. But if you don't want to play ball, you can always be a resident in my new prison." Casey squinted her eyes. "Hey, that doesn't seem too bad of a thing, does it?" Tenner moved closer to her. "I could come in at night, tell one of my guards to bring you to me, handcuff you to my office door, and do all kinds of fun things." Tenner touched Casey's cheek.

"What-ever," Casey said sharply. With surprising speed took his right hand and whacked her across her face. Casey grabbed the side of her face and whimpered.

"Watch your attitude, Casey. Do you understand?" Tenner walked over to the bathroom door and opened it, then walked back over to Casey. She was still holding her face but was anxious to see who else Tenner was bedding. "Come out here for a second, would you, Karen?" Tenner said, relishing the fact that he finally had both of his lovers in his presence at the same time. Karen came out of the bathroom, cautiously unsure what awaited next.

"Karen, I want you to meet Casey," Tenner said, standing in between them. "Casey, Karen." They looked at each other, both wondering why the introduction was needed. Casey took her hand off her reddened face and Karen stood still—silent, not wanting to know what Casey's face felt like herself. Karen was stunning—but surprising to Casey. She was black. In all of her years dealing with Tenner, Casey had never known him to date outside of his race. As Karen stood before her, Casey realized she knew even less than she thought she did about Tenner's intimate dealings. She always had known she wasn't his only playmate, she just didn't know what else—who else—Tenner was into. Karen and Casey just stared at one another. Casey looked at Karen's brown slender legs, straight black hair, and perfect makeup. Strange, but she was almost jealous. Karen looked Casey up and down, still recovering from the shock of seeing her in the room. Tenner noticed their competitive stares and was pleased.

"Well, good. I'm glad that you two have finally met," he said. "I thought it would be good to let you both know we'll all be spending a lot more time together. Lately I've had the urge to share." Tenner smiled. "Do I have any questions . . . any objections?" There was no reply. "Very well now, let's all get out of here."

The Housewarming

Artise stood atop the white balcony looking across their five-acre estate. *Nice,* she thought. *This is so nice.* She felt like an angel—her white gown covered her small pregnant tummy and blew emphatically with the light afternoon breeze that also swept across her face. Artise now understood the experience of a bird who had been let free from years of captivity. She was certain God was smiling down at her. Artise was on cloud nine.

On the grounds was a garden that surrounded a wooden swing and it was the first place she'd looked every morning since she and Vance had moved into their new dwelling. It was her spiritual awakening—the arousal of her daily spirit. She would look down, focus on the swing, and pray. She prayed for herself, Vance, and the birth of their new child. Artise gave thanks for her blessings and asked God to give her direction in her life and all the business affairs that always seemed to stray from her reach. She even prayed for her relationship with her mother; they hadn't spoken since she'd moved with Vance and decided on a small wedding, less the thrills and commotion of a formal ceremony. The couple's decision to marry at the earliest convenience had been an amicable one. They knew a message from the heavens had been sent, and had wanted to get married without losing another second. Vance had called his parents in Oakland and they gave him their complete blessings. Then he'd called Stubby, and Stubbs told him, "Yeah, yeah, marry dat little lady, Vance. I'm so proud of you. Dat's the same way Gloria and me got hitched—in a special, small, intimate setting." But Artise hadn't spoken to her mother since the night she'd called and told her that she had decided to get married. She knew her mother disapproved but she wasn't about to let that spoil her joy. Vance had arranged for a minister to come to their home and marry them on the front lawn. Ever since they'd tied the knot, Vance had been on a natural high—Artise even saw some of the confidence and happy spirit that led her to fall in love with him in the first place move back into his life. After they'd said their "I do's," she and Vance embraced and cried on the spot as the minister walked away. Vance had grabbed her—his new wife—then sat down on the soil and thanked God for bringing Artise into his life. He asked God to keep all the distractions that once bound their relationship from ever returning in the future.

Artise went down into the living room and tried to imagine what the night would be like, now that everyone had found out about their nuptials. It was like they'd all sat around on the dime line and called one another until it was unanimous that Vance and Artise were not going to get away without throwing a reception/housewarming party at the house. Artise had done the best she could with the little time she was given, and now she looked around and took a deep breath, waiting for their guests to arrive. There was no furniture, but they had rented enough chairs for everyone and the catered food had already arrived and was sitting pretty on a table against the wall. Vance sneaked up behind Artise and hugged her.

"Hello, baby. Everything looks good." Vance's hand went down to her stomach. "How's my boy?" Artise smiled. "You know I'm ready, right?" Vance told her.

"Yes . . . I know, and so am I. But let's get through with this party first, then enjoy the next six months together," Artise said, gently slapping Vance's hand as he began to touch someplace that would have got something serious started. "Boy, you betta' watch yourself!" she told her husband.

Vance smiled and gently turned Artise to face him, then the lovebirds began to slow dance as the music Vance had taped on his reel-to-reel began to energize their souls. Vance had taped enough music for six or seven parties. He had "ever'thang for everybody." There wouldn't be a person—young or old—who could refuse his music. Vance was determined they were going to have a good time. He grabbed Artise closer and kissed her on the cheek. Artise looked back at him and gave him one of her sexy looks. Her eyes traveled down to his beard, which he'd let grow back thicker this time. Artise began to outline his beard with her finger. From the bottom of his chin up to his cheek, past his sideburns into his soft mini afro and then her hand stopped when she reached the back of his neck. Artise felt Vance flinch. *He doesn't know how close I am from showing him one of the real reasons he married me,* she thought. Vance must have felt what she was thinking because he began to slowly grind her and kiss her softly on the ear and neck. Artise surprised her man and went straight for his belt, then the doorbell disturbed their flow.

"Oh, you goin' to get yours," Vance said seductively, looking down at Artise.

"I better," she playfully snapped back, then they walked over to the front door and opened it. It was Tassha and David.

"Hey! Is this where the party is?" Tassha shouted, stepping inside . . . then her hands went up into the air and her head toward the floor. "Ohh . . . ohhh no! Not the Controllers? Not my song? 'Distant Lover' . . . Oh my goodness! Come on, David, dance with me!"

"You ain't said nothing, girl!" David said, moving as smooth as butter. Artise saw the fun they were having and grabbed Vance by the hand, and they started to do a little somethin'-somethin' until the song was over.

"Now that used to be my song!" Tassha shouted, a little out of breath, holding on to David, who was smiling broadly. Then she looked around and threw her head up at the cathedral ceiling and bright white walls. "Y'all, this is sooooo sharp!"

"Thank you!" Vance and Artise sang proudly. They were indeed proud. The entire house was an expression of their love. The seven bedrooms, six full bathrooms, a very large octagonal kitchen which overlooked the family room and huge fireplace were all full of love. There was also a baby's nursery right next door to the master suite.

Nine-thirty and the reception was under way. The guests had been there at least an hour already and had removed their coats, relaxed, and begun to party. Ethan had a smile ear to ear as he made his way through the crowd, taking off his coat. He hugged and chatted with the people he knew and smiled gracefully at people he didn't know. He was looking for Vance, to let him know he had arrived, but he stopped when he noticed David. Ethan decided to greet him. He had seen this man—David Norman—many times on television asking the people of Columbus to elect him their next mayor.

"Hey . . . how you doin'? Ethan Cooper," Ethan yelled over the music, extending his hand to David.

"Hello . . . David Norman."

"Oh, there's no need to introduce yourself, my brother. I saw you last night on television talking about your candidacy." Ethan patted David on the back. "You sure made up your mind at the right time. I'm telling you, I have my ear to the ground and I'm sure that everyone is going to support you."

"You're with the media?" David inquired.

"No . . . no. I'm just stating the word that I hear out on the streets . . . that's all. But you're in good hands. You made up your mind at the right time. No doubt about it."

David was pleased with Ethan's enthusiasm. "Well, I certainly hope so!" he answered.

"I wish you every bit of luck," Ethan said, then he pointed to the lady who was starting to get wild as she danced. A thought passed through his mind. "So how long have you known Artise?" he asked, as he had never heard Vance utter anything about being an associate of David's.

"Ohh . . . I've known Artise for about three years now. She's such a delight."

"Yeah, she sure is," Ethan said. "Well, nice meeting you!"

"Yeah, you too," David said. Ethan continued to walk through the house. He couldn't have taken four steps before he ran into the Stubblefields.

"Hey, Ethan!" Stubby said. Gloria smiled, and looked like a distinguished queen on his arm.

"Hello to you too!" Ethan said, shaking his hand and bending down to kiss Mrs. Stubby on the cheek.

"You just gettin' here?" Stubby wanted to know.

"Yeah . . . yeah. Had to do a couple of things over at the store."

"Well, we're just about to leave this place. I've already danced and it's time for me to hit the sack!" Stubby exclaimed.

"You were out on the dance floor?" Ethan wanted to know.

"Oh yeah . . . we both were. You missed a treat. More than likely I brought back some of the old dances for these young jitterbugs." Stubby laughed. "Just ask Vance!"

"Where is he, anyway?"

"Over dat way, talking about his yard. You know, he's sounding like me more and more every day. Well, we have to be getting out of here."

"You need any help?" Ethan asked.

"No, no. We got us a driver tonight. We'll be okay."

"Okay. See you all later, and be careful." Ethan walked over to the area where Vance was standing.

" 'Bout time you made it!" Vance chastised. "I thought you were coming by early to help a brother out?" He playfully looked Ethan up and down. Ethan had a blank expression on his face, then remembered he had told Vance that he would be over early.

"Ohh . . . my bad! I completely forgot. I was over at the supermarket."

"That's all right. Speaking of work, I need you to do something for me."

"What is it?"

"I want to go to the doctor with Artise on Tuesday and I need you to check on the work the builders are doing for us. Can you do that?"

"Man, please . . . you know I can. Anything for my nephew."

Vance patted Ethan on the back. "Appreciate it."

"No problem."

"Now come on. . . . You're just in time to walk with me while I show some of the family the grounds."

Ethan looked at Vance. "Man, I haven't even ate yet."

"There's plenty—come on and roll with me."

"Are any of these family members females?"

Vance looked at Ethan and shook his head. "Yeah, why?"

"That's all I need to know, brother. You know you have some fine cousins."

Vance went out to the patio through the sliding glass door, where the family was awaiting the tour. As soon as the door shut Tassha and Artise came out of the study.

"I wonder where Vance is?" Artise said out loud. Tassha shook her head, then noticed David.

"Girl, he has to be around here someplace. Well, there's David. Let me go spend some time with him. I'll talk to you later, and good luck with your mother, girl." Tassha gave Artise a hug then reminded her of the conversation they'd had in the study. "Remember, stay positive, diva. Stay positive."

"Thank you." Artise scanned the entire family room for her mother. She was a little hesitant about seeing her; in fact, she wasn't even sure her mother was going to show up after the cold telephone conversation they'd had a few days earlier about her sudden marriage to Vance. Artise looked across the room and noticed Tassha grab David, and she smiled at them when they hugged. *Maybe Mama's out on the dance floor getting her groove on?* Artise thought. It had been such a long time since Artise had seen her mother dance and just have a good time, and she was really hoping to see her in the middle of the living room cutting the rug. Maybe she would grab her and dance with her just like the old days, but after looking over the entire dance floor, there was no trace of Cathy. Artise turned toward the kitchen and saw her mother sitting in a chair all by herself away from the festivities, and went over to say hello.

"Hi, Mom!" Artise bent down and kissed her on the cheek.

"Why didn't you tell me all these people were going to be over here? Artise, you know I don't like to be around a bunch of unsaved people."

Artise gave her mother a loving smile. "Aww, Mama, everybody here is just about family. Come on, let me show you around." Artise took her mother's hand and walked upstairs with her. She had been trying to get her mother to come over to see the house ever since she had been married, but her mother would always break their plans, citing a book club or choir practice she had to attend. As they walked up the stairs to the master bedroom Artise longed to feel her mother's excitement for her—but Cathy never said a word. Even the slightest compliment about something would have broken the ice and made Artise feel like her mother was happy for her. Artise tried to make herself feel better. She had gone over this occasion in her mind every single time she had walked up these steps since moving in. She imagined her mother saying kind words to her. *"I like how the walls are designed! Oh I like what I see so far, baby girl!"* Artise squeezed her mother's hand. It felt cold to her. Artise fantasized again. *"Girl, I know where you got your taste from!"* Her imagination didn't help her through her displeasure though. When they arrived in the bedroom, Artise extended her arms and turned around in a circle, showing her mother the room.

"Well, here we are! This is our bedroom!" Artise had a big schoolgirl grin on her face. She waited for her mother to say something—anything. It seemed as though the walls of the room had completely opened and let in a shot of cold air. Artise could see her mother's eyes graze the room, but still she didn't say a word.

"What's wrong, Mama?" Cathy tried to look into her daughter's eyes but couldn't. "Mama, what is wrong?" Artise pleaded. Cathy took a strenuous breath, looked around the room again, then quickly stormed out. "Mama . . . Mama? Where are you going?"

Tassha noticed Cathy coming down the spiral staircase while Artise followed quickly behind her. Without delay Tassha excused herself from David and met Artise at the bottom of the staircase just as Cathy was walking out the door.

"What happened?"

"I don't know, Tassha. I showed her my bedroom, she got real quiet, didn't say a word, then stormed out. I'm going after her—I need to find out what her problem is."

Tassha grabbed Artise by the hand. "No . . . just let her go, Artise. This is a special night for you and you need to stay calm. Don't forget about the little one," Tassha explained. "Just let this blow over and tackle it another day. Okay?" Artise looked at the door, knowing her mother was probably in her car already. "Okay?" Tassha asked again.

"You're right. . . ." Artise placed her hands on her hips and sighed with exhaustion.

"Artise? Where is your man? You know this party won't be complete until you and Vance dance in front of everyone. David has my camera, and all we need now is your man. Now where is he?"

"I don't know," Artise said, laughing.

"Well, let's go find him!" *Mission complete,* Tassha thought; she was determined to get Artise into a better frame of mind.

Vance and Ethan had finished giving the guests the tour of the grounds and were standing on the back patio. Ethan turned to Vance.

"Now you know . . . ain't nobody see shit you was talkin' about, Vance."

"What are you talking about, Ethan? It's always something with you."

"Brother, I'm just saying. You out here talking about valleys, dips, and hills, and shit. And it's dark as a mutha out here! That's all I'm saying. If you want to show people your yard, you need to have a barbecue or something. In the daytime . . . when people can see! Ain't got a bit of sense." Ethan started to laugh and Vance did too.

"Was I that bad?"

Ethan nodded.

"Man, I don't know what got into me. Really that bad?"

"Really. Don't worry about it. You're just excited. Hell, I would be too. 'Cause ten months ago, you was broker than a mutha!"

"I wasn't broke."

"You wasn't rich. And that's for damn sure!"

"Come on, let's go back inside," Vance said as he pulled back the sliding door.

"Here he is!" Artise said as Vance walked into the room. Vance grabbed Artise and gave her a hug. Tassha and Ethan locked eyes, almost like they were happy to see each other, then suddenly Tassha broke out of the interlock and turned around and walked away. "Come on, baby . . . they want us to dance!" Artise said to Vance.

"Let's go then."

"Here they are!" someone shouted out, then the dance floor opened up for Vance and Artise. Vance opened his arms to his wife, and she fell right into them as they danced to the Isley Brothers' "Smooth Sailin' Tonight." The lovebirds hadn't forgotten their steps, and soon looked like they were skating on the dance floor in a world of their own.

Ethan noticed Tassha standing next to David, who was smiling ear to ear as he watched Tassha take pictures of the newlyweds. Ethan was taken back a bit when David put his arm around Tassha and kissed her on the lips. So much, in fact, that after he made sure what he saw wasn't the gin and tonic playing tricks on his mind, he gave Tassha one more glance and quietly slipped out of the house.

Chattin'

Artise and Vance hadn't made it to bed until close to three in the morning. As soon as everyone left they went out to the patio, looked at the stars in the stillness of the night, then finished what they had begun before any of the guests had arrived. Vance was laid out flat on his stomach with legs spread, in his white pajama pants. He had spent most of the last hour looking at Artise curled up into a little ball sleeping peacefully. Suddenly Vance lifted his head up from the pillow.

"Baby girl. . . . Baby girl?" he softly said. Artise didn't move. Vance wanted to talk and knew the only way to wake Artise up without being the culprit of disturbance was to remove the covers from her body. The room had an early morning chill, his lover's worst nemesis to sleep. After looking down at Artise to make sure she was in a deep sleep, Vance moved his hand toward her, then thought twice about pulling the covers off her peanut-butter-colored back. But as his fingers moved closer to pulling the covers back, he suddenly felt like a gigglish school-boy. Vance couldn't wait to see what was under the covers again and tried to hide his face behind his pillow, pretending to be asleep as he began his assault. He gently pulled the covers, and they slowly made their way from Artise's shoulders down to the small of her back. Vance stopped and again pretended to be asleep; he knew it was only a matter of time. Sure enough, Artise began reaching for the covers with her head still buried in her pillow. She tried resiliently to pull the covers back over herself, but let out a sigh of disappointment when her fingers couldn't reach the covers.

"Hey, baby . . . you up?" Vance asked as sluggishly as he could.

"Um . . . um . . . not really. I need some cover. . . . It's cold in here," Artise said, raising up and pulling the covers all the way up over her body then curling back into a little ball. Vance had her talking to him, now was his chance.

"Yeah, it is . . . kind of chilly. Maybe I'll figure out how to work the thermostat today, to get it nice and comfy like you like it. You know what I mean? . . ." Artise didn't respond. "Artise?"

"Um-hmmm."

"Good . . . you're up. So what did you think about last night? Pretty good, huh?"

"What part of last night?" Artise said groggily.

"The whole night . . . ," Vance answered.

"Party seven. . . . Sex ten," she uttered. Vance smiled.

"Ten?"

"Umm-hmmm. Ten," Artise mumbled. Vance thought for a second.

"Why only a seven for the party? Don't you think everyone had a nice time?"

"Yeah . . . everybody except Mama."

"So your mother didn't have a nice time?"

"Nooo," Artise groaned.

"Come to think of it, she did look at me crazy when I asked her if she wanted to dance."

Artise turned over, interested. "You asked her to dance?"

"Yep. Sure did."

"And what did she say?"

"She didn't say anything. She looked at me crazy. Like I had some kind of nerve asking her. I don't know why either . . . 'cause you know yo' mama back in the day was always out clubbin'," Vance gibed.

"She was not." Artise giggled, then she hit Vance on his shoulder.

"No?" Vance asked.

"No."

"Well, all I know is, I went into the kitchen to get some ice for my aunts Emma and Reva. And I saw your mama sitting in the kitchen all alone. She seemed to be thinking about something really deep, because when I walked past her I asked her if she was doin' all right and she barely paid any attention to me."

"So she didn't seem right to you?" Artise sat up.

"Nope."

"Vance, I don't know what's wrong with Mama. I showed her our room last night and she just stormed out without saying a word. Why would she do something like that?"

"I couldn't tell you. Why don't you ask her?"

"I tried. But she wouldn't answer me. It's always something."

"You know what I'm getting ready to say, don't you?"

"Yeah. . . . What you've always said about me and my mother."

"Yep."

"Don't say it, Vance."

"But it's true."

Artise looked at him. "But you still don't have to say it," she said firmly.

"Then I'm right, huh?"

"Yeah, I guess . . . no. I don't know, Vance," Artise said, dropping her hands into a pillow that lay across her legs.

"You know what I think? I think your mother disapproves of your decision to marry me." Artise looked at Vance. "Just my point of view, the way I see it."

"I know . . . I know," Artise muttered. "But it would be nice to know that she's happy for me, you know?"

"You two just need to sit down and talk. Tell her how you feel, because as long as I've known you, you have always been at odds about something or other."

"I tried calling her last night to see if she got in okay. But she didn't answer."

"I told you . . . she was probably out at the club or something!" Vance taunted, then suddenly changed the subject. "What happened to Ethan last night?"

"What do you mean?"

"I didn't see him after we started dancing to the Isley Brothers song."

"Awww . . . we were smooth sailing, weren't we?" Artise smiled.

"Yep . . . doin' our thang! You forgot a brother could dance like that, didn't you?"

"Uh-uh. . . . I'm the one who taught you how to dance!" Artise said.

"But after we finished dancing I looked for Ethan and couldn't find him anywhere."

"Maybe he wasn't too much in a partying mood. You know he sure has been through a lot."

"True, but he seems to be handling everything okay. You know what he has been through would have torn some people's life apart. Just think about it. To see those three little boys in the tub dead. That's something else."

"Well, I'm just glad they locked the mother up. I would never leave my babies alone to do anything," Artise said, touching her stomach. "It's not like I haven't heard of women doing that before. But what could be so important to do that you can't take your kids with you? My motto is, If you're going someplace that your kids can't go, you probably don't need to be in there yourself."

"You're right. You are so right about that," Vance said, reaching over to touch Artise on the stomach. "I was thinking."

"About what?"

" 'Bout getting you some help around here."

"Some help?"

"Yep . . . some help. It's going to get mad crazy around here once the baby comes. We're going to have the baby and the museum will be opening soon after. We are going to be busy, baby."

"Well, we have about six months for the baby."

"Yeah, the baby will be here for the dedication of the museum," Vance said.

"Oh . . . that would be so nice," Artise confirmed.

"Well, just think about my offer, Artise. 'Cause I don't want you to have to go crazy around here. I know how you are, and you're going to try to cook, clean, take care of the baby, and put all the things you want to accomplish on hold. You don't have to do that now. I can handle things. We have enough money to get someone to help you out, okay? And what about your job? Are you going to quit or take a leave of absence or what? Whatever you want to do I'm going to support you. But you know I would rather you just quit."

"Vance, I don't know about that yet. Let me think about it?"

"You promise you'll think about it?"

"I'll think about it."

"So you still want a boy?"

"Yeah . . . for sure!"

"I've been thinking about a little girl lately," Vance confessed.

"Why?" Artise asked, noting Vance was all smiles.

"I have no idea!"

"Well, I'm claiming a boy!" Artise said. Then the phone rang and they looked at each other, puzzled.

"Probably yo' mama," Vance said and picked up the phone. "Hello?"

"Yo . . . Vance. . . . It's Ethan. We need to talk." Vance looked at Artise and whispered, "It's Ethan."

Artise sighed.

Vance said back into the phone, "Yeah, okay. Is everything all right?"

"Yeah. Just need to talk," Ethan said.

"Okay . . . cool. When?"

"I'll be over in about an hour."

"Okay, see you then." Vance hung up the phone.

Artise and Vance wondered what could be on Ethan's mind. Maybe he finally needed a shoulder to cry on, since they had never once seen him release his remorse for the little boys. But after they got into their oversized shower together, they were willing to wait to find out. It was the first shower they had taken together in their new home. From day one Artise had promised Vance that they were going to steam up the mirrors that surrounded the entire bathroom while making love, and that's exactly what they did. Newlyweds.

◆ ◆ ◆

An hour or so later Ethan arrived.

" 'Sup, man?" Ethan said as Vance opened the front door.

"Come on in," Vance told him, and they went directly into the study. Vance shut the door, walked over to a box, and pulled out a book. "You know what?"

"What's that?"

"I'm kinda glad you came. Now you can help me put these books on the shelves."

Ethan looked at all the books and all the shelves in the room. "Whose books are they?"

"Mine," Vance answered.

"You do it then," Ethan joked.

"Oh, okay. . . . It's like that!"

"Maaan, slide a box of them books over here," Ethan said.

"So what did you want to talk to me about?"

"I need some information."

"Information?"

"Yeah, that's right. I want to know how long Tassha's been dating the councilman and how long have you known about it?"

Vance was taken aback by the question. "Oh shoot, I don't know, maybe a year, close to two."

"She's been seeing him that long?"

"I guess, Ethan, I don't really know. That's Artise's girl. You know that."

"Well, Vance, why didn't you tell me?" Ethan wanted to know.

"Why didn't I tell you?"

"That's right," Ethan reiterated. Vance raised his eyebrows.

"I don't know. I didn't know you cared, I guess."

"I'm not saying that I do. I just thought you would tell me something like that."

"Ethan. You told her that you were going to marry her, and then you left her. Now why would I think that you would want to know anything about her? Matter of fact, I've been watching you two, and you haven't said two words to her since you got back—and believe me, you've had your chances."

"And she's had hers."

"I would expect you to be the one to say something first," Vance said. "I mean, look at the circumstances in which you left her."

Ethan began placing books on the shelves. "Believe me, Vance, I would have. But I don't know—maybe it's best to just keep my mouth shut."

"Just think about it, Ethan. We hang out. Artise and Tassha hang out. And me and Artise are married. Man, there ain't no getting over this. Eventually you two are going to have to say something to each other. You know what I mean?"

"Yeah, I know. . . . I know," Ethan said. "But I don't understand. What the hell is she doing with the councilman?"

"You know she works for him, right?" Vance asked.

"Yeah, I know. She started that job right before I left for Atlanta. Now that's a cozy arrangement, isn't it?"

"I ain't in it," Vance said. Ethan thought for a minute.

"So you really think it would be better if Tassha and I at least are on speaking terms, huh?"

"Yeah, I do. That's if she is willing to speak to you. Ethan, what you did to her was wrong, man. You left and didn't tell her why you were leaving."

"What can I say, Vance? I was confused back in those days—what can I say?"

Like It or Not

Ethan relaxed in his office chair as best he could, watching the small television set on a table across from his desk. The police chief was trying to reason with the media folk who had converged on his doorstep demanding to know why blacks were being singled out on city streets by police who'd been charged with racial profiling.

"Is profiling a new tactic that your force has taken on, Chief Harris?" a reporter shouted. Ethan turned his head from the set for a second as Casey entered the office.

"Hey," Casey said. Ethan waved to her and moved his eyes back to the screen, and Casey, too, became interested in what the police chief was saying.

"Absolutely not. Columbus, Ohio, police officers have not joined other forces around the country in profiling our citizens with respect to the types of cars they drive, the color of their skin, or the passengers who may be in a car."

"Well, the new law attached to the Fourth Amendment gives officers that right. Are you saying your officers will not take advantage of the new Senate ruling?" a female reporter wanted to know.

Casey looked over at Ethan. "What's this all about?"

"Oh, the NAACP has filed a lawsuit against the police for harassing black men when they're out and about in their cars. Nothing new. They call it profiling, but it happens all the time."

Casey tried to listen on. "Are you serious?"

Ethan laughed. "Yeah, happens all the time. You didn't know?"

Casey shook her head. "No. It's never happened to me. Why would they do that?"

" 'Cause we look suspicious, and we're a threat, and they can."

"Stop being sarcastic with me, Ethan," Casey said. "I know things are still not right yet."

Ethan turned off the set. "Well, at least you do. Because personally I'm getting tired of hearing about black men and women being shot or dragged on the ground for miles by some damn fools."

Casey noticed the box that Ethan had on top of his desk. "So, you packing it all in?" she investigated.

"Yep. . . . It's time to move on," he said. "After today you're going to be running the entire show around here."

"That's a scary thought," Casey joked.

"No . . . you'll do just fine."

"You think so?"

"Yeah, I do."

"Well, I do like it here. It's going to give me the experience I need so that I can move on with my master's degree. You know how important work-related experience is in working with the troops, and that's what this is for me," Casey said matter-of-factly.

"Yeah, this should be some good experience for you, that's for sure."

"So what are you going to do now?"

"Going to take a position with a nonprofit organization. Write the employee handbook, the whole nine yards."

"Well whatever you do . . . no unions, okay?" Casey teased.

"I know I've thanked you before, Ethan. But thanks again for all your help in breaking me in. It's going to make my transition a lot less painful. I have a feeling they're going to try and break the new little white girl in," Casey cracked. Ethan smiled.

"You'll do fine. Just make an example out of one person and you'll gain their respect and become more confident." Ethan placed a file into his box. Then his telephone rang and Casey got out of her chair.

"Well, let me go check on everyone." She walked away and Ethan picked up the phone.

"Hello?"

"Ethan . . . Vance."

" 'Sup, Vance."

"Just calling to make sure you're still going to make the appointment over at the museum. I left the plans for the coffee shop right on a chair in your office. I've talked to the designer already, and he seems to be on board with all of the plans. All you really have to do is let him in and let him take a look around the place."

"Yeah . . . that's cool. I want to get in there anyway and start to put some things away. I was thinking, Vance. This employee handbook is not going to take that long to work out. I mean, we don't have to negotiate anything, it's basically cut-and-dry. What do you think about going ahead and getting ready to hire some people?"

"Hey look, Ethan. You're the man running personnel. That was your area of study in school. You know what we need to start doing. Just make sure we get some good folk. That's what we're going to need. Some people who care about what the whole place is going to be about. You know what I mean?"

"Gotcha," Ethan said.

"As a matter of fact, I took Stubby to the bank today so that he could handle some business, and he ran into a friend of his who had some interesting things to say about employees. I kinda wish you were there."

"What did he say?" Ethan wanted to know.

"He just talked about making people feel like they were needed on the job. Saying nice things to them and not just on payday when everyone feels good. You know, just out of the clear blue sky. Do you do that over at the market?"

"With these fools?" Ethan asked.

"Yeah," Vance replied.

"Hell no," Ethan could hear Vance chuckling in the background.

"I'm serious. Not in here, brother. That's like a sign of weakness to these types. Half of them don't want to be here anyway."

"Well, that's what I want to do at the center. I want to make everyone feel needed."

"No problem. I can do that. Plus, the people I hire are going to want to be there. I'm going to bring in some dedicated souls," Ethan said. "Vance, let me ask you something."

"I'm listening."

"I thought about what you said about me seeing Tassha around and you're right, I need to tell her that I'm sorry for what I did."

"It would be best," Vance said.

"Yeah. Well, I don't know what good it's going to do. But I need to do it."

Vance started to laugh.

"What's so funny?"

"Nothing, man. I just been praying that you would see things differently before you took over at the center, that's all."

"Praying for me?" Ethan said, surprised.

"Yeah, man. Praying for you. Ain't nothing or nobody going to be in my life that I ain't going to be praying over. You know what I'm saying?"

"Yeah, I know what you're saying. It's just different to hear you say it," Ethan said back.

"Well, like I said, Ethan—I'm changing, man. Got to do what's right."

Ethan thought for a minute. "Vance, are you the one who put that book of Bible promises in my car?"

"Yeah. Take a look at it."

Ethan got quiet.

"Ethan?" Vance called out.

"Yeah . . . I'm here."

"Now don't go getting crazy on me. I know people look at you different when you begin to get spiritual about things."

"Naaw, man, it's cool. I've been thinking about going back to church myself. It's just different hearing you talk about God and praying and everything."

"Well, that's all right. 'Cause it's me now. This is the way things are going to have to be in my life. I've seen what God can do, and I'm not going to call on Him only when I need Him. I'm going to show and tell people what He can do," Vance testified. "So roll with me."

Ethan chuckled. "Okay, man . . . okay," Ethan said. "Well, let me get going. I want to make a phone call then get on over to the center. I'll call you when we finish up."

"Okay, talk to you later," Vance said.

Ethan put the phone down and picked up the piece of paper with Tassha's work number on it.

Tassha looked over at the phone and saw that it was an outside phone line ringing into the office. *"Let it ring!"* a little voice told her. She was sitting on top of David's desk, enjoying the kisses he was placing up and down her arm. The phone rang again.

"Are you going to get that?" David wanted to know. Then the phone rang again as David reached for the top button of Tassha's blouse. The door to his office was open and she could see her desk from where she sat.

"Yeah . . . I better. Plus, the door is wide open. . . . Wouldn't want anybody to come in here and get this on tape!" she teased as David was still trying to peek inside her shirt. Tassha tapped him on the hand. "Councilman . . . be a good boy," she said.

"That's exactly what I'm trying to do," David said as he assisted Tassha off of the desk and admired her body. The phone rang again.

"This better be good," Tassha said as she went out to her office. David sat down in his chair and began to look over papers on his desk. Tassha picked up the phone while at the same time buttoning up her shirt. "Hello, Councilman Norman's office. May I help you?"

"Uhh . . . hello, Tassha?"

Tassha looked into the phone. "Yes—can I help you?"

"Uhh . . . Tassha. It's me, Ethan." Tassha squinted her eyes and looked into the phone, then glanced back into David's office.

David was sitting back in his chair staring out at her, then he noticed the light blinking on the answering machine for his private line so he pushed the play button to see what it was. "Councilman Norman," the first message said on his machine. "Today is showtime. . . . It's time for you to give the reasons for our prison some pub," the voice said. "Sit by the phone. I will call you when it's time." David looked back out toward Tassha then erased the message.

"Ethan?" Tassha asked into the phone, still surprised.

"Uhhh, yeah . . . it's me," Ethan muttered awkwardly. Tassha didn't respond. "Uhhh . . . I'm calling to see if we can meet. Uhhh . . . I need to talk to you. There's something I need to say."

"Something you need to say?"

"Yes. I was wondering if you could come down to Front Street to the site where Vance is putting up the museum?"

"This afternoon?" Tassha asked, very skeptically.

"That's right. This afternoon. Please, Tassha, it took me everything I had to call you—I really need to talk to you."

Tassha could hear the urgency in his tone. "Well, okay. But only for a minute. Do you understand?"

"I understand . . . that's all I'm asking for, a little of your time," Ethan said.

Tassha hung up the phone and stood in her spot wondering what he could possibly want to talk to her about. David walked through his office door, bringing Tassha out of her confused thoughts.

"Baby girl? . . . Tassha?"

"Umm . . . oh, yeah, David."

"Are you all right?"

"Yeah, I'm fine. Just fine," Tassha managed to say.

Ethan hung up the phone and noticed his hands were shaking. He had never apologized to anyone in his life and he didn't know how he was going to do it once he and Tassha were face to face. *What will I say and how will I say it? Will she forgive me for what I did?* Ethan rubbed his eyes and took a deep breath. When he opened his eyes he noticed Kyle grabbing his time card and punching it with lightning speed, trying not to be seen by Ethan. Ethan had an idea. He would try Vance's recommendation of saying something nice—maybe it would help him get on track with his apology to Tassha.

"Kyle . . . Kyle," Ethan called out. Kyle stopped, stomped his foot, and turned around.

"Yeah? What is it?" Kyle asked, peeking his head into the open office door.

"Just wanted to say hello," Ethan said. "Glad to see you back."

"Is that all?" Kyle snapped.

"Yeah, that's it." Kyle was silent. He just stared at Ethan like he hated him with all his heart. Ethan shook his head and smiled. "Look, Kyle. I wasn't trying to start anything with you. I just wanted to say hello, that's all."

"Don't you know that you took money out of my pocket?"

"Yeah . . . I know. But it was necessary at the time."

"It wasn't necessary," Kyle insisted.

"I think it was. And it looks like it worked. Seems like you learned how it feels to be without the job you profess to hate so much. But you don't have to worry about me anymore. This is my last day. I'm moving on."

Kyle looked at Ethan for at least a good twenty seconds. He was standing in the doorway, seething hot. His mind replayed the feud that still lingered from their high school days. "Well, I have something to say."

Ethan invited him in with his hand. He waited while Kyle took a seat. Kyle came right out with it.

"I want to know why you think you are so damn better than me?" Kyle asked bitterly.

"Kyle, I've never said that," Ethan said, pointing to himself.

"You didn't have to. I see how you turn your nose up at me. How you shake your head when I walk by. And you've always done it. You did it in high school, you did it out on the block. And you've continued to do it since you started working here," Kyle said bluntly.

"Oh . . . so we're back at that again."

"We've never got into it," Kyle snapped.

"Okay, you want to know why?" Ethan asked.

"That's right." Kyle crossed his legs then placed his arm on the armrest of the chair and rested his head on his hand.

"It's just personal with me, Kyle. Don't get offended. But I think you try to push your sexuality around and try to gain the respect you could never get as a man."

"Ethan, get off of it, this is 1999. You ain't nothing but homophobic," Kyle snapped.

Ethan chuckled and shook his head from side to side. "I'm not fearful of anything you do, Kyle. Why do you sling that word around every time someone doesn't agree with you? If I didn't work here and have to answer for all of your insults and bad attitude toward the customers then I wouldn't have a problem with you and this would have never come up."

"What are you talking about? You've known me for years, and if someone doesn't respect me I'm going to stand up for myself," Kyle said, uncrossing his legs.

"Yeah, you're right. I've known you for a long time and that's why I have a beef with you, 'cause you never stood up for yourself in school. That's why people starting calling you punk. And questioning your sexuality. Look at the facts. You had a child and then started running around calling yourself the gayest man in the world."

"See, you didn't have to go there. I made a mistake when I slipped up and got Rhonda pregnant. But I'm the one who paid for it, because to this day I don't know where Rhonda is or if my son is dead or alive. So that should make you happy."

"I didn't say that," Ethan said, tossing a notepad into a box. At that exact moment Kyle began looking at Ethan with a lethal stare that could have easily turned into a murderous threat. "What? What's your problem?" Ethan wanted to know.

Kyle stood up. Ethan noticed that his shoulders were now pulled back and his chest was sticking out and his head was held high. "Oh, you want to know what my problem is."

Ethan scratched the side of his head and began looking around the desk to see what else he could throw into his box. "Kyle, you better get out of here with that," Ethan suggested, sensing Kyle's rage.

"I heard about you and Monica," Kyle said bluntly.

Ethan stopped reaching for his mug and looked sharply at Kyle. He was surprised to hear her name. "Yeah, that was too bad."

"Too bad?"

"Yeah, why?"

"Because, nigga, she's my sister!" Kyle screamed. Ethan's mouth was wired shut instantly. "That's right, now you're shocked." Ethan swiped his face with his hand. "I told her she shouldn't go out with your sorry ass. I told her that—now look at her. Locked up and grieving for her kids."

Ethan was in total shock. He took a moment to catch his bearings.

"Kyle, look. I didn't know Monica was your sister," he said solemnly.

"Yes, she's my sister. The first time you saw her here in the store she was just coming to return my pager I'd left over her house."

"But she didn't say anything about being your sister," Ethan testified.

"I know she didn't, Ethan. She's like you in a lot of ways. She didn't want anybody to know that I was her brother. She's younger than me, so she didn't have to go to school with me or anything. It was easy for her to keep it a secret. Hell, I was long gone out of the house when she got into high school. But that's not the point. The point is, like it or not, you are no different than me. You disrupt shit too."

"Uh-uh, you ain't going to blame that on me, Kyle. I didn't even know Monica had three kids. First of all, she told me she had one."

"Yeah, that's what she told you . . . because she heard about the bull-shit you pull on these women with kids. She had a crush on you since she was a little girl. You remember those days when you used to ride around in that damn Corvette? She was infatuated with your ass," Kyle explained. Ethan took a deep breath; he couldn't believe what his ears were hearing. "I had a feeling she was leaving them boys alone that night. But she didn't want them around me. She thought it would be too much for them to spend time around their gay Uncle Kyle." Kyle placed his hand on the doorknob. "But there's nothing we can do about it now . . . she's locked up and my nephews are gone. My family gone. But I tell you what—you need to quit looking at what I do, and look at your damn self," Kyle charged, then walked out the door.

"Kyle . . . wait a second," Ethan called out. But Kyle didn't return.

Ethan stood up and began throwing the rest of his things into the box. He was irate, flustered, and confused. *Damn, is Kyle right?* he wondered. *We aren't that different, are we?* Ethan looked around the office and made sure that he wasn't leaving anything. He definitely didn't want to come back again after what had just happened. He stood still for a moment. Right before he was about to pick up the box and walk out the door, Ethan grabbed a piece of paper, then sat back down and began to write. It didn't take long for him to finish. He stood back up, grabbed the box, and made his way out the door. He walked quickly down the hallway, and when he came upon the employee mailboxes, he deliberated a minute, looked at his note, placed it in Kyle's box, and walked away.

Just in Time

Tassha took her car out of gear and parked across from the building where she was to meet Ethan. As she looked at the front door of the building, she listened on the radio to David's opponent make crude remarks about her man not having the ability to lead the city into the new millennium. "That's all right, David. You'll get your chance on that show soon," she thought out loud. Tassha turned off the radio and sat in silence, wondering if she should just drive away without giving a damn what Ethan wanted to talk about. After all, Ethan had a lot nerve requesting that she meet him to discuss something—anything—with him.

Tassha looked at her watch. Exactly five forty-five. Enough time to go see what Ethan wanted then make it home to change before David picked her up for dinner. She looked across the street again. The windows on the building were still dirty from the work being done inside, and there were all types of debris sitting on the sidewalk. The front door had been left halfway open, and she could see the construction workers' bright lights glowing from the building. She started her car again. "Forget this," she said, putting her car in gear. Just then another car drew her attention to the front of the building again. Three men with masks on their faces jumped out of the car. Tassha didn't move. She put her car in park and watched the men dart to the back of their car, lift up the trunk, then grab several cans of gasoline. They quickly scanned the area for onlookers. Tassha slid down in her seat as all three men quickly ran to different sides of the building. The masked man who appeared to be the leader stood about fifty feet to the side of the front door of the building. He emptied his large gas can vigorously on and around the building, then stepped back and called out for the other two men, who were walking backward, also dousing parts of the building. When the leader joined them, he lifted up his mask, glanced around for a brief second, and looked directly in Tassha's direction. Tassha didn't move a muscle. It seemed like he was staring directly in her eyes, but her tinted windows were her saving grace. The man lit a match, threw it into the gasoline, and, instantly, flames shot toward the building. They were rising higher and higher by the second. Two of the masked men gathered together and stood admiring the crime they had just committed. When they saw the fire was uncontrollable they threw their cans into it. The leader ran back to the car and took out a glass bottle and lit a rag that extended itself from the bottle, then he ran like hell to the front window and threw it inside. Instantly there was an explosion. All three of the men then jumped in the car and sped away.

Oh my God! Tassha panicked. "Ethan!" she screamed, and without even thinking about the circumstances, opened her car door and approached the entrance to the building, which was now almost completely blocked by smoke. She stood there, frantically searching for help. She moved forward into the smoke, then put her head down and tried her best to make her way through the fumes. The flames inside were in the rear of the first floor, but began consuming the entire floor in no time at all. Tassha fought her way into the smoke-filled building, desperately wondering where Ethan could be. She could tell she was in the lobby, and she noticed wide, winding stairs that looked like they could fit in a mansion. Her eyes followed the steps up, past the elevators where she saw a light on in an office. She called out, hoping Ethan was inside.

"Ethan! Ethan! . . . Ethan!" Tassha shouted as the fire was beginning to move toward where she was standing.

Ethan was sitting in a chair, mute, still shocked from the revelation that Monica was Kyle's sister. Suddenly the sound of Tassha's voice brought him to, and in an instant he came out of the office and noticed the building was on fire.

"Ethan . . . hurry up and get down here! The building is on fire!"

Ethan was stunned and as he made his move toward the wide steps, the balcony began to buckle beneath his feet.

"Ethan, run . . . hurry, run!" Tassha shouted as the entire balcony began to collapse, and she watched Ethan fall down onto the marble floor with enormous impact.

"Ethan! Ethan!" she screamed. Tassha's first instinct was to get out, but she began to crawl in the direction Ethan had fallen. The smoke had become unbearable, the air almost impossible for her to breathe. She looked back and could still see the very top portion of the entrance and tried as she called Ethan's name to stay on a straight path so that she wouldn't have any problem finding her way out. Her energy was quickly depleting as she moved toward Ethan.

"Ethan! E-than! You better answer me damn it! E-THAN!" Tassha pleaded.

"Right here! I'm over here. . . . I can't walk!" Ethan shouted back. Tassha still couldn't see him. The fire was now out of control.

"Keep talking!" Tassha instructed, coughing. "Lead me to you!"

"I'm over here . . . Right here!" Ethan shouted as the fire popped and roared with authority. Ethan was stunned to hear Tassha's scream. "Tassha, get out of here! Get out!"

"I'm almost there. . . . Just keep talking!"

"Tassha, get out!" Ethan began to lose hope. "Go get help. You can't carry me out of here!" Ethan began to cough, and Tassha followed the sound. She fought her way and suddenly appeared right in front of Ethan. "I can't move!" he said. Tassha looked around and saw the fire was closing in on them by the second. Ethan's eyes were beginning to go back into his head. Tassha tried to keep him alert.

"Ethan, just hold on to me," Tassha encouraged. Ethan didn't respond, so she grabbed his arms and put them around her. She could feel that Ethan had passed out. "E-than. E-than?" she screamed as she felt his entire body weight collapse into her arms. "Just hold on," Tassha said, and with all her might, began to pull Ethan to safety as she held his arm over her body. Soon her body began to lose strength and she fell to the ground in tears. At the same time rubble from the ceiling began to fall. "Jesus help me!" Tassha called out. She was close to panicking, but she managed to pick Ethan up again and make her way through the thick smoke. Tassha could only walk a few steps until she stopped again. "Please, Jesus, help me!" she begged. Her eyes were stinging from the smoke and she realized that she could no longer tell if Ethan was breathing or not. There was nothing else she could do. Then miraculously a hand touched her shoulder and grabbed her by the arm. Two firemen were now bending over her. One snatched Ethan from her and the other picked her up and they were rushed out of the building.

Rescue workers ran over to Tassha and Ethan as they were brought out of the building. Tassha tried to catch her breath. She couldn't open her eyes and was extremely surprised when she heard David talking to a reporter as she was led to the ambulance. His voice seemed angered. He was busy working spin for Tenner and didn't see Tassha in the mayhem, although she walked directly behind him while he spoke.

"This is absolutely the reason why I propose that the City of Columbus come together and construct a private prison so that we can lock up slimy and inconsiderate thugs who have nothing better to do than burn down our precious city." David held up a smoldering gas can and showed it to the cameras. "This is where it started! We have to end this now!" David turned away from the camera, and instantly noticed Tassha sucking up oxygen that was being given to her as she sat outside of the ambulance. David ran over to the ambulance.

"Honey, are you okay?" David took his handkerchief and wiped the smoke from Tassha's face. Tassha nodded. "Tassha, what the hell were you doing in there?" Tassha took off the oxygen mask and the EMS technician stepped in.

"Easy now," he said as he rolled up Tassha's sleeve to take her blood pressure. David stood silently, waiting for an answer. As soon as Tassha began to explain, a gurney was rolled in front of her and David, then Ethan reached out to Tassha.

"Thank you," Ethan said. Tassha nodded her head and reached out and squeezed Ethan's hand as he was hoisted into the ambulance. David was left standing with a puzzled look on his face.

"Tassha, what's going on?" David asked.

"Not now!" the EMS worker told David. All of a sudden Vance and Artise pulled up and jumped out of his car.

"What happened?" Vance shouted. "Oh . . . my . . . where's Ethan? . . . Ethan!" Artise pointed toward the ambulance when she saw Tassha.

"Tassha! Are you okay?" Artise asked as she grabbed Tassha's hand.

"Is that Ethan in there?" Vance said, looking around, and Tassha nodded her head yes. Vance ran after the ambulance but couldn't catch up to it as it sped away. "Will somebody tell me what is going on!" he demanded.

"Somebody set the building on fire. I saw the whole thing," Tassha said, placing the oxygen mask over her mouth again.

"Well, who did it?" David asked, already knowing the answer.

"I don't know. I saw three men get out of a car, douse the building with gasoline, and the next thing I knew I was inside trying to get Ethan out."

"Tassha, do you think you can talk to the police now?" David asked.

"Maybe a little later." She began to cough again.

"Okay. I'll go let the lead detective know." David kissed Tassha on the cheek and walked away, remorseful that he'd put Tassha in harm's way.

"Girl, are you all right?" Artise asked again. Tassha nodded, sucking down more air.

"Okay. . . . I need to go to the hospital to see Ethan," Vance told Artise. "Look at this place!" he shouted, throwing his hands in the air.

Vance was getting in his own car to go see Ethan when David stopped him.

"Where's Tassha?" David asked.

"Artise is taking her home."

"Good," David said. "Vance, who would want to destroy your property like this?"

"I don't know."

"Well, whoever is responsible will be caught. No doubt about it. So what happens now with your property?" David inquired.

"I don't know. . . . I honestly don't know."

"Well, whatever I can do . . . you let me know, Vance?"

"Sure. Thanks, David, I will." Vance got into his car and raced after the ambulance.

Tassha was exhausted when she walked into her condo and collapsed right onto the couch. Artise looked at her sprawled out on the couch, making sure she was okay and thinking about how fortunate she was. Artise had to go into the trunk of the car and open up a box of cloth diapers she'd bought because Tassha was coughing up blood. Artise preferred that Tassha go to the hospital, but Tassha insisted that all she needed was lots and lots of water to put into her system. Artise went into the kitchen to prepare a pitcher of ice water for Tassha and could hear her coughing uncontrollably.

"Are you okay?" she called out.

Tassha tried to speak. "Yeah, yeah, I'll be okay," she said, still hacking while Artise came into the room with her water.

"Here, girl, drink this."

Tassha took the glass of water and drank it straight down and handed it back to Artise. While Artise poured, Tassha noticed her blouse was covered in blood. "Would you look at my blouse! This is terrible," she managed to say before she started back with her hacking.

"Here, drink."

"And to think it was completely white this morning," she joked.

"That's all right. At least you're alive and well enough to go buy another if you want. God was really watching over you tonight, you know? Are you feeling any better now?"

"Yeah, if I could only get this nasty smoke taste out of my system."

"Tassha, I don't know what you were thinking when you went into that building. You know you were really taking a big chance," Artise said over Tassha's continued coughing.

"I know, Artise," Tassha said apologetically. "But when I saw those men set the building on fire—like they didn't even care who was inside—it did something to me. Plus . . . Ethan was inside. I don't know what I would have done if I'd just stood there and not tried to help and he lost his life or something."

"You are one brave soul," Artise acknowledged.

"Well, what's a sista to do?" Tassha asked.

"Right now I want you to lay right here and get some rest," Artise directed.

When Vance arrived at the hospital, Ethan was still in the emergency room waiting for one of the attendants to take him to his room. Ethan was in pain. The way he was behaving you would think his entire leg had to be amputated. After thirty minutes he had already had his name on the hospital's Most Irritable list. He refused any medication from the doctor and had been complaining for the last fifteen minutes that he was being held in the emergency room instead of a private room because he wouldn't let anyone stick him in the arm with a needle. Ethan wanted to bear the pain; there was no convincing him otherwise.

"You doing all right?" Vance asked.

"Yeah . . . yeah. I'll make it," Ethan said, visibly suffering. "Man, what the hell happened? I was up in the office, next thing you know the whole damn place is on fire and I'm on the floor on my back."

"I don't know. Tassha said she saw the men who started it."

"What?" Ethan said. "I didn't see anything. I don't remember anything after the stairs collapsed. Except for . . ."

"Except for what?"

"I don't know, man. It's hard to explain. I just remember Tassha and me being together again."

Vance smiled. "You and Tassha? Together how?"

"Maaan . . . together . . . in the flesh together," Ethan said. Vance ran his hand through his beard, not understanding where Ethan was coming from. "I know, I know . . . it's freaking me out too," Ethan admitted. "All I know is . . . before I came to with the oxygen on my face I was out on the beach in the sand with Tassha and we were together. That's all I know."

Vance looked down at his friend, amused. "So explain this to me."

"You probably don't remember, but me and Tassha went to Myrtle Beach back in the day, Vance."

"Is that so? I think I remember that," Vance concluded.

"I think she hated it, though."

"Why do you say that?"

"I don't know. You know Tassha, she's high profile."

"Did she tell you she didn't like it?"

"No," Ethan said.

Vance laughed. "You have a feeling she didn't, though?"

"That's right."

"Are you sure they haven't shot you up with anything?"

Ethan grabbed his leg. "Yeah, I'm sure."

"Maybe you should take something, Ethan. You look like you're hurting bad and you're definitely trippin'."

"Nope . . . I'll be all right. But like I was saying . . . before I came to. I just kept seeing me and Tassha on that beach and she was telling me to hold her. Just hold her," Ethan confessed.

"I think that smoke messed your mind up, my man."

"I know what I saw in my mind, Vance."

Vance snickered. "I believe you . . . I do. But what does it mean?"

"I don't know . . . but I know that somebody—the man upstairs—is trying to tell me something. I've never in my life had things occur to me like they have been lately, and it's scary, man. I need to make some changes. First, Monica tells me her kids predicted my future. Now this. I have to turn around."

Vance smiled. "That's good. Real good, Ethan."

"I don't know what I'm going to do yet. But I have to do something."

"Try praying?" Vance said.

Ethan paused and stared at Vance for a while. "Tell me that wasn't David I saw talking to Tassha when they were putting me into the ambulance?"

"Hey, what can I say? It was him."

Ethan winced. "I don't see what Tassha sees in him, Vance."

"Why, what's wrong with him?"

Ethan arched his eyebrow. "What's wrong? First of all there is the age difference, and he's just not her type. Plus, if Tassha was completely happy with him there is no way she would have come to see what I had to say to her. I know her well enough to know that when she is serious about a man, she's a hundred percent committed and she doesn't go to see anyone, any time, for any reason."

"Ethan, what are you talking about?"

"I called Tassha and asked her to come over to the center so that we could have a talk. That's why she was there; if she was truly into this guy she would have never come to see me. That's just how she is."

"Let me get this right. . . . You think just because Tassha came to see you, she still cares for you."

"I'm not saying that she still cares for me. But what I'm saying is, she's not one hundred percent committed to who she's seeing now. That's what I'm saying." Ethan paused and then had a thought. "So what happens to the museum now?"

"Well, I have to assess the damage and move on, that's all."

"Good . . . because you know today was my last day at the market."

"Yeah, that's right."

"And the day I leave I had to find out that Monica is Kyle's sister."

Vance squinted his eyes. "Are you serious?"

"Yeah . . . no doubt about it. He told me today."

Artise stayed the entire night with Tassha. At one point during the night she thought seriously about insisting Tassha go to the hospital when she again began to cough uncontrollably, but after her bout with the leftover residue in her body Tassha began to feel much better. By morning she was almost as good as new.

"Rise and shine!" Tassha pronounced to Artise, asleep on her couch. The couch was full of pillows and it took a second for Tassha to realize exactly where Artise was.

"Hey you," Artise said, rising from underneath the cover. "Feeling better?"

"Girl, if you only knew."

"Good."

Tassha sat down next to Artise and pulled the cover over her lap. "Thanks for staying with me last night."

"Don't mention it. I know you would do the same for me."

"In a heartbeat," Tassha reinforced.

"Tassha, you never did tell me what you were doing in the building."

"Well, Ethan called me at work and asked me to meet him."

"He called you?"

"Yep. He said he wanted to talk to me about something or another."

"Oh?"

"He really never did say what. He was kind of talking in circles." Tassha thought about the situation for a while, then tried to shake it off. "So how was your day yesterday, Artise?" she said, changing the subject.

"Well, the baby is fine. My checkup went well, plus Ms. Cathy called me today." Artise smiled.

"She did?"

"She wanted to know if I wanted to attend a book club meeting with her."

"A book club? Yeah, that would be fun!" Tassha said.

"Why don't you come along with me?"

"I don't know, Artise."

"Yeah . . . come on with me. Then it won't be so much pressure for me and Ms. Cathy to talk."

"Okay . . . I can do that. Just let me know when. What did the doctor say about the baby?"

"Everything is fine, I'm four months pregnant, and I have to go back to see the doctor once a month until the baby comes."

"I am sooo happy for you, Artise," she gushed.

"Thank you, girl."

"You and Vance are doing it right."

"Yeah, the only thing that I regret is that we didn't get to share the romantic evenings and serious lovemaking to make our baby," Artise joked. "Now that was my dream—that's how I wanted to do it."

"The fact that you didn't means this child is just a blessing," Tassha said. "I know you try to plan these things. But when He says it's time—"

"It's time," Artise interrupted.

"Exactly," Tassha confirmed. "Aren't you scared a little bit?"

"Yeah, a little. But I think having everyone around me will help me get through this. You know how I am. I like my family and friends around."

"Well, I'm here for you. Whatever you need, and I mean that."

"Thank you, Tassha."

"You're welcome, Artise. I can only imagine, but having a child is a very serious matter. I mean, the world is so crazy and cruel, and with everything going on nowadays, I figure you're going to need all the help you can get."

"You have that right. Sometimes I cringe when I think about what kids have to go through. It just frightens me, Tassha."

"I understand."

"I mean, look at those boys who just shot up the entire school in Colorado. Now tell me, what kind of sense does that make? Those boys just walked into the school and started shooting and throwing pipe bombs. What's going on?"

"I don't know. It's terrible," Tassha said.

"I know, Tassha. My heart stopped while I watched how they just shot those kids in cold blood. But that's where the world is coming to. Kids shooting their parents and killing one another; they don't listen to their elders or anything. That's what really bothers me, because I don't want my child to ever blame me for bringing it into this world."

Tassha grabbed one of the pillows and placed it on her lap. "I remember we could ride our bikes all over the neighborhood, go to the recreation centers and not even worry about if we had the right color on or not. Didn't have to worry about none of this craziness relating to getting our shoes and clothes taken off of our backs at gunpoint. These damn kids have lost their minds."

"I definitely feel ya," Artise agreed. "Shoot, girl, there are already so many things running through my head. Just think . . . when I'm fifty-two my firstborn will be twenty."

"Good thing we look ten years younger than we are!" Tassha bragged.

"Ya know!" Artise said, running her fingers over her eyebrows and laughing.

"Well . . . look at it this way. At least you aren't like some of these women our age who have kids and are running around still chasing their damn dreams and don't give a damn about anything or anybody," Tassha said. "Like that girl Ethan went out with. Now that was a shame. And I can't even blame him for that. Not totally anyway."

"No . . . Vance told me that Ethan didn't know she had three kids, and the one he thought she had was supposed to be at the sitter's. She almost got Ethan in a lot of trouble for that," Artise said.

"Yeah, I imagine. When you have children your life changes. You're no longer living for yourself, and too many sisters are not seeing it that way."

Early One Sunday Morning

 "Umm . . . baby, it feels so good when you touch my leg like that," Artise said, delighted.

"Well, I like the feeling I get every time you tell me you're having my baby," Vance said flirtatiously.

"Do you really?"

"Oh, yeah. . . . As a matter of fact . . . I love it."

Vance kissed Artise on her cheek and she melted into his arms as they lay in the bed. Artise was on cloud nine. Her man was pleased and she was full of life and courage to take the gigantic step into motherhood. Vance laid still in the bed—like a king—with his mind drifting toward the responsibility of fatherhood, even though his building had been set ablaze.

"Baby, we're going to need protection," Artise told Vance, moving as close as she possibly could to him and touching his lip with her finger.

"Uhmmm . . . uhmmm. Not until after the baby comes," Vance said.

"What are you talking about?" Artise asked.

"Protection. Why do we have to use it now all of a sudden?. . . You're already pregnant," Vance said as he rubbed his hand all over Artise's stomach. Artise pulled her head off of Vance's chest.

"Not that type of protection, silly!" Vance looked at Artise. "I'm talkin' about for the baby."

"Oh! I was getting ready to say, I've been pulling out all these years and the bank is about to get some real deposits. You know what I'm saying?"

Artise nodded in agreement. "I know what you're saying, Vance . . . but I'm not talking about sex."

"Then what are you talking about?"

"It's just that me and Tassha were over at her house, talking about children and bringing them up in this cruel world. . . . It's kind of scary, you know?"

"Oh, so you two were over there dropping science, huh?"

"Yep . . . after the fire. Things like that make you think."

"I know, baby. It's one big mess, too. The good thing about it is that none of the floors were damaged except the lobby, and I had a great idea last night."

Artise waited for him to continue.

"Well, I want to extend the lobby a little and put an auditorium in there. We can use it to show movies and you can give your presentations in there when you're ready, instead of in one of the small rooms. I'm going to have it so they hook up a podium that comes up from the stage—and everything."

"Awww, Vance, that's a great idea!"

"I just want to make sure you have somewhere to do your thang, baby."

"You are so nice," Artise said. Then she kissed him.

"But getting back to what you were talking about. You might as well relax, because we're together and there's absolutely nothing . . . nothing in this world that I'm going to let happen to either you or my child."

"I'm glad you said that, baby. . . . It makes me feel much, much better."

"I meant every word, Artise. Because look at it like this. For the last eight or nine years, we've been planning and waiting for the right moment to get married and have children. I mean we went through the temperature taking and chart readings so that when we decided to have kids, we would know the best time to do it. But look what happened, after all these years, we got pregnant without any of it. That's how come I know this baby is truly a gift from God. He made his mind up for both of us about our child."

"He sure did! There's no denying that!" Artise said.

"And I want to make sure we squash all of this fear right now, baby. Look at me." Artise's and Vance's eyes locked. "You don't know how much it means to me that you're having my child."

"Thank you, Vance."

"We've been through so much together, and the strength that we've drawn from one another all these years is now combining to make the most wonderful child the world has ever seen. A lot of men don't take seriously . . . this father thing . . . or even know what it takes to be a good father."

"Vance, you are wonderful."

"And truthfully I can't tell you what it takes. But I can tell you this . . . right off the bat. You and my child—boy or girl—will receive the love that you deserve, and if that means doing things that I've never in my life dreamt of doing . . . then so be it . . . because I love you with all my life . . . because you are my life."

Artise kissed Vance gently on his chest. "Thank you, baby. . . . Thank you."

Reconciliation

After the doctor told Ethan he only had a stress fracture on his knee and a few bruised ribs, he struggled out of his hospital bed onto his feet and limped right out of the hospital. He'd had a very hard time sleeping and he was tired. His mind had been at work thinking about how close he'd come to dying and all the people he'd hurt over the years. The many issues that touched Ethan as he lay in the hospital bed made him realize that he was truly spared for a reason. For a short period after Vance left him at the hospital, Ethan managed to doze off, but he was awakened abruptly after dreaming that he was lying in a casket. In his dream the room was filled with all of the WWKs he'd ever been involved with. Ethan broke down and cried when he thought about what he would have left behind if God decided to take him from the world.

Nothing . . . absolutely nothing, Ethan told himself over and over again. He thought about how difficult it would have been for a preacher to deliver a eulogy on his life, because he hadn't done anything at all for anyone to be proud about. It didn't take long for him to realize the job at the museum was going to be a worthwhile project for him, and he was so thankful that he was being given another chance—so much, in fact, that on Sunday Ethan found himself someplace he hadn't been in years . . . church.

When Ethan stepped into the church, he instantly began to feel his burdens lessening. The peace and serenity that overtook his body was refreshing and seemed to give him the energy he had been missing all through his bones. Ethan accepted a program from one of the ushers and waited until the doors of the sanctuary were open to take his seat. The doors opened and Ethan limped slowly and sat down at the first open seat he came to in the back. He was ashamed that he hadn't been to church in such a long time, but at the same time he had a smile on his face because it felt so good to be back in the same church he had attended as a young boy.

Just as Ethan settled in and got comfortable a joyful noise arose from the parishioners, and the sound of music along with beautiful voices began to bless his ears. The choir began to walk down the middle of the aisle to the choir box located behind the pulpit. Ethan was surprised at how much the choir had changed since the last time he had attended. Everyone stood up as the choir members made their way down the aisle, but Ethan stayed seated because of the pain that was still shooting through his leg and because he didn't want to disturb his bruised ribs. He wondered, *What happened to the song they used to sing?* The choir was almost completely in their spot—Ethan tried to remember the song. *"We Shall Overcome." Yeah, that's it!* he thought. It had always put him in a depressed mood, even though it's message was meant to uplift. But that song was no more. The words coming from the choir were positive and full of direct absolutes, and everyone had their hands raised in praise of the Lord. Ethan forgot about the pain in his body and stood up to see what was going on. It was so much different from what he remembered. *Have I been away that long?* he thought to himself. Ethan's eyes were fixed toward the front of the church, where he noticed a group of musicians. "Oh snap, a guitar . . . horns . . . and bass player!" he mumbled, joining the other members and raising his hands as they sang. Ethan clapped his hands and let the beat of the music fill his soul. The song that the choir was singing sounded like something he used to blast on his radio in his car as he drove down Broad Street trying to look good—but the lyrics had all been changed. Ethan looked up into the balcony without moving his torso and saw hundreds of people participating in this joyous praise and worship. Ethan had heard that his old church was now the largest church in the black community, and he was pleased that it had flourished. It seemed that since his departure the church had gone through great strides to involve the whole community and he was feeling more at home than ever. No longer were people staring down their noses at their guests or even members. Everyone in the church was there for one thing and one thing only. To praise the Lord. After the first song the musicians slowed down the tempo of the music and the lights of the church were dimmed as the choir along with the praise leader began to sing. The entire congregation was now placing their hands upward toward the sky as they sang in praise. Ethan was deeply moved and began to feel how blessed he truly was for being saved from the fire. He raised his hands and dropped his head then began to pray as the Spirit seemed to just flow through his entire body.

"Oh God," Ethan prayed. "As soon as I walked into this place I felt your presence through my entire being, and I quickly realized that I have been away from you . . . way too long. Father, I want to thank you for giving me the strength to get up out of the bed this morning so that I could come give thanks to you. I want to thank you for saving my life. I heard Tassha call your name as she picked me up, and I want to thank you for giving her the strength to move me from the flames." The spirit, music, and sounds of the other members sending their individual prayers to the Master were starting to get to Ethan, and when he heard a lady next to him begin to cry . . . tears began rolling down his face too. He continued to pray, "I know that all of these years I have not been all that You have intended me to be. I haven't even been all that I wanted to be. I don't even know if I have the strength or the courage to put my past behind me and start anew, but please . . . please help me to do just that. . . . Please, Jesus . . . please . . ." Then Ethan began to remember the things that he was not at all proud of. "Please . . . take care of those three little boys, Father . . . and their mother too. You know that I had no idea they were in the house alone, but I do take the blame for being shallow and self-serving by preying on women who I knew deep down inside were looking for more than I was willing to give. Please . . . please help all those who feel that I have hurt them to forgive me." Ethan couldn't take the emotions that were running through his body, and he took his seat and wept openly as the choir and congregation continued to give praise. Ethan had never in his life cried in a public forum, let alone in church. Everything that had happened to him in the last couple of months was a bit too much, then to walk into church and know that God still embraced him took Ethan over the limit. He sobbed uncontrollably—then a hand touched his shoulder and he looked up slowly.

"It's going to be all right, Ethan," Tassha said with tears in her eyes.

Ethan tried to wipe his face, but it was too late. Tassha saw his sorrow and sat down right next to him and held his hand until the choir stopped singing.

Ethan couldn't bring himself to look Tassha in the eye. He was truly embarrassed. *First she pulls me out of a burning building, now sees me crying my eyes out like a baby,* he thought. But Tassha didn't seem to mind. One thing was for sure: she didn't let go of Ethan's hand during the entire sermon, and Ethan didn't try to remove his sweaty hand from hers. It felt good as they sat there listening to the pastor addressing the congregation in a voice that could move a mountain.

"In order to have real intimacy in your relationships, you've got to have all three levels of intimacy," the preacher said. "I don't think y'all hear me this morning!" Pastor Grier shouted.

"Oh, we hear you!" the congregation responded. "Take your time, Pastor!"

Wiping the sweat from his brow, the large, dark-skinned man continued. "There's a spiritual level, which is the highest level of them all. Then there's an emotional level, which involves your soul. And last but not least—I said last but not least—there's a sexual level, which I like to call the entry level, that some of y'all know too much about!" Pastor grabbed his handkerchief again and wiped his mouth and took a second as laughter was heard throughout the church. "That's right, you heard me. . . . I said it! . . . There is a sexual level that some of us never get past and choose to put before the other levels the majority of the time!" For the first time Ethan looked at Tassha out of the corner of his eye and saw a smile on her face as she was enjoying the sermon. "That's why our relationships suffer. But added to that, our relationships suffer because many of us have unforgiving spirits. We want forgiveness, but we are not willing to give it up. Everybody repeat after me. Give it up!"

And everyone said "Give it up" as Pastor Grier took a sip of his water.

"Read with me for a minute, Matthew 6:14–15. When everyone has it . . . let the church say 'Praise God.' " Tassha opened her Bible and quickly found the scripture and placed it across her and Ethan's laps.

"Praise God!" the church said.

"Okay, now read," the pastor instructed, and magically, as they read aloud, Ethan's voice was the only voice that Tassha could hear, and Tassha's voice was the only voice that Ethan could hear.

" 'For if you forgive men when they sin against you, your heavenly father will also forgive you. But if you don't forgive men their sins, your father will not forgive your sins.' " Tassha and Ethan raised their heads from the Bible and stared into one another's eyes. Tassha gave him a sentimental look, then placed her eyes back on the pastor as Ethan stared a little longer at his ex. The scripture made both Tassha and Ethan lose track of what the minister was saying for a moment.

Now that's some righteous teaching, Ethan reasoned as he looked up at the pastor.

"I know some of you have feelings of unforgiveness for much more serious reasons than others, but in order to improve our relationships with God and with others we must forgive. Sisters and brothers must forgive; fathers and sons, husbands and wives, mothers and daughters . . . we all must forgive. It doesn't matter, you can change the relationship today, start today. You can't have a true relationship with God or anybody else . . . until you forgive. . . ."

Two hours later, over a cup of tea, Tassha had her eyes fixed on Ethan sitting across from her. She was unsure what he was trying to say to her. Ethan read her expression. "See, it was really me being Ethan that took me away." Tassha squinted her eyes and took a sip from her cup, still not understanding. "Put it this way. I didn't have eyes for only you. You know what I mean?"

Tassha had a puzzled look on her face. Ethan gave her a nervous smile.

"It didn't have anything to do with you. . . . Look, it was like this. If I was in a grocery store buying a loaf of bread in aisle one, I would see a sister, and want to know everything about her. Literally glance at her, pick up my bread, and at the same time wonder all kinds of things about her. Things I had no business wondering about. And the scary thing about it—if I would see a different sister in the same store in the next aisle over? I would do the same thing again over and over again. Woman after woman after woman."

Tassha shook her head, trying to understand.

"I know—weird, huh?"

Tassha's bright eyes were still reading Ethan's, then she blinked and put her fingers on the handle of her cup and raised it toward her mouth and took another sip.

"So my mindset was, how could I think so deeply about every single woman I would see and then say that I love you and I wanted to be with you forever? I'm telling you the truth—that's what was on my mind when I left. I just couldn't control it. It had nothing to do with you, and I want you to believe that. I could've been in a *real* freaky relationship with—you, Lisa Bonet, Toni Braxton, and Janet Jackson at the same time and I still would've had those crazy thoughts in my mind about every woman that crossed my path. It wouldn't have made a difference. So I began to think about what would have happened if I had acted on my thoughts, Tassha, after we were married? So I decided it would be best if we didn't get married at all, and I didn't have enough backbone to tell you about what I was going through. I had to make a decision, and knew I was going to hurt you either way. So I took the easy way out. I'd never seen your face while you were hurting. I took pride in never once hurting you, and I didn't want to ever see you in pain that I caused."

Tassha kind of smiled. She remembered how Ethan would go through great lengths to make sure she was just fine—all the time.

"As selfish as it may be, that's how I wanted my thoughts of you to remain."

"Interesting. . . ." Tassha said.

"Does that make any sense?" Ethan asked.

"Yeah . . . yeah, I guess," Tassha said. Then she got a burst of energy and lightened up the conversation. "Sooo . . . do you still look at women that way?" she teased, catching Ethan off guard.

"No . . . well, not as much as I used to," Ethan quickly suggested. "I do it now 'cause I'm single."

"Oh . . . so that's the only reason, huh?"

"I hope so. I mean, I don't want to get committed to a mental hospital for having some type of mental disorder!" Ethan joked.

Tassha smiled. "Yeah, that wouldn't do you any good."

"Who you tellin'? They have women in there too!"

It became quiet for a few seconds. Ethan looked at Tassha while she stared down into her cup as though she was looking for something. She raised her eyes and Ethan looked at her for a second then down into his own cup. Tassha's voice brought their eyes back on one another.

"I'm really glad you finally opened up, Ethan," Tassha said, nodding her head up and down.

Ethan was relieved. "Just thought it was time for understanding," he said in a lower tone.

"And forgiveness," Tassha said back. Ethan's eyes widened. "I forgive you, Ethan."

Ethan was surprised. "Really?"

"Yes, really," she said.

"Thank you." Ethan raised his cup toward Tassha. "Friends?"

"Friends." Their cups gently met.

Paperwork

Casey made her way across the intersection. She could smell the smoky residue floating in the air from the fire that Tenner's boys had initiated. Casey hated the smell of smoke and was beginning to have a queasy feeling about being under Tenner's complete control. When he'd instructed her she would be delivering the insurance paperwork on the site his goons had set ablaze, Casey's first response had been, "When did I start working for an insurance company?" After she'd spoken, Tenner grabbed her words, put them back in her mouth with a brutal backhand, then shouted, "After I asked a friend to do me a favor. That's when!" He had become tense and goosey over the last couple of days. After she'd endured the sting of his hand, Casey dared not provoke him again. Tenner was in one of his zones, ranting and roaring about the strings he had to pull to get his operation under way; his impatient and agitated nerves were running a mile a minute. He had been informed the site for his future prison was being restored. His attempt to get his family's former property back had failed. The fire hadn't forced Vance to consider selling or walking away from his endeavors. "I have to take things to another level. And you're going to help me," Tenner instructed Casey before filling her in on his plan. "I want you to seduce this Mr. Vance Butler, and we're going to tape it, then blackmail him. I understand he has a thing for women."

Tenner chuckled. His boys in the street had gotten the 411 on Vance and relayed to Tenner everything they could about his past. Vance's history was full of lovers and deceit, and Tenner decided to place Casey within his grasp so he could get what he wanted. There was no doubt that Casey could get the job done. Men had a weakness for her. On Tenner's command, she had wrecked one marriage and forced another man to change his vote on a board he sat on. Casey carefully stepped into the dusty building. She stood still for a minute and looked around. Casey was dressed perfectly for the part. She had on a brown blazer, a white V-neck shirt, Dockers, and brown loafers. There were workers everywhere. Some were sweeping up the debris from the fire and others had just watched an outside wall fall. Dust, ashes, and dirt began filling the air, making it difficult for her to breathe.

"How can I help you?" a masked man said.

"I'm looking for Vance Butler." Casey choked as the dust seeped into her lungs.

"That's me!" Vance mumbled through the mask. "What can I do for you?" Casey looked around and turned her nose up at the mess. Vance took notice. "Come on, let's go to my office, it's a little bit neater in there." Casey followed Vance into the elevator and as they waited noticed the balcony was being replaced. Vance took off his mask and helmet when they reached his office. "Whew . . . that's a lot better. Now, how can I help you?"

"My name is Casey Adams, with Prestige Insurance." Casey ruffled through her carry bag and Vance watched her fumbling hands. "I'm your claims examiner and I wanted to come out personally to give you the report on what we, along with the fire department, have determined to be the documented cause of the fire." Casey nervously handed Vance the papers.

"That was fast," Vance noticed.

"It's pretty cut-and-dry. We had determined the day of the fire it was arson and the liquids used were gasoline along with kerosene—this report verifies that." Casey handed the report to Vance. "Later today we'll have the important stuff." Vance looked at Casey, stumped. She smiled. "Your money, Mr. Butler."

"Ohh."

"I would have brought it with me but the accounting department wanted to double check and make sure everything was correct. We like to keep the owners up-to-date on every aspect of our operation," Casey said, trying to sound as knowledgeable as she could.

"Good, because I've never done business with you guys. The insurance on this place was already in place when I took over, but I like what I see so far," Vance told her as he noticed the dust on his jeans and brushed it off.

Casey turned around and peered through the glass windows down into the lobby. "I see you're adding on as well?"

"Yeah, I thought it would be good to have an auditorium where we could show movies and give presentations during seminars."

"What a great idea."

"Thanks. You know, someplace for people to come right in from work and see a movie before they go home."

"Well, it looks like they're moving right along."

"Yeah, they are. . . ." Vance moved closer to the window himself. "Luckily we had enough land to extend out a little. All they had to do was tear down the wall that was burnt the most then start the remodeling."

"Looks great," Casey said, turning back to Vance, trying to dismiss that she was there to do evil. Every time Casey tried to smile at Vance or look him in the eyes with more than business in mind, she couldn't get herself to do it.

"Well, I better be going. Your check should be ready around four o'clock and I can bring it to you if you like," Casey offered.

"Four o'clock? It's going to be real dusty around here around that time. They're going to be sweeping all this mess up. How about we meet across the street at the diner?" Vance suggested.

"Okay, that works for me. Maybe you can tell me more about the museum?" Casey forced herself to say. "You know, I took a class at Ohio State my freshman year on Harlem Renaissance literature and I always thought it was so interesting."

"You went to Ohio State?"

"Sure did."

"So did I."

"Get out."

"So you say four o'clock, huh?"

"Yeah, why not," Casey affirmed as she opened the door and walked out.

Casey turned the napkin sitting in front of her over and over again while she waited for Vance. She was apprehensive about the staged meeting. When she'd gone to pick up the check for Vance, Tenner's assurance of the swift harm that would come to her if she tried to get out of her assignment changed any thoughts Casey had of refusing to harm a man who had done absolutely nothing to her. She had seen Tenner at his most ruthless moments. He reminded her of the night she'd witnessed his thugs beat a man who had refused to do as he was told to within inches of his life while his wife was made to watch. Once again the thought of getting out of town and leaving her awful situation popped into her head, but her thoughts didn't make sense. Tenner had every piece of information on her—social security number, names and addresses of family members, every background detail necessary to enable him to track her whereabouts. Casey sighed, trying to dispel the nervous look she knew was plastered over her face. Then she noticed Vance walk through the door. *Showtime,* she thought.

Vance stood looking for Casey but didn't recognize her. She had changed clothes. She had taken her hair from the ponytail, and it was now the full length of her back. Her hair must have been wet, because it was curly. She was wearing a white tank top, black leather pants, and a thick bronze costume bracelet on her right arm. She had on red lipstick and her eyes were lined with dark pencil. Casey had to stand up and wave to Vance to get his attention.

"Hello there," Vance said as he looked her up and down.

"Hello."

"I didn't recognize you. Sorry I'm late."

"That's okay. I'm meeting a couple of friends after so I thought I'd change clothes." Casey looked down at herself. "Hope you don't mind?"

Vance shook his head no. Casey pulled the check out from her briefcase. "Here you are."

Vance took the check and looked at it. "Thanks," he said.

"So how does it feel starting something so important. So uplifting?" Casey wanted to know.

"It's fun . . . it really is."

"I bet," Casey said before the waiter arrived. Vance and Casey were tentative to order. But he was hungry, and Artise was beginning to hate the smell of food cooking, so he ordered himself something and carry-out for Artise.

"So what did you study at OSU?" Vance asked.

"Business administration. My minor was vocal music. I was more into my music than anything else though."

"Is that so? Writing lyrics is a passion of mine," he told her. Casey noticed Vance had finally smiled.

"That's wonderful."

"Well, I've never sold anything—or recorded anything, for that matter—but it's my lifelong dream to write a song and hear it played over the radio. I mean, it don't get no better than that," Vance explained.

"Yeah . . . wouldn't it be awesome?"

"No doubt. I bet people who do that for a living are in heaven," Vance cited. "So how long have you been with Prestige Insurance?"

"Just two years," Casey quickly sputtered. "I stayed here after graduating instead of moving back to California. You know? For a change of pace."

"You stayed in Columbus for a change of pace?"

Casey nodded her head.

"Well I'll be." Vance chuckled.

"What?" Casey sang, hoping to keep Vance happily distracted.

"My partner just came back to Columbus and I can't understand why. I mean, I lived here all my life and this place sometimes just itches at the core to me. But soon I'm going to start traveling, give myself a break."

"Awww . . . come on, it's not that bad, is it?"

"Well, yeah. . . . There are a few things to do. But it's just not as prosperous as I think it could be."

"But you're about to change all of that, right?"

"I'm going to try. But we need more. A heck of a lot more. This is supposed to be the capital of Ohio, ya know?" Vance said.

"You're right about that, but I like it here. It's quiet, traffic is not that bad, and it's different for me."

Vance smiled. "Well, I'll be sure to call you in a couple of months to see how you're doing then," he said, poking fun.

"Really . . . you would do that for me?" Casey flirted, and she began her assault.

Panties and Jerseys

Just as Artise expected, the mall was jam-packed for the annual Shop 'Til U Drop weekend. Every single store was offering their best deals of the year, and Artise was stepping into each one of them to see if anything would catch her eye. Every time she saw a mother-daughter combination she would think of her mother. It reminded her that she and Cathy had gone to the event together for the last fifteen years and it was the first time she had ever attended without her mother by her side. It was usually automatic that they would go together. First croissants and coffee at their favorite breakfast spot then hours of shopping, buying one another whatever they wanted for tradition's sake. But Artise's phone never rang—and she never picked up the phone herself to see what her mother's plans were. When Artise made up her mind to go she promised herself that she wouldn't focus on the problems they were having, and would make it a point to enjoy herself. She had become tired of worrying about her troubles and was adamant about placing positive vibes into the atmosphere so that when she saw her mother at the book chat they could possibly put their troubles behind them and move forward. Artise was on a mission, anyway. That morning, Vance convinced her to stand beside the bed and model for him, and afterward Artise told him, "That was your last show until six months after the baby comes." Her mission at the mall was to find something to wear for Vance when he got into his naughty moods that would not put all her assets, which she was becoming self-conscious about, into the atmosphere. *If I got to suffer with this weight . . . then he can too. He can see all of me when we get under the covers, but not until then,* Artise decided. While Artise was shopping she passed by an athletic-shoe store, and a pair of infant-size Jordan basketball shoes caught her eye and she almost died. Artise stood still in front of the glass that held the shoes. She smiled then put her hand on her stomach. She began to wonder if she was going to have a boy or a girl, and thought how fun it was going to be to shop for her and Vance's child. Artise took a moment to browse at the rest of the infant shoes, then she heard a voice.

"Those baby shoes sure do cost an arm and a leg!" a lady mentioned as she joined Artise at the window. Her comment brought Artise back.

"Hmm. . . . What did you say?" Artise asked.

"Child, I'm just talkin' 'bout those shoes right there in the window. I just can't see paying that much for a pair of baby sneakers. Those cost as much as the big boys' and girls' shoes!"

Artise smiled. "Yeah, they sure do," she said in a lower tone, not really noticing the lady draped in a knit white sweater, long flowered sundress, and comfortable walking shoes holding a used oversize shopping bag.

"I don't see how parents can afford such a thing today. You know, in my day, we didn't care what type of shoes our babies had. We just wanted them to have something on they feet!" Artise smiled again. "But I tell ya, if it's ever a day to buy 'em . . . today's the day! Looka there." She pointed. "They sixty percent off, plus you buy one and get one free. Shoot, I might get my grandson a little something," she said. "What about you?"

"Noooo . . . I'm just looking. I have a baby on the way, and I thought they were cute," Artise said. The lady struggled to see Artise from the front.

"Honey, you don't look like you pregnant!"

Artise smiled. "Yes . . . I'm five months."

"Five months! Five months! Oh my goodness. At five months I was three times your size," she said. The woman stood about five inches taller than Artise, was heavyset with brown skin and her hair pulled backward. Her lips were thin and eyes beautifully brown, and she used them to help exaggerate her words. Her arms and hands were heavy, almost wide, but it didn't seem to bother her at all as she stood firm and tall. "You're to be commended, sweetie. That is wonderful!"

Artise blushed. It was exactly how Vance felt about her physique. *It must be true,* she thought for a brief second, and it felt good to hear.

"Where's my manners—my name is Melba!" the lady said, then she extended her hand to Artise.

Artise looked at her, astonished—she didn't meet many people in Columbus so open, so eager and zealous to strike up a conversation. Artise shook her hand cautiously.

Melba felt her hesitation. "Honey, don't mind me! I'm a Southern girl, born and raised, and where I come from, we talks to each other!" Melba snickered. Her revelation soothed Artise a bit.

"Hi . . . I'm Artise. Sorry about that."

"Don't be sorry, child. It's the way of the world," Melba counseled. "So let me guess?" Melba put her hand on her chin and sized Artise up. "You are here not only to browse around and get an idea of things for the baby. But you probably here to get something nice to wear for your husband."

Artise laughed out loud. "How did you know that?"

"Child, I know how men get when they find out they're getting ready to be daddys. They just get all frisky like you wouldn't believe."

Artise looked around hoping no one could overhear their conversation. She was almost embarrassed. Then she uttered quietly, "You're right . . . you're right about that . . . My husband has been nonstop since he found out."

"See, I knew it. I've been around it much too long—I have experience with these things, you know."

"You have kids yourself?"

"Yes, I have two boys and one girl. They're all grown up now. But more than that—I just retired from being a baby-sitter of thirty-five years, and I've seen how the men run after their wives when they're with child. Mine ran after me too—God rest his soul."

"He did?" Artise wanted to know.

"Oh yes—it just does something to a man. And it's pretty good to the woman too!"

"Yeah . . . my husband practically begged me to pick out something nice to wear for him tonight."

Melba's eyes lit up. "Well, I'm not doing anything—why don't we look for something together. It's always fun to have someone to shop with. Come on, I'll go with you!" Melba said with a burst of energy.

Artise nodded her head. "Okay . . . why not?" she said.

About an hour or so later Artise and Melba found themselves in their third store searching for something special for her to wear for Vance. Artise wanted to wear something sexy but not revealing. She huffed after she put down yet another garment that didn't suit her taste.

Melba sensed her displeasure. "Let me ask you something?"

"Go ahead." Artise looked at Melba.

"What's your husband's favorite football team?"

"Football team?"

"Yes, what's his favorite team?"

"Hmm . . . I think it's the Cowboys . . . and I hear him talking about the Vikings too. He likes Cris Carter; they went to college together."

Melba tapped Artise on the arm. "Come on, follow me." Melba walked a couple of aisles over into the underwear section of the store and picked up a pair of panties. "These should work just fine. Get these, then we have to go down to the sports store," she said, smiling.

"The sports store?"

"Trust me, baby," Melba said. "Your husband is going to go crazy seeing you in your outfit . . . just trust me! He's going to think you're the sexiest woman in the world!"

Artise inspected the panties that were in her hand, then looked skeptically at Melba. "Okay. . . ." she sang, as she was already out of ideas for what to get.

Melba was a blast. She had Artise almost in tears in the sports apparel store. When she asked the gentleman who was helping them if he would like to see his lady friend surprise him in a football jersey and matching panties and he answered with a thunderous "YES!" Melba looked at Artise and said, "I told you!" Artise and Melba meshed so well together that they decided to make a day out of it, but when Melba saw an inviting bench right across from the Cookie Factory stand, she walked right over to it.

"Whew! I was wondering if we would ever run up on an empty seat! Have a seat, young lady," Melba insisted. Artise was already busy making herself comfortable. She sat down next to Melba and put her shopping bags between her legs. "You know? I haven't had this much fun in a very long time," Melba said enthusiastically.

"Without a doubt, this has turned out to be a very fun day," Artise agreed.

"I tell ya, this feels just like the time I found out my daughter was pregnant. We drove up to Pittsburgh and put a hurtin' on the shoppin' malls up there. It was such a good time. Took us five hours both ways just to get there and come back home, and you know that's just a three-hour drive. But we were just so happy, we just took our time. . . . I wanted my baby girl to know everything there was to know 'bout having my grandchild and being a good mama."

"What did she have?" Artise wanted to know.

"Oh, she had a boy! A big ol' handsome dark-skinned boy. She's going to have to beat the ladies away from this one, child. Just get her a bat and keep it by the front door, 'cause they going to come a knocking and that's for sure," Melba said proudly.

Artise had a thought. "Can I ask you a question?"

"Sure," Melba replied.

Artise thought about her question first. She wanted to word it right. "Ummm . . . did you and your daughter always have a good relationship?"

Melba smiled and clasped her hands together on top of her purse like she was in prayer. "Ahhh . . . yes. For the most part we did and still do. You know there have always been times when she and I don't agree on some things. That's just a part of life. But we have a beautiful relationship." Melba noticed Artise daydreaming, gazing at the marble floor of the mall. "You care to talk about it, darlin'?" she asked sweetly.

"Well . . . my mother and I just haven't been getting along. I think it goes back to when I was younger. For one, I've always felt like she disapproved of me for some reason and that I was just in the way when it came down to things that she wanted to do with her life. It's always something with us. Sometimes we get so mad at each other for so long that we forget about whatever we were mad at each other about in the first place. We just have issues, that's all."

"I understand. Believe me. You're not the only person going through troubles with their parents. My mother and I were the same way. We looked alike, talked alike, liked the same styles of clothes and cars—we were just carbon copies of each other, but we never seemed to get along. And when I sit down and think about the things we argued and fussed about—it all adds up to foolishness. But guess when I realized all of this?" Melba looked deep into Artise's eyes. "Artise, I realized that we were foolish when she was in her casket, as I sat right in front of her when they were putting her into the ground." Melba saw Artise flinch. "That's right, it took her death for me to realize that all our disagreements were not worth the time of day. We really wasted a lot of good times. We never had a chance to build memories that I could cherish later on. Believe me, neither you nor your mother want to find out after—God forbid, if something ever happens to one of you—that you don't have happy memories to fall back on. It's hell, baby. Hell on earth."

Artise clung to Melba's every word. "Well, I just don't know what to do. I just got married, I'm about to have my first child, and she has distanced herself from me," Artise said. "I always thought these are the type of things that brought mother and daughter closer. I really need her to just be there for me right now, to call me every day to see how I'm feeling, to come over to the house for a visit and have dinner."

"I understand," Melba said and patted Artise on her knee. Artise looked down and felt a special energy passing through Melba to her. Something she had been missing.

"You know, my husband asked me if I wanted to get some help around the house so things wouldn't be so hectic once the baby comes. I always thought my mother would be there for me, but I don't know. Maybe I should just start looking for someone to help me out."

"Well, darlin', there's never nothin' wrong with a little help. I helped other people raise their kids for years, and if you can pay someone to help you out, then I would truly recommend that you find someone who can help."

A light went off inside of Artise's head. "How about you?" Artise asked with a little tap on Melba's leg.

"Me!"

"Yes, Miz Melba! You're very comfortable to be around, and just face it. I've probably already spent more time with you than anyone I would ever interview to watch my child. We clicked right off the bat. I know you're retired . . . I don't know—maybe you can just spend a couple of hours over at the house. You just don't know how frightened I am about this whole thing!"

Melba saw the desperation in Artise's face. "Okay . . . okay, Artise," Melba said with a warm smile on her face. "How can I turn down someone as nice as you? But it will only be for a short while, honey. . . . I'm enjoying my retirement something special. But it would really be a blast to hold another little baby."

"So you'll do it?"

Melba smiled. "Yes . . . yes, I will, Artise."

"Good. We can decide later when you can start, okay?"

"That's fine. You need to look over all my references, anyway, and give them all a call. And just listen what they say about Miz Melba. I'm good at what I do, child . . . I'm good," Melba flaunted. "I just love me some babies."

"I'm sure you do!"

Artise couldn't wait to get home and tell Vance about Miz Melba. Melba's revelation about her own mother made Artise think that she really needed to patch things up with hers. *Nothing,* Artise realized, *could ever be that bad between us. We need to get it together.* As she dropped her packages next to the study Artise made up her mind that when she saw her mother at the book chat they were going to have a heart-to-heart.

"Hey, baby, did you have a nice time?" Vance wanted to know as he took a sip of his soda.

"Yep . . . sure did!" Artise said back.

"That's good." Vance noticed right away that she was glowing. "Hmm, you really did have a nice time, didn't you?"

"I did. . . . And guess what?"

"What's that?"

"I met this fantastic lady named Melba and she said that she would help us out with the baby."

"You did?"

"Yep, I met her at the mall, when I was looking at some baby shoes. We spent the entire day at the mall shopping together and just talking."

"Artise, that isn't even like you."

"What?"

"To just shop with someone you don't really know."

"I know, Vance. That's what makes her so special. You know how sometimes you might have a couple of words to say to someone at the mall about something or another. But this lady has a personality out of this world. She's just real nice people."

"She must be," Vance said.

"Ummm-hmmm, she is." Artise reached into one of her bags. "She even helped me pick out something nice to wear for you. Close your eyes."

"What?"

"Close your eyes, I want to show you what I got."

Vance started to close his eyes then opened them back up. "Teese, how old is this lady?"

Artise stomped her foot. "I don't know, Vance . . . late fifties, sixties. Come on, close your eyes."

Vance started to, then opened them again. "And she helped you get something to wear for me?"

"Sure did. Now shut up and close your eyes." Vance did. "She knows . . . trust me . . . she knows." Artise pulled out a pair of sexy underwear then placed them on top of Vance's head. Then she pulled out the Minnesota Vikings jersey with number 80 plastered on the front and held it up to her body. "Want to play some ball?"

Vance opened his eyes. "Dannnnnnng, baby. That is sexy! You goin' to wear this for me?"

"Ummmmmm-hmmmmm," Artise purred.

"I think I like Miz Melba too!" Vance decided.

Book Chattin'

Artise turned her head to Tassha and let out a sigh of relief. The discussion on Oprah's recent book club reading was finally over and Artise enjoyed it more than she thought she would. It was her first time ever attending a meeting where people get together and discuss books. Artise promised herself that she was going to run out and purchase the book for herself, but at the moment she wanted to talk to her mother and see what was going on between them. She had been antsy the whole two hours of the meeting. Artise wished that the ladies would take a break and mingle a little to give her a chance to speak with her mother, but it didn't happen. They stayed seated in their chairs, which had been placed in a circle in the small living room at Dorothy's house.

"Okay, sisters. What's going to be the next book that we read?" asked Dorothy, the president of the Sisters We Are Book Club.

"Well, I think we should delve into Alice Walker's new book next," Lidia said.

Artise looked over to Lidia and kind of smiled. She liked her. Lidia was the out-loud reader for the group, and she read with passion and zeal. Artise could tell that she took her reading seriously. It was Lidia who inspired Artise to want to read the novel under discussion for herself. The other eight or nine women were also delightful. Half were head nodders and concurring folk, and the other half were objectionaries and introspectives who spoke freely and at times very loudly when trying to get their point across. Added to the mix was Cathy. She was a combination of all the book club members. She spoke and said what she wanted whenever the thoughts came to her mind, in a conservative way.

"Well, I still think we should read *Zenzele* by J. Nozipo Maraire. I read it almost two years ago, but it was such a passionate read." Everyone looked over at Dorothy.

"Dorothy, what is your fascination with this book, darling?" Lidia asked from across the room.

"Well, Lidia, sisters," Dorothy commanded their attention. "It's a beautiful book. It's a book about a mother who writes her daughter a letter and tries to give her wisdom and lessons on life. They both are from Zimbabwe, and I found it fascinating how even sisters across the water have similar concerns as our own. Being a mother is being a mother and having a daughter is universal. It's really interesting and I think you'll all agree after you read it. If I remember, it's almost two hundred pages, so if we wanted to we could combine it along with something else. Since I know all of you divas love to get your read on!" Dorothy teased.

"Well, sounds good to me," Stacy agreed. Everyone turned around, surprised because she hadn't said anything to anybody the whole meeting. "Don't you know that my daughter has not come home to see me yet?" she informed everyone. Tassha raised herself up in her chair. Stacy sounded like she had some things on her mind.

"When was the last time you talked to her?" Dorothy asked.

"Well, I talked to her just the other day. She seems to be doin' all right. But when I asked her when she was coming home for a visit she just got very quiet and said that she didn't know."

"Um . . . now that's something else. My daughter comes to see me whenever I ask her to. But the problem is, once she gets here it's just so dang-on hard keeping her all to myself. Y'all know she lives in Chicago. She always drives here to see me whenever I mention that I want to see her. We usually sit around early in the morning and talk for an hour or so then BAM!" Dorothy said, clapping her hands together, eyes wide open. "She's out the door to see some of her friends. And to tell you the truth, that really makes me upset 'cause I asked her to come see me"— Dorothy pointed to herself—"not her friends. But it's a whole lot better when I go see her in Chicago, because she doesn't like to leave me alone in the house by myself. Then it's just me and her, and we have a good time." Dorothy paused with thought. "Stace? Do you ever go see your daughter?"

Stacy hesitated. "No . . . no, I sure haven't. I haven't gotten a chance to visit her yet. She just moved to Charlotte."

Dorothy looked amazed. "How long has she been there? I seem to remember that she was in Philly for a while."

"Um-hmm," Stacy said. Artise could hear the dissatisfaction in her voice. "She was . . . she was, then from there she moved to Orlando and six months later she moved to Charlotte. That job really has her moving from place to place since she graduated from college. As a matter of fact, I can't believe it's almost been ten years since she graduated from Howard."

Artise tried to get her mother's attention. Maybe they could sneak into the kitchen or outside to talk for a while. But Cathy was into the conversation and didn't catch Artise's glances.

"Has it been that long?" Lidia asked.

"Yes. . . . Girl, it's been ten years!" Stacy said.

"But I seem to remember she used to come home all the time." Dorothy interjected.

"Yeah . . . she did. But the last three or four years she's just stopped coming to see me."

"I can understand why," Dorothy said, grabbing the attention of those who'd tuned out of the conversation.

"Excuse me?" Stacy asked.

"How do you expect your daughter to come and see you and you yourself have not taken one step whatsoever in visiting her. Girl, that ain't right," Dorothy insisted.

"Well, I don't know why I have to travel all over the country to see my own daughter. I am the one who gave birth to her, and she should want to come home and spend some time with me," Stacy said with plenty of attitude. Stacy polled the group. "What do you think, Cathy?"

Artise's eyes opened wide. She kept her hand on her stomach and waited intently for her mother's answer.

Ahhh . . . shoot. Here we go! Tassha thought to herself.

Cathy glanced briefly at Artise. "I don't know. My daughter has been here with me all my life, so I can't really comment on it."

"But don't you think Stacy should go see her daughter?" Dorothy asked, not letting Cathy off the hook.

"I think Stacy needs to do whatever Stacy feels like doing," Cathy snapped. "I can kinda see her point. We do so much for our children over the years, and it's like they just don't care about what we have done for them."

Stacy pointed to Cathy. "Thank you," she quipped. "All that damn diaper changin', crying, first day of school blues, first love jones heartaches, sweet sixteen passion, temporary license driving, boy craziness, Mama what should I do questions, and college homesickness—hey, that stuff was tough."

"Ooooooh, girl, you hit it right on the nose!" Cathy blurted out, never minding that her daughter was sitting two seats away. Tassha looked at Artise. Artise was surprised by Cathy's comments. Then Dorothy took over.

"Well, I don't look at it like that."

"Oh, you don't?" Stacy asked.

"No, I don't. I enjoyed watching my daughter grow up and going through all the phases that children go through. And I especially enjoy the ones daughters go through while they're adults. I've never felt my daughter has been a burden to me. Quite frankly, I don't know how I would have gotten through my life without her."

"Child, please! I know how I would've gotten through my life without mine," Stacy shouted in a joking way, and Artise noticed her mother smirk at the comment.

"Not me. My daughter made me strive to do better because I wanted the best for her, and I wanted to lay a foundation for her so that she could see that things could be accomplished. Time could have stood still forever for me and Sherise," Dorothy said. Artise felt good about Dorothy's answer. It was the answer she would have loved to hear her mother say.

"I don't know if I can say that, looking back at all the things I've sacrificed in my life for my kids. Don't you know I've said no to many men—I mean some fine men, now—just to spend time with my daughter and give her what she needs. One man in particular really stands out in my mind, and to this day I still wonder what our lives would've been like if I didn't have to make that choice. It was in seventy-six. I think Jai was in the sixth grade—ummm-hmmm, that's right, sixth grade. I remember 'cause me and Herm listened to Richard Pryor's *Bicentennial Nigger* album over and over again. Do y'all remember that crazy-ass album?" Stacy asked the others.

"Yes, girrrl," they said in unison. Even Tassha and Artise, who were the youngest in the group, knew about it. They used to listen to the album at friends' houses.

"Those were the days!" Stacy said. Artise and Tassha exchanged knowing glances.

"Well, that man wanted me to marry him something awful. I mean, he asked me over and over again like his life depended on me being his wife. I just adored this man. He had a good job as a manager over at the Gilbert Shoe factory. Y'all hear me? I said a management position back in seventy-six, now!"

"He must have been a special breed," Cathy said. Some of the others agreed. Artise had almost forgotten about her mother's earlier statement.

"That's right, he was. And I mean in every way. Whew! This brutha dressed like Super-Duper Fly . . . he listened to Curtis Mayfield and Al Green. Herman had a Cadillac with a diamond in the back and a sunroof top!"

"Go ahead, tell it!" someone shouted.

"But I just couldn't marry the man. Jai's father and I had just broken up about seven months before I met Herman. And she was so confused. I mean, the first night her daddy didn't come home from his job and sit down at the dinner table with us, she thought it was the end of the world. She took it soooo hard and just cried and cried for her daddy. Even though I had gotten rid of one problem I instantly inherited another. I thought Herman would step right in and take the place of the rotten apple. Uh-uh, no way. The first time Jai met the man she was so cold and disrespectful that I didn't know what to do. I had never in my life seen her act that way, and Herman wasn't takin' no stuff from no little ten-year-old girl. Y'all hear me—he was a manager. So he grabbed his apple hat and walked straight out of my house. I never saw him again."

"Oh no, he didn't," Dorothy said.

"Yep . . . he did. Um-hmmmm, and believe it or not, I haven't found a man that has made me feel that good again after all these years. I could have forced Jai to like Herm, but I made the decision not to for her good, and the only one who has suffered for it is me."

"Well, that's what it's all about," Dorothy concluded. "Our children will always be here for us no matter what, and ain't no man that important to break up a mother and child's bond."

Tassha had been silent too long. "That's right," Tassha declared. Artise smiled at her.

"Well, I don't know about that," Cathy said. Tassha watched with compassion as Artise's grin disappeared.

"Say what?" Dorothy said.

"I said I don't know about that." Cathy turned toward Artise and her eyes flickered before she spoke again. "I mean, look at Stacy now. Look at all of us now. We did whatever we could for our children when they were coming up. But look at us now . . . all tired and lonely with only our stories of what we did for our kids to get us by. Now we're lonely as hell and our kids still come to us for advice and don't listen when we give it to them."

Artise was in shock, and when her mother finished talking it seemed like everyone turned their heads toward her, waiting for her response. Artise felt like she was being chastised, loud talked, belittled. "Wait a minute now," she said firmly but with respect. She had a surprised smile covering her face. The others were amazed that quiet Artise had spoken up. Everyone had their eyes on her except the person she was really addressing. "Now, I can't believe what I just heard. I've never in my life tried to stand in the way of you getting a man. And I'm going to go out on a limb and say to everyone here that I don't believe any of your children would do that." Artise looked around the circle. "And as far as coming to get advice. Who are daughters supposed to run to?" Tassha patted Artise on the leg. She could hear the hurt in her voice. The book discussion had suddenly turned into a mother-daughter dispute.

"Well . . . ," Cathy stopped. She wasn't sure if she wanted to continue in front of all of her girlfriends. But it was on her mind. "I'm just saying that when a mother tells her daughter what's good for her after she is asked, it hurts like the dickens to see her do the opposite after you try your best to show her the best way to go."

"Well . . . it's important that daughters still live their own lives. Mothers can tell their daughters what they would do and let us think about their decisions. But mothers really need to understand that their daughters are grown and will make their own decisions." Artise put a touch of class on her statement. "Does anyone feel differently?" she asked. Lidia and Dorothy looked at each other and shrugged their shoulders. Tassha took a deep breath and was glad things hadn't gotten totally out of hand like she'd feared.

"Soooo . . . is it going to be *Zenzele* or something a little lighter?" Lidia changed the subject.

"*Zenzele!*" Cathy spurted out. All eyes were on her again. "I think it would be important to see if the author addressed some of the things that we have just talked about here. So yeah, why not?" And *Zenzele* it was.

Artise tapped Tassha on the arm when the ladies began to disperse into the kitchen to fill their plates with food and drink. She was heated and panting harder than she had in months, and she was ready to go. On the way home Tassha noticed her breathing.

"Artise, are you okay?"

"Yep. Just fine," Artise said.

"Try to relax, okay? I know that you're upset. I know I would be; but take it with a grain of salt. You know you're better than that."

Artise turned to her friend. "Thanks. Just so unbelievable, that's all," she said, taking another deep breath. "So are you ready for the ball tonight?"

"Oh, girl, yes. David bought me this red dress that is out of this world, and I'm going to wear it well. We don't have many functions around here, so I'm planning on having a good time." Tassha was glowing. "David told me that he knew that I was going to be the sexiest woman at the benefit—even without the dress, but he wanted to do something special for me."

"That was nice," Artise confirmed as she struggled to get comfortable in her seat.

"You know? I was supposed to go with David last year to this very ball, but I wasn't ready to go out with him yet. Now look at me being all adventurous and things—spreadin' my wings."

"Not only that, you've gotten a chance to reconcile with Ethan, and that's one less negative vibe you have to deal with in your life."

"Oh, girl, who you tellin'? When Ethan and I had dinner I saw a glimpse of the man I fell in love with years ago."

Artise looked curiously at Tassha. "Oh really now?"

"Years ago," Tassha repeated. "I just hope that he can stay on the right path. Sometimes it takes things to happen in your life to make you move forward."

"Yeah, like today. I didn't know my mother felt like she does, Tassha. She has never said anything to me like that. And for her to say it in front of all of her friends. You know that really hurt. Maybe it's time for me just to move on without her."

Tassha felt Artise's emotion. She saw Artise wipe a tear from her face. "Do me a favor, Artise?"

"Yeah . . . what's that?"

"Try to relax, okay? It's going to be all right."

At the Ball

The atmosphere at the ball was exactly the way Tassha envisioned it would be. Elegant, dignified, with an abundance of distinction floating through the air—almost too perfect for the city. Tassha was all smiles as she stepped out of the flawless shining black stretch Lincoln limo. David was close behind. His eyes were so tight on how well Tassha's rear end looked in her dress that he almost forgot about all the media in attendance. But when the first flash bopped David in the eye he was brought back to reality. The ball was in honor of the Columbus Youth Program, a biannual event that was held at the Franklin Park Conservatory, and it was already in high gear. The inside of the Conservatory was decorated immaculately. There were fresh flowers on every table, and the greenhouses inside that held all types of exotic trees and plants were trimmed in gold. The ceiling had been made to look like they were partying outside under a beautiful starlit sky.

"Baby girl, this ambience fits you so well!" David said into Tassha's ear as he straightened out his tie and posed for the cameras.

"Why thank you," Tassha said while they began walking up the plush red carpet leading into the Conservatory. "Oh . . . that music is sooo nice!" she reveled as they entered.

"Oh yeah, I forgot to tell you. . . . That's the Lincoln Center Jazz Orchestra from New York City! They were flown down here exclusively for this event. . . . Aren't they great?"

"Yes, amazing!" Tassha tapped David on the shoulder. "Isn't that Mr. White singing with them?"

"Oh yeah . . . that's Carl. . . . He can go!" David said.

"He sure can! Wait until I see him downtown. I knew he was one of the best opera singers in the country. But he's up there singing jazz!" Tassha waved to Carl. When he noticed her wink he acknowledged Tassha with a wink of his own. "He's soooo smooth!"

"Watch out now!" David yelled over to his longtime friend. "Well, sweetheart, here's our table. After you." David pulled Tassha's chair out for her. Tassha thanked her escort, and David took his seat and began to stare at Tassha as they listened to the music. David took Tassha's hand. "God can just take me right now," he proclaimed to Tassha.

"What?" Tassha giggled.

"When tonight is over, Tassha. God can just take me. He's allowed me to be in the presence of the most beautiful woman I've ever known. You are so beautiful."

"Thank you, David." Tassha blushed.

"I'm just not saying that, you know? I really mean it. Do you ever get tired of hearing that from me?"

"Please!" Tassha said. "I love to hear it. What woman wouldn't?"

"Truthfully?" David asked.

"Yes."

"I knew a lady . . . who couldn't stand being called beautiful. Which actually made her repulsive."

"Well, Councilman-soon-to-be-mayor-of-our-city . . . she was a fool," Tassha said bluntly. David laughed and looked at the age of the bottle of wine sitting on the table.

"I really enjoy the time we share together, Tassha," he said as he briefly acknowledged a supporter of his campaign. "You really make this old man realize what life is all about. Especially at a time like this. You're really something. A real woman, that's what you are."

Tassha beamed. She wanted to stay in control tonight and knew she was becoming ever so close to just being putty in David's hands.

"Sweetheart, are you okay?" He began to fill their glasses.

"I have a question, David," Tassha timidly admitted.

"Sure, anything. . . . What is it?"

She looked around and cleared her throat. "I want to ask you something about what you asked me in the car tonight."

David smiled. "About getting married?"

"Yes. . . . Exactly. David, are you being more aggressive because I had dinner with Ethan the other night after church?"

David took a relaxed breath, like he was turning on his seasoned charm. "Tassha, in all honesty, I remember you telling me everything that you went through with him. It took you a hell of a long time to get over what happened between you two and I didn't want any of those old feelings to come back and haunt you. Especially after meeting him at Artise's housewarming. You know I've been around a time or two, and I know how things happen. So . . . yes. I decided to step it up. But I really do mean the things I've said to you about being together. Everything that I've said since we've been sitting here—and everything on the way here in the limo. You do take me seriously, don't you?"

"But, David, you asked me to marry you . . . right now. As soon as possible. I guess I'm just a little dazed that you want to get married all of a sudden. I mean, what brought this on?" Tassha persisted.

"Time, for one, Tassha. Plain old time."

"I understand."

"And I simply love being around you."

"And I enjoy being with you also, David. But marriage as soon as we can? Wow!"

"I'm just ready to take care of you, that's all, and I don't want to bring finances into this. And I meant what I said about everything that I have will be yours. No prenuptial—there will be no need for that. I want to marry you because I love you and want to take care of you."

"I know, David. It's not just about that. I just have to think about this. That's all." Tassha put her hand on top of David's. "It's so serious to me and . . ." Tassha stopped talking. David was no longer paying attention to her. His eyes had shifted toward the front of the Conservatory where Tenner was standing with Casey and Karen. They were both draped on his arms as he strolled up the red carpet. Casey's hair had been cut into a short bob. She was wearing a perfectly-fitting black gown that showed her shoulders, her arms, the sides of her breasts, and all of her back. She had on diamond earrings, a matching necklace, and a sparkling bracelet, and her dress was so long that you could see just the tips of her silver pumps. Karen was standing taller than both Tenner and Casey. Her hair was pulled back into a ponytail. She was draped in a shiny bronze shawl over the same color dress and had a stunning necklace around her neck. She was standing with her hands holding the shawl together and a radiant smile on her face. Tenner knew all eyes were on him with his dates, as he stood in his all-black suit, black shirt, and black tie. Tassha looked at Tenner then back at David, who seemed to be steaming.

"What's wrong, David?" she asked. David took a couple of seconds. He hadn't even thought about Tenner being at the function and was annoyed that he was.

"Uhhh, yeah."

"Why are you looking over there so hard?"

"Oh . . . oh. That's just Ronald Tenner."

Tassha looked at Tenner again. "Yeah, I know who he is. He's trouble."

David gave Tassha a fake smile. He hadn't returned any of Tenner's messages left on his home line ever since the fire. "That's what they say."

"Well, that's what I know. Look at him standing there like some New York City Mafia thug with those women hanging on his arms. I would never let myself be paraded around like that. Don't you know there's buzz about him being a womanizer?"

David was still staring at Tenner, so Tassha didn't see any reason to continue their conversation.

"David . . . would you excuse me for a second? I have to go to the ladies' room." Tassha stood up. David didn't stand up as he had always done for her when she left the table. Tassha was surprised and followed David's eyes over to Tenner again. "David, I'll be back, okay?" she pronounced loudly.

"Oh . . . sure . . . sure," David said, and he finally stood up as Tassha walked away.

Tenner's eyes locked on Tassha's beauty like an infrared light. He marveled at her fabulous dress, then he saw David. Tenner flashed a sleazy smile and made his way over to the table with his dates.

"Well, well, well," Tenner said. He stood directly over David and his table. David stood up—they barely shook hands. Both Tenner and David looked tightly at one another. "How are you, Mr. Councilman?" Tenner asked smugly over the loud music.

"I could be better," David told him.

"Is that so?"

"Yes, it is."

"Well myself," Tenner said, looking at his dates, "I'm feeling like five hundred thousand dollars."

David glared sharply at the ladies and, shooting Tenner's sarcasm right back at him, said, "I think you're overestimating a little." Then David sat down to signal the conversation was over. Tenner looked at Karen and Casey and nodded for them to sit down at the circular table. David's eyes widened just a little.

Tenner examined the room and waited a beat before he said anything at all.

"Is that Carl up on stage singing? Now that's a singer there. Yes indeed," he said. Then he scooted his chair up to the table a bit and turned directly to face David while Casey and Karen focused on the ensemble. "David . . . I'm so glad that you're here. Haven't you received any of my calls?" Tenner asked, moving Tassha's glass aside. David watched him, and he took offense at Tenner's rearranging his table.

"I've been busy. No time to play phone tag," David said. Tenner grinned at his dates politely, not happy that David was copping an attitude with him in front of them.

"Busy doing what? Busy promoting my prison? I don't think so," Tenner said, gritting his teeth. "I don't think you know what's at stake for me, but I do know I've done a lot for you. My money has made you the number one candidate. Now I want results."

David leaned in. "Listen, I don't know if you're aware of this, but you almost killed someone very, very special to me in that fire, and I take offense to that."

Tenner swiped his face and moved up toward the table as close as he could. "You do, huh? Well, maybe next time you won't be so lucky—and that goes for your woman too."

David's eyes cut deep into Tenner. "Never . . . threaten her. Do you understand?"

Tenner looked over at the ladies, visibly seething. "Ladies, would you excuse us for a minute?" he asked with concentrated calm. Casey and Karen obeyed without a peep. "Look, David, I have just made arrangements with a major corporation and they want my inmates to make clothes, sneakers, and do a little telemarketing on the side." Tenner eased up a little. "Now, I know you can't make anybody move out of the building I want. I have to do that myself, and it will get done. But what you can do . . . let me put it like this. What you'd better do is talk up the prison to the public. Make it seem like it's the best thing that ever happened to this city." David didn't get to answer because he noticed Tassha coming back to the table. David stood up for her. So did Tenner. Tassha looked at David questioningly, wondering what Tenner was doing at their table.

"Sweetheart, let me introduce you to Ronald Tenner," David said, hating every second of the introduction.

"Hello," Tassha snapped.

"Tassha!" Tenner said with excitement. Tassha was amazed Tenner knew her name. "It sure is a pleasure to finally meet you. I've heard so much about you." Tenner pointed at David. "You know this guy really thinks a lot of you." Tenner pulled out her chair for her. David's breathing became heavier, and Tenner could see that he had him. They all had a seat and Tassha was bewildered, sitting in between them. "So where were we, David?" Tenner asked, preying on his victim. David was numb. "Ohh . . . yeah. My prison." Tassha stared at David, whose face was riddled with discomfort. He had been exposed. "As I was saying . . . ," Tenner continued.

Karen followed right behind Casey as though it was what she was supposed to do. This was the third time they had been with Tenner together, but this time they were going to be seeing a little bit more of each other than either one of them really wanted to. Tenner had been all over them during the limo ride to the function. "Oh what a time we're going to have tonight!" Tenner had said as he sipped some Moët, not at all offended when his ladies would not drink with him. He was going to have them, if they drank or not. Karen was facing the mirror when Casey came out of the stall. They had never talked with one another, just exchanged stares while Tenner pawed over one or the other. Casey walked over to the sink in the restroom and turned on the water as she proceeded to wash her hands. Karen was putting on her lipstick in the mirror. Karen caught Casey's stare, and they looked at each other in the mirror. There was silence; both had something on their mind, but dismissed it and continued with their personal business. Then Karen checked to make sure no one else was in the restroom with them.

"Casey?" she whispered. Casey turned off the water.

"Umm-hmmm?"

"Casey?" Karen whispered again.

"Yes?"

Kyle scanned the room. "Girl, it's me, Kyle," he spit out with lightning speed speaking in Karen's voice.

Casey looked into the mirror and tried to see behind Karen's heavy makeup, to erase the eye shadow and blush and lipstick to determine if the voice she heard was really Kyle's. Kyle turned his face left, then right, and tried to help her. Casey let out a surprised scream and tried to catch it as soon as it released from her body.

"What the hell is going on?" Casey's voice echoed.

"Shhhhhh. Shut your ass up! You're not supposed to know."

"Is this some kind of joke?" Casey asked.

"This ain't no damn joke. Ronald has been my lover for years, and if he finds out I'm telling you this he's going to beat both of us, so hold it down."

"What!" Her voice echoed again.

"Damn it, Casey . . . please be quiet," Kyle begged.

"I think I'm going to be sick," Casey said.

"Well, if we don't figure out how to get out of what he has planned for us tonight, we're both going to be in trouble," Kyle assured her.

Tassha didn't want to believe what she was hearing and David sat still and silent while Tenner rambled on, implicating David for taking campaign dollars from him for his prison. David dared not look at Tassha. He could feel her tension rising as she listened.

"So that's where we stand now, David," Tenner said. "I'm to a point where we're going to need more verbal push from you so this thing can get done." He noticed his dates approaching the table carrying glasses of Moët. Tenner extended his hand to Tassha. She looked at him like he was crazy and turned away. Tenner dropped his hand. "Well, Tassha . . . it was a pleasure meeting you, and I really hope—and I do mean this—to see you later."

"Don't bet on it," David fired as he stood up. Tenner raised up then cut his eyes at David.

"I didn't know you were a betting man, David." He snickered then joined his dates. David stood there, almost afraid to sit back down, as he watched Tenner slither to the other side of the Conservatory, dates in hand. Then he sat back down. Tassha wouldn't look him in the face.

"Tassha, I can explain this. . . . Please hear me out . . ."

Tenner was set. Here he was, finally in the middle of his fantasy, and feeling like a champion because he had just made David's night miserable. Tenner, Casey, and Kyle, dressed as Karen, were alone at last. When he opened the door to the hotel room, his dates had no question what was on his mind. Tenner walked directly over to the Moët chilling in the bucket. Casey and Karen stopped at the door.

"Come on in ladies," Tenner said, sly as a fox and eyes focused as such. "No need to act shy now. The moment of truth has arrived. . . ." He hooted.

"Oh, we're not shy," Casey said as she walked over and grabbed herself a glass. "Hmm . . . pour me some of that," she said, almost demanding. Tenner grabbed her around the waist.

"Ummmm, Casey, as long as I've known you I've never seen you drink like this," he said, himself completely intoxicated. "You damn near drank all the booze in the limo."

"Well, you know what they say. You never know people as well as you think," Casey revealed, then she tipped her glass and the Moët found her lips. Tenner began to chuckle.

"You know . . . you're sooo right, and you're about to find that out

. . . ain't that right, Karen!" Karen smiled and sat her purse down on the table. "Ronald, you are sooo damn crazy!" she squealed. Casey looked at Kyle, because it was the first time since they'd been together that she truly recognized his voice. Karen sat down in the chair and kept her eyes on Tenner.

"So, ladies, why don't we get this party started?" Tenner said. He took off his suit jacket then turned and gave Casey a prolonged kiss. When he finished with her he walked over to Karen. Casey immediately wiped her face and mouth with her hand. "Come here you . . . ," Tenner said to Karen as he sat down on the bed. She walked over to him, and at the same time gave a quick glance and wink to Casey. Karen sat down on the bed, and instantly Tenner began kissing her all over. Soon he was on top of her, groping and fondling for what seemed like hours to Casey. Never in her wildest dreams had she believed that Tenner was as freaky as he had turned out to be. She watched him act with Karen pretty much the same way he had always been with her. She wasn't going to have any problems at all going through with the plan she and Kyle had come up with. Tenner raised up from Karen and began to take off his shirt.

"Casey, come on over and join us, huh?" Tenner reached for his glass on the nightstand.

"You want me to come over there with you?" she asked.

"Yes . . . that's what I said. Get your ass over here. There's something I want to do with you." Casey took her glass, drank the remainder of her champagne, then slowly begin to walk over to the bed as Tenner began with Karen again. Casey had never imagined herself being in such a position; she hated what she had become, and even more the very steps that she was taking. Casey watched closely as Tenner devoured Kyle's mouth. Tenner pulled up Kyle's dress and ran his fingers passionately down his recently shaven legs, the exact way he had done to her in the past. Another step closer and Casey could hear Tenner's moans. When Casey was as close as she could get she saw the pleasure on Tenner's face. His indulgence was giving him gratification and fulfillment. While Casey watched in shock, Tenner stuck his tongue into Kyle's mouth, and it was the last straw. Her mind snapped and Casey churned her stomach on purpose and instantly vomited everything she had eaten all over Tenner and Kyle.

"What the fuck!" Tenner jumped up and shouted.

"Oh . . . my!" Karen cried. "Casey, you must be sick, honey!"

"Damn it!" Tenner yelled again. "What the fuck is wrong with you!" Casey covered her mouth, looked at the mess she'd made, then clutched her stomach.

"I'm sorry, you guys . . . sorry, I must have drank too much," she admitted.

"Fuck . . . fuck . . . fuck!" Tenner yelled, looking at the mess all over his body. "Karen, get me something to get this shit up with!" Karen went into the bathroom to get a towel.

"Look at me!" Tenner said, disgusted.

"I'm sorry, Ronald—I couldn't help it," Casey said. Then Karen came out with the towels and gave one to Ronald.

"Shit . . . Casey, I think you need to go home," Tenner suggested. "We're going to have to finish this some other time. Go down to the car and tell Delmar to drive you home."

"Ronald . . . I'm so sorry," Casey reiterated.

"Go, Casey . . . just go, damn it."

Casey looked around and grabbed her purse. Tenner noticed Karen looking for her purse as well. "Where the fuck you think you're going?" Tenner asked.

"Oh . . . huh . . . I just thought I was leaving too," Karen said dejectedly.

"Sit your ass down!" Tenner instructed. "You're not going anywhere."

Casey's and Kyle's eyes locked as Casey glanced back from the hallway of the hotel, then Tenner slammed the door.

❖ ❖ ❖

Tassha rushed to her door and couldn't unlock it fast enough. David was steps behind her, walking with his head down, trying to figure out what to say to her.

"Tassha?" David called out. Then he heard the bolt lock unlatch. Tassha didn't turn around. "Listen. I'm sorry that you had to find out about the finance dollars for my campaign like this. But what was I supposed to do?" Tassha still didn't answer. "Tassha . . . the son of a bitch set me up. He took all of my campaign financiers. Then promised them back to me if I backed his prison." Tassha listened to what David said and huffed. She started to turn around, but she didn't—she pushed the door open and walked away. "Tassha . . . ," David called out. Tassha locked the door behind her and immediately sat down on her couch. Two minutes later the phone rang.

"Hello?"

"Tassha?"

"Yes. . . ."

"It's Ethan. . . . Is everything okay?"

"Sure. Why do you ask?"

"You just don't sound like you looked tonight."

"Huh?"

"I saw you on the news tonight at the ball."

"You did?"

"Sure did."

Then Tassha's call-waiting chimed in. "Hold on a sec, Ethan, okay?"

"Sure."

"Hello?"

"Hi, Tassha. It's Vance. Listen, I had to take Artise to the hospital tonight."

"What!"

"When you dropped her off after the book club meeting she wasn't feeling too well. She seemed to get worse, so I brought her out to Riverside. We've been here about thirty minutes. She's in with the doctors now."

"Is she okay, Vance?"

"They haven't said anything yet."

"Well, I'm on my way," Tassha said. She clicked over the phone. "Ethan?" she said in despair.

"Yeah? What's wrong?"

"Artise is in the hospital."

"What?"

"Vance just called me, and he sounded like it was serious."

"Listen, I'll be right over to get you. We'll go together. Okay?"

"Okay. . . . ," Tassha answered. Then she hung up the phone and bent her knees to pray.

Moving On

Five days later Artise was back home, but all was not well. Her doctors placed her on mandatory bed rest because her blood pressure had soared and they'd diagnosed her with hypertension due to stress, complicated by her pregnancy. Vance was a nervous wreck but thankful he hadn't listened to Artise's insistent cries that she was okay even when her feet, ankles, hands, and face began to swell. When the doctors explained to him that if Artise didn't receive medical attention, there was a good chance of the baby being born with growth retardation or oxygen deprivation, Vance took it upon himself to make sure Artise had everything she needed. He cooked, cleaned, sat for hours at her bedside, and tried his best to make sure Artise was comfortable as could be. He had not slept more than three hours at a clip since Artise's release from the hospital. The everyday optimistic spirit she'd always possessed was a thing of the past, and it was beginning to worry him. She barely responded when he tried to lighten her worries about her mother and the incident at the book chat, and when he brought up the subject of the baby, Artise would just gaze uneasily at the television without saying anything. Vance wanted to see Artise smile. He wanted her to be happy about their new beginning, but Artise refused to break out of her rut. The Stubblefields, Ethan, and Tassha and their constant phone calls were the only thing keeping Vance together. Ethan stepped up and began to handle matters at the museum to keep the opening on track. The auditorium was near completion, and Ethan authorized the contractors to hire additional workers for the center. Vance thought about calling Cathy to let her know about her daughter's condition, but after he continued to notice that Cathy was really the only thing on Artise's mind, he decided against it. Vance called Melba instead, who without hesitation accepted his invitation to begin working for them at once. Vance felt a tremendous amount of his stress release from his body when he finally heard the doorbell ring.

"Hi . . . Melba?" Vance asked expectantly.

"That's right. . . . That's me!" Melba said as she stood with her hands full of brown paper grocery bags. Vance reached out for the bags.

"Let me take that for you. Come on in."

Melba followed Vance back into the kitchen, her head moving up and down, left and right, as she looked through the house. "Oh, this is gorgeous," she admitted.

"Thank you very much," Vance said as he placed the bags on the counter. "Miz Melba, you didn't have to buy any groceries . . . there's plenty here." Vance smiled.

"But you don't have what I brought. I brought some food over that's going to get everybody in this house back to normal. When we were talking over the phone I could just hear the stress in your voice. I know you must be ready to just fall to the ground from exhaustion. So this is what I'm going to do. I'm going to go check in on Artise, say hello. Then I'm going to get this house smelling like a home with a home-cooked meal, and then you and Artise are going to get some rest. How's that?"

"Oh . . . that sounds good to me!" Vance said.

"So is Artise awake?"

"The last time I checked she was." Vance took a deep breath. "She's really got me worried."

Miz Melba grinned. "Dear, don't worry. Nothing we can't take care of together. She's just been worrying a little too much."

"Well, I told her that I wanted her to relax and take her mind off her mother. She worries so much when they're not on the same page. I think all of this is crazy, if you ask me."

Melba gave Vance a serious look. "Let me tell you. This is something that you wouldn't understand. This is a mother-daughter thing. I talked to Artise about it at the mall when we met. She wants her mother to be more involved in her life than she is." Melba smiled. "See, you men, you're happy when you just call y'all's mama every now and then to hear her voice." Vance laughed. "Don't ask me how I know . . . 'cause I got boys of my own." Melba patted Vance on the arm. "But girls are different, don't ask me why . . . it's just the way it is. But don't worry, you hear." Vance looked at Melba, still visibly concerned. "I'm going to get your wife as good as new!"

Who Did It

Ethan awoke at the sound of the phone. He raised his head and looked around for the cordless but couldn't find it. So he laid his head back down and tried to finish sleeping, but the phone kept ringing over and over again. "You would think if I didn't answer after twenty minutes a mutha would stop calling," Ethan mumbled to himself as he arose from the bed and noticed he still had his clothes on. Ethan was dead tired and his leg was sort of stiff. He had been at the museum all day while the contractors finished putting in all of the seats in the auditorium and installed a state-of-the-art movie screen. Ethan glanced at the clock while he looked around for the phone. He felt let down after he realized he had twenty more minutes of peace and quiet before he was supposed to get prepared to go back to the museum to receive a very important shipment of out-of-print books. Ethan had to keep pushing, though, and he was actually enjoying the decisions he was being forced to make. He was finally realizing the job was worth the effort. Ethan picked up shirt after shirt as he tried to find his phone, and then finally he saw it sticking out from under the side of his bed.

"Yeah . . . yeah, hello," Ethan strained to say.

"Hi . . . Ethan?"

"Yeah, this is Ethan speaking."

"Uh, yeah, hi . . . it's Casey. . . ."

"Casey. What's up?"

"Wow, you sound tired."

"I am. What can I do for ya?" Ethan said as he sat on the edge of his bed.

"Well, I'm calling to ask you a favor," Casey uttered, her voice fading off.

"Sure . . . what is it?"

"It's about Kyle," Casey rushed.

Ethan thought for a second. "Kyle? What about him?"

"Well, he hasn't been here in a couple of days, and I'm really kinda worried about him."

"Worried about him? Why?"

"I just am. . . . He's been doing pretty good, and I . . . just want to make sure he's all right."

"Well, did you try to call him?"

"Yes, I did, but there was no answer."

"I don't know what to tell you, Casey. I mean, what can I do?"

"You really mean that?"

"Mean what?" Ethan became confused and rubbed his eyes.

"What you just asked . . . what can you do?" Casey badgered.

Ethan looked into the phone. "Yeah, Casey, what can I do?"

"Well, you can do me a favor and go over to his house and see if he's okay."

"Go over to his house?" Ethan said, surprised.

"Well, you asked. I can give you his address."

"Casey, I know where Kyle lives. I went to high school with him. Known him damn near my whole life."

"Will you do it?"

"Casey, for what? I am not going to go over to his house and ask him why he hasn't been to work at a place that I don't even work at anymore."

Casey was silent. "Well, Ethan, I just thought you meant what you said in the note to Kyle."

"Note?" Ethan asked.

"Yeah, the note you left him the day you left. He was telling everybody about it. I think he was kind of touched by it."

"He showed everyone?"

"He sure did. So will you do it? I haven't known him long enough to just pop up at his house. Plus I have to be someplace in thirty minutes." Ethan was very quiet. "Please, Ethan. . . . I will owe you big time . . . I mean big time," Casey said.

Ethan huffed. "Okay . . . I'll go by there."

"Thank you, Ethan."

"I'll call you later."

Kyle opened the door for Ethan on the first knock. He turned around and started to walk in the opposite direction, and Ethan stepped in and followed behind him.

If he didn't want me to come in, he wouldn't have walked away, Ethan thought as he looked around. Kyle had all the blinds drawn and had one candle flickering on the table next to a bottle of rum. His place smelled like incense. There wasn't much furniture, just a large pillow on the floor and on the other side of the room a couch. His component set was lit and Ethan could hear Angela Bofill's "I Try" playing softly.

"What are you doing here?" Kyle grumbled.

"I got a call."

"From who?"

"Casey."

Kyle turned around and looked at Ethan. He tried to figure out if Casey had told Ethan anything.

At the same time Ethan wondered why Kyle was looking at him so intensely. "She wanted me to check on you." Ethan got his first good look at Kyle in the dim setting. "Damn. . . . What the hell happened to you? You look like you need to go to the hospital." Kyle's face was beaten to a pulp. Both of his eyes were black-and-blue and his lip looked to be three sizes larger than normal.

"Already been," Kyle snapped.

"What happened to your face?"

"I'll be all right," Kyle managed to say. Then he grabbed his jaw. "They just gave me some painkillers." Kyle's face looked like someone had taken a baseball bat to it.

"Well what the hell happened, Kyle?"

Kyle walked over to the rum that was sitting on his table and poured himself a shot.

"I know you're not going to drink that while you're on painkillers?"

"Sure am. Hell, what else could happen to me?" Kyle asked.

"Okay, Kyle, what's going on?"

Kyle was tired of telling lies. He looked up at the ceiling. He knew that he wasn't supposed to say anything—his life depended on it.

"It's way too deep, Ethan. That's all I can say."

"Way too deep? You standing there with your eyes almost out of your head and you're telling me it's way too deep?"

"There are just some things that you don't want to know. Because if it gets out that you know, you might end up like this," Kyle confessed.

"I tell you what. There is not one man that can kick my ass that bad. . . . Trust me," Ethan boasted. Kyle took a sip of his rum then placed a painkiller on his tongue, swallowed the medicine, then finished what he had left in his cup. "So, Kyle, are you going to tell me or what?"

"Why, Ethan? Why should I tell you?" Kyle said, slamming down his cup. Then Kyle picked up the bottle of painkillers again and shook another one out into his hand.

"How many of those are you supposed to have?" Ethan asked.

"I don't know. Does it matter?" Kyle popped the pill in his mouth then poured himself another shot. Ethan walked over to the table and snatched the bottle of painkillers out of Kyle's hand. He took the bottle of rum and placed it on the counter next to the sink.

"That's some type of shit a friend does for a friend," Kyle recognized. "You trying to tell me that we friends now, 'cause you feel bad for getting my sister locked up?"

Ethan thought for a second. He didn't want to get into it. "Let's just say we're friendly," he conceded. "Now who the hell beat you like that?"

Kyle walked over to the album playing and placed the needle back on "I Try." "You know, I can't get enough of this song," Kyle slurred. "It just rings so true." Ethan watched Kyle as he stood still, soaking in the pain of the song. "No matter how hard you try to please, you never can get it right," Kyle said over the music then looked over at Ethan. "You know what I mean?"

"No, not really." Ethan sat down at the round kitchen table.

"Yes you do. . . . You know when you just give your all to one person because you believe that they truly care for you but it turns out that they couldn't give a rat's ass about you," Kyle explained.

"Yeah, yeah. I been there a time or two," Ethan admitted.

"With who? That dark-skinned slim babe who stormed out of the store when she saw your face maybe?" Kyle sat down across from Ethan.

"Hey, now, that's my business," Ethan lashed out.

"Shit, you've been all in mine. So she's the one?"

"Yeah, we have history, so what?" Ethan downplayed.

"You hurt her or she hurt you?" Ethan's eyes fell from Kyle. "You hurt her, didn't you? I knew it anyway by the glance she gave you when she saw you. It's the same way I feel sometimes."

"What glance, Kyle? What are you talking about?"

"That look of pain everybody has when they've been done wrong. But she's lucky she's able to show her frustrations without ending up—" Kyle stopped.

"What?" Ethan inquired.

"Nothing." Kyle began to take another sip of his rum but placed it back down on the table. "Tell me something. Did you ever tell her you loved her?" Ethan remained silent. "Come on, Ethan, you can tell me," Kyle pressured as he grabbed his aching jaw and took a quick sip of his rum.

Ethan thought about his question and nodded. "Yeah, I told her." The candle between the two drew Ethan's eyes toward its flicker. He glanced at the candle then at Kyle. He wondered how the hell Kyle was able to get him to talk about something so private.

"So, what happened after that? What did you do?"

Ethan took his fingertips and ran them over his right eyebrow two times. "I asked her to marry me," Ethan said. "Then I left town."

"That explains her glance then. Now I understand. One thing about being duped is—it will surely make you act strange—Why do you think I act so crazy at the store sometimes?" Kyle noticed Ethan's wondering eyes. "I know what you're thinking. How does a fag have so much insight, huh?"

"Not in those exact words," Ethan admitted. "But yeah, I was."

"Too deep for you right now. Maybe later."

"Well, tell me who did that to you then. That's what I want to know."

"You really want to know?"

"Yeah I want to know?"

"You know Ronald Tenner?" Kyle asked sharply.

"Yeah. The rich cat with all the women. Who doesn't? Why?"

"Because he's the one who did this to me."

"Why? For what?"

"Because he was my lover and he was having a bad day."

"Your lover?"

"Umm-hmm."

Ethan walked over to the bottle of rum on the sink counter and picked it up. "The glasses are overhead on your right," Kyle told him. Ethan turned to Kyle. "Ronald Tenner, the biggest player this city has ever seen?"

"Yep. My lover for the last two years."

"Kyle, what the hell are you talking about?" Ethan asked. He began to think Kyle was lying to him.

"Just what I said," Kyle spurted out. "We're involved. He's the one who did this to me."

Ethan kind of smiled. "You mean to tell me Ronald Tenner is a—"

Kyle cut him off. "Watch your mouth, Ethan," he warned.

"You mean to tell me Ronald Tenner, one of the most influential men this city has ever seen, is gay and is involved with you?"

"What's wrong with me? And for your information, Ronald is bi."

"Do we have to go there?" Ethan asked.

"Yes—yes, we do. Since we are friendly."

Ethan paused. "I just would think that a man like that could have any woman he wants, that's all."

"He can . . . believe me, he can."

"Well, what's going on then?" Ethan asked.

"Dang, Ethan. You want to know everything, don't you?"

Ethan nodded.

"Well, put it like this. Ronald loves the way I look when I dress," Kyle said bluntly.

"When you dress?"

Kyle nodded.

Ethan tried to laugh off his question.

"Like I've always said, Ethan. I have female tendencies and I like to dress like a woman from time to time." Kyle tried to smile. "I remember the first time I met Ronald. I had put on my tight black dress and some makeup and walked down Broad Street, and next thing you know, his driver in his Mercedes pulled over to the side of the street and called me over. I gave Tenner my number, and that night he called me—and he told me I was so beautiful and that there was something very special about me. We were on the phone and I didn't know his ass from Adam so I told him what was so special about me."

Ethan focused hard on Kyle's worn, beaten face. Kyle was becoming very emotional.

"Ethan . . . you should have heard the laughter in the phone after I told him that I am a gay man and like to dress like a woman. You should have heard the surprise in his voice. Then all of a sudden he told me that he didn't care. I was still the sexiest woman that he had ever seen, and it filled my cup right away."

"So you love him?" Ethan couldn't believe he asked that question. He hated himself for it. It was like he was talking to a female friend. Kyle looked at him.

"Yes . . . I do. Yes, I love him." Kyle took a deep breath. "It wasn't like this when we started out. Over these last couple of months he has become so damn violent. . . . I just don't know what to do."

At that moment Ethan wished he'd never written Kyle the note and slipped it in his mailbox at Snyders. He didn't want to hold to the words that he'd written to Kyle: *If there is anything you need, let me know.* But he couldn't let the conversation end. "Why did he beat you, Kyle?"

"He just didn't like something I said, that's all it was. . . . Looking back on it, it was all my fault."

"All your fault? You think because you said something he doesn't like he has the right to beat you?"

Kyle was quiet.

"Look at you, man."

Kyle shot Ethan a sharp look.

Do I owe this guy? Ethan asked himself, examining the situation. Kyle peered across the table at Ethan. Ethan tried to look him directly in his eyes, but the bruises caused him to turn away. Kyle chugged down what rum he had left. "Look, where can I find this guy?" Ethan blurted out. Kyle slammed down his glass.

"Ohhhh, no, Ethan. You don't even know what you're talking about," Kyle pleaded.

"Oh yes I do."

"Ethan, Ronald is dangerous. He told me if I ever told anyone about us he would kill me," Kyle cautioned.

"He said that?" Kyle nodded his head yes then exhaled as he looked in his cup of rum and saw there was nothing left.

Hello

Thirty days later

"No . . . no Miz Melba." Artise smiled. "Ain't nobody got no time to fix no collards after they get off of work and taking care of three and four kids!" She and Melba were sitting around the counter in the kitchen while Vance sat an earshot away in the family room, watching the Miami Dolphins play the New York Jets.

"Oh . . . yes they do sweetheart . . . yes they do," Melba insisted.

"How?"

"You cook those bad boys on a Sunday. As a matter of fact, cook all the meals for the week on Sunday right after church then store everything in the icebox. Then, when you get home all tired and spent, you throw everything on the stove and let it warm up. Now that's what you tell them to do. These women today are feeding these kids way to much of that Mickey D. stuff—that's why they can't get their grades and have no energy at the end of a day to help around the house and clean."

"Now that's not a bad idea. Let me jot that down," Artise said.

"I told ya, Miz Melba been around a time or two."

Vance looked over at Artise and smiled. He was truly relieved that she was almost back to normal. Artise fought through the turbulent issues she had with Cathy, and realizing that Vance and Melba were right and that she had to heal herself for the good of the baby. Artise started to focus on her future instead of the on-again-off-again relationship with her mother. Vance enjoyed the fact that Artise was beginning to smile again, and Melba's ability to fit right in the household worked wonders for him because he was able to get back to work at the museum without having to worry about Artise as much. It was just a good old-fashioned Sunday afternoon.

Suddenly, the telephone rang and everyone stopped what they were doing.

"I'll get it!" Miz Melba sang. She wiped her hands on her apron then picked up the phone. "Hello! Butler residence."

"Hello?" Cathy said at the other end of the phone.

"Yes . . . can I help you?" Melba asked. Vance turned to Melba, wondering who it could be.

"Who is this?" Cathy investigated.

"My name is Melba. Can I help you?" Melba smiled and shrugged her shoulders as Vance got up from his chair and walked into the kitchen.

"I'm looking for my daughter, Artise," Cathy said, almost defiantly.

"Oh . . . okay, just a minute," Melba said as she walked over to the table to hand Artise the cordless phone. "It's your mother," she whispered. Artise kind of brightened; she was surprised. It was the first time her mother had called since before the book chat. Vance took the phone from Miz Melba then looked at Artise.

"You sure you're up to it?"

"Yeah, I'm sure," Artise said, reaching for the phone. Vance handed it to her but kept a protective eye on his girl. "Hello," Artise said.

"Hey, Artise?"

"Hey, Mama."

"What's going on?"

"Huh? What do you mean?"

"Who was that lady who answered the phone?"

"Oh—that's Miz Melba. She's helping us out around here." Artise looked at Melba, who had just pulled the roast out of the oven.

"Helping you out?" Cathy asked. Vance saw Artise take a deep breath.

"Yes. . . . She's been coming over ever since I got out of the hospital."

"The hospital!" Cathy shouted.

"Yeah," Artise said, looking at Vance.

"When were you in the hospital and for what?"

"I went after the last time I talked to you. The doctor said I've had too much stress on me and needed to relax, that's all."

"Well, why didn't you call me?" Cathy wanted to know. Artise looked at Vance again.

"What? I thought Vance called you the night I was in the hospital. He told me he would take care of everything," Artise said back.

"I didn't even know you were in the hospital," Cathy said with a mixture of hurt and anger. Artise took a couple of seconds to think.

"Well, it doesn't matter anyway, because it shouldn't take me landing in the hospital for you to call to see how I'm doin'. After all, I am carrying your grandchild."

Melba looked at Artise, then at Vance. Vance was not going to let this get out of hand.

"Let me have the phone, Artise," he demanded.

"Hello, Cathy?"

"Yes."

"This is Vance. . . . Look, Artise is restricted by her doctor. She isn't supposed to be getting her blood pressure up or anything like that. I don't know, but you two always seem to upset each other. So I'm going to ask you out of respect for me and your unborn grandchild if you would give Artise some time alone, so she can focus on the baby."

"Out of respect!" Cathy shouted. "Where is the respect for me, Vance, when my daughter is laying up in some hospital and you don't even call me? Huh?"

"Cathy, the way you are acting now is exactly the reason why I didn't call you," Vance said. "Talk to you soon." Vance hung up. Artise looked at him, surprised. "I can't take this anymore!" Vance said, then he walked back into the family room and plopped down in his chair.

"Vance, why did you do that?" Artise asked.

"Do what?"

"You know what. Why did you say that to my mother?"

" 'Cause it's true. You get upset every time you talk to her, Artise, and you almost lost our child because of it. So I just tried to stop the dispute before it started," Vance said.

"Well, I don't think that was right. And where do you get off not calling her when I was in the hospital. What if I would have died in there?"

"If you would have died, Artise, she would have found out. The reason I didn't call her is because the day you got sick all you were doing was complaining about the things she said at the book club meeting and for weeks before the meeting you were complaining about her. So what am I supposed to do when I know the reason you're in the hospital . . . What? Call the reason up and invite it to the hospital to see you? Uh-uh, I wasn't doin' that."

Miz Melba had never seen Vance and Artise argue like this. "I don't mean to interrupt. I really don't. But please, y'all two take it easy. Artise, in this instance I have to say, if you'll let me, Vance is right, darling—your health is more important at this time. I'm sure you and your mother will work things out, but right now you need to be in the best health possible. You understand?" Artise took a deep breath then rolled her eyes at Vance. Vance went back to watching television, hoping and praying that he hadn't raised Artise's blood pressure, because his was sure enough pumping like pistons in a race car. He had been holding back his explosion about Cathy ever since Artise had gotten back from the hospital. And more than that, he'd been putting up with their little spats as long as he had known Artise. Vance was never the one to get involved, because he thought well of Cathy. It was the relationship between her and Artise that he didn't like. He had even begun praying for the deliverance of their relationship. But he couldn't keep his mouth shut any longer. He had to speak for his wife and child.

After dinner Artise was still following her doctor's orders. She dejectedly told Vance good night and went to bed. Vance was quiet. He placed his napkin on the table and watched Artise walk up the steps, then he looked at Miz Melba.

"Well, can't always have perfect nights," she said.

"That's for sure. I really thought I was doing the right thing by not calling Cathy," Vance confessed.

"I think you did. She needs to get stronger. She's going to need all the strength she can muster when it's time to deliver the baby."

Vance thought about what Melba said and wiped his brow. "She scares me so much, Melba. Artise used to walk around smiling and having fun. Now that she's pregnant I would think that she would be happy, but this is ridiculous. All I do is worry about her twenty-four-seven. I intended for us to have fun during this time, not to be trying to keep her away from her mother for the sake of our baby. This is not how I envisioned it."

"Well, we have to roll with the punches, Vance. Roll with the punches." Melba thought for a moment. "Hey . . . why don't you go out for a while?"

"Huh?"

"Yeah. Why don't you go and get out of here for a while. I can probably count on one hand how many times you've been out of here in the last couple of weeks. It will do ya some good."

"You think so?"

"Yes, I do." Melba smiled. "I'm a firm believer in that old saying, 'If you can't stand the heat, get out of the kitchen,' " she explained.

"So you think I need to cool off, huh?"

Melba nodded.

Vance thought about it for a second. "What about Artise?"

"Shoot . . . I'm not going anywhere tonight. I'll be right here."

Vance tapped the table with his knuckles. "Well, that's what I'm going to do then."

For a Sunday night, Whispers was packed. Vance was lucky and got a booth ordinarily reserved for two. He liked Whispers. It was actually the only place that catered to the thirty-something crowd in Columbus and the only place on Sunday that played jazz. It was almost eight-thirty when Vance arrived, and he was astonished to find out that David Sanborn was in the house from four to six. Vance put his bottom lip back into place and enjoyed his private booth. The individual booths in Whispers were surrounded by black-tinted Plexiglas, and each had its own jukebox on the table with small round speakers within. Vance pushed the intercom and ordered himself a brandy. Afterward he turned right to the jukebox. The only thing he wanted to hear was his girl Anita Baker.

Vance leafed through all the selections offered by Anita on the jukebox and programmed song after song after song. Vance was absolutely in love with the songstress. Anita's voice reminded him of Sarah Vaughn, smooth and inviting. Vance was so head over heels with her ability to make a song feel like real life that he wrote all of his lyrics intended for her sweet voice. Many times he would fantasize about being across from her in a recording studio hearing the words from one of his songs blaring passionately from her soul. Vance had lyrics for Anita he'd written in college locked away in his Taurus. Most of his songs he'd written for Artise, but he'd always been too embarrassed to show them to her or anyone else.

Vance finished his drink and was ready for another. The brandy had him feeling very mellow. *Thank God for the tinted windows,* he thought, pretending to be a piano player as Anita's "Body and Soul" pounded inside his booth. Then he switched positions in the orchestra and began displaying his conducting skills, pretending to direct the symphony that played behind Anita's dynamic voice.

Originally Vance was planning to have just one drink, cool off, and go back home. But this night was all about the music, so he pushed the intercom to order another drink. When Vance turned to look for his drink he was forced to take a second glance at the white girl who was being shown the booth right next to his. Vance focused his eyes and beamed in on her features. He couldn't figure out for the life of him where he knew her from or who she was, then he sprouted up from his seat and opened the door of his booth.

"Hey, you!" he said.

Casey stopped. "Hi, Vance! Imagine running into you tonight," she said.

"Yeah, I know. I almost didn't recognize you with that short haircut."

Casey blushed. "Well, this is my spot on Sunday nights. I never go anyplace else."

"You want to have a drink?" Vance offered.

"Sure, why not." They got situated back in the booth.

"What are you having?" Vance asked.

"White zinfandel, please." Vance pushed the intercom and ordered for her. Casey could tell from Vance's eyes that he was already feeling good.

"Listen. . . . Listen," Vance said, tapping Casey on her arm. Casey tuned in.

"That's nice and soothing," she said, bobbing her head to the rhythm.

"Yep . . . that's my girl Anita Baker; matter of fact, you got her hair-cut!" Vance recognized. "Don't you know I've followed her career ever since I was a sophomore in college?"

"Get out!" Casey said.

"That's right. She has been my favorite since her first album. It was called *The Songstress.* What a name for an album. I still remember the day I went to the record store and they were playing it, and her voice caught my attention right away. I'm talking about when albums were albums. Vinyl . . . thirty-threes! Do you remember those?"

"Sure do!"

"Now back in those days . . . Damn, listen to me sounding like an old man." Casey laughed. "I made sure that I went to the record store every week just to see what new albums had been released."

"You know, I still do that, too? You have to really love music to do that. I used to want to be a singer in a band. I bet all the kids did, though," Casey said.

"Matter of fact, I used to get dressed up like the Temptations when I was growing up and perform for my mama. I remember running into the bathroom and throwing water on my face so I could look sweaty, just like I imagined them looking when they did their thing on stage."

"You were a true groupie, Vance!"

The waitress came with their drinks and set them on the table.

"Oh, yeah. Now getting back to Anita. When I bought *The Songstress,* I took it right back to my room—I mean right back—and I cleaned off my needle and placed the thirty-three on my stereo. From the very first note I realized how special she was, that music came from her soul. It was one of the best nights I ever spent with a woman."

"You sound like a serious fan, Vance."

"No . . . tell the truth. I sound drunk!" Vance admitted, looking down into his glass. "You know, it's not every day that you find some-one—myself included—that keeps themselves true to what they do and who they are. And as far as her music is concerned, Anita has stayed true. . . ." Vance took a swig of his drink then looked at Casey. "But let me tell you. These lyrics in these songs they play on the radio nowadays, I'm talking about this stuff that's goin' platinum. Shooot, ninety-five percent of it is bull. Except for, of course, Erykah Badu, Lauryn Hill, Mary J., Chante Moore," Casey interrupted. "Patti Patti, Whitney, Faith, Tamia," she added, grinning.

"I see you know your music . . . but let's not forget, uh . . . uh Debra Cox and, last but not least, Monifa. She doesn't know she can sing yet, but she'll get it," Vance rattled off. "Sounds like a lot, but it's not. Not compared to all the singers out there. The majority of that booty-shaking, tongue-licking, mack-daddy, thuggin'-lifestyle bull they're playin' is for the birds. Now don't get me wrong, I still like my rap 'cause the beats are fierce, but the lyrics all sound the same to me. That's why I couldn't even tell you the last time I listened to the radio."

"Oh, I know," Casey agreed, as her index finger touched the top of Vance's hand. That's when he noticed her red nail polish. "It seems like everyone is trying to sound alike."

" 'Cause they don't have anything to say. They need to live a little, experience some things. But I don't blame them 'cause it's all about the money nowadays anyway."

"My . . . you sure are in a serious vibe tonight," Casey said. Vance nodded his head.

"Yeah, I guess so."

"Want to talk about it?"

"No . . . no thanks. Sometimes things are best kept unsaid. Too bad people don't realize that."

Casey and Vance locked eyes. She was trying desperately to figure out what Vance was talking about—but his dark eyes didn't give her a clue. Vance let his thoughts pass, then punched in another tune on the juke-box and conducted Anita's orchestra under the watchful eye of Casey.

After Vance had his third drink he knew he'd had enough. He was feeling the bang. Maybe in college he would have a few beers then call it a night. But that was years ago. Vance wasn't a drinker at all, and drinking three strong drinks was definitely not in his character.

Casey had barely touched her drink. She had drunk enough with Tenner and Kyle to last her a lifetime. She had enjoyed their conversation. Vance took her mind off of everything that had been bothering her. Casey wasn't thinking about Tenner or what she owed him, nor was she thinking about the dreadful night in the hotel after the ball. Casey was thinking about Casey and the needs that she hadn't fulfilled in ages. There was something about Vance that Casey enjoyed. He was a different breed than Tenner, who was the only man she had been with since becoming in arrears to him. Tenner had taken the passion and tenderness out of the entire act of intimacy, had reduced it to fury and resentment for Casey. She could relate to Vance, and managed to smile when he talked to her. She quickly turned the friendly setting into a romantic one in her mind, and began to make it known.

It took Vance forever to finally catch on to Casey's hesitant flirtatious movements, gestures, and signals. She was hesitant because deep down she didn't know if she was flirting with him because she had been told to or because she was legitimately turned on by Vance's non-come-on conversation. But when the old Vance senses came alive, he tried to straighten up and clear his head. He remembered, even with the liquor in his system, what Stubby had told him about the devil and how he would try to work mischief in his life. Stubbs told Vance that even though he had found his inner spirituality, the devil was still going to attack him, especially with his weakness for women. Stubbs was right. Casey had tried everything from sexy winks to playing footsie under the table to coming back out of the restroom with her shirt almost completely unbuttoned. Vance was in his first battle with the devil since his newfound fortune, and in no time he was hearing instructions from Lucifer the liar.

"Maaaan, you can have your way with her. Look at her sitting there exposed and ready. Ummmm . . . look at her. Hey, she likes you . . . she wants you. It's not like you don't want to have her. I've traveled your eyes six times over her entire body already. Up and down her silky soft body. You don't always get a chance like this, Vance. Shit, an alibi from Melba. She can vouch for you. That's been your problem in the past. No one vouched for you. No one has seen you behind these tinted windows—and if she leaves first, you two can drive away free as birds! You know you want her—look at her staring at you, just waiting for you to ask." Vance looked, then Lucifer changed his tone. "And you know, Vance . . . you've bedded many women. But never . . . never a white one. Here's your chance. A chance at a one-night stand like you've never had before."

Vance kept his eyes on Casey. She sat there gazing at him. She licked her lips, then took her hand and placed it on top of Vance's. She ran a single finger across his hand, and Vance dropped his head to watch her finger tantalize and tease his senses. *How did she know I loved that?* Vance asked himself. *This must be right.* Vance thought some more. *It would be a wonderful ending to a dreadful day. Hell, I can't win them all. So what do you say we go to your place?* Vance thought, with his eyes glued on Casey. Casey smiled. She understood without hearing a word.

"I thought you'd never ask," she said back.

Casey left and Vance waited behind to pay the bill. He then followed her to her place, which was only about five minutes away.

"So here we are," Casey said before she opened her front door.

Vance smiled then looked behind his back and Lucifer chimed in again. *No one in sight, no cameras overhead.* "Yeah . . . here we are."

Casey took Vance by the hand, and they both walked inside, and there was celebration in hell.

> *This is how I get within*
> *Place everything on the mind you don't like*
> *To lure you in*
> *Some of y'all good folk like to call it*
>   *Sin*
> *But it's my job, y'all, to lure you in*
>
> *Make it look good*
> *No matter if it's wrong*
> *Make it look good*

Give you something in common
Like a good song

Well my job's done now
I got to move along
Got to look for the next one
To make 'em do wrong

The Reason Why

Tassha released a very long surge of air from her lungs and let go of all the excruciating pain she felt within. *Maybe this will make him understand,* she uttered to herself as she slammed down her pen in frustration. She was tired of talking to David about Tenner until she was blue in the face, and had written him a letter to tell him so. David wouldn't change his position or his relationship with Tenner. He had explained to Tassha that it was too late to back away. He had already taken the money—and the first poll had him in the lead for the election, which was six months away. Tassha saw David's mindset as selfish, and she'd told him so. They had been working together toward something good, or so she thought, and now she felt violated and ashamed to be associated with him. She picked up the letter to review it one last time before she sealed it and laid it on David's desk.

Dear David,

By now you must know by my distance that I am very upset by your actions. It's been a month or so since I found out about you backing this prison, and, David, I am hurt because I know you know better. I know deep down in your heart you don't believe that this city needs a private prison. You are doing nothing but helping one man. I always thought you were about repairing and rebuilding communities so that others can dream, instead of constructing walls to cage people in. I have been trying to deal with what you told me about Tenner and how he took all of your campaign supporters. But, David, really, do you want your name on the mayor's door that bad that you are willing to forget about your morals and what you truly believe in? Over these last few weeks I have done my own research on private prisons. They are all about money, and are being used to put more and more of our black men in jail. David, just take a minute and use your wisdom, which I have always admired. Why do you think politicians have pushed so hard for the "three strikes and you are locked up for life" policy? Why do you think they made it so five pieces of crack results in more time in prison than five ounces of powdered cocaine? It's to fill these new prisons that are going up all over the country to capacity. Prisons that politicians, lawyers, judges, and very influential people own stock in. That's right, David, stock. I was flat-out flabbergasted to find out that we have private prisons on the stock exchange under names the ordinary person would never recognize. They are paying prisoners twenty to forty cents an hour for doing anything from making leather for car seats and other car parts to telemarketing airline reservations and making blue jeans and shirts. There was even a case where prisoners were shuttled into retail stores to stock shelves at night. I think it's a shame that you're going to back such a thing. Our kids can't get a job on the street but they can go to prison and find all types of work. What kind of society is that? I think you need to be trying to stop this from happening instead of letting these companies manipulate people who are paying a debt to society and who are basically working for free, which, let me remind you, is the definition of slavery. You probably already know this, David. You have associated yourself with one of the most notorious men on this planet, and if you do win the election, you won't be running the city—he will. You will be at his every call, and I don't want anything to do with it. I've decided to move on, and as of today I resign. I don't really think I need to tell you that our relationship is over as well.

I looked up to you not only as my lover, but as a great man. My opinion of you has changed. I'm really sorry that things had to end this way, but I really do feel it's for the best.

Tassha was happy it was Saturday, because she was able to seal her letter and place it on David's desk in solitude. She wasn't wasting any time moving on with her social life either. Ethan had asked her out, and she accepted. They had talked on the phone a couple of times in the last month and it had been delightful. Tassha wanted to move forward with her life even though she was going out with her past, and as she told Artise, "At least I'm going out." She was excited but concerned at the same time about doing so. For the last couple of years she had been seeing David, and he had done everything for her—always picked her up, always drove or had a driver. But this was different. Ethan had asked her to meet him at the museum. Something about venturing out alone sparked her interest. It took the "Daddy's little girl" edge away that David had made his forte. When Tassha finally stepped into the museum it was almost completely dark except for the small lightbulbs that lined the baseboards leading to the auditorium. *Much different from the last time I was in here,* Tassha thought. It was strange to her that Ethan was not waiting for her in the lobby, but the door to the auditorium was wide open. It looked inviting, so Tassha went to take a look. She stood at the entrance and looked down into the auditorium. The lights were dim and Tamia's new album was playing softly over the speaker system. Tassha examined each row of seats, then when her eyes met the center rows of the auditorium she saw a silhouette.

"Ethan! Ethan! It's me, Tassha. Are you here?" she said at the top of her lungs. Tassha squinted her eyes when the silhouette stood up.

"Here I am, Tassha," Ethan said. Tassha smiled.

"What are you doing down there?"

"Waiting for you," he said boldly.

"Waiting for me?"

"That's right. Waiting for you. So we can go on our date."

"Well, are you ready to go?" Tassha asked, still standing in the door.

"Um-hmmm. I'm ready. Come on down here."

"Down where?"

"Down here. Come on and sit with me."

"Ethan, what are you up to?"

"Nothing." Ethan looked into his hand. He took the remote and turned the lights up a little so Tassha could find her way to where he was. "You look very nice, Tassha." She was wearing a dark blue silk pants suit. Tassha giggled but she didn't move. "So are you going to come down here or what?"

"Ethan?" Tassha cried, not understanding what was going on.

"It's okay. Trust me."

"Okay . . . if you say so." Tassha made her way down toward Ethan and at the same time Ethan took a bottle of wine along with two glasses out of the ice bucket that sat on the floor.

"Are you ready for our date?" Ethan asked as Tassha appeared.

"Are you serious?" she asked him.

"I'm serious." Ethan pointed to a roller tray that had chips, dips, M&M's, and other goodies on it.

"Ethan, you are sooo crazy!"

"You think so? Come on, have a seat."

Tassha took a seat and Ethan began to pour the wine into their glasses. "Now that's not the imported stuff that you've been drinking. That's Alize, baby!"

"I like Alize!" Tassha said excitedly. "Don't try to play me like I'm brand-new. Pour me a little more!"

"Are you sure?"

Tassha nodded.

"Well, if you're hungry I have all types of snacks right here on the tray. You know, snacks are good for you when you're watching your favorite movie."

"My favorite movie? You remember my all-time favorite movie?"

"Yep. Sure do. How can I forget a movie in which you think the star looks just like me?"

"Ohh, brother. What is it, then?" Tassha said, taking a sip of her drink. Ethan turned around in his seat until he was looking up at the projector, then pressed the remote. The theme music for the movie came on. Tassha began playfully hitting Ethan on the arm. "Oh, Ethan, no you didn't!" Tassha said, taking another sip and getting comfortable in her chair.

"Ohhh, yes, I did."

"New Jack City!!!" Tassha screamed.

"Dat's righ'! Dat's righ'!" Ethan shouted. Things were looking good.

"I never understood why you cry at the end, Tassha," Ethan snickered.

"I always thought you knew. You want to know why?" Tassha asked.

"Yeah, I want to know."

"He just reminds me of you . . . that's why I cry. He really does."

"Who? Nino?"

"Yep . . . except you have your hair cut shorter. But back in the day, Ethan, you looked just like Nino!"

"You did always used to say that. . . . I just thought you were joking on me. So you think a brother looks like Wesley, huh?" Ethan said, putting his arm around Tassha.

"But you ain't," she teased, then put his arm back where it belonged.

"Ohhh . . . that's cold," Ethan said, equally flirty.

"Ethan, this has been so fun."

"You think so?"

"Yes, I really do."

Ethan paused a second. "At first I didn't know what to do . . . where to take you, Tassha," he admitted. "Seeing how much you have grown."

Tassha shot around and gently hit Ethan on the arm.

"Grown?" She demanded explanation.

"Mentally, Tassha . . . that's all I'm sayin'."

"Oh . . . okay. Well, go ahead then," she said, settling down.

"I just didn't know where to take you, seeing that you've been privileged to the finer things in life since I've been gone."

"Well, Ethan, I'm still the same old person."

"I know. . . . I know," Ethan said, full of thought. Then he noticed she was sitting back in her seat and gazing. "What's wrong?"

"Just thinking about something that has been on my mind for weeks."

"Well, what is it?" Ethan turned to face Tassha.

"Oh, it's just about David."

Ethan sat back in his seat and looked up at the blank screen.

"Oh," Ethan said.

"No . . . no. He just came to mind when I said I was still the same old person."

"Is that right?"

"Yeah. He's changed something terrible, Ethan," Tassha said.

"How so?"

"Well, when we went to the ball I found out that he took campaign money from Ronald Tenner to finance his campaign."

It took a while for Ethan to register what she said. He had thought Tassha was going to start talking about all of the things that David had done for her. Ethan quickly sat back up.

"Tenner?"

"Yeah. That's right."

Ethan just shook his head back and forth.

"David took the money in exchange for his backing of this new private prison Tenner wants to build in the city."

"Man, this guy Tenner has his hand on everyone in the city, doesn't he?"

"What do you mean?"

"Well . . . ," Ethan thought about it for a minute, because Kyle had sworn him to secrecy.

"What is it, Ethan?" Tassha asked.

Ethan looked at Tassha firmly. "You have to promise you won't repeat this, Tassha. I've seen the damage this guy can do."

"I won't say a word."

"Well, you remember the girl I went out with that left her kids in the house alone . . ."

"I remember," Tassha interrupted.

"Well, unbeknownst to me, her brother is the guy you had it out with at the grocery store sometime back, but I never found out that they were related until after she was in prison and her kids—God bless their souls—were in the ground."

"So what's this have to do with Tenner?"

"Well, Monica wasn't on good terms with her brother because he's gay. And this guy supposedly is having an affair or whatever you want to call it with . . . guess who?"

"No," Tassha said, wide-eyed.

"Yep. With Tenner himself."

"Ethan, now, this is crazy!"

"You're telling me?"

Tassha thought for a minute. "But if I remember right, he was with two women the night of the ball. A white girl and a black girl."

Ethan thought for a minute. "What did the black girl look like?" he wondered.

"I didn't really pay attention to her features. But she was pretty though."

"Hmmmm."

"What's wrong?"

Ethan shook his head. "Nothing, but listen to this. The manager who works over at the grocery store asked me to check up on Kyle, and when I went to see him, his face was bashed in."

"And Tenner did it?" Tassha wanted to know.

"That's what Kyle said."

"I warned David about that man. He's just ruthless."

"Oh well," Ethan said. "If David doesn't want to listen, then that's his fault."

"Yeah . . . I know. That's why I decided to start looking for something else to do. I refuse to be working for the possible mayor of this city if he's being controlled by a man like Ronald Tenner."

"You're looking for another job?"

Tassha nodded her head yes.

"Why don't you work here?"

"Here?"

"Yes, here. There's going to be plenty to do—once this place starts jumpin'. We're going to be the only museum of its kind in the country."

Tassha smiled. "Well, you sure seem energized, Ethan."

"I am, Tassha." Ethan looked around. "Look at this place. It's destined for greatness. I'm finally part of something that is meaningful."

Tassha looked at Ethan; his excitement reminded her of earlier times. "Well, I don't know."

"Why not? You and Artise are working on your business venture anyway, and Vance told me that Artise was already talking about the seminars you two will be giving right down there on that stage."

"Well . . . I'll have to think about it. Plus I'll have to talk to Artise and Vance about it."

"Hey, hey now, I'm the director of personnel up in here," Ethan said proudly. "If you want it, you got it."

"Oh, it's like that, huh?"

"Just like that," Ethan said and smiled. Tassha thought for a minute.

"Then that means I will be working for you?"

"Funny how things work out, huh?"

"Well, do you think we can handle that? I mean, we've got history."

"Yeah—I know. And I'm trying to create some more."

"Oh really now?"

"Really. I just need a little time."

"Is that all you need?" Tassha asked.

"I think so. I just need to work on some things which will make me stronger and more committed. Hell, I'm a man, Tassha, and right now, not a very good one. I have to work at it."

Tassha tapped Ethan on his hand. "We all have to work at it, Ethan. All of us."

Have You Ever

"Come on in, son." Stubby had been waiting on Vance since he received his early morning call. Vance had gone home and slept on the couch after his night out with Casey. In the morning he'd slipped on his jogging shoes, sweatpants, and sweatshirt, then told Miz Melba as she stood over the stove cooking breakfast that he would return shortly.

Vance stepped into the screened-in porch and looked around. Mrs. Stubby was usually always a beat behind Stubby, wondering if he needed anything. Stubby noticed Vance was wondering where she was.

"Oh, she's out. Wanted to go handpick some flowers to send to the Clarke family in New York City. One of the sisters from church carried her over so that she could pick out something special for Dr. John Henrick Clarke. We just found out he died, and she's really grieving. He's the gentleman that helped to start the Harlem Writers Guild. Another one of our great leaders in literary history is gone," Stubby agonized.

"Oh yeah, yeah," Vance remembered. "Ethan called to tell me that we received copies of his books. He sure was responsible for a lot of work."

"Yeah, that sure was nice of him. He also had a library of about twenty thousand books. His peoples say they goin' to send us some of those vintage works, too. What a man. We've known him since he proclaimed himself as a Nationalist and Pan-Africanist. Dr. John Henrick Clarke, one of our great literary leaders," Stubby said solemnly. "But we all have to go yonder sometime. . . . What a legacy." Stubby snapped out of his remembrance. "Soooo . . . sit on down. What you want to talk to me about?" They both took a seat on the porch. Vance smiled nervously, embarrassed by the question he was about to pose. He took a deep breath.

"Well . . . it's about suddenly having something you've never had before put in front of your face."

Stubbs's eyes traveled over Vance's whole body and soul. "Boy, what are you mumbling about?" Stubbs asked. "I don't have time like dat to be playing no guessin' games."

Vance swiped his face with his hand. "I'm trying to tell you."

"You're trying to tell me what?"

"Okay . . . okay. Let me put it like this. You remember telling me how the devil was going to test me and throw things at me?"

"Yeah, yeah . . . I remember. I don't remember what day I told you dat. But it sounds like me and it's true," Stubby voiced. Stubbs tried to put two and two together, looking Vance precisely in the eye. Vance looked back at him. "Oh, Vance . . . don't tell me?"

"I'm not saying anything. I just want to know if you ever wanted something that you couldn't have, and what you did when it was time to make your decision."

Stubby shook his head. "No . . . no, son. It's not that easy," Stubbs gritted. "Now, tell me, who she is?"

Vance stared out into the yard, then turned back to Stubby. "Stubbs, this is hard, man."

"Vance, life is hard. . . . Now what's so different about her that you've never had before? Huh?"

"She's white," Vance blurted out. Stubby moved his shoulders back, stunned. Then he glanced around his own house like he was making sure no one could hear them and whispered, "Vance . . . you done got you a white gir'?"

"Wait a minute. Hold on. I didn't go get nobody. She just happened to come into my life, that's all."

"Boy, now you know you're wrong. Even if she was black. You married, boy, and getting ready to have a kid any day."

"Stubby, I know this. That's why I wanted to know if you've ever had something come to you that you never had before. . . . How did you deal with it?"

Stubby thought about his question while he carried the look of disappointment on his face. "Now that I know what you are talking 'bout. Yeah—I've always wondered what it would be like." Stubby raised his eyebrows as best he could. "But I never went and did it," he whispered defiantly. Vance paid attention to his concealment again. "Don't you know . . . back in my day, you get killed for looking at a white gir'?"

"I know . . . I know. But it ain't that day anymore."

"Well, Vance, let me tell you something." Stubbs's eyes shifted right to left. "I don't think there's a black man alive that hasn't thought about bedding a white girl. Oh yeah, Vance, plenty of black men have thought about it, but in my day, you betta' not act on your thoughts or you would find yourself dead somewhere. But I can indeed see why it might cross yo' mind. 'Cause of all the powerful things done to our people. My advice to you is to forget about what you done. You got to move on—try to make amends. What I think you did is horrible, though, Vance. Dang-on horrible." Stubby chuckled a bit, then scratched his head. "My, my, my. You know? Back in my day there was a poem that everybody knew. All the men believed it and everybody treated the words like it was a part of life." Stubby pointed at Vance. "I ain't good at recitin' no dang-on poetry. It ain't what I do. But I know this one like the back of my hand. And I want you to listen, 'cause it make good sense—and right now that's what you need." Vance sat back, not moving his eyes off of Stubby. Stubby cleared his throat.

> *"Ohhh . . . dere's Miz Salley Jay*
> *Turn yo' eyes better not look dat way*
> *No matta' how nice she looks*
> *Eyes stay straight or find yo' neck*
> *In a good tight noose*

"I heard her granddaddy owned a bunch of us
Heard he was father to some of the boys
Who hang out in da cut
Betta' not even think of doing the same
If you plan on taking another breath today

"Don't seem right we can't touch
Her granddaddy touched most of our grandmamas
When he should've been at chu'ch
He tell our grandpappies go . . . and serve da Lord
But make grands' wives stay home keep his bed warm

"Oh dere's Miz Salley Jay
Turn yo' eyes . . . betta' not look dat way"

Stubbs gave Vance a scolding look. He struggled to get to his feet then opened the door to the house. "Son, you listen to me. You got a wife and a kid on da way. Nuffin' is more important than dat. Damn you, Vance, straighten it out, you hear. Straighten it out." Then Stubby walked inside. The gentle sound of the closing door hurt Vance more than if it had been slammed shut.

Something to Tell You

Vance sat on Stubby's porch for thirty minutes trying to make a conscious decision on whether or not to make known to Artise what he had done. Vance hoped that Stubbs would come back out—and tell him what to do. *Besides, I didn't get to tell him everything,* Vance recalled. But it was clear that he had upset the old man something terrible. Now it was time to do what others had always done to him. Tell instead of being told on. Embarrassment and confusion were the components holding Vance's tongue. But he was calm and unruffled because he knew deep down inside what happened was meant to be. Nothing like the other times when he would let the lust and his mighty urge control him. This was ancestral, inherited, passed on through the generations, and it was just his time. Surely Artise would grasp Vance and tell him that she understood. She was his wife now, his helpmate and supporter, with the knowledge to understand. When Vance made it back home Artise was asleep on the couch. Miz Melba told him that she fell asleep right after her breakfast, so Vance watched her slumber while preparing what to tell her, unaware that she was dreaming.

Cathy, Artise, and a little big-eyed baby boy they both called Nadif were enjoying themselves as they played on an oversize blanket at the park. Artise was sitting on one half of the blanket and Cathy on the other side. Both were smiling and looking at Nadif, who had on the exact same pair of Jordans that Artise had seen in the mall, with a matching shorts set and baseball hat, getting ready for what they hoped would be his first steps.

"Okay, Mama . . . you ready?" Artise called over after they had been guiding Nadif with their hands.

"I sure am. I know he's ready now!" Cathy called out.

Artise whispered into her son's ear, "Okay, baby . . . get ready, I'm going to let you go!"

Nadif began to move his legs and mumbled uncontrollably with excitement to his audience as Artise let him go . . .

"Artise . . . Artise . . . Artise?" Vance interrupted, shaking her lightly. Artise awoke from her sleep and saw Vance standing over her. "Baby, I need to talk to you," he told her.

"Awwww, Vance . . . why would you wake me up like that?"

"What?" Vance asked.

"Why did you wake me?"

"Well, you've been sleeping a couple of hours and I've been sitting here waiting for you to wake—I just thought it would be all right."

"Damn it, Vance . . . why did you wake me?" Artise wanted to know and Vance stepped back.

"Look, I'm sorry, baby. I already told you."

"That's no kind of excuse!"

"That's okay . . . go on back to sleep, okay," Vance said then walked toward the door and slowly shut it. Artise stared up at the ceiling and tears began to form in her eyes, knowing her dream might be the last time she would ever see her mother and child together.

Later, in the still of the night, Vance turned to Casey.

"Whew! Now that's the way I like it!" he boasted.

"It really felt good to me that time, Vance. Really good," Casey agreed.

"I don't know how long we can keep this up."

"Why? . . . Why would you say that? It's safe here," Casey said back to Vance.

"Yeah, I know . . . but you don't know my history of being seen when I'm not supposed to in this city. It's like someone follows me around with a damn zoom lens or something."

"Ohhh . . . so you have history?" Casey quipped.

"Don't we all?" Vance joked back.

"So how did I do?" Casey wanted to know.

"You were great, of course."

"I never dreamed what we've done would make me feel this way," Casey acknowledged. "I mean, it's been so enjoyable and peaceful at the same time. It's like an awakening."

"That's what I tried to get you to understand the other night, when I suggested it to you. It feels like you're in an entirely different world."

Casey looked at Vance and seriously deliberated if she should tell him about Tenner's plan. She looked at him as he sat still, his eyes gleaming; he was also in thought about the moment. *Why should I?* she suddenly decided while Vance caught her eyes and smiled. *He doesn't need to know, no one does. This entire situation has turned enormously personal and I really feel like it was meant to be, and to hell with Tenner.* Casey returned from her thoughts with all sorts of energy. "You want to do it again?" Vance shook his head no. "What's wrong, Vance?"

"I tried to tell Artise today."

"You did!"

"Yeah . . . I thought it would be for the best."

"What happened?"

"Nothing. . . . I woke her up so that I could talk to her, and she just about had a heart attack, so I didn't say anything about it."

"Vance, think about it. It's probably better she finds out when the time is right. The less on her mind the better, don't you think?"

"Yeah . . . you're probably right. You're probably right. Well, we better go. I have a big day tomorrow," Vance said.

"Do you mind dropping me off at Whispers?" Casey wanted to know.

"Whispers?" Vance asked.

"Yeah. I'm in the mood to hear a little more music, after a night like tonight. I'll take a cab home from there."

"Okay . . . yeah, sure. I can do that."

After closing the car door for Casey and beginning the short journey to Whispers, Vance began thinking about the poem Stubby had recited. He began to feel uneasy while he drove down the dark city streets. Stubby's passion and realism hadn't sunk in back on the old man's porch, but with Casey in the car with him in the still of the night his words found their way into the car. Vance looked over at Casey and gave her a nervous smile. He pushed the electric locks down in his Taurus, and they locked after a slight delay. Casey could feel Vance's nervousness and looked over at him. Suddenly three sharp blasts of light illuminated the whole car, forcing Casey and Vance to squint their eyes. Vance tried to look back and see who was behind him in the rearview mirror, but the high beams were flashed again and his eyes were overtaken by rays. Vance pulled over to the side of the road, then he raised his rearview mirror so that the lights reflecting off of his mirror would have less of an effect on his eyes.

"Why would the police pull us over?" Casey asked. Then she suddenly remembered the special news report concerning racial profiling she had watched with Ethan and became nervous. Vance was frantic; all he had on his mind was Stubby's poem. He went into his glove compartment to retrieve his license and registration before he was even asked, then he placed his hands on the steering wheel so they could be seen: he wanted to be ready; he didn't want any trouble. In seconds there was tapping on the driver's-side window. Vance rolled down his window.

"What's up!" Ethan said, smiling from ear to ear before he noticed Casey on the passenger's side.

"Ohhh, Ethan. . . . Negro, you almost gave me a heart attack!" Vance said, sighing with relief.

"I bet I did." Ethan took a closer look into the car. "Hey, Casey—small world, isn't it?"

"Hello, Ethan!" Casey said back to him, blind to his sarcasm.

"So what's going on? I didn't know you two knew each other," Ethan said.

"Just dropping Casey off at Whispers," Vance said.

"No joke? That's where I'm going! Well, let's all go, so you can fill me in on how you two met," Ethan said as he turned to walk back to his car.

Casey turned to Vance. "Well, looks like you finally get to tell someone."

Just Sweatin'

Melba looked over at Artise while she slept on the couch. Artise was resting easy now after the two had watched television for most of the night. Melba was tired as well. She'd had an excruciating day, and as she began to play back what had gone down, she drank the rest of the water she couldn't seem to get enough of.

She had never been in a sauna, Miz Melba thought as she wrapped herself in towels and prepared to step into very unfamiliar waters. Melba had never been big on fitness—maybe a walk or two or occasional diet—but with all the years of chasing down kids, cooking, and cleaning, there was no need for her to sit in a hot, steamy box and sweat. But she reminded herself that she had to enter the sweltering chamber to cool down a situation which was about to blow out of control. Melba didn't like the decline she saw in Artise, and she thought that if she didn't get any better she might even have trouble delivering her baby. The strong, courageous, independent lady full of dreams and aspirations that Melba had met at the mall had become bitter, snappy, quick-tempered. It was not how Melba thought Artise should start the new chapter in her life as mother and wife.

"That's Cathy," Melba said to herself as she stood close to the entrance of the sauna. Artise had pictures of her mother all around the house, and from all Artise's talk about her mother's comings and goings, anyone could have figured out she went to the spa three times a week at twelve noon. Cathy had never seen Melba before, so when Cathy walked past her to enter the sauna she had no idea who Melba was. Melba held her breath, opened the door, then walked in after her. She exhaled deeply and tried to find her regular breathing pace.

"Whew! It's hot in here!" Melba sat down next to Cathy. "No wonder nobody else is in here," Melba said.

"Yeah . . . that could be the reason," Cathy said back to her.

"I believe it is!"

"Is this your first time here?" Cathy asked. "I've never seen you here before."

"Yes . . . as a matter of fact it is. My name is Melba."

Cathy looked at Melba because her name quickly registered. Cathy put a how-dare-you smile on her face. "Unbelievable." Cathy continued to shake her head, then she adjusted her towel around her chest as if to shield herself from Melba. Melba sensed her attitude immediately and didn't want to waste Cathy's time or stay in that damn sauna any longer than she had to.

"You don't have to worry, I'll make this quick."

"Why would you say that?"

"Just noticed your posture when you figured out who I was."

"So . . ." Cathy thought about Artise for a second. "No wonder Artise likes you so much. You seem to do the same thing she does."

"Which is?" Melba asked, broadening her eyes.

"Analyzing. . . . Always trying to piece together how I'm feeling, what I'm thinking."

"Well, you know? Body language, facial expression, and attitude always give a person away."

"Listen. I think it was a bad idea for you to come here. I don't know what you thought you were going to do by coming to meet with me. But I don't have anything to say to you."

Melba wiped the sweat that had started to bead up on her face. "I just wanted to come and see for myself."

"See what?"

"Just see if things were as bad off between you and your daughter as it seems."

"I don't know what Artise has told you, but—"

Melba cut her off. "Artise hasn't said anything to me to make me form an opinion of you. I just know there's a problem between you two, and I know it needs to stop. Quite frankly, I believe you both need to ease up."

"Umph. . . . It's none of your business," Cathy told Melba.

"I think it is. Any time I see a bright young lady that I care about begin to let her problems affect her health and her relationships, I'll make it my business if I think I can help."

"What do you mean? Affect her health?"

"Cathy . . . Artise isn't well. She had in her mind for so long that you were going to be in her life when she became pregnant and now that you've shut her out it's affecting how she is carrying that baby."

"Well, I don't know why."

"Maybe because you always told her that you were going to be there for her . . . to help her out when this time in her life came along. But she's pregnant now . . . and you're nowhere to be found. And, Cathy . . . she's hurting."

"I don't think you know what you're talking about," Cathy sharply replied.

"Cathy, come on. We're both women. Women who are old enough to know when enough is enough. I have seen changes in Artise that are dangerous."

"I don't see how any of this has anything to do with me."

"Well, I can tell you, Cathy. It has everything to do with you because you are the only topic that seems to be on her mind when we're talking. Let me tell you something. Eight out of ten conversations that I have with Artise a day are about the two of you." Cathy turned her head and wiped her forehead . . . not wanting to hear. "So that's telling me you have everything to do with this."

"No it doesn't."

"Cathy, why are you so quick to say this problem has nothing to do with you? Whenever my daughter and I have any type of disagreement, we just settle it. Life is too short."

"Not that it's any of your business . . . but Artise and I have always been like this," Cathy said.

"Well, that doesn't mean things can't change. I think you two need to seriously sit down and talk. There are too many issues between you two."

"That's just the nature of our relationship."

"Well, is it the nature of your relationship for your daughter to ask me to be with her when she delivers her baby instead of you?" Melba could see Artise all through Cathy.

"She asked you that?" Cathy was surprised.

"Yes, she did. And to tell you the truth, it's not my place."

"Well, don't do it."

"But she wants someone with her besides Vance, and if you don't do it I will."

Cathy looked at Melba and wiped at the sweat that was really beginning to pour down her face.

Early in the Morning

Ethan looked at his watch: 3:45 A.M. "I'm calling anyway," he mumbled. "I can't believe this." Ethan continued to ramble. There was no hiding his passion—he was being pulled by vindication. He had silently exonerated himself on the way home from Whispers. *Doesn't look like I'm the only misguided soul around here after all, does it,* Ethan had told himself. All the info Casey knew about Tenner and everyone he had under his command had been told. The facts about the prison, the fire, David, and Kyle had all been laid on the table, including why Casey was under Tenner's dominate control. It nearly gave him the feeling of happiness. But seeing Vance with Casey was mind-blowing to the point where he wanted to take Vance to the woodshed. But so much had been thrown into his lap at one time. Ethan was down to his last sip of coffee when the night's events began to run through his mind again.

"So tell me, what's going on?" Ethan quickly said to Vance as he picked up his glass of water and slurped it down. Vance looked around. Casey had gone to the restroom.

"What do you mean? I told you before, I was giving her a lift."

"Uuh-uh. Nope," Ethan grumbled, wiping his mouth. "How did you meet her and what were you two doing before you decided to give her a ride is what I want to know," Ethan said in a disdainful tone of voice. Vance took a deep breath.

"Well, I met her through the insurance company. She's a claims examiner." Ethan's eyes crumpled. "What are you talking about? She works at Snyders. Matter of fact, she's doing my old job."

Vance's eyes widened. "No . . . no . . . no . . . no . . . no . . . She works for the insurance company that insures the museum. She brought

over the report from the blaze and check for my claim. That's how we met."

"Well, looks like she has two jobs, then—and I don't know how she's doing it with the hours she's working at the store," Ethan pointed out.

"I couldn't tell you," Vance said.

"Well, let's just wait and see, because something's not right."

"Yeah . . . let's do that." It was quiet for a couple of seconds.

"So how's Artise?" Ethan didn't hide his sarcasm. He waited for Vance to answer while he stuffed his mouth with pretzels.

"She's fine." Then Casey came back to the table.

"Okay, guys, I'm back." One look at Vance's and Ethan's faces and Casey knew she had some explaining to do, and that's what she did.

"Who would have thunk it?" Ethan mumbled as he chugged down the rest of his coffee. "That sucker ain't getting my vote now." He dialed Tassha's phone number. "Come on, Tassha, pick up," he said into the phone as he looked at the coffeepot and realized he had drunk a whole pot while obsessively going over what he had learned. Soon afterward he heard the most disturbed voice in the eastern standard time zone.

"Hel . . . llo," Tassha struggled to say.

"Hello, Tassha?" Ethan asked, speaking way too loudly.

"Ummmm-hmmmm," Tassha answered, pulling the phone away from her ear.

"It's Ethan."

"Ummmm-hmmmm."

"We need to talk."

"Ummmm-hmmmmmm."

"Damn. . . . There's so much I need to talk to you about, I don't even know where to start." There was no response. "Tassha?"

"Ummmm-hmmmmm," Tassha said again.

"Look, you need to get up for this."

"I'm up. . . ."

"Listen . . . I was going out to get something to eat at Whispers tonight, and guess who I ran into?" There was no answer. "Tassha?" Ethan called out.

"Yeah. . . . Who, Ethan? . . . Listen, if you expect me to talk to you like it's the middle of the day, you might as well forget it. . . . So take my silence as listening."

"Okay, got it. Anyway, I ran into Vance. And if things weren't as deep as they are, I would never, ever tell you this, because Vance is my boy." Ethan sounded like he'd had more coffee than his body could handle. Ethan was still waiting for some response from Tassha. "Anyway, I spot his car driving down Broad Street. This was about ten-thirty, eleven. So I flash my brights right into his car and he stops like I'm the police or something. I don't know what was on that boy's mind. So I get out my car. Tap on the windows, and as soon as he rolled down the window I see Vance in the car with this white girl named Casey, who I used to work with at the supermarket."

"What?" Tassha said. She sounded like she had raised up from her bed.

"I knew that would get you up. That reminds me . . . Vance never did tell me what they were doing together," Ethan rambled on.

"Ethan, what's all this about?"

"Tassha, it's all about deception, fraud, arson, blackmail, trickery, and sex."

"With who. . . . Vance?" Tassha asked.

"No. With Vance, Casey, me, you, Kyle . . . and David."

"With David? . . . Who's Kyle? Ethan, have you been drinking?"

"No, I just found out some things tonight that are going to rock your world."

"Ethan, what are you talking about?"

"Go fix yourself a hot pot of coffee and call me back."

"What?"

Ethan slowed down his frantic pace. "Tassha, I'm serious. We need to talk," he explained.

"Okay . . . give me fifteen minutes." Tassha struggled out of her bed and Ethan hung up the phone, remaining still until it rang.

Fess Up

The wide double doors to David's office were flung open and there stood Tassha looking directly at David. What Ethan told her about David's role in the fire that had come close to killing her had put her over the top. But she wanted to hear it from the culprit's mouth. *And he had the nerve to act like he cared about me after the fire,* Tassha had thought on her way over. *David told me he loved me. That's not love, it's betrayal.* She had other things on her mind as well. She couldn't believe how Ethan let Vance and Casey duck his questions about the two of them being together. But she and Ethan had evaluated the situation, looked at Vance's history, and come up with the conclusion that once again he was playing foul. All she could do was think of her little friend Artise, carrying the weight of their child and trying to hammer out her problems with her mother at the same time. There was no way Tassha or Ethan was going to upset Artise with the information—not now, anyway. From David, to Tenner, to Casey, to Karen or Kyle. Tassha had the brought-up-to-date blues, and she was ready to get some answers. David rushed out from his office to see Tassha, thinking maybe she had changed her mind about quitting her job.

"Tassha, sweetheart," David said in a rushed manner.

"David, please. Don't 'sweetheart' me."

David pulled back. "I honestly think I owe you an explanation concerning the things you said in your letter."

Tassha looked stunned, then hauled off and smacked David. "I'd rather hear about the fire!" she shouted. David stood rigid. The fact that Tassha knew about the fire hurt him more than the stinging handprint that was left on the side of his face. "So . . . ?" Tassha persisted, arching her eyebrows. David walked a few steps away then turned back around to face her.

"Tassha, it's like this."

"I'm listening."

"I didn't have anything at all to do with the fire. You have to believe me."

"David, it will be hard for me to believe anything that comes out of your mouth."

"Well, I'm telling you the truth. I got a phone call from someone, and they told me to go out to the site because there was something that I had to do."

Tassha thought for a minute. "Like what?"

"Tenner wanted it to be a forum for me to pitch the new prison. You know, work spin on the situation."

"And you did it!" Tassha screamed.

"I had no choice, Tassha. I didn't know you were going to be in the fire. . . . I had already taken the money," David said dejectedly.

"David, you really disgust me. You're letting Tenner pimp you. That's what he's doing, David. David, you're nothing but a ho!" Tassha screamed out loud. David had never seen Tassha so animated, and there was no way that he could handle her—her anger was too thick. "I think everyone needs to hear about this—everyone in the city," Tassha said, then spun around and began to walk out.

"Tassha, wait . . . wait. You don't have to do this."

"Yes I do, David. You're working for a thug who is trying to set up a venue to put most of the people who are going to vote for you in jail. I thought you were a lot smarter than that!"

David sunk into the office chair. "So, what . . . what do I have to do?" David said, defeated. Tassha turned back, shut the door to his office, and sat down across from him to give it to him straight.

Breaking It Down

The more Tassha thought about David's dealings with Tenner, and everything she ever learned from her father concerning justice, the more fuel was put on the fire. She wanted to bring Tenner down. She couldn't do it alone though and asked Ethan to help. The two made off like private detectives through the night, drinking coffee after coffee, putting two and two together, attempting feverishly to figure out everything that had been unfolding right before their eyes.

Ethan turned to Tassha, who was driving her car. "So that's everything you know about David and Tenner, huh?"

"That's it," Tassha recalled. "Tenner got all of David's financiers to stop backing David's campaign. Then the scumbag approached David about backing the prison that he wanted to build in the same building as the museum. He said if David got behind the prison, he would return David's endorsers."

"Then he set the museum on fire, hoping Vance would give the building up," Ethan interjected.

"And almost killing us at the same time, I might add," Tassha remembered. "Did you tell Vance about any of this?"

"Yes, I told him, but I'm not over him stepping out with Casey on Artise. And to make things worse, he still sidesteps my questions about what they were doing together." Tassha gave Ethan a quick sarcastic glance up and down. "What?" Ethan wanted to know.

"You're just saying that?"

"Tassha, I'm surprised at you," he responded. His voice was higher-pitched than normal. "Yeah, Vance is my boy. But Artise is about to have their child. With all I've been through, you know I can't condone what he's doing." They were silent for a moment.

Tassha tapped Ethan on the leg as she began to park the car. Ethan smiled at the touch of her hand. "Okay, I believe you," she said.

"Thank you. And you don't have to move your hand."

"So how well do you know Kyle?"

"I've known him for a long, long time."

"I hope he doesn't start that attitude he had with me at the grocery store."

"Naww, doubt it."

"Why?"

" 'Cause he was just going through some things. I think that's why he was acting up with all the customers."

"Must have been serious."

"He told me that he loved this guy Tenner."

"Loved him?"

"And said that Tenner told him the same."

Tassha thought for a minute. "Guess that goes to show you how deep love really is."

"I guess."

"So you think he'll talk?"

"He has been lately. I spent an hour or so over at his place and I have to be honest, he really surprised me with his insight on love."

"Oh really now. Want to share it with me?"

"Naww, but I'll tell you this. Most of what he said to me was concerning you."

"Me? What about me?"

"Aww damn, we're here. Maybe later," Ethan teased.

Ethan knocked on Kyle's door and Tassha stood right beside him. They could hear music and singing from inside.

"Somebody's in a good mood," Tassha said as the door opened.

Ethan looked confused. "Is Kyle here?" he asked the lady who opened the door.

"Hey, Ethan!" she sang as she stood in the doorway draped in a housecoat and slippers. "Come on in."

Ethan looked back at Tassha and shrugged his shoulders. Tassha squinted her eyes trying to remember where she had seen the lady before.

"I don't think I remember you," Ethan said as he stepped inside. He focused his eyes on the dark-skinned lady. She had long, straight black hair. Her face was flawless and her cheekbones were beaming and went perfectly with her eloquent, slanting deep eyes.

"Ethan don't be silly. It's me." There was a pause and Ethan looked at Tassha, stumped.

"Me who?"

"Kyle!" Karen sang.

"Kyle?" Ethan and Tassha both let go. Tassha covered her mouth.

"Uh-uh. Karen." Then Karen turned her head to Tassha. "I see you're making progress, Ethan. How are you, Ms. Thang, nice seeing you again."

Tassha smiled. "Hey, girl." Ethan turned his head quickly toward Tassha and put his index finger up to his lips and Tassha pushed it away.

Karen smiled. "It's okay, believe me it's okay. So what brings you over?"

"Well, uhhh, see, this sure is a shock." Ethan couldn't believe how different Kyle looked and was very uncomfortable looking at him while he spoke, so he turned his eyes to the ground. "Kyle, I mean, Karen, we need to talk to you about Tenner," Ethan stumbled.

"What about?"

"We need you to help us bring him down. He's done some terrible things. We're trying to get together everyone he's hurt and make him realize that if he doesn't stop his ruthless tactics then we're going to the press about him. But we need everyone to be a part of this or it won't work." Ethan looked at Tassha when he was finished.

Karen blew on her nails. "I don't have anything to say against him. Matter of fact, I'm seeing him tonight."

"Tonight?"

"Hmmm-hmm. He called me this morning and told me that he wanted to see me. I told you Ethan, he loves me," Karen said, relieved.

"He doesn't love anybody. He can't love," Ethan said.

"Sorry, but he loves me."

Ethan shook his head, not believing what he was hearing. "Did he love you when he beat you?" he asked.

Karen took her eyes off her nails and stared directly at Ethan.

"Look, I'm sorry, okay? It's just that David, Casey, and Vance are all down with this. All we need is you and we can move forward and forget about all of this."

Karen shook her head. "Ethan, I know you said we were friendly. But really, I have to get ready. It takes some time to do what I do and tonight sounds like a big night for me."

Ethan gasped. "No problem . . . ," he said, then he and Tassha turned around and walked out the door. Then Karen peeked her head out the door.

"Ethan . . . I'm going to see Monica next week. You want to go with me?"

Ethan huffed. "I'll have to get back to you on that, okay?"

"Okay," Karen said back. "Bye, Ms. Thang."

Later the same night, Ethan and Tassha ended up on the couch in his apartment, waiting for Vance to arrive. Tassha took a good look around at Ethan's place. The walls were covered with nice pictures and the leather on his couch was soft as a feather.

"I don't remember you having this nice furniture when we were together."

"Hey, what can I say. When I moved to Atlanta I became a connoisseur," Ethan boasted.

Tassha ran her hand across the leather. "Where did this leather come from? Italy?"

"Naww, southside of Atlanta," Ethan joked.

"You still crazy."

"And still know a deal when I see one too." He moved over closer to Tassha. "So, you want to go out on a real date, once this is all over?"

"I thought we already had a real date."

"Well, a real second date?"

"Sure. Why not?"

Ethan put his arm around Tassha and looked at her deeply. "You know, I sure have missed you," he said as he began moving forward to kiss her lips.

"Is that right?" Tassha purred as she licked her lips, getting ready to see if Ethan could still kiss. Then the doorbell rang and Tassha pushed Ethan away. "Better get that," she instructed.

Ethan opened the door and Vance walked in and surveyed the mood.

"Bad time?" Ethan and Tassha shook their heads no. Vance sat down across from Tassha in one of the two chairs that flanked the couch.

"So is everyone coming aboard for the plan?"

"Just David and Casey. Kyle doesn't want anything to do with it. Matter of fact, he's going out. Well, Karen's going out. With Tenner, tonight."

"We'll just have to do with what we've got and hope it's enough."

Tassha moved her body up from the couch. "Before we start talking about our plan, Vance, I want to know what you and Casey are up to. Because if you're doing what I think you are, I'm telling you, after Artise has your child, I'm going to tell her."

"You won't have to because she'll know by then."

"What?" Ethan asked.

"Look, don't worry about it, okay? All you have to know is that I love my wife and I would never do anything to hurt her and that's all I'm saying." Tassha and Ethan looked at one another then the phone rang.

"Hello?" Ethan said.

"Hello, Ethan, it's Karen, I mean Kyle. Can we talk?"

The Deal

It was finally time to talk to the man behind the drama. All the players were to assemble at the DoubleTree Hotel at exactly twelve noon to put their plan into motion. Kyle surprised everyone when he called Ethan and told him he would help them bring Tenner down. He was fed up. Tenner had once again become violent on their date and began to use Karen as a punching bag. But this time Karen managed to get away and realized while she struggled with Tenner's drunk arrogance that he was never going to change. Kyle was nervous and didn't know if he could go through with the plan, though, because the surprise they'd arranged for Tenner would surely give him the shock of his concealed homosexual life.

David was extremely happy he was being given another chance to renew his political career without his misdeeds ever reaching the media and ruining his political future. He was determined to get back on the right track and capitalize on his front-runner status as soon as he had cleared his business with Tenner. David hadn't gotten a chance to express his regret to Tassha in the proper setting. Tassha had become distant, but it was on the top of his list to let her know that he was truly sorry for betraying her trust and hoped that they could remain friends.

Casey, on the other hand, was relieved that her situation was going to be settled. She no longer bore the burden of knowledge about the terrible accident which Tenner turned into a stone-cold blackmail scheme despite his promise to straighten everything out for her.

After finding out how ruthless Tenner actually was Vance had no problem going along with the plan and wanted very much to get the whole situation behind him so that he could prepare for his child and the surprise for Mrs. Stubblefield.

Casey started it off. She called Tenner and told him to meet her in the lobby of the hotel. She had good news about her successful seduction of Vance, she told him. There wasn't a tape, she said, but if need be, she could easily get Vance in bed again. Tenner didn't waste any time and arrived at their designated meeting spot five minutes early, dressed as sharp as a knife. He made himself comfortable in the lobby, sitting with his legs crossed. His goons were only steps away from him. Then all of a sudden David walked through the revolving door with Vance at his side. Tenner noticed him right away.

"Tenner," David said strictly, as he and Vance stopped right in front of where he sat. Tenner waved his boys off.

"David? What brings you out this way?" Tenner looked over at Vance for explanation.

"Just thought I'd introduce you to someone." David pointed to Vance. "This gentleman here is the owner of the property you are so enthused about setting your prison on."

"Now, David, you know I don't discuss those things in public," Tenner said smoothly. "How did you know I was here, anyway?"

"You're not hard to find," David said back. "Soon it's going to be my job to make sure I know where everyone is at all times."

"That's the spirit!" Tenner said. "Have a seat. You know, you're starting off on the right track, David, by bringing him to me so that we can strike a deal. I would never want his wife to find out about this. Cheating these days can be very, very messy. So, you here to strike a deal or what?" Tenner lit up a smoke. Vance gazed at him, then he and David sat down.

"There won't be any deals here, Tenner," Vance said with plenty of attitude.

"You wait one minute, boy," Tenner directed and Vance fought like hell to control himself. "You're in no position to make any type of decision here. Any minute now the details of your infidelity will be in my possession, and I'm quite sure your wife would like to hear about it too. Don't ya thank?"

"That's what we're here to talk about," David interrupted.

"We?" Tenner smiled. "Now, David, have you done gone to the other side? Now that's not good politics. I'm sure you know that."

"Shut the fuck up, Ronald," David said. "I'm really tired of your mouth."

Tenner's boys looked at Tenner and he calmed them down with a hand signal. Tenner smiled. "What's this all about, huh? . . . You want to give me the land for my silence? Or give me some money to take it off your hands? What's it going to be?"

Vance looked at David. "This guy does think he's Al Capone, doesn't he?" Vance asked David. "Look, we're not here to deal anything. You got that, boy? I am here to save you some trouble."

Tenner took a drag from his cigarette then pointed the cigarette in Vance's direction. "What the hell is he talkin' about?"

"I think you better listen to the man," David said. Tenner took another drag from his cigarette, still unfazed. Vance inched up from his seat and clasped his hands together.

"Now, it's my understanding that you want my property to build some private prison so that you and a gang of crooked business partners can make millions of dollars."

Tenner blew smoke into Vance's face. "Along with the mayor, here," Tenner said. Vance gave David a knowing glance.

"Sorry—he rolls with me now," Vance said. "Now look . . . this doesn't have to be difficult. There are only a couple of things that I want . . . and I want them all . . . and won't settle for any less."

"You must be out of your mind. You don't hold any cards here." Tenner sneered.

"That's where you're wrong. I hold all the cards."

"Like what?"

"I hold the blackmail card. I hold the arson card. Oh yeah, and the assault card and the illegal campaign funding card."

Tenner looked over at David, and David shrugged his shoulders.

"Looks like a full house to me," David chimed in.

"I have no idea what you're talking about," Tenner said.

"Well, I don't like to reveal my hand, but in this case I will."

Tenner cocked his head to hear better, at the same time taking a puff of his cigarette.

"Blackmail card—that would be Casey. Casey has been doing dirty work for you for years, not to mention holding down bedroom chores as well, for your silence. You've been blackmailing her ever since she came to you after accidentally hitting that little boy on his bike. She wanted to go to the police and you told her not to because she was running one of your illegal errands, so you smoothed things out."

"I did no such thing."

"We have evidence that you did."

"So, so what?" Tenner asked, unfazed.

"I want you to leave her alone and let her go, for one. She no longer works for you. Is that understood?"

Tenner snickered. "Casey would never tell you anything about me."

"Are you sure about that?" Casey appeared suddenly, as if on cue. She looked right into Tenner's eyes and nodded her head yes, as she walked past them and took a seat across the lobby in the dining area. "Do you think I'm bluffing now?" Tenner didn't answer.

"Here's my illegal campaign funding card." David smirked at Vance's nerve.

Vance pointed to David. "David here will have no problem at all going to the authorities and telling them about your thugs who torched my building and the money you had his supporters take from him."

David interrupted. "I'll let them know how you showed up and offered me the exact same money that I had already raised from my supporters, you asshole." Tenner gave David a snarling look.

"He wants out and he owes you nothing," Vance said.

"You know . . . these are nothing but threats," Tenner said, looking a little nervous.

"Oh, you think so?" Vance asked. Then he moved closer to Tenner so that his bodyguards couldn't hear what he was saying. "I want you to do me a favor and look over to the right at the gentleman standing by the front desk."

Tenner turned his head and looked.

Kyle was standing in a white buttoned-down shirt and blue jeans. When his eyes made contact with Tenner it was like he was frozen. Tassha and Ethan were sitting in the lobby watching Tenner look at Kyle. They noticed the frightened expression on Kyle's face, then Ethan made his way over to Kyle.

"So, what about him?" Tenner asked.

"So? Is that all you can say?" Vance said back to him. "Well, I know that man's real name. But you know it as Karen."

Tenner's eyes became violently red-shot and he sat up in his chair. He stared at Kyle. He had never in his life seen Karen as a man. Kyle looked back at Tenner, full of hurt feelings from the beatings and abuse, and his eyes began to water.

"Hang in there, friend," Ethan said, coming up alongside Kyle. Kyle took his eyes off of Tenner and smiled at Ethan and nodded his head.

"Looks different, huh?" Vance provoked. "You should've seen him after the night of the ball when you beat him senseless for no reason." Tenner snapped his head around and looked at Vance, surprised that he knew.

"My . . . my . . . my. I bet all of your big brutal bodyguards and all of your big-time associates would be surprised at what you do behind closed doors . . . huh, Tenner? You think I should tell your boys here who that guy really is standing over there? Let them know what type of ladies' man you really are? I'm sure they remember Karen." Tenner gave Vance a doubting glance, so Vance leaned back in his seat and pointed to one of Tenner's bodyguards.

"No . . . no," Tenner said, clearing his throat. "We don't have to do that. Listen, there's no reason at all why I can't build my prison some-place else."

"Not in my city," David snapped.

"No . . . no, of course not," Tenner whimpered.

"And David, Casey, and Kyle? You'll leave them alone, right?" Tenner scanned the room at them. "Yeah . . . sure," he agreed.

"Now let me show you one more thing," Vance said, "just to let you know how serious I am about this. You see those gentlemen standing over there?" Vance pointed to two men who were standing by a window in the lobby next to Tassha. "They work for Channel Ten, and they were asked here because I told them there was going to be a big scandal that their viewers might think was very newsworthy. Now, if I ever hear of you harassing anybody else, I promise to you"—Vance moved closer to Tenner's face—"I will personally make sure they get the story of a lifetime about the Great Ronald Tenner." Vance and Tenner locked eyes, then Vance looked down at the cigarette in Tenner's hand and took it out of his hand and smashed it in the ashtray that sat on the table between them. "And I mean that. Deal?"

Tenner stood up, straightened out his suit, and looked at Vance and David. "Deal." Tenner gathered his horses and walked away.

Three Weeks Later

Vance was a nervous wreck. He'd been sitting at the kitchen table going over his personnel roster—which now included Tassha as the public relations manager, and Kyle as the circulation manager—when he heard Melba holler for him at the top of her voice.

"Vance—go get the car! It's time for your child to come into the world!"

When Vance had heard those words, a great big smile appeared on his face and he darted out to get the car. Melba had told Vance earlier that morning that she had a feeling Artise would soon be ready, so they had prepared together for the stress and worked on how to keep Artise nice and calm during the short drive to the hospital.

Vance hadn't become nervous until Artise answered a loud and thunderous "No!" to the doctor when asked if she wanted a shot of epidural anesthesia. Vance was happy she'd decided not to take the shot. His knees buckled when he saw the long needle the doctor wanted to insert into her back. Vance had almost thought he would faint after the doctor took off his gloves and told everyone that Artise was at least an hour away. Miz Melba grabbed a room pager and said she needed to sit down a spell in the lobby, but Vance didn't move one bit. He stood beside Artise and held on to the bed rail and helped her get through her thunderous contractions.

312

"So . . . maybe I brought you in a little too early, huh, babe?" Vance asked as he wiped Artise's forehead with a wet cloth.

"It's all right, baby. Better early than too late."

"So you ready to do this?" Vance asked.

"Ummm-hmmmmm," Artise sang as she felt another contraction coming on. Vance could see the anticipation and pain on her face. . . . There was nothing he could do. So he just let nature take its course. Vance stood there feeling Artise's pain like he was having the contractions himself.

"You all right? Do I need to ring for the doctor?" Vance asked. Artise shook her head no. "Baby, you're doing well. I'm proud of you, okay?"

"Ummm-hmmmm," Artise answered.

"I just need you to stay focused. Stay mental and concentrate for me all the way through . . . and it will be just fine. Try to close your eyes and relax." Artise nodded then laid her head back on her pillow, taking deep breaths. Vance thought it was a good time to just let her rest, so he stayed quiet. About twenty minutes had passed by when the hospital door slowly opened. Vance looked at Artise as she rested, then left her side.

"Hey. How are you?" Vance whispered to Cathy.

"Fine," she said.

"How did you know?"

"Mamas always do," Cathy whispered. Vance smiled and gave her a hug. "I'll be right outside the door, okay?"

"Sure . . . sure," Cathy said, looking over at her daughter. Cathy walked over to the bed and just stared at Artise. Cathy kept an eye on her while she positioned herself for another contraction.

"That's right, baby. You get yourself comfortable," Cathy encouraged. Artise opened her eyes.

"Mama!" Then her contraction grabbed her and she had to deal with it.

"That's right, baby . . . just breathe . . . breathe," Cathy instructed. Artise couldn't wait until her pain subsided to talk to her mother.

"Ohhh . . . Mama. . . . Thank you for coming."

Cathy smiled. "I wouldn't miss this for nothin'," she said. "Now, baby girl, just relax. I don't want you to waste any of your energy, okay?"

Artise didn't say a word, she just reached over and grabbed Cathy's outstretched hand and felt all the unwanted stress in her body slowly evaporate. Artise pointed to the table next to the bed.

"Mama?"

"Yes?" Cathy answered.

"I want some water."

Cathy took the cup off of the table and moved it up to Artise's mouth. At the same time Artise raised her hand and put it around the cup. Their hands touched and together they controlled the cup.

"Thank you," Artise said.

"You're welcome," Cathy told her.

Thirty minutes had passed and Artise was still struggling with labor pains. They were hitting hard now, becoming closer and closer. Melba and Cathy along with the midwife were calling out instructions, then all of a sudden the doctor came in, put on his gloves, and hollered, "Showtime!" as Vance watched with pride.

Four weeks had passed, and both Artise and Vance had gotten the change of their lives. Nadif was only sleeping two or three hours at a clip before he started letting the entire house know that there was a new boss in town. Melba was still coming over to the house during the day, but Artise was really in heaven when her mother started coming over to the house at six every night and staying until Melba arrived the next morning. Melba's talk and very welcomed phone call when Artise was in labor had brought the two back together again, and now Cathy wanted to make sure her grandson was getting everything he needed. Artise and Cathy hadn't talked yet about their problems, but one day out of the blue, while Nadif slept carefree within the confines of Grandma's arms, they began to talk.

"Mama, do you still drink your coffee black?"

"Sure do. Until I die."

Artise shook her head. "I don't know how you do it."

"I've always drank it black."

"I know. But the taste—I'm going to put three sugars and cream in mine," Artise boasted. Artise set Cathy's coffee down in front of her then reached into the cabinet and pulled out a basket of Mrs. Fields cookies. "This should do it right here!" Artise took a sip of her coffee. It seemed to give her a charge. "So what do you want to talk about?"

Cathy looked at her cup and ran her fingers around its contour. "About the visitor I had weeks ago who made me realize that we needed to sit down and talk."

"A visitor?"

"Ummm-hmmm."

"Who?"

"Melba." *Miz Melba,* Artise thought, *the guardian angel, the peacemaker.* She shook her head and smiled. "You know . . . she's all right. We have a lot in common," Cathy said, as if reading Artise's mind.

"Is that so?" Artise smiled.

"Sure do. You know she met me in the sauna at the club and we talked."

"Miz Melba in the sauna?" Artise giggled at the unbelievable image.

"She hung in there too," Cathy confirmed.

"Wait until I see her tomorrow." They became quiet for a while. Artise grabbed a chocolate chip cookie from the basket. "So what did she have to say?"

Cathy looked at Artise. "Well, it's really what she made me understand," she confessed.

"Oh?"

"Yes. We sat down and talked about mother-and-daughter relationships and what they are all about."

"Now, Mama . . . I didn't ask her to do that."

"I know, I know. She told me. We talked about so much, and the one thing that really stuck in my mind was the relationship that you and your father had. You were too young to remember this, but your father and I were at odds with each all the time. There wasn't a time that we argued in front of you, though. That was one thing about your daddy. If he had conflict he would not let it happen in front of his baby girl."

Artise smiled, then looked at Nadif lying content. "So during the conversation with Melba she realized something and made me realize it too. I wasn't having problems with you, Artise. Now don't get mad at me . . . but it was Vance I had problems with." Artise's look questioned her mother. "He just reminded me of your daddy, baby. Your father was just like him—always talking but never doing, and I noticed that about Vance from all the stories you would tell me over the years. But I never wanted to say anything. Your father filled my head up the same way. And Artise, God is my witness, I did not want the same thing to happen to you. So when you told me you were pregnant and that you'd decided to marry Vance, I guess my mind just did a complete three-sixty to the time when I was first starting out—then got my heart broken and was left to take care of you by myself. I don't know . . . maybe the devil put those thoughts in me . . . because I do want the best for you two, and when I think of all the trouble I caused you during the time you were carrying little Nadif, I could just die." Cathy leaned over and kissed the baby.

"Well, I guess the devil got into both of us . . . because I wasn't exactly the nicest person. I mean, not making sure you knew I was in the hospital. But, Mama, let me tell you something."

"What's that?" Cathy asked, her head nestled in Nadif's little neck.

"Vance loves me . . . I know he does," Artise said, running her finger around the top of her cup.

"Are you sure?"

"You know, he told me something that he didn't have to."

"Ohh?"

"Umm-hmm. That's right. He got himself in a situation that was tempting him to do evil and betray our wedding vows." Cathy looked up from Nadif and gave Artise a wondering stare. "No . . . no. Not this time. Not my Vance. Vance confided in me that he went all the way into the devil's chamber and locked the door behind himself without a soul to see him with this woman and guess what he did?"

"What?"

"Vance grabbed that woman by the hand and dropped to his knees and prayed."

"Well, praise God," Cathy said.

"He prayed the devil right off of them, and when he did, God gave him an idea."

"An idea?"

"Ummm-hmmm." Artise got up from the table and walked toward the CD player on the counter in the kitchen. "Mama, Vance finally recorded one of his songs and the woman, Casey, is now a close friend of ours—and she sang the lyrics to it."

"Well, how did they do all this without you finding out, Artise?"

"Vance said they met at the recording studio three or four times and recorded it. Wait until you hear it, it's beautiful." Artise turned the CD player on then sat back down at the table with her mother. "Listen, listen," Artise said. Cathy began to nod her head and suddenly Nadif opened his eyes and smiled.

"Awww . . . look at him," Cathy cooed. "Oh . . . it sounds so nice, Artise."

"Doesn't it?" Artise said, grooving her head back and forth to the love song Vance made for her and Nadif.

"Let me tell you something, sweetheart. If Vance did all this for you and laid all of his burdens with the Lord, there's no doubt in my mind that he's nothing like your father and you two are going to be all right!" Cathy exulted.

"Thank you, Mama," Artise said as she stood up from the table and kissed her mother on the cheek. Then they sat side by side drinking the rest of the coffee and eating way too many cookies.

Cut the Ribbon

One month later

"Hey! They told me you was supposed to be here!" Jesse, the peanut man, shouted in his high-pitched voice to everybody that walked past his stand. He had sold peanuts on the very block of the museum for years, and Vance had decided to let him set up shop and become a fixture of the ambience of the site. "I'm so glad that you came out today," he said to each patron as they walked past. "I haven't seen you since high school! Come on, now, I got fresh roasted peanuts for a dollar a bag!" he hollered.

The turnout for the opening of the museum was beyond awesome. At least one thousand supporters came out for the historic moment, and Vance and everyone else who had assisted in putting everything together were elated as can be. Vance bellowed internally when he realized he had done something that was worthy of becoming a legacy. He had kept his word, his pledge, his vows to those he loved. As Vance sat on the risers he saw Mrs. Stubblefield grasp the hand of her mate. Stubby kissed her on the cheek and followed with a hug; it moved Vance to see he had been able to do right by them, to fulfill their vision. Artise noticed Vance's proud stare and took his hand supportively. Vance looked deep into her eyes, and they didn't have to say a word, because they knew their cup was forever full. They were one passionate, united covenant, not afraid to lay their burdens down. They were linked together without end, with a life full of joy awaiting them. Their friends were happy too. Ethan, Tassha, David, Casey, and Kyle were all there to herald the big day. David had begun to really concentrate on his upcoming mayoral race and had surrendered his love for Tassha. He saw in her eyes the passion that was growing between her and Ethan, and he never wanted to stand in the way of her happiness. Kyle and Casey were free and clear and were happy to start their lives anew. Cathy and Melba both sat next to Artise, watching Nadif, who didn't realize what was going on but had a smile of happiness all over his little face. When Mrs. Stubblefield arose from her chair on the podium, the crowd silenced; it was time to hear the address that would open up the doors to history and many future years of enjoyment.

> *"I remember talking to Chester*
> *He was upset about how they wouldn't let us*
> *Put on a page how we saw it*
> *It was so, so sad*
> *There was regulation—on how we done it*

> *"Langston was on the same type of thang*
> *Wondering why freedom couldn't ring*
> *And all of us—looking from the outside in*
> *Would look at their goodness and tell them*
> *Shoot . . . y'all brothers ain't got no problems*
> *Uh-uh y'all in . . .*

> *"Instantly there was a picture that*
> *Those from the Renaissance didn't like*
> *Truth be known they were just like*
> *You and I*

> *"Wanting to display the beauty within*
> *To a point when L.H. said*
> *Hell I just don't care, everybody who reads mine*
> *Going to take me as I am*

"*That's why we must show the world*
Yes that's what we have to do
Show the world . . .
The goodness the depths
Reasons we have endured

"*Let's show the world*
We're descendants of kings and queens
Display the knowledge
Which comes from our seed

"*Let's make visible our worth to the cause*
By exhibiting our importance and demonstrating
What we have done
For if we don't show the world
The best we have of thee
How are children going to know the legacy

"*I'll be long . . . gone, when some of them read the pages of*
these books
I'll be long . . . gone, when the evidence of our magnitude is
known
I'll be long . . . gone, when some of the young ones read this
poem
Long gone with the heavenly father, shawl draped over my
shoulder

"*So make me proud and show the world what we can do*
It's an everlasting struggle
Let's show the world
We can do it, my sister and brother."

May God bless you . . .